The detective, who'd been sitting on the wall watching the exchange, picked up the camera and began to shoot as each new bone was uncovered.

"Gonna get my people out here to get the remains ready for transport," Patton said. He took the phone from his pocket and made his call.

"Yeah, Harve, I'm up here on Turner's Hill with Chief Duffy and a couple 'a her people and the FBI. Got us some bones. Bring me up a bag to bring them back in."

"Two," Joanna said. "Tell him to bring two bags."

"What?" Patton turned to the grave where the techs had stopped digging.

"Two sets of remains, two bags." Joanna stood and wiped the sweat from her brow with the back of her right hand. She glanced from the ME to the police chief to Portia. "There's a second body in here."

"Are you sure?" Portia leaned into the grave.

"Yes, ma'am." Joanna nodded certainly. "Unless the boy you're looking for had two heads, there're two people buried here."

Books published by The Random House Publishing Group
are available at quantity discounts on bulk purchases for
premium, educational, fund-raising, and special sales use.
For details, please call 1-800-733-3000.

mariah
STEWART

Forgotten

A Novel

BALLANTINE BOOKS • NEW YORK

Sale of this book without a front cover may be unauthorized. If this book is coverless, it may have been reported to the publisher as "unsold or destroyed" and neither the author nor the publisher may have received payment for it.

Forgotten is a work of fiction. Names, characters, places, and incidents are the products of the author's imagination or are used fictitiously. Any resemblance to actual events, locales, or persons, living or dead, is entirely coincidental.

2008 Ballantine Books Mass Market Edition

Copyright © 2008 by Marti Robb
Excerpt from *Goodbye Again* copyright © 2008 by Marti Robb

All rights reserved.

This book contains an excerpt from the forthcoming mass market edition of *Goodbye Again* by Mariah Stewart. This excerpt has been set for this edition only and may not reflect the final content of the forthcoming edition.

Published in the United States by Ballantine Books, an imprint of The Random House Publishing Group, a division of Random House, Inc., New York.

BALLANTINE and colophon are registered trademarks of Random House, Inc.

ISBN 978-0-345-50611-5

Printed in the United States of America

www.ballantinebooks.com

OPM   9 8 7 6 5 4 3 2 1

For my dad

ONE

No two ways about it. Dying was a bitch.

There would always be too many important things—good things—left undone.

Madeline Williams wept for all the books she'd never read, all the music she'd never hear, all the sunsets she'd never see. The grandchildren she'd never hold. On a bad day, she made lists of all the *nevers*.

Today had been a particularly bad day.

She shifted her tired shoulders and eased her head back upon the pillows she'd stacked behind her on the bed she'd slept in almost every night for the past twenty-nine years. It was just after four on a Tuesday afternoon, but already her eyes were closing in spite of her wanting to stay awake long enough to watch the sun drift down behind the row of evergreens that ran along the far edge of her property. She remembered the day her ex-husband, Greg, planted them the year they moved into this sweet Cape Cod on Higham Road. They'd put in gardens and shrubs and had taken such joy in the shared work. But things had changed over the past decade, and when he left her, he left for good, leaving behind the house and the gardens and the joy as well.

Divorce was a bitch, too.

She wondered if he ever looked back. Most days it seemed all she did was look back.

One of the things she hated most about the disease that was siphoning away her life was the way it kept nibbling at the precious time she had left. It seemed that every day, she lost a little more to her body's demands for sleep. It was the medication, it was the treatment, it was the disease. She knew all that. She just hated that it was happening to her, and happening so quickly. She'd hoped for more time.

Yesterday her daughter, Lisa, left work at noon to hit the bookstore and pick up the long-awaited new release from Maddy's favorite author, and had hurried over with it as a surprise. It was a book she had long anticipated, but she'd not been able to get past the first page. The chemical fog in her brain had seemed to absorb the meaning of the words, and the ever-present fatigue had gotten the best of her. Before she'd realized what was happening, she'd fallen asleep, the book on her chest.

Maddy hated knowing that she wouldn't live to finish it. In frustration, she'd hurled the book to the floor.

There was one thing she'd sworn she'd do before

she died, and it was weighing heavily on her mind today. Her greatest fear was that she'd fail in that, too. The energy it took to dispose of the book left her weak, and she closed her eyes, letting exhaustion take her to that dark place where these frightening truths could not follow. But they'd still be there tomorrow when she woke up, and they'd be there the day after as well—would be there, she knew, until the end, which, if the doctors were to be believed, wouldn't be all that long now.

She slipped into sleep, the promise of death so close she felt its breath, even as it stole hers. It was, they said, only a matter of time.

She awoke in a dark room, the only light that of the night-light Lisa had plugged into an outlet outside Madeline's bedroom door. With great effort, Madeline pushed herself up and reached for the clock on her bedside table. It was twenty minutes after eight. She'd slept for four hours.

She pulled the covers aside and sat on the edge of the bed in the pink cotton nightshirt that Lisa bought for her last Mother's Day. She dangled her short legs over the side of the bed for a moment before making her way slowly to the bathroom. She'd just closed the door when she heard Lisa outside the bathroom.

"Mom, are you all right?" Lisa stood in Madeline's bedroom, anxiously awaiting an answer.

"Yes, fine, sweetheart. I just got up and needed to use the bathroom."

"Are you sick? Do you want me to come in and help you?"

"No, baby. I just needed to go to the bathroom." Maddy fought the sharp edge in her voice. These last few days, she'd been short-tempered, and it hurt her as much as she knew it hurt Lisa. "I'll be out in a minute."

Madeline finished up, flushed, washed her hands, and pulled open the door. Lisa sat on the end of the queen-sized bed looking nervous and scared.

"Do you think you can eat something?" Lisa asked.

"In a while," Madeline smiled to reassure her. The last thing she wanted was food, but she was hoping that, in another hour or so, she'd feel like eating. "I just woke up, and you know I never like to eat right away."

"Carolyn called a while ago to see how you're feeling today," Lisa said.

"I'll give her a call in the morning." Maddy knew her lifelong best friend checked in at least once a day, every day. It was breaking her heart to know that Carolyn was having such a hard time facing the inevitable. Right now, though, as much as she appreciated her friend's love and concern, she lacked the strength to deal with anyone else's sadness. It was all she could do to cope with her own.

Maddy stood in front of her dresser, wondering

who the sick old woman was who looked back at her from the mirror. If she'd been vain, which she was not, she would have been more upset at the sight of her reflection. Mostly, these days she was resigned to her appearance. She knew the woman the mirror had reflected once upon a time was long gone, and would never be back.

"I had a thought." Maddy turned to her daughter. "I woke up with something very important on my mind."

"Do you remember what it was?"

"Don't interrupt, I'm liable to lose it." Madeline tried to make a joke. She opened the top drawer of her dresser and moved several things around. "Ah, here it is. I can't believe that after twelve years, it's still where I put it."

She handed Lisa a card.

"What is this?" Lisa frowned.

"What does it look like?" Madeline sat next to her on the side of the bed. Her body was already craving sleep again.

"John Mancini, Special Agent, FBI." Lisa read the faded business card, then looked up at her mother. "This is the agent who investigated . . . when Chris . . . ?"

Madeline nodded, and despite her best intentions to go downstairs and watch TV with Lisa, she slid back into the bed and pulled the covers around her.

"I want you to go to him, Lisa. I want you to ask him—beg him, if you have to—to go to the prison

and ask the monster where he buried my son."
Madeline's eyes suddenly filled with tears.

"Mom, he might not even be in the FBI anymore." Lisa held the card between her thumb and
forefinger.

"Shouldn't be too hard to find out. You call the
FBI and you ask." Madeline reached for her water
bottle but it was just out of her range. Lisa shot up
and handed it to her.

"What makes you think he'd do something like
this? He might not have time, you don't know
what other things he's working on . . ."

"Then he can look you in the eye and tell you
no," Madeline said simply. "It's the last thing I will
ever ask of anyone, Lisa."

"Mom, you can ask anything of me, and I'm
more than happy to do whatever . . ."

"No, you don't understand." Madeline removed
the lid from the bottle and took a few sips. "There
is nothing that I want except to bury my son. I
want them to find Chrissy and bring him back,
whatever is left of him, and bury him properly next
to me. That's all I want, Lis." Madeline reached
out and took her daughter's hand. "Can you try for
me, please?"

"Of course, Mom." Lisa leaned over and kissed
her mother's pale cheek. "First thing in the morning. I'll find him."

"Thank you, baby." Madeline lay back against
the pillow and smiled. "I can't leave him out there,

you know? I just can't leave this world, knowing that my little boy is still out there all alone somewhere."

"I understand, Mom." Lisa smoothed the blankets out over Maddy's wasted form and kissed her forehead. "I'll call, I promise. First thing in the morning . . ."

TWO

The newly leased sports car inched past the short row of identical brick townhouses for the third time before parking directly across the street from one. The driver turned off the engine and studied the façades as a child might study one of those *Can you find the difference between these pictures?* exercises in a workbook. Fifteen minutes passed before the car door opened and a tall, deeply tanned woman with short black hair and mile-long legs emerged. Dark glasses covered part of her face, and a pale green scarf draped the neck of the simple white shirt she wore with black linen pants. She leaned against the car for another few minutes, then walked across the street and directly to the house marked 712.

She rang the doorbell and waited.

Her hand was raised to ring a second time when the door opened. A dark-haired man wearing glasses, a gray T-shirt, and worn khakis stood barefoot in the doorway, a wide grin on his handsome face.

"Hey! Portia!" He greeted her with a bear hug, scooped her up, and swung her into the foyer. "Welcome back. Great to see you!"

"Thanks, Will." Portia Cahill allowed herself to be totally engulfed by her sister's longtime love and fiancé.

"Miranda's not home, but I expect her any minute now." He let her down and pushed the door closed with his foot. "But come on in, sit."

"Sorry to pop in unannounced," she said as he led her toward a comfortably furnished living room. "I'd have called but I wasn't sure what time I'd be getting in. My plane was late leaving London and late getting in to Newark, so I missed my connection to Baltimore."

"Hey, I know the drill. Travel's a bitch these days." He stood in the doorway. "What can I get you? I know you have to be hungry, thirsty, tired . . ."

"Actually, I would love a cup of tea."

"Great. I'll just be a minute."

"I'll come with you." She followed him down the hall to the back of the house.

"We might have some kind of cookies in the pantry there, if you'd like a snack." He filled a kettle with water, placed it on the stove, and turned on the burner. "If we'd known you were coming, we could have . . ."

"I'm sorry I didn't call. I should have," she conceded. "But you don't seem all that surprised to see me."

"Well, we've known you'd be coming back for about a week now," he admitted. "We just didn't know when."

"I suppose John told you?" she asked, annoyed that their mutual boss had shared her relocation plans with her sister. Then again, she reasoned, why would he not? John couldn't be expected to know that Portia hadn't been in touch with her, wouldn't have known about the strain between them.

"He did mention it to Miranda. He assumed she already knew." Will turned his back to get mugs from a glass-doored cabinet.

"So I guess she's pissed off that I didn't call her."

Will shrugged. "You're going to have to take that up with her, Portia. I'm not getting in the middle of the two of you."

"I suppose she was almost gleeful when she heard I got the bounce overseas," Portia muttered.

"That comment wasn't worthy of you." He turned around and faced her, his eyes solemn. "You know her better than that."

Her lack of response was a silent admission that Portia did, in fact, know that her sister would not find pleasure in her twin's downfall.

"All that crap between you and Miranda and your father . . ." Will shook his head. "That's stuff the two of you have to work out on your own."

"Well, she'd be right if she said I brought this transfer on myself," Portia sat on one of the wicker chairs in the corner and rested her elbow, chin in hand, on the kitchen table. "I should have kept a lower profile. I should have been more aware of the press."

"I hardly think you'd have expected some tabloid reporter to mistake you for one of Jack Marlowe's girlfriends."

"Everyone but me was highly amused when it was revealed that I was in fact his daughter." Portia made a face. "Not funny to have people think you're your own father's playmate. Disgusting, actually."

"But understandable, since so many of Jack's girls are our age or younger these days." Miranda Cahill came into the kitchen and tossed her bag onto the counter. "And since he really has never publicly owned up to having sired us, you can't blame the press for thinking you were our dear daddy's girl *du jour*. Whew, this heat's a killer, isn't it?"

"Good to see you, too, Sister Love." Portia rose and watched Miranda warily. "And for the record, Jack's owned up to it now."

Miranda stared back into eyes the exact shade of green as her own. "Well, that certainly makes up for, oh, thirty-some years of neglect."

"I *am* glad to see you, Miranda," Portia said softly.

"Oh, shit." Miranda opened her arms and hugged her twin. "I'm glad to see you, too. I'm so glad you're home and safe."

"I was safe overseas," Portia told her as she backed away slowly from the embrace.

"Really? Because I never feel safe when I'm being shot at. There's something about the sound of bullets whizzing past my head that makes me just a tad jumpy." Miranda shrugged. "Of course, maybe it's just me . . ."

"It wasn't that bad, really," Portia assured her. "I admit there were some dicey moments, especially in Afghanistan, but all things considered, it could have been worse."

"Well, that's all behind you now, right?" Miranda sat opposite Portia at the table. "You've been reassigned stateside."

Portia made a face. "For the time being, I suppose. At least until this dies down, and people forget what I look like."

"Sorry, but no one will ever forget what you look like," Will interjected. "Once your face is out there, it's out there, and people will remember you. It's part of that whole cursed-with-beauty thing. People remember beautiful faces."

"I know you meant that as a compliment, Will, but it's not making me feel better." Portia sighed. "I love undercover work. I love counterterrorism, I really do. I could have stayed overseas and ended my career there."

"Unfortunately, if you'd stayed overseas once your cover was blown, your career would have ended permanently, a lot sooner than any of us would have liked," Will pointed out.

The kettle whistled and Will tended to it, pouring tea into one mug and serving Portia. He then poured coffee from a glass carafe into mugs for himself and Miranda. He was setting a carton of half-and-half on the table when Miranda said, "Oh, we're drinking tea, now, are we? How very British of you."

"Lots of people drink tea."

"You never did. You never liked it. But I guess all that time you spent in London, being wined and dined by Jack . . ." Miranda paused. "Or do you call him *Dad* now?"

Portia's eyes narrowed and she wrapped her hands around the mug.

"Don't, Miranda," she said. "Just . . . don't."

Miranda bit the inside of her mouth but didn't speak.

"I think I'll just go on up to my office and check my e-mail," Will said. "Maybe water the plants. Feed the goldfish."

"The goldfish died last month, Will," Miranda reminded him drily.

"Yeah, I know. I'm still in denial. I sure do miss the little buggers," Will said as he backed out of the kitchen. "Besides, I know you two have a lot to catch up on . . ."

Portia watched through narrowed eyes as Miranda added more cream to her coffee. It seemed to take longer than necessary, and Portia knew she was struggling to get her temper under control.

"Go ahead and say whatever it is you have to say, Miranda. Let's just get it out and over with once and for all so we can move past it."

"There is no 'once and for all.'" Miranda looked up. Portia saw a touch of sadness in Miranda's eyes and was painfully aware there was nothing she could say to make that sadness vanish. "Not as long as you continue to defend Jack, as long as you refuse to acknowledge what he is and what he did to our mother thirty-odd years ago."

"I don't need to defend Jack. He is who he is. And for the record, Jack loved Mom. She was the one true love of his life. I know you find it hard to believe, but . . ."

"Oh, ya think?" Miranda snorted. "Well, narrow-minded me. Just because he left her pregnant and unmarried while he courted some of the great beauties of their day. Oh, hell, he's courted some of the great beauties of *our* day. And he's been married what, four times? A couple of supermodels, an actress. A princess, for Christ's sake. But somehow, he never found time to marry Mom." Miranda scoffed. "Love of his life, my ass."

"Look, that was between the two of them. If Mom could understand—if she could accept it—I don't know why you can't."

"I don't know how you can." Miranda made a face. "He left us . . . flitted in and out of our lives for years, though the blame for that is on her as well. She let him hurt her, over and over again. Even after she married Roger—a really decent guy who loved her—Jack couldn't stay away, and she couldn't say no when he came back. He just couldn't leave her alone. Even when she was dying."

"I think she wanted to love Roger—I think she really tried—but she never really did. She liked him a lot. Respected him. But she never loved him. I think she wanted to be a good wife to him," Portia reminded Miranda. "And I think Roger really tried to overlook Mom's feelings for Jack. He knew that she'd never love him the way she loved Jack."

"Yeah, well, after a while, poor Roger couldn't take it anymore. Hence the divorce. But I will never forget the look on that man's face when you brought Jack into Mom's hospital room that last time." Miranda averted her eyes. "Mom was dying. Roger thought that at last, he'd have her all to himself. He wanted to be her rock, wanted to be the one who was there for her at the end. He wanted to be the one who held her while she passed. And then you had to go and bring Jack back in at the last minute . . ."

"First off, I did not *bring* him." Portia's eyes blazed. "Mom specifically asked for him. She wanted him there. And knowing how close to the end she was, he asked me to come with him. If it hadn't been for him, I might not have been with her at the end, either, since you weren't in any big hurry to share that bit of news."

"That's just not true." An indignant Miranda slammed her mug on the table. "Mom may have shared her bad news with Jack, but she never told me how bad things were. I found out from Roger the morning the two of you showed up." Her eyes narrowed as she studied her twin's face. "How could you even think I'd have kept that from you?"

"Oh, I don't know. Maybe because you've been so pissed off at me because of my relationship with Jack that you hadn't spoken to me for months before we found out that Mom was sick."

"No matter how angry I was, I would not— could not—keep something like that from you," Miranda whispered. "I have no use for Jack, that's true, but I would never have kept you from Mom, if I'd known how close we were to losing her. I'm afraid I was in a bit of denial then. I didn't want to see how bad she was. It was easier to tell myself that she was going to beat it, that she was going to be fine. I couldn't imagine it turning out any other way."

Portia bit her bottom lip to hide its quiver, but it was too late. Miranda had already seen and recognized her sister's attempt to cover up her emotions. She got up from her seat and stood behind Portia's chair to rest her head upon her sister's.

"All those years, it was just the three of us, remember?" Miranda sniffed back tears. "You, me, Mom. The Mighty Cahills."

Portia nodded, not trusting herself to speak.

"She faced the censure of a small town to raise us by herself, and never regretted it, as far as I could tell."

"She didn't. She told me she wouldn't have changed one thing in her life, not for anything." Portia swallowed hard, fighting her own tears. "She said we were the best thing that could have happened to her, and she thanked God every day that she had us."

Portia lifted her face to her sister and said, "Mom loved deeply, Miranda. Deeply and forever. That's how she felt about us, and even though you don't like it, that's how she felt about Jack. He was the love of her life."

"Too bad she wasn't the love of his."

"Ah, but she was," Portia told her. "That's the part you don't understand. He never loved anyone but her."

"Did he tell you that?" Miranda sneered.

"Many, many times."

"And you believe him?" Miranda shook her head. "Then you're as blind as Mom was about him."

"If you got to know him, you'd understand. His life hasn't been a normal one."

"Ah, yes. Mad Jack Marlowe. Sixties rock idol. Guitar god. International superstar." Miranda shook her head. "I understand all too well. Why bother to tie yourself down to one woman when you could have *all* the women?"

"That was part of it, probably. I'm sure it was, especially when he was younger. Jack's way of life has taken him down some very strange roads. Mom wasn't interested in traveling those roads with him. She wanted to stay home, with us."

"I'm sure that's what she told herself . . ."

"It's how she really felt." Portia shook her head from side to side. "Do I understand that? No, frankly, I don't. But I respect it. It was her choice."

Miranda rolled her eyes. "Jack would have tired of her in no time if she'd tried to follow him."

"Which is why she never did." Portia smiled. "And why he always came back to her."

"We will never see eye to eye on this, will we?"

"Probably not."

"I don't want to see him."

"You don't have to." Portia reached over and took her sister's hand. "But don't get upset if I do."

"I don't want him to be my father."

"Now *that's* something we can't do anything about." Portia smiled.

Miranda got up and refreshed her coffee. A moment later she turned and said, "I read somewhere that he has this yacht that's supposed be like a floating palace. It supposedly has luxury staterooms and an incredible chef and a full staff."

"All true." Portia nodded. "He leaves it in Greece."

"Have you ever been on it?"

"For a whole week last year." Portia smiled at the memory.

"Is it truly glorious?"

"Ridiculously so," Portia assured her. "Everything you've read and more."

"*Damn,*" Miranda whispered between tightly clenched teeth.

THREE

The black SUV eased into the first reserved parking spot, the name on which read simply, J. MANCINI. No first name, no title, but anyone arriving at this nondescript four-story redbrick building in a Baltimore suburb knew that the J stood for John, and that John Mancini was the head man in one of the FBI's most elite investigative units. The SUV's engine was cut, the driver's door opened, and a man emerged carrying a briefcase in one hand and a take-out cup of coffee in the other. He slammed the car door shut with his elbow and was inside the building in less than half a dozen long strides. He greeted the security guard and headed straight for the elevator. He got off at the third floor and acknowledged his assistant, Eileen, by raising and tipping his cup as he hustled past her on the way to his office.

"Uh, John," she called to him. "You have . . ."

"A conference call in fifteen minutes, I know."

"Yes, but right now you have a visitor," Eileen said softly, tilting her head in the direction of the modest reception area where a young woman sat watching.

As he turned to look, the woman got up and approached him.

"Mr. Mancini? You're John Mancini?" she asked.

"Yes, I am."

"Mr. Mancini, you wouldn't remember me. My name is Lisa Williams," she told him. "My brother was Christopher Williams. He . . ."

"I remember the name." John nodded. "I remember your brother. We always thought he was one of Sheldon Woods's victims but we couldn't prove it." He paused for a moment, then asked, "How is your mother?"

"Actually, I'm here because she asked me to find you." The young woman's eyes welled with tears.

"Here, come into my office." John led her toward his door, then glanced back over his shoulder and said to Eileen, "Hold my calls for a few minutes, okay?"

Once inside his office, John dropped his briefcase on the floor next to his desk and closed the door.

"Can I get you something? Coffee? Tea?" he asked as he sat his own cardboard cup on the desk.

"No, nothing, thank you. I appreciate you seeing me without an appointment, and I'll try not to take too much of your time." Her voice quivered with emotion.

"You said your mother asked you to find me." John sat on the corner of his desk. Less intimidating, he figured, than sitting behind it in that big leather chair his wife, Genna, had bought for his birthday last year.

"My mother is very sick, Mr. Mancini. She might have a few weeks left, not more than a month, according to her doctors." Lisa took a tissue from her pocket and wiped her eyes.

"I'm so sorry to hear that. I admired your mother very much." Madeline Williams's valiant effort to have her son included on the list of Sheldon Woods's victims was still clear in John's mind. Woods had capped the list at thirteen—his "Baker's Dozen," he called them. But he wouldn't admit to having killed Christopher Williams. For some reason, he'd adamantly refused to add that final name.

"My mother really believed that he'd killed Chris."

"Well, she wasn't alone in that. I believed it, too." John's head began to pound. The Woods case had changed his life. There was hardly a day that passed when he didn't think about some aspect of it.

"Well, that's what she asked me to talk to you about." Lisa took a very deep breath. "She wants to know if you would please try one more time. If you would go to him and ask about Chris."

"She wants me to ask Woods if he killed your brother?"

The young woman shook her head. "She knows

he killed him, Mr. Mancini. She wants you to ask him where he left the body."

After a long moment, he said quietly, "Lisa, I am probably the last person on the face of the earth that Sheldon Woods would give that information to."

"But you got him to reveal where all those others were buried," she protested.

"No, that's not the way it happened. He gave up the others because that was the deal he and his attorney made with the prosecutor. That he'd tell where to find the remains of those thirteen boys in exchange for thirteen concurrent life sentences without parole, instead of the death penalty." His voice dropped again. "I found him, I brought him in, but I was not involved in the bargaining. His attorney was the deal maker."

"But you found the graves. I remember seeing the pictures in the newspapers and on TV . . ."

"Yes, I found the graves, and I was part of the recovery team. But I was responsible for arresting Sheldon Woods. He has no great love for me, Lisa. He wouldn't give me the time of day."

"So what do I do now? What do I tell my mother?" Her face fell. "The only thing she wants before she dies is to find Chrissy. She wants to be buried next to him."

John looked out the window and watched two squirrels chase each other around the trunk of a maple tree. For a moment he wished he was out there with them.

"Lisa, I'm sorry," he said softly. "I don't know how I can help you."

She nodded her head and began to weep. "I understand. My mother just thought that maybe . . ."

John's private line began to ring. He glanced at his watch. It was the call he was waiting for.

"I'm so sorry, but I have to take this." He went behind his desk. "Leave your number with Eileen. Maybe I can think of something. I'll give you a call if I do."

"Thank you." She backed out of the doorway, clutching the tissue in her hand. "Thank you so much, Mr. Mancini."

Portia Cahill watched the elevator doors close and felt as much as heard the creak as it began its ascent. She blew out a long breath and resigned herself to the fact that she was going to receive an assignment she knew she wasn't going to like. It almost didn't matter what it was; domestic investigations just didn't have the panache or sense of danger that undercover work had.

A weeping young woman was waiting for the elevator when the door opened on the third floor, and Portia held it for her before stepping into the quiet of a brief hall. Beyond a glass door to her left sat a receptionist, and after showing her ID, Portia was directed through a maze of gray fabric-covered cubicles and small peripheral offices to an area clearly presided over by a red-haired woman in her sixties.

The woman glanced up from her phone and did a double take when she saw Portia. Then, smiling, she pointed to a seating area and raised her index finger to indicate she'd be free in just a moment, though it seemed to Portia the woman took her time wrapping up the call. When she finally hung up, it wasn't to address Portia but to make another call.

"Portia Cahill is here to see you," the woman said into the receiver. Hanging up, she turned to Portia and said, "John can see you now, Agent Cahill. His is the door straight ahead."

"You're either a psychic or you know my sister," Portia said as she passed the woman's desk.

"Everyone knows your sister. Everyone knows she has an identical twin. Besides, John told me you'd be in this morning first thing." The woman smiled broadly. "Welcome back, Agent Cahill. By the way, I like the short hair. I'm used to seeing Miranda with that long mane, but I do like the short cut."

"Thank you. It was easier to take care of where I've been for the past few years . . . Eileen," Portia added, reading the nameplate on the desk.

The woman nodded. "You've been gone for quite

some time, I know. I'm new since your last state-side assignment."

"All of this is new," Portia noted, looking around at the spacious office. "Last time I worked for John, we were crowded into a little warren of offices in Virginia."

"John thought—and the director agreed—that it was best all around to move the unit into space of its own. We're close enough to headquarters to get something if we need it, but of course, with so much on the computers these days, we hardly . . ."

"Eileen, perhaps you could fill Agent Cahill in after we have our 'welcome to the rest of your life' chat." John stood in his office doorway, his arms crossed over his chest. "I have to leave here in about thirty minutes."

"Well, hopefully, it won't take you that long to fill me in," Portia said as she walked toward him. "How are you, John?"

He took the hand she offered him and sandwiched it between his own. "Couldn't be better. I'm glad to see you, Portia. You look great. I guess all that covert stuff agreed with you."

"Thanks. And yes, it did." She followed him into his office. He closed the door and pulled out a chair for her.

"I've heard you were very good at what you did over there. Your superior was very unhappy to transfer you out."

Portia's face hardened slightly. "He didn't really

have to . . . I mean, he could have found something else for me to do. I shouldn't have had to leave."

"You can't seriously believe that." John took his seat behind the desk and stared across at her. "Once your face is out there, once you've been identified, it's over, Portia. That's what *undercover* means. You get your face all over the British tabloids, that's the end of it."

She tried to mount a protest, but knew he was right, so she sat silent.

"Anyway, we're glad to have an agent with your investigative skills back with our team. We have a lot going on right now." He glanced at a stack of files on his desk. "Any particular area of interest? We've got a couple of serial killers, a serial arsonist in Pittsburgh, serial rapist in South Carolina, abducted children in three states . . ."

Portia shrugged. "Whatever."

John's smile faded. "Your enthusiasm is overwhelming me, Portia."

"It's no secret that I didn't want to come back to domestic work, John. I don't see any reason to pretend that I'm thrilled to be here. But I will do whatever job you assign to me, and I'll do it to the best of my ability."

"If I thought otherwise, you'd be at home, polishing your résumé." His stare ate right through her. She could feel his ire from across the desk.

"So we both know I'll do a good job at whatever." She averted her eyes. "Just give me my assignment and I'll get on with it."

"Let's get one thing straight, Agent Cahill." John's voice dropped an octave and she raised her eyes to meet his. That stony gaze she'd seen trained on other agents who'd met with his disapproval was now turned on her. "I know you think the work you did undercover over there was much more important than anything you could be doing here. I get that. Counterterrorism *is* important. But the fact of the matter is that you are *here* rather than *there* because of a colossal blunder on *your* part. And while the domestic cases that we get may not require you to crawl through mountain passes on your stomach in the middle of the night or any of the other exotic things you may have experienced over the past few years, the work we do here is damned important."

He paused, then added, "There's a lot of misery in this world, Portia. A lot of pain. It isn't all confined to the Middle East." John leaned forward slightly, pronouncing each word slowly, distinctly, as if speaking to a child. "When you're dealing with demons, it doesn't matter where you find them or what language they speak. Torture is torture. Pain is pain. Fear is fear. It isn't confined to one part of the globe. The demons are everywhere."

Portia felt her face flush as she uncharacteristically struggled for a retort. By the time something came to her, John had moved on and was dialing an extension on his desk phone.

"Eileen, would you bring in the file we started this morning?" He replaced the receiver and turned back to Portia. "A situation came up today that I'm going to assign to you to look into before I give you anything else."

"All right." She sat up a little straighter and tried to look enthused, though she suspected he could see right through her. She'd worked with John before he'd been named the head of this elite unit, before she'd gone overseas. She knew without question that he was a good man, a great agent, and she had immense respect for him. He wasn't an easy man to bluff. Still, she felt obligated to give it her best. She put on her most interested expression and sat back to listen.

"Back in nineteen ninety-six, the first of what became a long series of child abductions was reported in Kingsley, Maryland. Over the following three years, several dozen young boys disappeared from Maryland, Pennsylvania, Delaware, Virginia, West Virginia, New Jersey . . ." His face was taut, his eyes dark.

"Sheldon Woods. I remember," Portia said to spare him from repeating the details. She knew the case well. It was the case that had almost ended John's career, had almost taken his sanity, had almost cost him the woman he loved. There was no need for him to say more. Portia knew. "The press called him the Pied Piper. You worked it."

He nodded and was quiet for a few minutes. Then he said, "Anyway, he admitted to killing a certain number of these missing boys . . ."

"Thirteen. A 'Baker's Dozen,' " she said softly.

"You do remember." John looked out the window. "Thirteen sets of remains were found buried around the region. Woods made a big deal out of identifying each victim and his burial place. Wouldn't *tell* where they were, he had to *show*. And wouldn't give up the child's name until they were at the grave site. Then he'd tell us who he'd buried there, how he'd abducted him. What he'd done to him . . ."

"Made you all listen . . ."

"It shook the soul of every man and woman who was there." John continued to gaze at the sky.

Portia knew he was thinking about how Woods had latched on to John, the agent in charge, and had made his life a living hell, often calling John to taunt him, to force him to listen while he tortured and killed his victims. John had stoically seen the case through after finding Woods hiding in the basement of an abandoned bungalow in western Maryland. She'd heard how he'd made certain Woods was not touched except to handcuff him, that he'd been read his rights, that everything about the arrest was by the book. He'd completed the paperwork, he'd been present at the hearings.

And once Woods had entered his plea and had been sentenced, John quietly disappeared for months while he tried to regain the bits and pieces of himself he'd lost through the ordeal.

Of course Portia knew. Everyone who had ever worked with—or for—John knew. He was just shy of being a living legend because of it.

"Anyway, there were others. Kids who'd disappeared during that time who were never found. Kids we knew Woods had killed, but without his confession, without any evidence, not even the bodies . . ."

"He couldn't be convicted." She finished the thought for him.

"Right. We all knew he was holding on to the others as bargaining chips, for some future date when he could use it to his advantage." He turned and looked at her. "And that day just might be here."

"What does he want?" Portia asked.

"This time it's not about what he wants."

There was a quiet rap on the door. Eileen stepped into the room and handed John a folder.

"This is all I have right now," Eileen told him, "but I've requested the rest of it from headquarters. We should have it by tomorrow. Also, I'm printing out everything I was able to access from the system for Agent Cahill. As soon as we set her up with a password and get her cleared for one of the department computers, she'll have access to the information herself."

"Thanks, Eileen. Does she have an office yet?" John glanced up at his efficient assistant.

"Please. You insult me." Eileen rolled her eyes and feigned indignation. "Third door on the right."

"You *are* good." John smiled.

"Damn right, I am." Eileen winked at Portia and closed the door behind her as she left the room.

"So, you have an office. Eileen will get you set up on the system, show you what you need to know here in the office, give you whatever paperwork you need . . ." John pushed the folder across the desk in Portia's direction.

"Wait, you didn't tell me what I'm supposed to be doing. What's my assignment?"

"Oh. Right. Well, there was a boy—eight years old back in nineteen ninety-seven. Boy from Maryland, up near the Pennsylvania border. Kid's name was Christopher Williams. Disappeared on his way home from soccer practice, less than two blocks from his house. The more I looked at that case, the more I knew it was one of Woods's but I couldn't get him to admit it. Even when the boy's mother confronted Woods in the courtroom—pleaded with him—he wouldn't give us an inch." His eyes had darkened again, and Portia suspected his mind was replaying the scene. "Said he'd agree to thirteen, he'd given us thirteen, and that was all we were getting."

"I'm assuming that something has brought this case back to active status?"

"Active only in the sense that I'd like to see if we can get Woods to tell us where he buried Williams."

"Why now?"

"Because the boy's mother is dying. She wants to be buried with her son."

"Oh, that's rough," Portia acknowledged. They'd all faced a lot of rough scenarios. Very few of their cases ever had happy endings.

"This woman—Madeline Williams—courageously sat through every minute of the hearings. Sat by and listened while Woods described in horrific detail what he'd done to these children. Sat there, knowing that he'd done pretty much the same to her boy, but she never said a word." John swallowed hard. "After the sentencing, as Woods was being led away, Mrs. Williams reached out for him, begged him to tell her where they would find her son. Woods asked her who her son was. 'Christopher Williams,' she told him. He just smiled and looked at this grieving woman and said, 'I'm sure he was a lovely boy.' Turned his back and they led him away, leaving her standing there, sobbing, *knowing*."

"One of those moments that just stays with you," Portia whispered.

"It's one of the great regrets of my life that I wasn't able to protect Madeline Williams from that moment. That I wasn't able to find that boy and return him to his family. I promised her that I'd do whatever I could to find her son, but once the case was over, there were others . . ." John shrugged his shoulders. "There was never any time. Now she's dying, and if there's any way we could give her this . . ."

"I understand," Portia said, and she did. Every agent had at least one case that haunted him or her. The unsolved case, the missing closure for heartbroken loved ones, the killer who was never found. "I just don't understand how I fit into this."

"If I could do this myself, I would. But if Sheldon Woods had any reason to suspect I had an interest in this, he'd never give an inch."

"Because you arrested him."

"That and other reasons."

"What other reasons?"

"Woods felt that by sharing his kills with me, by letting me 'witness' his depravity, that we'd become sort of soul mates."

"Jesus. Was he serious?" Portia's stomach turned.

"The bastard felt I'd betrayed him by arresting him."

"It never occurred to him that maybe you were only keeping him on the line long enough to try to pinpoint his location?"

"At first he'd cut the conversation short so we couldn't trace the calls. Later, though, it was as if he'd lost all sense of fear of being found. Almost as if he really believed I wasn't actually looking for him, but somehow participating, *sanctioning . . .*"

"Dear God, John."

He stood and ended the meeting abruptly.

"I want you to go to Arrowhead Prison and talk to Sheldon Woods. Find out how to persuade him to give up Christopher Williams's body."

"All right." Portia picked up the file and tucked it under her arm.

"Madeline Williams's daughter tells me that her mother only has maybe three weeks left," John told her. "That's how long you have to make a deal with Woods and find the boy's remains. Use the time wisely."

FOUR

The air in the tiny, windowless room was stale and smelled of sweat, Lysol, and anxiety. Portia grimaced before taking a seat on one of two orange plastic chairs, both marked with questionable smears and bolted to the floor. Whoever had cleaned the room last had apparently focused all his efforts on the floor, which was spotless except for a few black heel marks under the table. Fortunately, Portia'd had the good sense to wear old pants and a matching jacket in a dull shade of brown. Whatever the last visitor left on the chair would probably blend right in.

When the door opened, she watched Sheldon Woods shuffle in. His ankles and wrists were chained together and secured to another chain wrapped around his waist. Inmate and agent took their time sizing each other up, each studying the other's face while initially avoiding direct eye contact. Portia had seen photos of the man, but somehow had missed any references that may have been made to his size. He was in his late forties, was around five foot five or so, and weighed about 120 pounds. His appearance was youthful as well. His hair, though thinning slightly, was still as blond as it was in the photos taken over twelve years ago, his skin smooth and relatively free of lines, his fingers long and thin, the nails trim and clean. His eyes, however, were those of an old man: a pale, watery blue, with thin lashes. Portia noted they were totally devoid of any sign of humanity.

Woods calmly took the seat across the table from Portia, in no more hurry to speak than she was.

"Ma'am," the guard, whose badge identified him as CO DeLuca, broke the silence. "I'll be right here on the other side of the door if you need me." To his prisoner, the guard said, "You behave yourself, hear?"

Sheldon Woods smiled. "I always behave for the ladies. And we'll do fine, don't you think, sweetheart?"

"It's Agent Cahill." Portia could barely disguise her disgust. "Not a good way to start, Woods."

He raised a questioning eyebrow.

"Playing games," she said flatly. "I really don't have time for that."

"Pity." He leaned back against the chair. "I have all the time in the world."

"Then it looks like this will be a very short visit." Portia rose. "I have better things to do."

"Whoa, whoa, hold up there." He raised his manacled hands and held them in front of his chest. "You were the one who called this meeting. Surely you wouldn't walk out without even telling me why?"

"Unless you can keep the bullshit to a minimum, yes." She nodded. "I would have no problem ending this interview."

"Interview, eh?" His rubbed his cheek close to the right side of his nose with a finger. "The FBI already interviewed me. Many times, as a matter of fact. Now, why at this late date would someone think they missed something?"

She was halfway to the door and paused to think about how best to answer without giving away too much.

"Ahhh, of course. Of course." He grinned as the thought occurred to him. "You must want something from me. Now, what could that something be, Agent . . . forgive me, I didn't catch your name."

"Cahill."

"Yes, of course. Agent Cahill. I'll remember." He nodded with more animation now. "Come sit back down and tell me what it is that you want from old Sheldon."

She continued to stand. "Nineteen ninety-seven. Palmer, Maryland. Eight-year-old Christopher Williams disappeared on his way home from soccer practice. He was never seen again."

"And . . . ?" Woods smiled and gestured with his hands for her to continue.

Bastard knows what's coming, she realized, as an urge to knock him off that chair, chains and all, threatened to overtake her. It was an effort to maintain a neutral demeanor.

"I understand that following your sentencing hearing, the boy's mother approached you and asked you to tell her where you left her son's body."

"She assumed so much, didn't she?" His eyes narrowed and he studied Portia's face. "She assumed that I had something to do with his disappearance. Or at the very least, that I knew what happened to the boy."

"You're doing it again," she said stonily.

"What's that?"

"Playing with me. I don't care for it."

"And just who are you, Agent Cahill, to take that attitude with me?" He lowered his voice to a near whisper. "You came here to ask a favor of me. I don't think I'll grant it."

He prepared to stand.

"Did you kill him?" She asked point-blank. "Was Christopher Williams one of your 'boys,' Woods?"

"You ask as if you expect me to say, 'yes, Agent Cahill, I did do this boy.' " He shook his head. "So I say yes, and you charge me with his murder, and the government gets to go back to court and get me that death sentence it wanted so badly so many years ago?" He laughed. "Is everyone stupid now except me?"

"No one wants to charge you with anything. That isn't what this is about."

"Then what is it about?"

She debated about telling him the truth. "Christopher Williams's mother has less than a month to live. She wants to recover her son's remains before she dies so she can have him buried near her."

From the look on his face, Woods was taken aback. He studied her for a long moment, then said, "That's very good, Agent Cahill. Very good indeed."

"It's the truth."

"So who's the good Samaritan at the FBI, hmmmm?" He pretended to ponder. "Wouldn't be my old friend John, now, would it?"

"John?" She frowned as if she didn't know who he meant.

"Oh, please. You talk about *me* playing games?" He laughed harshly. "This has John Mancini's fingerprints all over it."

"I don't recognize the name." Portia shrugged. "He must be in a different office. The assignment was on my desk when I came into work on Monday."

"Who is your supervising agent?"

"Will Fletcher," she responded without missing a beat, Will's being the first name that popped into her head. "Your guy either retired or got transferred, but he's not one of the agents assigned to my unit." Which technically was true, since John was in *charge* of the unit.

"So what happened here?" He leaned forward slightly in his chair. "Walk me through this."

Portia sat back down again and rested her elbows on the table. "I don't know what instigated it. I just got reassigned to this office myself."

"From where?"

"Philly." Again, a stretch of the truth. Portia had worked in Philly before she volunteered for counterterrorism duty.

"Okay, so you get transferred to this new office and the first day you're there, you're assigned to . . . to what?"

"To do what I'm doing right now. Talk to you, ask you about the Williams boy, try to find out where you left his body. Couldn't be more simple than that, Woods."

"Again, there's that assumption of guilt." He smiled and the urge to smack him returned.

"Are you denying it?"

"Depends."

"On what?"

"On what I get in return for the information."

"You get my word that you won't be prosecuted for his murder."

"I'm not being prosecuted for it now, so you're offering me nothing I don't already have. You can do better, Agent Cahill." He leaned even closer. "Assuming I did the boy, and assuming that I could remember where he is, what are you willing to give me?"

"My undying gratitude?"

He laughed out loud. "You're something, aren't you? I'd almost be tempted, just because you have such balls. But no," he shook his head. "You have to do way better than that."

"Like what?" She crossed her arms over her chest and leaned back in the chair, giving no sign that she recognized him for what he was—a malevolent, soulless aberration. "What would it take, Woods?"

"I don't know. I hadn't expected to have to make a deal today, so I don't know what it's worth to me." He stared at the wall behind her, obviously contemplating the situation. The room was so quiet, Portia could hear her own pulse beat in her temples.

"I don't know," he repeated after several minutes. "I'll tell you what. I'll think on this, and get back to you. Come back two weeks from today, prepared to make a deal."

"Christopher Williams's mother doesn't have two weeks." She stood and went to the door and called for the guard. "I'll be back in two days."

Portia left the prison and drove directly to Miranda's townhouse, where she was staying until she had time to find a place of her own. She was grateful to find no one else at home. She unlocked the door and went straight upstairs to the guest room, stripping off her jacket and blouse. Once in the bathroom, she tossed her clothes on the floor and turned on the shower. Being in Sheldon Woods's presence for almost thirty minutes had made her feel dirtier than a week climbing through mountain crevices and crawling through caves. She stood under the steaming water for almost as long as she'd spent in his company.

When she finished, she dried her hair, changed into fresh clothes, and reapplied her makeup, but did not feel free of the taint of Sheldon Woods's presence. It clung to her like a stain she could not remove from her skin.

"How long before you no longer felt contaminated?" she asked John when she returned to the office. She stood in his doorway, her bag tucked under her arm.

"You've been to see Woods." He looked up from his desk, and for a moment appeared distracted.

"Yes. This morning."

"Then if I told you the feeling has never gone away—that I've never been able to cleanse my soul of the taint—you'd understand?"

She nodded. "I've met a lot of wicked people in my time, John, but I've never come across anyone so blatantly evil."

"I'm sorry, Portia," John said quietly. "I should have just gone myself."

"Uh-uh. He asked right away if you were behind

this, and I denied knowing you. Your first instinct was spot-on: If he thought he could get to you through this, he would, and there'd be no chance of getting Mrs. Williams's son returned." She shook her head adamantly. "No. This is the right way to do it."

"So what happened? How did he react?" John motioned for her to come in and sit down. "Were you able to persuade him to talk about the Williams boy?"

"He was clearly caught off guard at first and thought I was there to try to trick him into confessing to a murder he hadn't admitted to in the past so that he could be tried and given the death sentence."

"That's an idea worth revisiting at another time." John smiled. "But go on."

"When I finally convinced him that there was no plot to entrap him, he perked up a bit and told me we'd have to make a deal, give him something he wanted in return for what we want."

"What does he want?"

"He told me to come back in two weeks and he'd let me know. I told him he has two days. I'll go back in on Friday and see what it is he has in mind. Like I said, he hadn't been expecting a deal, and I guess he wants to take advantage of the opportunity and ask for something he really wants." She tapped her fingers on the arms of the chair. "How much leeway do I have here, John? What are we willing to give him? What *can* we give him?"

He shrugged. "It's going to depend on what he asks for. With him, it could be damned near anything. Let's wait until Friday and see what he comes up with. But I'll tell you this: After all Madeline Williams has gone through over the past twelve years, I'll move heaven and hell to find her boy. So unless he wants something totally outrageous, we'll do our best to make a deal."

"You want *what*?" Portia leaned forward in her seat slightly, not certain she'd heard correctly.

Sheldon Woods smiled, with no small amount of self-satisfaction. "I want to go horseback riding. For an entire hour."

"Are you crazy?" She all but laughed in his face.

"Not at all. I'm just bored. I'm sure the FBI can find at least one indoor riding facility within an easy drive of the prison. After all, this *is* horse country, you know." He tried to cross his arms over his chest. The wrist restraints prevented action, so he let his hands drop to his lap. "Shouldn't be all that hard for you to arrange."

"I don't know that the prison would let you go, and besides, I'm not sure . . ."

"Oh, please." He laughed at her. "You're the FBI, girlfriend. You can make it happen."

"Don't call me girl—"

"Oh, and I want James Cannon there." He ignored her protest. "In the car with me, sitting right next to me, to and from."

"Who?" She frowned. The name was vaguely familiar but she couldn't quite place it.

"Cannon. My lawyer. Well, my ex-lawyer. He doesn't represent me now, but he did back then. And I must say, he did one hell of a job, don't you think? An admitted child killer, for God's sake, in a death penalty state, and he gets me life sentences." Woods winked at her. "The man's a genius."

"He sounds charming," she said sourly. "I'm sure you deserved each other."

"He actually is charming, in his own way. You'd like him."

"I've never had much use for men who make deals with the devil."

"Oh, meaning me, of course. You flatter me, Agent Cahill." Woods chuckled. "You might change your mind about Cannon after you meet him, though."

"I doubt it."

"Anyway, that's what I want. One hour, out of here, to ride. Immunity. And Cannon has to be there or there's no deal."

"Why is his presence so important if he's no longer representing you?"

"Because he's the only truly honest man I've ever met." Woods grew serious, the light banter set aside. "And if he's there, there won't be any accidents."

"Accidents?"

"You know. Like me falling off the horse and breaking my neck. Or falling out of the car and having a truck run over me. Or a made-up story about how I tried to escape so they had to shoot to kill. Accidents like that." He shrugged. "If Cannon is there, I know I'll be safe. So that's it."

"What if he's out of town?"

"Then we wait until he gets back."

"We don't have time to wait. Mrs. Williams is . . ."

"Please." He wiggled the fingers of one hand dismissively. "If you're so damned worried about Mrs. Williams, you'll get Cannon there, one way or another." He turned toward the door and called over his shoulder for the guard. "CO DeLuca? We're done in here!"

"Wait a second." She held up a hand to hold off the corrections officer as he opened the door. "I don't remember hearing about the part where you tell us what we want to know."

"I'll tell you when I'm sitting high in the saddle, Agent Cahill. Not a second sooner."

"I don't know that that will be acceptable to . . ."

"To . . . ?" He raised his eyebrows.

"To the SAC. Fletcher. He's the one I'll have to go to with your request."

"Oh, right," he said, a touch of sarcasm in his voice. "Special Agent in Charge 'Fletcher.' Well, you just do your best to convince him that he needs to make this happen. I'm sure Mrs. Williams's peace of mind is every bit as important to him as it is to you."

"I'll have to get back to you." She waved the guard in.

"Now it's my turn to remind *you* that time is running out." He stood and began his shuffle to the door. "And don't forget about Cannon. If he's not here to go with me, the deal is off."

FIVE

"Do you believe the nerve of this guy?" Portia had called John the minute she got into her car.

"Yeah, I do. No one's ever said Woods didn't have balls, Cahill. He's pretty damned smart."

"Smart enough to figure out that you're behind this. I told him Fletcher was the SAC, but when Woods mentioned him, there were definite quotation marks around Will's name, if you know what I mean."

"Let him suspect all he wants, as long as he cooperates and gives up the burial site." John paused. "Do you think he's serious about that?"

Portia drove to the gate and rolled down her window. "You tell me; you know him better than I do. Is he likely to go back on the deal once he gets what he wants?"

She handed the visitors badge to the guard through the open car window, and nodded in acknowledgment of his "Thank you."

"Would he renege if he could get away with it?

Sure. We just can't give him an opportunity to do that."

"Is what he's asking even possible? I mean, can you arrange for this to happen?"

"Arrange to get him out of prison and to a secure indoor riding facility where he can be brought in and taken out without anyone knowing he was there?" John fell silent for a moment. "Yeah, I think I can, as long as I have the assurance of everyone involved that no one leaks this to anyone. No press. No rumors. Obviously, the fewer who know about it, the better. All we need is to have it get out that we're making deals with the likes of Sheldon Woods, or that he's getting some kind of special treatment."

He blew out a long breath. "At least he didn't insist on you taking him to the burial site, the way he did back then. No way I could arrange that again. It would call too much attention to the situation, and attention is the one thing I don't want."

"But there will have to be clearance on several levels through the prison system, right?" she asked. "And there will have to be guards, and transport . . ."

"I can pull the right strings and get the clearance, and we can probably keep the prison personnel to a minimum. The warden, of course, will have to be involved, and maybe one guard, maybe two at the most. We'll provide the rest of the security. As for the immunity, well, hell, he already got life for killing thirteen kids. After all this time, what the hell difference does it make if he isn't prosecuted for this one?" After another silent moment, John said, "Yeah, I can make this happen. I just have to talk to a few people."

"Speaking of talking to people, Woods had one other condition: He wants his attorney—his former attorney, the one who handled his defense back then—in the transport vehicle with him as a sort of security. He's afraid someone will try to take him out, but thinks he'll be safe if this lawyer is present."

"He wants Cannon there? Strange . . . Well, then, give the guy a call, go see him, whatever. We can't have this thing go south because the lawyer didn't show up. Take care of it, Cahill. I'll get back to you when I have the details wrapped up, then you can tell Woods everyone's on board."

A phone began to ring in the background.

"That's my private line," John said. "I'm going to have to take it. Meanwhile, you get in touch with Cannon and get him on board."

He paused before adding, "But God help the little bastard if the Williams boy isn't where he says he is."

It took Portia less than five minutes on her computer to learn that James Cannon was thirty-six years old and had the reputation for being one of the best criminal defense attorneys in the region.

Well, duh. Get a serial killer life in prison instead of the death penalty, and you're bound to have a path beaten to your door.

Back in 1999, when he defended Woods, Cannon would have been just a few years out of law school. How, she wondered, did someone that young end up representing the defendant in a case that big? Did he take on the case figuring to make a name for himself? It would have been a gamble though, wouldn't it? Defending a serial killer who'd murdered, at the very least, thirteen young boys?

Well, the gamble apparently paid off for him, she thought as she looked for and found his website, which showed a picture of his well-decorated office in a tony suburb of Baltimore.

"Apparently, crime does pay sometimes," she muttered as she dialed the number. "And it looks as if it's paid very well for Mr. Cannon."

The call was answered on the second ring by a most efficient-sounding voice. "J.P. Cannon and Associates."

"I'm calling for James Cannon. May I speak with him, please?"

"I can put you through to his assistant. Your name, please?"

"This is FBI Special Agent Portia Cahill."

"One moment, please."

Almost a full minute later, another equally efficient voice came on the line.

"This is Ms. Bennett. How may I help you, Agent Cahill?"

"I'd like to speak with Mr. Cannon."

"I'm afraid Mr. Cannon is out of the office at the moment, but I'd be happy to take a message."

"What time will he be back?"

"I don't expect him back till after five, but I'd be happy to—"

Portia glanced at her watch. She'd already figured out it would take at least ninety minutes to get to Cannon's office from hers.

"Will he be in by six?"

"Yes, he is expected, but—"

"Please tell Mr. Cannon that he can expect me at six and I'd appreciate a few minutes of his time."

"I can't guarantee that he'll be here precisely at six—this is Friday, you realize, and we normally do not make appointments for Friday evenings. But if you'd like to make an appointment for another time—"

"I would not. Please let him know that I'll be there at six."

The efficient voice was becoming increasingly terse.

"May I tell him what this is in reference to, Agent Cahill?"

"Tell him it's about Sheldon Woods."

"Mr. Cannon no longer represents Mr. Woods."

"I'm aware. Six P.M. today. Thanks so much."

The law offices of James P. Cannon and Associates were located in a handsome redbrick building in an area just outside the northern city limits. By getting off the interstate before rush-hour traffic clogged the arteries leading into Baltimore, Portia was able to pull into the small parking lot at exactly five fifty-three. Not bad, she thought as she scanned the names on the reserved parking places. A dark blue Jaguar sat in the space bearing the name J.P. Cannon. She parked her rental car in the visitors' space next to it.

"Right up there by the front door," she mused as she turned off the engine. "Must have paid a little extra for that little perk."

Nice. She nodded to herself as she walked around the back of the Jag. Very nice. It was a similar model to one Jack owned, one he'd let her drive occasionally when she visited. Portia loved that car. Even now, walking around this one, her fingers itched for the keys, her hand for the gear shift. She did appreciate a little speed, a little luxury.

Then she remembered what James Cannon did that permitted him such luxuries.

Right. Criminal defense. We bring 'em in, he gets 'em out.

She stepped away from the car and walked through the front door.

Portia stopped at the security desk in the center of the lobby and showed her credentials.

"I'll call up to let them know you're here, Agent Cahill," the uniformed woman told her. "Mr. Cannon's office is right there where you get off the elevator on the seventh floor."

"Thank you." Portia kept her ID in her hand as she headed into the elevator. She'd probably need it again very shortly.

As Portia suspected might be the case, Cannon's highly efficient assistant was waiting for her. The shapely young blonde in the blue silk suit appeared to be assessing Portia even as she stepped off the elevator.

"Agent Cahill?" she asked crisply.

"Yes. Ms. Bennett?"

"Yes. May I see some identification?" She held out a hand attached to an arm that sported a row of gold bracelets.

How, Portia wondered, did one type with all that hardware hanging off one's arm?

Portia handed the woman her ID, which she seemed to take a long time studying. While she did so, Portia scanned the firm's list of attorneys on the plaque on the wall facing the elevator. It appeared Mr. Cannon had amassed quite a staff since his Sheldon Woods days.

"This way," the woman said, Portia's credentials still clutched in her hand.

Portia followed her through a central reception area where several spacious glass-walled offices lined the outer wall of the building. The door of the back corner office was open, and it was through this door that Portia was directed.

"Agent Cahill is here to see you," the woman announced as she entered the spacious office.

Portia wasn't sure what she was expecting, but it wasn't James Cannon. He was leaning against the front of his desk, his arms folded across his chest, as if he'd been waiting for her. He was tall and broad-shouldered and had the look of a former athlete, one who refused to let himself get out of shape. His eyes were dark blue and his sandy brown hair fell across his forehead in the front, and in the back, just brushed the top of his collar. He held out one hand, and his assistant passed him the small folder holding Portia's ID. He looked it over, then handed it directly to Portia.

"What can I do for you, Agent Cahill?" he asked.

"I understand you represented Sheldon Woods." She had crossed the room to take back her ID, and remained standing several feet from Cannon.

"Represented—past tense—being the important word there," he said.

"Excuse me, is there anything else you need from me?" the assistant asked from the doorway.

"I don't think so, Danielle." He smiled at his assistant. "I know you like to leave on time on Fridays, so go ahead and wrap it up for today."

She cast an uncertain glance at Portia.

"I think I can take it from here," he told her.

"Okay. I'll see you later." Danielle started out of the room, then turned to Portia. "Agent Cahill."

Portia nodded as the woman left.

"Have a seat." Cannon gestured to one of the wing chairs near his desk.

"Thank you." Portia sat on it and crossed her legs.

"Now, what's brought Sheldon Woods back onto the FBI's radar?" Cannon asked.

"Long version or short?"

"Short. It's been a very long day."

"The mother of one of Woods's suspected victims is terminally ill. She'd like to bury her son before she dies. We'd like to help her do just that."

"Since when has the FBI cared so much for the little guy?"

"Since the man who runs the unit I work for was the agent who brought Woods in twelve years ago."

"John Mancini?" Cannon raised an eyebrow. "He's still around?"

Portia nodded. "You sound surprised."

"I'd heard he'd . . ." Cannon hesitated. ". . . had a hard time after the thing with Woods. Took a leave for a while, or something."

"He took some time off, yes." Portia wasn't willing to concede more than that. Few people knew just how bad things had gotten for John after Woods's trial. "But he never left the Bureau."

"I'm glad to hear it. So—we have a woman dying who wants to bury her son." Cannon turned one of the other wing chairs to face Portia, and sat. "Since all of the 'Baker's Dozen' victims were recovered, we're talking about someone Woods hasn't previously given up?"

Portia nodded. "Yes."

"Is there any proof that Woods was the killer?"

"The boy—Christopher Williams was his name—was eight years old, disappeared on his way home from soccer practice, no ransom note. This was in nineteen ninety-seven, northern Maryland . . ."

"In short, he fit Woods's MO and victim profile."

"To a tee."

Cannon's forehead creased as he seemed to think back.

"There was a woman who came to court every day . . . I think her name was Williams. She spoke with Woods on the last day, at sentencing. She had a picture of a boy . . ."

"That was Madeline Williams." Portia nodded. "I wasn't there, of course, but John told me how she'd approached Woods, begged him to tell her where her son was buried. She was convinced that Woods had killed him. As was the FBI, by the way. They just couldn't prove it at the time."

"So how do you propose to go about proving it now? And what does it have to do with me?"

"I've been to see Woods. . . ."

He arched an eyebrow but did not interrupt her.

"And he's pretty much agreed to tell us where the boy is, but he did have several conditions."

"Of course he did," Cannon muttered. "What does the bastard want this time? Oh, let me take a wild guess—immunity for the boy's murder."

"Naturally, he doesn't want to be punished for the crime. That was a given going into this. What he wants is an hour of horseback riding."

"He wants . . . *what*?"

"That was my reaction too, but that's it. He wants to ride a horse for an hour."

"Of course, you're not going along with this."

"Of course we are. It's being arranged in an indoor riding facility as we speak."

"That's total bullshit."

"Tell that to Madeline Williams."

"Why would Mancini agree to this?"

She shrugged. "Oh, I don't know. Maybe because he wishes he'd been able to hold out for the names of a few more victims before you made that deal locking them into thirteen."

Cannon stared at her, his eyes dark, his expression unreadable.

"And I fit into this how?"

"Oh, that's the third condition," Portia told him.

"He wants you there. He wants you to ride with him to and from the prison."

"I'm no longer his attorney." Cannon shook his head. "I don't want anything to do with him. You can count me out."

"Then there's no deal, and Madeline Williams goes to her grave never having found her son." Portia looked directly into Cannon's eyes, anger rising within her. "But I suppose any man who'd craft a deal to get a child molester and murderer life in prison rather than the death penalty—a penalty he so richly deserved—shouldn't be expected to give a damn about the families of his client's victims."

Cannon's face hardened.

"I'm sorry I wasted your time, Mr. Cannon." Portia rose, unable to meet his eyes, afraid of just what more she might say.

She turned her back and walked out of the office.

"Agent Cahill," he called to her when she was almost to the elevator. "Wait."

She paused midstride and looked back over her shoulder as he approached.

"Let's get one thing straight. I did not choose to represent Sheldon Woods. I was appointed by the court to defend him. And while I understand your feelings about the deal he got, I had a moral and ethical obligation to do the best I could for my client, odious as it might seem."

"It looks like it all turned out well enough for

you." She glanced around meaningfully at the well-appointed reception area, with its Oriental rugs and plush seating. "I'll bet that case made your reputation as the criminal defense attorney to go to when the going gets tough."

"Everyone deserves an honest defense."

"Even an animal who rapes and murders children?"

"You don't get to pick and choose who gets to be defended and who doesn't. Everyone is presumed—"

"—innocent until proven guilty, right," she snapped. "Yeah, yeah, I've heard it before. Better a guilty man should go free than an innocent man punished."

"It's the principle our system of justice was founded on," he pointed out.

"I've seen too many of the guilty go free. Very often, they're set free to kill or rape again."

"You don't believe that everyone deserves a fair trial?"

"Fair trial, yes. Sweetheart deals, like the one you got for Sheldon Woods? Uh-uh." She shook her head. "Frankly, I don't know how you sleep at night."

"Well, actually, for a long time, Agent Cahill, I didn't." He stuck his hands in his pants pockets, looking unexpectedly self-conscious. "But before you condemn me, keep in mind that thirteen families got to bury their sons. I regret that I was not able to return the remains of every murdered child to his loved ones, but that was the best I could do. Woods would not give up more than thirteen.

"And for the record? Lethal injection would have been far too easy a death for him."

"Well, that's one thing we can agree on." She turned to the elevator where the doors stood open, waiting for her. She stepped in and pressed the button for the lobby without looking back.

Jim Cannon watched the elevator doors close and the light above them descend, floor to floor, as the car made its way to the lobby.

"Well," he muttered, "I guess she told me."

He'd been taken to task many times by cops and family members of victims whom his clients had been accused of killing or assaulting, so it wasn't as if the FBI agent had expressed sentiments he hadn't heard before. Usually he did his best to not dwell on other people's opinions of the work he did. He had his reasons and they were damned good ones. His motives were no one's business but his own.

So why was he still standing here, feeling chastised, because an FBI agent had looked at him as if he were the lowest form of life on the planet?

Something about Special Agent Portia Cahill announced that she was not a woman to be taken lightly. It was in the degree of contempt that had hung on her every word, the way her eyes had challenged him. The way she'd assumed so much about him, about his morals and his ethics.

The words he'd spoken were the truest words he knew. He did believe that every man, every woman, was entitled to the best, the most honest defense possible. He did believe, with all his heart, that no innocent man should ever pay a price for a crime he did not commit, and that if everyone involved did their job the way they were supposed to—the cops, the prosecutors, the defense attorneys—the guilty would not walk free. But all too often someone got lazy, skipped a step or two, lost evidence, missed a witness, and the wrong verdict came down, and the guilty got to walk.

The problem was, you couldn't always count on everyone to do their best every time. He should have tried to explain that to Agent Cahill.

I suppose any man who'd craft a deal to get a child molester and murderer life in prison rather than the death penalty—a penalty he so richly deserved—shouldn't be expected to give a damn about the families of his client's victims.

That had stung the most. The families of the victims were always in the forefront of his mind. Had she intended the insult to cut so deeply? Did she really believe that he had so little regard for the victims of violence?

For all the research she'd done on him, she'd missed some very salient details.

He should have defended himself better, he chided

himself as he walked back to his office, but he'd
been somewhat distracted by her. She'd come strid-
ing into his office, all cool confidence and bold attitude and had thrown him off his best game by
knowing way more about him than he knew about
her. She'd done her research before she arrived,
so the advantage was clearly hers. Was that it, he
had to ask himself, or was it because he'd been so
struck by her beauty and by the fierceness of her
sense of justice, that he'd neglected to explain that
crafting the deal for Sheldon Woods in a manner
that assured families that their lost sons would be
returned had been one of his best moments?

He'd heard those arguments before—that he
should have let the state find Woods guilty at trial
and given him the death penalty that he so richly
deserved. Jim had not exaggerated when he'd said
that lethal injection would not have been sufficient
retribution for all the terrible things Woods had
done.

But those who condemned him for the deal he'd
struck had not been in the courtroom to witness
the procession of heartbroken parents, brothers,
sisters, and friends, whose pain was a palpable
presence. They were the ones whose prayers had
not been answered, the ones who had nothing left
to pray for, the ones who could no longer pretend
that their loved one would be found alive and that
somehow they'd been caught in a very bad dream.
These were the families whose only remaining hope

was that the remains would be found so that they could bury their dead. They were the ones who, in the end, he'd best served. By finding a way to spare Sheldon Woods's life, he'd given the victims back to their families. He'd not sought to defend Woods, but once he'd been assigned to handle the case, he'd been determined to make of it what he could, not for his sake, but for theirs.

He wished he'd been able make Special Agent Portia Cahill understand that about him. He wished he knew why it mattered so much to him that she did.

He packed his briefcase with some work he needed to finish at home, wondering if he was bothered more because she'd so easily dismissed him and questioned his value as a human being, or because she'd had the last word.

SIX

Portia stood in the dark outside the indoor riding ring and swatted at the mosquitoes that had been feasting on her various body parts for the past five minutes. Not yet dawn, the air was still and heavy and smelled of night. A smattering of low fog, ghostly white, drifted eerily across a nearby pasture.

"Give it a rest, will you?" she pleaded as she smacked her left forearm with the palm of her right hand, only to miss once again.

"You talking to me?" the tall young agent standing at the doorway asked.

"No, I'm talking to these vicious little bastards that seem to think I'm breakfast." She ducked as another circled her head, its buzzing loud, defiant, purposeful in the morning air. "That's it. I'm waiting in my car."

She hurried down the paved drive not caring if she looked like she was running away, though in the dark, she reminded herself, who would know? There were certain things she just couldn't tolerate. Blood-sucking insects were close to the top of the list.

"The sun doesn't rise for another two hours and already I'm wimping out," Portia grumbled as she got into the car and turned on the ignition.

Opening a window would be tantamount to an invitation to the mosquitoes: *Come on in. Drink up!* Figuring she'd done her part already that morning to ensure that the little bastards would live and prosper, she started the car and turned on the air-conditioning.

She toyed with the radio before accepting the fact that her only choice was country music—with or without static. She opted out completely and turned it off. She hummed a few bars of a song, then realized it was one of Jack's. It reminded her about the CDs he'd given her before she left London— advance copies of his newest album for her and for Miranda. She hadn't had the nerve to give Miranda her copy. She could kick herself for not having had the presence of mind to have stuck one in her bag before she left the house that morning. Of course, it had been practically the middle of the night; one of the prison's stipulations for going along with the FBI's request was that no one within the prison community—except for the warden and one carefully selected guard—would know that Woods had been permitted to leave the compound. Fair enough. It wasn't something the FBI wanted publicized either. Portia glanced at her watch. The transport should be arriving any minute now.

Portia hummed a few more bars, wishing she

could figure out a way to get her sister to at least try to understand Jack. True, he'd never been much of a father to any of his children while they were young, and granted, he hadn't been much of a husband to any of the women he'd married. He'd been in and out of her own life when she and Miranda were young—Miranda hadn't exaggerated that— but he had taken to Portia as an adult. She thought perhaps he just might be one of those men who didn't relate well to small children. Not that that was an admirable thing, but sometimes, that was just how it was. Something you could accept, or not.

Of course, Portia reasoned, she could just be making excuses for him because she'd found that she really liked him, lousy father or not. He was an intelligent, interesting man, and an incredibly gifted musician. He made no excuses for the way he was and never tried to pass off his deficiencies as anything other than what they really were—flaws in his character. That made him one of the most honest people she'd ever met.

Sheldon Woods, she reminded herself, had said the same thing about James Cannon, but what would be Woods's idea of an honest man? One who knew but didn't tell where all the bodies were buried?

Woods had been everything she'd thought he'd be, but Cannon hadn't been what she'd expected. She'd thought he'd be older, maybe, heavy on the sleaze factor, a bit of a hustler. Shifty-eyed, perhaps, unable to make or maintain eye contact. The James Cannon she'd met the day before yesterday had been none of those things. And while he'd been unapologetic over his role in orchestrating Woods's plea bargain, he'd certainly not gloated over it, either. Within the criminal defense community, Woods getting life without possibility of parole instead of the death sentence had been a definite coup—a win for the bad guys—but Cannon had given her the distinct impression that the deal he'd orchestrated had been as much about the victims and their families as it had been a fulfillment of his obligation to provide a proper defense for his client. Then again, he might just be a very good actor. But he had agreed to get up in the middle of the night to do this today, and for that she was grateful.

The crunching of tires on the gravel drive drew her attention to the light-colored van that cautiously approached the barn. It pulled up to the very front of the building and came to a stop. Moments later, two men emerged from the vehicle's front, then four more came out of the rear, all dressed in dark blue shirts with FBI in white on the backs. In the lights from the barn, Portia watched the van's rear side panel slide back. She recognized the guard who jumped out as CO DeLuca, who'd brought Woods into the visitors' room both times she'd been there. As all the agents stood by, James

Cannon hopped out, followed by Woods, still dressed in his orange prisoner's garb, his cuffed hands and ankles secured by chains to a ring around his waist. He was led into the barn, his gait encumbered by the hardware, agents on either side and behind him, Cannon the last in line.

Portia got out of her car and hurried to catch up. Once Woods was inside, the doors would be locked behind him, and she'd be embarrassed if she had to bang on the door to be let in. Her long legs carried her quickly across the distance, and she arrived at the door just behind Cannon. Hearing her approach, he looked over his shoulder, but did not greet her. She filed in behind him, and the door was closed and locked by a tall, sleepy-looking man who she recognized as being from Bureau headquarters, though she couldn't remember his name. She nodded to him as he locked the door, and noted that he, like all the others, was heavily armed. Portia smiled to herself. John Mancini was taking no chances. If Sheldon Woods was going to try to escape, he'd look like a piece of Swiss cheese before he came within ten feet of the door.

Inside the riding ring, a burly man wearing jeans and a frayed T-shirt held the reins of a chestnut mare. The horse stood calmly by as if being saddled up and led out of her stall in the middle of the night was an everyday occurrence.

"So, who's got the keys?" Woods demanded,

looking from one guard to the other. "Come on, get these things off me. I only have an hour."

"Ummm, Sheldon?" Portia stepped forward. "Aren't we forgetting something?"

"What?" He turned to her, an annoyed expression on his face.

"You're supposed to give me information, then you get to ride."

"No, first I ride, then you get to ask your questions."

"There aren't going to be any questions," Portia stood with her feet apart, her hands on her hips. "You're going to give me exact instructions on how to find Christopher Williams's grave, then you get a leg up."

"Actually, what I believe I said was, I'd tell you what you wanted to know when I was high in the saddle. Not before."

Portia gestured for the man holding the mare to step forward, then turned to the guards.

"Undo the ankle and waist restraints, but keep the cuffs on his hands." To Woods, she said, "Once you're in the saddle, you give me what I want, then your wrist cuffs come off. You mess with me, you're back off that horse faster than you can blink. Understand?"

"Agent Cahill, you insult me. We had a deal. You kept your end of the bargain, I will keep mine." His eyes lit up as he watched the horse approach.

"Ah, aren't you a lovely thing. A bit long in the tooth, as they say, but lovely."

He shuffled closer. "And I'll bet you had some fire when you were younger, eh? Well, didn't we all?"

The guard holding the key glanced at Portia and she nodded. With a wary look at Woods, he knelt down to unlock the ankle cuffs, but Woods barely noticed. He was still crooning to the horse.

"Help him up," Portia told the man holding the reins.

"No, no, I don't need any help." In one surprisingly smooth movement, Woods had leaped to grab the pommel and swung himself into the saddle. He closed his eyes and smiled as he put his feet in the stirrups. "My, but it's been a long time. But as they say, some things you never forget."

He addressed the groom, asking, "What's her name?"

"Molly Blue" was the response.

"Nice. Well, Molly Blue, let's take us a little . . ."

"Woods." Portia made no effort to disguise her impatience.

"Oh, right. Sorry. I forgot." Woods smiled down at her. "You wanted some directions."

She took a small recorder from her pocket.

"Go 'head," she told him.

He leaned forward to pat the horse's neck. "From here, you want to head north . . ."

He rattled off a series of highways and back

roads leading increasingly close to the Pennsylvania border.

"Once you get to Oldbridge," he continued, "you want to head out of town past a large red barn. I don't recall the name of the road, but you can't miss the barn. About a mile farther down the road, you'll look to your left, and you'll see a hill with a tall straight tower rising up from its crest. There will be a road that intersects there. Take a left and follow it until you get to the dirt road that leads up to the tower."

"What kind of tower?" Portia frowned. "Like a cell phone tower?"

"No, no, it's some kind of monument. Stone. It's the highest point around." Woods fixes her with a withering stare. "If you can't find it, you're not much of an investigator."

"Okay, so we see the hill and the monument . . ." She ignored the jab.

"It's maybe a quarter mile down the road after you make the turn," he told her.

"Then what?"

"Then you stop the car at the top of the hill and get out."

"Don't try my patience, Woods, it's hot in here and it's going to be a long day digging in the heat."

"Hey, your choice."

"Get. On. With. It."

"Okay, so you're at the top of the hill—there's an old cemetery there, did I mention that? Pre-

Revolutionary War, I think, judging by the dates on some of the headstones."

Portia gestured with her hand for him to continue. She was rapidly running out of patience.

"There's a cluster of pine trees off to the left, and a sort of rock pile behind the trees. Again, you can't miss it. You'll find what you're after right in front of the rocks, between the tallest two trees— they sit about twelve feet apart, or did, last time I was there." He nodded to her, then turned back to the groom, who still maintained a hold on the mare. "I'd like my ride now."

"Woods." She called to him as he edged into the ring on the horse, walking it as if trying to get a feel for it. "Woods. I'm talking to you."

He threw a glance over his shoulder, but did not stop.

"God have mercy on you if you're lying."

Woods laughed and nudged the horse into a trot. "Haven't you heard, Agent Cahill? God has no mercy for the likes of me."

Portia walked to the door and without being asked, the agent at the door unlocked it. She was halfway to her car when she heard someone calling her name. She turned to see James Cannon jogging toward her. He wore washed-out denims and a blue polo shirt that matched his eyes.

"I'd like to come with you," he told her.

"Why?"

"I was there when every one of the other boys

was found. I want to be there for Christopher Williams as well."

"Sorry. You have to ride back to the prison in the van with Woods. That was the deal, counselor. Cannon in the van on the way out, Cannon in the van on the way back."

"You got what you wanted. What difference does it make now?"

"Because maybe—just maybe—he might decide to play this game again sometime. But if I break my word now, there won't be a next time."

The barn door swung open, thumping dully against the outside wall, and two agents emerged. As they walked toward her, Portia called out to one, "Shay, find out who has the jurisdiction in and around Oldbridge, Maryland—local, county sheriff, the state. Call them, talk to whoever's in charge and tell him or her—and only that person—what's going on. Have them meet me there with a crime scene team. If Christopher Williams is there, we're getting him out today and I don't want to step on anyone's toes while we do it."

To Cannon she said, "Mr. Cannon, thanks for doing your part to make this happen. We appreciate it."

She walked away and got into her car. Making a U-turn in the drive, she looked back, but he was gone.

Two hours later, the car's external thermostat read eighty-five degrees, and Portia knew that the temperature would only continue to climb as the day progressed. Combined with the rising humidity, it was sure to become increasingly uncomfortable. She parked at the foot of the tower that stood just as Woods had described it: by itself, atop a hill, the tallest point around. There were pines exactly where he'd said there would be, and she could see the makeshift rock wall that ran behind them. The tower did appear to be some sort of monument, as Woods had suggested. She got out of the car and walked closer to see if she could read the words inscribed about eight feet up, but they were badly eroded. She started toward the pine grove that Woods claimed marked Christopher Williams's resting place.

There was no path to follow, and here and there pale granite headstones, almost flush to the ground and worn by wind and weather over the years, were obscured by grass long overdue for cutting. She knelt to push aside the tall green leaves from one on which the date was barely visible—12 DECEMBER, 1723—and the name, not at all. When they were children, she and Miranda used to make rubbings of the headstones in an old cemetery not far from where they lived. Today the thought of two young girls playing in a graveyard made her shiver.

Portia was careful to watch where she walked, not wanting to willingly tread on the ancient graves, but it was almost impossible to avoid. Several times she stubbed her toe on stone that only rose above the soil by inches.

At the pines, she hesitated momentarily, then walked between the two largest and looked for the spot Woods had described. If he were to be believed, Christopher's grave lay just two feet from where she stood. Silently she prayed for the lost boy beneath the ground.

Sorry, Christopher. So sorry it's taken so long to find you. She thought about that for a moment, then added, *If in fact we have found you. Your mother's sick, Chris—did they call you Chris? She needs you. They sent me to find you, to bring you back to her, so that you could make the journey together. She's holding on until we bring you home. I hope we can do that today.*

Reminded of the recent death of her own mother, Portia was near tears. She pushed aside her grief and cleared her throat as the procession of vehicles began to climb the dirt road toward the monument and raised a hazy cloud of dust in the early-morning sun.

OLDBRIDGE TOWNSHIP POLICE DEPARTMENT was painted in red on the side of the white vehicles. A tall, slender woman emerged from the second car in the line. She had latte-colored skin and wore a white baseball cap, brown slacks, and a tan T-shirt. She shielded her eyes from the sun with one hand as she gazed around the field. Seeing Portia, the woman slipped on a pair of dark glasses and walked toward her.

"Agent Cahill?" the woman called.

"Yes." Portia met the woman halfway.

"I'm Elena Duffy. Chief of police here in the township. I got a call from your boss about ninety minutes ago. Something about a child being buried some years ago up here on Turner's Hill? Previously unknown victim of Sheldon Woods?" The chief frowned. "What the hell's that all about?"

Portia told her.

"Shit, and it has to be here, in my township?" Elena Duffy shook her head. "Okay, let's get to it then."

She turned and waved on several casually dressed members of her force. "Your guy said we needed some recovery, so I brought what personnel I could get on short notice. Joanna there is a real good crime scene tech, Alvin is as well. I do have a call into the ME's office but haven't heard back from him yet. I suppose we should start digging—carefully, of course."

Portia nodded, eager to get on with it.

"I have to tell you straight out, we don't have much of a crime lab here in the township," the chief said. "Depending on what we find, we generally send it to the county or the state."

"What's their turnaround time?" Portia asked.

"Probably a lot longer than either of us would like."

Portia pretended to mull that over for a moment. "There's the FBI lab . . . that is, if you don't mind . . ."

Elena Duffy waved a deeply tanned hand. "I don't mind at all. The way I see it, you did me a courtesy by notifying me, respecting my jurisdiction. But there's no case to be investigated, since you already know who the victim is."

"Assuming that Woods is telling the truth."

"Right. There is that." Chief Duffy nodded. "But let's assume he told you the truth. You know the victim, you know who killed him. The fact that Woods left the boy in my backyard doesn't make the case mine. I have no problem with you taking it from here."

"Thank you," Portia said, grateful there would be no turf war. "Christopher Williams's mother will thank you, I'm sure."

"After all that lady's been through, no way am I going to be the one to stand between her and her son now. So if you have someone you want in on this recovery, get them out here, let 'em work with my team. Let's get this taken care of as soon as possible."

"How's your ME?"

"Top notch."

"Then we'll go with him to examine the remains and determine cause of death. The lab might not be necessary but we'll need a death certificate and that's going to have to come from the ME."

"Good enough." Elena Duffy turned and waved on her CSI's.

"This is Special Agent Portia Cahill," she told them. "She's going to show you where she thinks you're going to find some remains. Be real careful with them. It's someone's little boy."

Portia led the pair to the spot where Woods had indicated the grave would be found, then stepped back while they began to carefully remove the dirt. She leaned against the stone wall next to Elena Duffy for a while, both women silently watching the painstaking dig. A half hour later, the perimeter of a makeshift grave had been uncovered. Elena had dismissed all of her crew except for one detective, who photographed every stage of the excavation, and the two crime scene techs.

"Man, I can't even imagine what it's like, waiting all these years, like this kid's mom has had to do," Elena said softly. "If it was my kid, I'd have dug up half the state by now."

"You have children?" Portia asked.

"Two sons. Seven and twelve." Elena shook her head. "Just about the same age as . . ." She pointed to the spot where the digging was under way.

"Usually we've found the body by now," Alvin said to no one in particular after they'd dug for another twenty minutes. "Most of the time, the body's in a shallow grave. We're two feet down, and there's nothing." He glanced up at Portia. "You sure this is the right place?"

Portia removed the tape recorder from her bag. After rewinding for a moment, she played back Woods's words.

"There's a cluster of pine trees off to the left, and a sort of rock pile behind the trees. Again, you can't miss it. You'll find what you're after between the tallest two trees, right in front of the rocks. They sit about ten feet apart."

"Okay," the tech nodded. "Asked and answered." The digging resumed.

Portia noticed a light-colored SUV approaching the top of the hill and parking near the monument.

"That your ME?" she asked the chief.

"That would be him." Elena got off the wall where she'd been sitting for the past fifteen minutes and waved to the man who was exiting the car, but he didn't appear to notice.

She took off in the direction of the new arrival. Portia squatted and sat on her heels, watching the techs remove shovel after shovel of dirt.

If he lied about this, if this is all a game to him, I will personally find a way to make that little shit fry, she thought. *If he thinks putting Madeline Williams through this is fun . . . shit, if doing this to John is his idea of a good time, I will . . .*

"Agent Cahill, meet Tom Patton, the county medical examiner." Elena returned, leading the way for a portly man in his sixties for whom the walk up the hill had not been an easy one.

"Thanks for coming out." Portia stood and extended her hand. He took it in his own fleshy, overly warm one.

"That's the job." He took a deep breath and tried to get his breathing under control. "Asthma," he told her. "Asthma and allergies. All these damned dandelions, the wildflowers, tossing their damned pollen in the air, this blasted humidity . . ."

"Dr. Patton . . ." Elena began.

"Tom. How many times have I told you all to call me Tom?" He grumbled and stared down at the hole in the ground. "Where's the body?"

"It's still in there," Portia said, gesturing toward the hole. "We think it's in there."

"This is the emergency that had me tracked down at the dentist's office?" He raised an eyebrow.

"We thought the remains would have been closer to the surface," Portia told him.

The ME frowned at Elena across the open excavation. "What makes you so sure there's a body here?"

"The killer told Agent Cahill he'd buried a boy here," Elena explained.

"How long ago?" he asked.

"Sometime between 1997 and 1999," Portia responded.

"We're looking for old bones?"

"Yes."

"Well, for cryin' out loud, Elena, you brought me out here to look at something that may or may not

even be here, that may be ten, eleven years old?"
He glared equally at the two women.

"Got something," Joanna said, and three heads
turned to look at the same time. "Looks like a
hand. A very small hand."

The detective, who'd been sitting on the wall
watching the dig, picked up the camera and began
to shoot as each new bone was uncovered.

"Gonna get my people out here to get the remains ready for transport," Patton said. He took
the phone from his pocket and made his call.

"Yeah, Harve, I'm up here on Turner's Hill with
Chief Duffy and a couple 'a her people and the FBI.
Got us some bones. Bring me up a bag to bring
them back in."

"Two," Joanna said. "Tell him to bring two
bags."

"What?" Patton turned to the grave where the
techs had stopped digging.

"Two sets of remains, two bags." Joanna stood
and wiped the sweat from her brow with the back
of her right hand. She glanced from the ME to the
police chief to Portia. "There's a second body in
here."

"Are you sure?" Portia leaned into the grave.

"Yes, ma'am." Joanna nodded certainly. "Unless
the boy you're looking for had two heads, there're
two people buried here."

SEVEN

"Yes, I'm serious. Two bodies." Portia paced on the hillside, barely able to contain her anger and all but spitting her words into the phone. "He knew. That little fucking bastard knew there were two."

"Both children?" John asked.

"Yes. The one on the bottom looks to be considerably smaller than the one on top—the one we think is the Williams boy because there's what's left of a leather belt with a large C on the buckle. Neither of the skulls appear to be completely fused, which you'd expect to see in young children, but the shape of both indicates male."

"Cause of death?"

"Tough to tell. The one on the bottom hasn't been examined because they're still removing the top one. I can tell you that in the first one—the one I think might be Christopher—the hyoid bones are in three pieces, but the ME said he'd expect that if we're looking at kids, that it starts out in pieces.

The bones don't fuse together into one until sometime later."

"Woods maintained that he'd strangled all his victims, and the ones we recovered—his 'Baker's Dozen'—had all been strangled. I wouldn't expect to see any deviation."

"Yes, and these victims might have been as well. We just don't know by looking at the hyoid, as you could with an adult." Portia paused. "The reports I read in the file indicated that Woods had used different methods of strangulation for different victims."

"Make sure the ME knows to look for other signs. Fractured vertebrae, maybe."

"Will do." Portia noticed a black van heading up the dirt road. "Looks like the ME's people are here. They're going to try to separate the remains. Could take a while, they're so close in the grave."

"Are the remains intact?"

"Mostly, but some of the smaller bones are commingled, and a few of them are missing. Probably small animals took off with them. The techs will continue to dig around after the bodies are removed, see if they can find the digits." Portia set her bag down on the hood of her rental car and removed a bottle of water. She twisted off the cap, then took a quick drink. "We're going to need Christopher's dental records for a positive ID."

"I'll call Lisa Williams immediately," John said.

"Let's have them sent directly to Tom Patton, the

ME. I realize that time is working against us here, so if this is Christopher, I know everyone wants to see him returned to his family as quickly as possible. I'll let the ME know to expect them, then I'm out of here," Portia said. "Sheldon Woods and I are going to have a little chat."

"No." Sheldon Woods sat back in his chair in the little interview room and stared blankly at Portia.

"Don't fuck with me, Woods, I am seriously not in the mood."

"Your moods are irrelevant, Agent Cahill. You wanted Christopher Williams, and I gave him to you. I'm not obligated to give you anything or anyone else."

"What will it take, Woods?" She sighed deeply. "What do you want this time?"

"Nothing. I'm not giving you this one," he snapped. "This one is mine."

"Odd choice of words, Woods." Her eyebrows knit in thought. "Very odd."

"Do feel free to run it past your behavior people, your profiler, whatever you're calling your mind-benders these days." He waved a hand breezily. "It won't be the first time the FBI has tried to analyze me."

"This boy's family has been waiting years to find out what happened to their son."

"Then surely by now they've accepted the fact

that he isn't coming back," Woods said calmly. "And don't try to play on my sympathies, I haven't any. It only serves to annoy me."

"Annoy you?" She laughed hoarsely. "Trust me, Woods, before I'm through with you, you're going to be more than *annoyed*."

"CO DeLuca?" Woods said over his shoulder. "I'd like to go back now. Agent Cahill is being a pain in the ass today."

The guard glanced at Portia with empathy. She watched Woods shuffle out, envisioning herself wrapping both hands around his neck and holding him off the floor, his short legs kicking wildly, until he gave her the name of the boy who'd shared a grave with Christopher Williams for the past decade. She'd never been one to act out against a prisoner, but if there was ever a man who had earned her wrath and disgust, it was Sheldon Woods.

Okay, you little bastard. Don't want to tell me his name? Fine. I'll find out on my own, and then I'll prosecute you for his murder. Think you're going to play games with me? Think again, pal. This is one you will not win.

Portia sat at her sister's kitchen table and toyed with a spear of asparagus. Given everyone's work schedule, it was the first time since she'd arrived in town that she, Miranda, and Will had been able to have dinner together.

"I hear Woods is a first-class asshole," Miranda said after Portia brought her up to date on the case. "I know he got to John big-time. Genna told me once he still has nightmares about that case."

"Woods could definitely have that kind of effect. He is in his own class of creepiness." Portia pushed aside her plate and rested her forearms on the table. "There's an aura about him, a malevolence that I've never encountered before, and I've dealt with some really sinister characters over the years. But this man has no soul. He reeks of depravity." She looked at her sister and said, "I don't know how else to say it."

"I think you said it quite well." Miranda stood and took her plate and Portia's to the counter and set them down. "We've all had those cases where the suspect is so vile, so immoral, that they have a sort of malignant air about them. But from all I've heard about Sheldon Woods, he pretty much wins the malignancy trophy."

"Are you thinking it might not have been Christopher Williams in that grave?" Will said as he got up from the table and started to make coffee.

"I have a feeling it is," Portia told him. "They recovered a belt buckle with a *C* on it, which of course is not conclusive, but I think it's him. We should know for certain tomorrow, though. The ME will have the dental records and that should make a positive ID easy. There will be a match, or there won't be." She looked up at her sister. "It's the other boy that I keep thinking about. Woods would not—*would not*—discuss him. Said that one was his, whatever that meant. When I questioned him, he all but dared me to talk it over with a pro-filer."

"Did you?" Miranda removed the remaining ves-tiges of their dinner.

"I have a call in to Annie. I'm curious to see what she has to say about him." Portia got up, took mugs down from the cabinet, and placed them on the table.

"Surely someone has gone over his case before?" Will asked.

"There are several reports in the file from differ-ent psychiatrists. They all concurred that he's a so-ciopath." Portia sat back at the table and watched Will fill the coffeepot with water and pour it into the coffeemaker. "I still want Annie's take on him, though. I mean, with all his kills, why would he be so protective of this one?"

"Maybe he's just playing with you. Trying to piss you off, just because he can," Will suggested.

"That's a possibility, I suppose, but if you could have seen his face . . ." Portia shook her head. "I don't know, Will. I can't help but think there's something more there."

"What are you doing to identify the second boy from the grave?" Miranda asked.

"Well, that's where I was hoping Will could give me a hand," she said. "I was hoping I could sweet-talk you into running a list of all the missing male children that were reported to NCIC from nineteen ninety-five through 'ninety-nine from the states where Woods was active. Maryland, Virginia, Delaware, Pennsylvania . . ."

"I know the territory," Will grimaced. "I remember reading about the case while I was at the academy."

"I don't have a lot of identifiers for you to input," Portia told him, "but I have enough to start out with. Once the ME is finished with his examination I can probably add to it."

"You know the time frame, that's good." Will nodded. "And you know the sex."

"We'll go with the characteristics of the rest of Woods's victims. All white males between the ages of seven and thirteen." She paused and thought for a moment. "This boy did appear to be pretty small even for a seven-year-old, so maybe we should lower the range and start with missing five-year-olds. Of course, this one could be the exception. Or he could be really small for his age."

"We'll do five through fourteen. That should give us a lot of hits. You can narrow it down later if you have to," Will said. "The ME probably isn't going to be able to fill in some of the other blanks, like eye color and hair." He paused. "Unless there was hair attached to the skull . . ."

"It was really hard to tell," Portia told him. "The remains of the unknown boy were under those of the body we believe to be Christopher Williams, plus the bones were all brown from being in the soil for so long. If there was hair attached to either skull, it wasn't readily apparent while I was there. They were still trying to extract them when I left."

"I'll bet John has a list of probable victims," Miranda said, "though some of those could have been resolved by now. Of course, the NCIC report would show if the reporting agency removed the record."

"Meaning that the person has been found, one way or another," Will added.

"Good idea. John mentioned that he suspected Woods had killed a lot more kids than he gave up. Mrs. Williams probably was not the only parent of a missing boy who showed up at the courthouse." Portia toyed with the spoon her sister had placed on the table next to her mug. "And I can ask the lawyer, Cannon, if he has names of any possible victims."

"Would he be able to hand them over, even if he did?" Miranda asked.

"I guess it would depend on how he got the list. If Woods gave him the names while Cannon was representing him, I'd think Cannon would be violating attorney-client privilege if he gave them to me," Portia said thoughtfully. "But maybe he has some thoughts on the case. It doesn't hurt to ask."

"What's he like?" Miranda asked. "The lawyer?

I saw pictures of him in *Baltimore* magazine. He looks hot."

Portia shrugged as if she hadn't noticed, though in fact she had.

"He's a criminal defense attorney. Bottom-feeder. His job is to keep his clients out of jail, guilty or innocent. He's obviously successful at it, so I'd guess there could be a 'six degrees of separation' thing at work here between him and us."

Miranda turned and gave Portia a blank look.

"There's a good chance that he could have defended someone we busted our humps to bring in," Portia explained.

Turning to Will, she said, "I know you have other cases that you've been working on. Your mad computer skills have made you a very popular guy within the Bureau. But if you could fit this in sometime soon, I'd really appreciate it."

"Tonight soon enough?"

"Tonight would be awesome."

"Ask and ye shall receive. Besides, it only takes a few minutes." He started to fill Portia's cup, then hesitated. "Would you rather have tea?"

"Coffee's fine, thank you."

He poured Miranda's, then his own. Taking his mug, he told Miranda, "I think I'll just go tinker in my office for a while."

Knowing he'd be working on her request, Portia told him, "No, no, sit. Drink your coffee. I didn't mean for you to—"

He waved away her protests. "Some people like an after-dinner mint, or a drink. Me, there's nothing I like better with my coffee than a good puzzle."

He leaned over to kiss the top of Miranda's head. "If you need me, you know where to find me."

She smiled and turned to watch him leave the room. "One thing about that man." Miranda turned back to her sister. "He does have a good rear view."

"That he does," Portia agreed. "The front view isn't bad, either."

"If you like that slightly bookish type, which I do." Miranda got up and locked the back door. "All this creepy-guys-I-have-known talk has me a bit antsy. Did I mention that I leave for Maine in the morning?"

"I heard about the case on the news. That's yours?"

Miranda nodded. "Seven women in four months. John said when the call for an assist came in, the local sheriff told him they thought they might have a serial killer." She shook her head. "Ya think?"

"You know the locals don't like to panic too soon . . ."

"It's never too soon to panic, not when the bodies are piling up like that," Miranda noted.

". . . And they don't like to call us unless they have to."

"That's always been true. But now, with so many agents in counterterrorism, there aren't as many agents available to be sent out. A lot more of the local agencies are having to deal with this stuff on their own," Miranda reminded her. "Which makes our unit even more valuable than it had been. John set up this unit by handpicking his people, and he's only taken the best from the field since then. Not too many of us have left, so we haven't had too many new agents. There have been some over the past couple of years, of course . . ."

"Oh, right. The Shields thing." Portia had heard about one rogue agent going bad and killing another, who happened to be his own cousin. Since several members of the family were in John's unit and had taken some time off to recover from the tragedy, they'd been shorthanded for a while. "I heard Andrew and Connor are back in the fold now."

"Yeah, they're both back, but Mia left. She's a cop in some small town on the Chesapeake now. Got herself a great guy, I hear, and is happy as a clam."

"I wonder if John is going to assign some new cases to me now that it looks as if we have Christopher's remains." Portia stirred her coffee.

"You're going to have to discuss that with him."

"He hasn't said anything to you?"

"He wouldn't." Miranda shook her head and looked away. "Not about his plans for you, anyway."

Portia put her mug down. "What is it that you're not saying?"

Miranda stared into her mug as if searching for an answer. Finally she said, "Word is that you don't want to be here."

"That's no secret. I didn't want to come home. You know that." Portia sipped her coffee. "It's my own fault that I'm here, as John pointed out to me on Monday, but I'm not happy about it."

Portia took another sip, then asked, "Who'd you get the word from, anyway, and what are they saying?"

"I just heard it around the office. Someone overheard you and John the day you came back. Said he chewed you a new one for letting yourself get outed by the tabloids and basically that he laid you out in lavender for your attitude."

"Well, that's certainly an accurate recollection. Someone must have been damned close to the door to have heard all that." Portia frowned. "So everyone thinks I'm . . . what?"

"Just that you'd rather be back where you were."

Portia sighed. "Crap. Nothing like making a name for yourself your first day back."

"It doesn't matter. Everyone who's ever worked with you knows how good you are. I wouldn't worry about it." Miranda went to the coffeemaker and lifted the pot, waving it at Portia.

"No, thanks, I still have some."

"Are you upset? Annoyed? Pissed off?"

"No." Portia shook her head. "I probably deserve whatever dirt is out there. I wasn't as gracious as I should have been to John. I shouldn't have been so blunt about not being happy at being reassigned. He could have just left me out there, to be sent to any shit-hole office that needed an experienced agent."

"You were part of his team before you left for counterterrorism. He wanted to give you the opportunity to come back here."

"Where the elite meet and greet."

"More or less, yes." Miranda drained her cup. "This much I do know: He called the director immediately when he found out, asked for you to be sent here."

"He told you that?"

"Not exactly. Oh, he did say something to me about you coming back, thinking I already knew. Which I did, but only because I happened to be in Kit's office when John got the call about you being given the boot," Miranda admitted.

"Ah, a little eavesdropping of your own, eh?"

"I couldn't help it. He had a bad connection and he was talking very loud."

"Oh, swell," Portia lamented. "So the whole office heard . . ."

"No, it was close to nine at night. He and I and Kit were the last people there. Kit was in the ladies' room, so no one else heard that part." Miranda stood and took her empty mug to the sink and rinsed it. "At least, not then, and not from John. I think bits and pieces were patched together over a few days. Everyone knows why you were sent back but no one's been talking about that in front of me, because apparently everyone knows how I feel about Jack."

"How would they know that?" Portia frowned.

"You know how it is in a small office, sis. One person tells one person, that person tells two . . ."

"And so on and so on. Yeah, I know how it is. I hope it hasn't made things uncomfortable for you."

"Nah. It's chatter, but it's not mean-spirited chatter."

Portia stood and stretched. "Thanks for such a great dinner. I didn't realize you'd become such a terrific cook."

"I have my moments." Miranda grinned. "Maybe only once or twice a week, but I do have them."

"Well, it was delicious and I'm happy that I was here on one of your nights. And thank you again for letting me stay in your spare room. I promise I'll be out of your hair as soon as I can find a place of my own."

"No hurry. Will and I like the company."

"I'll be looking at a few apartments tomorrow, actually." Portia opened her bag and waved a piece of paper at Miranda. "I went online today and made a list of all the places that looked decent. I have my first appointment at ten in the morning."

"Please don't feel that you have to do that. Seriously. We love having you here."

"Of course you do. Nothing like having a third wheel crash into the love nest."

Miranda laughed. "It's all right. We hardly know you're here." She thought about that for a moment, then added, "Of course, we haven't all been here at the same time except to sleep since you got here. And I'll be away for a few days." She thought for a moment, then added, "Actually, Will is leaving tomorrow for a few days—he's going to Texas through at least midweek, maybe longer—so you'll actually be doing us a favor by staying around for a little while."

"How so?"

"You could . . ." Miranda looked around the kitchen. "You could watch the house. Water the plants."

"I thought you only had fakes because you always forget to take care of them and they die."

"Will brought a few real ones when he moved in. He tossed out the fakes."

"Well, isn't he optimistic?"

"Yes, he is," Will said from the doorway. "And with good reason."

He tossed several sheets of paper onto the table and pointed to the clock on the wall. "Let it be noted that it didn't take me past eight o'clock."

"You're finished already?" Portia frowned. "Damn. I heard you were good . . ."

"It's all true." Will pulled out a chair.

"Your modesty is overwhelming."

"Hey, some got it, some wish they had it." He grinned and turned the sheets of paper to face Portia. "Actually, you could have done this yourself on your laptop if you had the right codes and passwords. These are the names and all the identifiers of all the boys within the age range who disappeared during the time frame we discussed, from the states we're interested in. Reporting law enforcement agency is here." He pointed.

Portia pulled the pages closer to take a better look. "I guess the reporting agencies would know if their missing kid has returned alive or if his remains have been located."

"In that case, they should have removed them from the list, though I suppose sometimes they forget that detail."

Portia studied the list. "So many kids, Will . . ."

"Yeah, I know." He stood and smacked the back of the chair he'd been sitting in. "No one said it was a pretty job."

"Thanks, Will. I really appreciate this."

"Not a problem." He shrugged. "I hope it helps you to identify your boy."

Portia headed for her room, eager to start an Internet search for anything she could find on the missing boys. She turned on her computer and shot off an e-mail to John Mancini, asking him to send her his list of suspected victims of Sheldon Woods to match against the list Will had prepared for her. Then she used a search engine to look up the boys whose names had shown up on Will's search. From there, knowing their hometowns, she went on to read about the cases in the victims' local newspapers.

So many of their stories were the same. Young boy, snatched from the street, on his way home from an innocent childhood activity—soccer, baseball, Peewee football. The library. A friend's house. All missing from their own neighborhoods—mostly from within a few blocks of their own homes, where they should have been safest. Gone without a trace. Almost every one of them, in broad daylight.

No one saw . . . no one heard.

It was after three when she turned off the light and stumbled off to bed, the names of the missing and their sad stories echoing in her head. Tomorrow, she would start the search for the name of the boy in the grave. It might take a while, but sooner or later, she would discover who he was, and why Sheldon Woods wanted to keep his identity a secret.

Then she'd hand over her file to the U.S. Attorney's Office. She would be there, right in the front row of the courtroom, when Sheldon Woods went on trial for his life.

EIGHT

Portia turned over lazily, awakened by sunlight streaming through the bedroom window. She opened her eyes and looked at the clock, then sat straight up. It was after nine A.M. She couldn't recall the last time she'd slept that late—even on a Saturday. She swung her legs over the side of the bed and listened. All she heard was the clock ticking away on the bedside table and a passing car or two outside the window. She grabbed her robe and went to the top of the stairs.

"Miranda?" she called over the banister. "Will?"

When no one answered, she realized she was alone. Miranda had told her she'd be leaving this morning for her trip to Maine, but Portia hadn't realized she'd be leaving so early. *Will must have driven her to the airport,* she thought as she went down the steps to the kitchen. A note was pinned to the coffeemaker.

Hey, P.—Help yourself to some morning caffeine and breakfast—you know where to find every-

thing. See you on Tuesday or Wednesday, depending. Love, M.

Portia poured a cup and grabbed a yogurt from the refrigerator, a spoon from the drawer, and ate standing up. She watched a hummingbird at the feeder near the small deck at the back of the townhouse before heading back upstairs. She'd almost forgotten she had appointments to look at apartments this morning.

While she showered, she questioned why she was bothering to look at places to live when she wasn't even sure she wanted to stay with the Bureau. It had occurred to her that perhaps a private security firm might be a better fit. They were always looking for people with her experience, especially in the Middle East. *That's where I really want to be,* she thought, *isn't it? Isn't that where I belong? The work I was born to do?*

She had to admit that there were some aspects of being back in the States that were highly appealing, things she'd missed while camping in the mountains. Like hot showers. Electricity. Indoor plumbing. Things that were taken for granted here were luxuries where she'd been in Afghanistan. As much as she enjoyed the work, she had to admit that this stateside gig had a lot going for it.

The list of apartments was at the bottom of her purse. She looked it over, debating whether or not to cancel her appointment. She hated to waste anyone's time showing her places she wasn't likely to rent. On the other hand, it could take some time to find another job, and in the interim, she'd be imposing on her sister and Will. Not that either of them seemed to mind, but how would they feel after six weeks? Six months?

She was almost dressed when her phone began to ring.

"Portia, it's John. I got your e-mail. The information you asked for should be in your in-box right about," he paused, and she could hear the tapping of fingers on a keyboard, "now."

"That was fast." She placed her laptop on the bed and sat next to it, booted up, and waited for her mail to appear.

"I've had that list for years," he said. "It was just waiting for someone to find a reason to look into it."

"Well, now we have two reasons."

"If we could positively identify the remains that were found yesterday—both sets of bones—that would take two names off the list. That means two more families will have peace of mind, two more families will be able to bury their dead. No small thing, Portia, when you think about it."

"No," she agreed. "It's no small thing."

"What are you planning on doing with the list, now that you have it?"

"First I want to compare it to the NCIC list Will pulled off the computer for me last night, info on boys who'd gone missing during the period we knew Woods was active. Some of them may have been located, some could have been runaways who have since returned." She opened the e-mail from John and scanned it. There were twenty-three names on it. "Jesus. You think Woods was responsible for twenty-three more kills than he'd admitted to?"

"At the least, yes."

"Good God."

"Yeah." John sighed heavily. "So go on. Your plan . . ."

"Right. I'm going to start calling the reporting police departments and try to find out the status of each one of those kids, see what's new. Since Woods didn't seem to travel too far with his victims, chances are the other boy we found yesterday was from the Pennsylvania/Maryland area, as the Williams boy was. I think his family home was within twenty miles of where we found him."

"Sounds like you have a handle on things." He paused again. "It would feel really good to cross two more names off."

"Yeah. I hear you."

"Let me know what the ME comes back with. Keep in touch." John hung up, and she turned off her own phone.

Portia forwarded the list to her office computer and grabbed her bag. She was halfway out of the room when she remembered the appointments she'd set up for that morning. She went back into

the room, picked up the paper with the addresses
and phone numbers and stuffed it into her purse.
She'd call and cancel. Apartment hunting could
wait.

When Portia arrived at headquarters, the lights in
several of the offices were on and the individual office doors were closed. Eager to work, she closed
her own door and booted up her computer. While
the machine went through its paces, she sipped the
container of drive-through coffee she'd picked up
on her way in, and dug the apartment listings out
of her bag. She made four quick calls canceling her
appointments, then set about comparing her notes.

All of John's twenty-three names were on the list
compiled by Will, but Will's list was much longer.
She read them over, one by one, before picking up
the phone and beginning her calls. She realized that
since it was Saturday morning, she'd most likely be
leaving messages. She knew she would have to wait
a few days while the message slip went from desk
to desk until finally it landed in the hands of someone who'd return her call. *Might as well get the
process started,* she thought, *get step one out of the
way.*

It took her most of the day, but she did manage
to call all fifty-seven police departments on the list.
She'd left both her cell and her office numbers, and
hoped that by Tuesday she'd be getting some re-
turns. She sorted through her notes, looking for
James Cannon's phone number. While he probably

wouldn't get her message until Monday morning, it would be one more step finished. She dialed the number and listened to it ring.

"Cannon."

"Uh . . . ," she stammered, caught off guard. She hadn't expected a real person to pick up.

"Hello?"

"Mr. Cannon, it's Agent Cahill. I'm sorry, I was caught off guard. I didn't expect you to answer the phone."

"Who did you expect to answer?"

"An answering service. Maybe a recording."

"Disappointed?"

"No, of course not. I just didn't expect to find you in on a Saturday afternoon."

"So why did you call if you didn't think I'd answer?"

"So that I could leave a message." She realized she was speaking through clenched teeth.

"Ah, we're back to that again." He sounded mildly amused.

"Mr. Cannon, I'd like to talk to you about Sheldon Woods."

"I assumed that was why you were calling. How'd you make out looking for the remains?"

"We found what we were looking for."

"That's terrific. Congratulations. I'm sure Mrs. Williams will be very happy."

"Yes." She cleared her throat. "But there was something else . . . someone else. Buried there."

"What do you mean, someone else?" He paused. "Wait a minute, you mean there was more than one body?"

"Yes, but I'm hoping that doesn't leak to the press. Actually, I don't want any of this to get out. Everyone who has a missing son will be calling, wondering if it's their boy. We don't need for people to be getting their hopes up." She shuffled through her lists. "Some of these people have been waiting so long . . ." She sighed. "Actually, that's what I'd like to speak with you about, if you have some time."

"I have time right now. Shoot."

"I'd rather do it in person, if that's all right with you." She wanted to read his face when she asked about Woods's victims. Would he tell her the truth? Would he cover for his former client? Would she know the difference?

"You can stop over if you're in the area. Otherwise, I could meet you someplace."

"I'm about ninety minutes from your office."

"So we'll meet halfway. How about Dalesberg? There's a nice little Italian restaurant on Clark Road. Giorgio's. They have the best chicken piccata you'll ever taste. I can meet you there at six."

"That's not necessary, we can wait until Monday."

"Actually, I'm pretty hungry right now."

"I meant, I'm sure you have better things to do on a Saturday night."

"Trust me, I don't." He hesitated. "Unless you've got other plans . . ."

"No, actually, I don't. Fine. I'll meet you at Giorgio's in Dalesberg at six." She hung up the phone, then frowned.

Had she just agreed to a date with Sheldon Woods's lawyer?

No big deal, it's a fact-finding mission, she told herself. *Exchange of information. Nothing more. So unimportant that I'm not even going to stop in the ladies' room to put on some makeup or fuss with my hair. It's just meeting at a convenient time.*

Yeah, she reminded herself, grimacing at the implications. *The dinner hour on a Saturday night. Way to advertise that you have no social life, Cahill.*

"Well, then, apparently, neither does he," she said aloud. "Besides, it's fact finding," she repeated. "Just . . . fact finding."

James Cannon was already seated at a window table overlooking a fast-moving stream when she arrived. He stood when she approached and held her chair. *Not necessary,* she'd wanted to say, but thought it would sound peevish, so she bit back the remark and merely said, "Thank you."

"You're welcome." He sat opposite her. "Did you hit a lot of traffic on your way?"

"No, it was fine."

The waiter appeared at the table and she looked up. "I'll have a Yuengling."

"What? A woman who doesn't drink light beer?" Cannon feigned shock.

"I make it a point to avoid anything with light on the label." She opened the menu and scanned the offerings, then closed it again.

"Know what you want?" he asked.

"I'm here for the chicken piccata," she said as she unfolded the list of names she'd typed up before she left the office. "But mostly, I'm here for this."

"What is that?"

"A list of lost boys." She passed it to him. "Boys who were reported missing during the time Sheldon Woods was out there doing his thing."

She watched his eyes as he read down the list. When he got to the bottom, he said, "None of these boys ever came home?"

"I'm not sure. I have calls into each one of the law enforcement agencies that reported into the system. They're supposed to remove the names if the boy is located, but you can't always count on that. Frankly, I don't expect to hear from anyone until midweek. But I had to start somewhere."

"It's a lot of names." He shook his head. "Do this many kids disappear every year?"

"Way more than that. These are just the boys from Woods's self-professed killing grounds. When you start adding up all the minors who are reported missing every year, the number is staggering."

"How many of them are found alive?"

"Way too few."

The waiter came back with Portia's beer and took their orders.

She sipped from the glass and smiled. "One thing I missed while I was away. Good old Pennsylvania beer."

"Where were you?"

"I've been working with the counterterrorism unit of the Bureau for the past several years."

"Must have been exciting."

"It had its moments."

"Where were you?" he repeated, but this time, she knew he wanted specifics.

"Here and there." She smiled. "Anyway, back to the case at hand. I'm assuming you didn't recognize any of the names on that list."

"Did you expect me to?"

"I thought maybe Woods might have mentioned the names of some of his victims whose whereabouts he hadn't given up."

"Are you kidding?" He lifted his beer and took a drink. "I had to fight tooth and nail to get him to give up the thirteen. Until it became obvious to him that it was in his best interest to start naming names and drawing maps, he wasn't going to admit to a thing. But even if he had, I wouldn't be able to give you the information. Anything he told me back then, when I was representing him, would be privileged."

"I figured as much, but I thought I'd give it a shot."

"Agent Cahill, I know you don't think much of me and what I do—it's okay, I get that from law enforcement types all the time—but I do try to stay true to the oath I took." His eyes darkened and his mouth tightened. "Sometimes it's easier than others, but I do try to conduct my business ethically."

"Well, forgive me, Mr. Cannon," she couldn't help but ask, "but how does an ethical man justify having defended someone like Sheldon Woods?"

"I was appointed by the court," he said simply.

"You could only have been in your midtwenties back then. How does a reasonably fresh-out-of-law-school attorney get appointed to a major capital case? And a notorious one at that?"

"Just lucky, I guess," he replied wryly.

"Seriously."

"I was in the wrong place at the wrong time," he explained. "None of the established lawyers in the county wanted the case. For one thing, no one wanted their name associated with Woods. Then there was the matter of the assumption that the case was going to be open and shut—meaning fewer billable hours—and the fact that the evidence was overwhelming. Woods was going to be tried and convicted in short order—the idea was to try him for the one victim he'd had with him when he was arrested—and given the death penalty. Not worth anyone's time, plus there was no question he'd be convicted."

"So how did you get from being the new kid on the block to making a deal where he gave up thirteen victims in exchange for life?"

Cannon sat back while the waiter served their salads.

"Can I bring you another beer?" The waiter asked. "Perhaps a bottle of wine?"

"I'm fine for now," Portia smiled at the man, and after he left the table, she urged Cannon to continue. "Go on. This is getting interesting. How did you get the case?"

"I had the luck—good or not so good, depending on how you look at it—to stop in to the judge's chambers at the exact moment when he was trying to decide who to assign. He told me later he'd asked three other defense attorneys, all of whom claimed a schedule conflict. I was relatively new, the judge knew I hadn't been practicing long enough to have so full a calendar that I couldn't take on the case. The defendant needed a lawyer, I was right there, in his face, asking for a favor. The favor was granted and Woods got representation."

"What was the favor?"

He shrugged. "I was asking for an extension to file some papers. Which I would have gotten anyway."

"So you get assigned to the case, you talk to

Woods, then what . . . Woods said, 'How 'bout I offer to tell them where I buried some of my victims if they'll agree to a life sentence instead of lethal injection?' "

"Not exactly." He started in on his salad, his head down, avoiding her eyes.

"Then what?" She took a sip of beer. "If I'm not out of line. Or, if you think it's none of my business . . ."

For a few moments, his attention appeared to be on the plate in front of him. When the waiter reappeared and asked him if he'd like another beer, he nodded and said a quiet "Thank you."

Portia figured she'd overstepped, and opened her mouth to apologize. Before she could speak, he said, "At every hearing, there were parents, siblings, grandparents, friends—of the boys Woods was suspected of killing. The DA didn't have enough evidence to charge him with those killings. The bodies were never found, so the defense would have been that there was no proof that the kids were even dead, let alone that they'd been victims of Sheldon Woods."

She set her fork down on her salad plate. "You didn't really think he was innocent of all those murders, did you?"

"It didn't matter what I personally thought of him, or what I suspected he did or didn't do. What mattered was that I was obligated to give him the best possible defense I could."

"I guess I can understand someone coming out of law school, being idealistic . . ."

"I'd do the same thing today," he told her without hesitation or apology.

"Because everyone deserves a fair trial. Innocent until proven guilty." She rolled her eyes. "I think we've already had this discussion."

"Then there's not much point in having it again." He smiled. "My opinion hasn't changed. I suspect yours hasn't either."

"True enough."

They finished their salads in silence, and watched the waiter remove the plates and serve their entrées with more interest than either of them felt.

"Well, you were right about the chicken," she said, after a few awkward moments. "It is exceptional."

"At least there's one thing we can agree on."

"I suspect there may be more than one."

"Based on . . . ?"

"The fact that you did show up at the prison to accompany Woods to the farm." She cut another small piece of meat. "And the fact that you did make the deal for the thirteen bodies to be returned."

She glanced up at him and caught him watching her.

"Let me ask you this, Mr. Cannon . . ."

"Oh, I think we're past the 'Mr.' and 'Agent'

stage," he said. "Let's go with Jim and Portia from here."

"All right, Jim. You said that Woods didn't want to give up names and locations of his victims. But he did. Thirteen times. So how did he go from 'no,' to 'here's thirteen'?" She put down her fork and touched the corner of her mouth with her napkin. "It obviously wasn't his idea. I'm going to guess it was yours."

"I suppose it was."

"Was that your way of providing the best possible defense for your client? A means of saving him from the death penalty?"

"Well, it worked, didn't it?" He was trying hard to be cavalier. Portia saw through his act.

"You know what I think?" She leaned forward and lowered her voice. "I think you're a sham. I don't think you took the case to make sure he got a fair trial. I don't think you gave a shit whether he got life or not." She lowered her voice even more. "I think you took the case so you could talk him into giving up his victims."

"And that would be a bad thing because . . . ?"

"Well, he hasn't had to answer for any of those murders. He wasn't even charged with any of them. Do you really think justice has been served?"

"Do you really think that makes a difference to the families whose sons and brothers were returned to them?"

"But given time, they might have been able to

build strong enough cases against him to have charged him."

"And who do you think was going to do that?" He pushed his plate aside. "John Mancini? He was off somewhere repairing his damaged psyche after going toe-to-toe with Woods for all those months." Cannon shook his head. "Everyone knew there were more victims, everyone wanted those bodies recovered. You referred earlier to those kids as 'lost boys.' That's exactly what they were. They were lost, and without Woods, none of them would ever have been found. He buried them in out-of-the-way, ingenious places . . ."

She thought of the grave where they'd found Christopher Williams and the still-unidentified boy.

". . . and there are more bodies out there, as you well know. If Woods had been executed, it's unlikely any of them will ever be found. As long as he's alive, there's always the chance he'll want something badly enough to give up another one now and then. Just like he did this week. Do you think the family of the Williams boy cares if Woods is ever charged with his murder, as long as they get his remains back?" He'd picked up the teaspoon that sat next to his plate and began to tap it on the table. "You asked me if I thought justice was served. Hell yes, but unfortunately, not for everyone whose child was taken by this monster. If I thought for one minute he'd given up all his victims, I'd have injected him myself. As it stands, as long as there are other names on that list of yours, there's a chance they'll be found, as long as Woods is alive. So yes, justice was served. It was damn well served."

Portia sat quietly, feeling chastised, not sure why, and not liking the feeling at all.

"Any other questions?" he asked.

"No." She shook her head. "No other questions."

"Then tell me about the second boy."

"There's nothing to tell, except that he was in the grave with the Williams boy."

"You're positive one was Christopher?"

"Well, we won't know for certain until the ME checks the dental records, but I'm pretty sure he was the larger of the two. I can't imagine Woods giving us anyone else in his place."

"But he gave you Christopher, knowing you'd find a second victim. He didn't say who the boy was?"

"No. As a matter of fact, he totally shut the door on that subject."

Their plates were cleared. She leaned an elbow on the table and rested her chin in the palm of one hand.

"And he said the oddest thing," she continued. "He said, 'That one is mine.' Strange, don't you think? I have a call in to one of our profilers to see what she thinks of that statement. If you could have seen his face . . . he looked totally defiant when I brought it up."

"Maybe the boy in question had been a favorite of his. Or the first. Or the last. Who knows what goes through that perverted mind of his?"

"Anyway, the purpose of this meeting was to have you go over the list, see if you recognized any names," she said. "I thought maybe you'd have some information, that maybe he'd told you something, or said something in passing . . ."

"I'm sorry, no. I wish to God I could help you, but as I said, I had to fight for every last name we got. He wouldn't have given me anything for free."

"Well, it was worth asking."

"It was certainly worth it for me." He smiled, and for the first time since she sat down, there was real warmth there. "I got to have dinner with you."

"Even if we don't see eye to eye on certain legal issues?"

"It helps to know that you're willing to concede when you're wrong," he grinned.

"When did I concede anything?" She frowned, trying to remember what she'd said.

"When you didn't have a snappy comeback after I said that justice was better served by making a deal with Woods and letting him live in return for the names and locations of his victims, rather than going to trial and letting him get the death penalty."

"I still think he has to answer for his sins, Jim."

"With any luck, maybe someday someone will find a way to make him do just that."

NINE

Jeremy Potter. Age nine in 1997. Disappeared from a playground while waiting for his older sister's softball game to end. His mother told the police that one minute he was there, the next minute he was gone. It was as if he'd dropped off the face of the earth. As if he'd never been.

Steven Craeger. Age twelve in 1996. Older than Woods's usual victims, but according to reports, he was small for his age. Disappeared from a parking lot where he was waiting for his father to come out of a drugstore.

David Chandler. Age seven, 1998. Disappeared while on his way home from school, three blocks from his home. His older brothers were walking ahead of him and claimed to never having seen or heard a thing. He was behind them when they got off the bus, but he never arrived at the house.

And on it went, article after article, story after story, boy after boy. A knot settled in the back of Portia's neck and a painful lump balled up in her throat. Her fingers trembled on the keyboard, and with every new name, she found herself hoping against hope that this next child might have somehow escaped to tell a story of survival. But none of the boys on the list had survived. She'd known that when she'd turned on her laptop that morning. Still, the knowledge hadn't kept some small part of her mind from holding out for one happy ending.

But there were no happy endings when Sheldon Woods was involved. *Unless, of course, you considered recovering remains a happy ending,* she thought wryly. For some families, that was as close to *good* as they were likely to get.

The amount of suffering caused by this one small man was incomprehensible. When you counted the children who still had question marks next to their names, it was beyond horrific, beyond unspeakable. *How in the name of God do abominations like Sheldon Woods exist?*

She took a long drink from a bottle of spring water and cleared her aching throat. *What,* she wondered, *had he been like as an infant? Had he been a sweet baby, an inquisitive toddler, a charming young child? Had something monstrous happened that transformed him into the devil he'd become? Or had he been born with the hideous seed within him? Had he been terrorized as a boy, or had he been born to terrorize others?*

Nature or nurture, she thought. It always seemed to come back to that.

Portia put down the newspaper articles she'd printed off the Internet and rubbed her eyes. She'd been reading since she got up that morning, and it was now almost eight at night. The loud rumblings of her stomach reminded her that she hadn't eaten anything since breakfast, which explained why she had such a pounding in her head.

There was chicken in the refrigerator, leftovers from the meal Miranda had prepared a few nights earlier. Portia heated up a generous portion and ate it on the little back porch where she found a small table and two chairs. *Just perfect for the two of them,* she thought as she sat on one chair and rested her feet on the other, and noted there were no extra chairs for guests.

She'd need to make some decisions, and soon, she reminded herself. She was wondering if it was possible to find a three-month lease when her cell phone rang.

"Cahill."

"John Mancini, Portia." John wasted no time getting to the purpose of his call. "I just got off the phone with Tom Patton, the ME up there in Old-bridge Township. Lisa Williams drove her brother's dental records up to him yesterday, and he got right to it."

"And? Did he find a match?" Her heart rate sped up, anticipating the news.

"He sure did. It's Christopher Williams, no doubt about that," John told her. "He's a good man, that

Patton. Went to work right away, X-raying the skull and making impressions. Called me as soon as he'd made a positive ID."

"Terrific. That's wonderful news. Who's going to tell Madeline and Lisa Williams?"

"I am, first thing in the morning. Would you like to accompany me?"

Portia hesitated, then said thoughtfully, "No, I think this is yours, John. It's always been yours."

"You found him, Portia. You're entitled to be there when I give them the news." He hastened to add, "And you'd be welcome."

"Thank you for offering to include me, but this is something between you and Madeline Williams. You've both waited a long time for this moment. As much as I appreciate your offer to include me, I think I'll pass."

"If you change your mind between now and tomorrow morning, give me a call. Make it early, though."

"Will do. Thanks again. Have a safe trip."

Portia disconnected the call, placed the phone on the table, and turned her attention back to her dinner. It would be wonderful to be there when someone got some good news for a change, but she'd meant it when she'd said this was a moment for John and the Williams family to share. She'd have felt like an outsider there. She may have found the remains of the missing boy, but it had been John who'd kept Christopher and his mother in his heart all these years, John who'd arranged the meeting where the killer gave up the location. Convinced she'd done the right thing by passing on the invitation, Portia took her plate back into the kitchen, rinsed it, and stacked it in the dishwasher. She poked around in the freezer for the carton of almond fudge ice cream she knew was in there, and scooped out a few tablespoons before she talked herself out of it. She took the bowl outside and sat on the back steps, which were still warm from the heat of the day.

Fireflies were just starting to light up the tiny backyard, and the cicadas were still humming. Before she knew it, she found herself envying her sister's life. *It must be really nice to sit out here and watch the seasons with someone you love,* she thought. From the yard next door, she heard the hushed voices of children as they stalked and caught fireflies. From the steps she watched the specks of yellow light dance across the air, and remembered other summers, when she and Miranda were the kids chasing the small flying insects, catching them in cupped hands, studying their glow before setting them free again.

Thinking of the games of children reminded her of the boys she'd been reading about all day, boys who had probably chased lightning bugs on summer nights. Boys who'd laughed and played with their friends, who had been young and innocent, until their paths had crossed with a soulless man who took their lives without shame or remorse. *How is it possible to do such unmentionable things,* she wondered, *to cause such terrible pain to so many people, and simply not care?*

Tired of asking such questions of herself, she went back inside, and called the only person she could think of who might have answers. The number rang several times before the recording picked up.

"You've reached the voice mail of Anne Marie McCall. I can't take your call right now, but please leave a number so I can call you back."

"Oh, damn, Annie, I missed you again." Portia sighed with frustration. "This is Portia Cahill, and I was hoping to maybe pick your brain about . . ."

"Portia?" A breathless Annie picked up. "I'm sorry. I left my phone in a pocket and couldn't remember where I put the shirt. I know you've been trying to get me; I'm sorry I didn't return your call sooner but I was out of town and just got back a little while ago." Annie took a breath. "So how does it feel to be back on the A team?"

"It's okay. Different from what I've been used to, but okay."

"That bad, eh?"

Portia recognized a touch of what sounded like disappointment in Annie's tone, and hastened to explain.

"No, no, not bad. Just . . . different."

"How are you adjusting to the change?"

"I'm adjusting."

"If there's anything you want to talk about, even off the record, I'm here."

"Thanks, Annie. I appreciate that. If I ever felt I needed to talk something out, you'd be the first person I'd call." The offer had made Portia smile. Annie was a friend first, a psychologist second, and a highly respected profiler third. She never hesitated to help a friend or a colleague. It comforted Portia to know that she was there. "Actually, I was calling you for help, but not for myself."

"Sheldon Woods." Portia could almost see Annie's eyebrows knit together in thought. "Yes, I certainly do remember the case. I didn't get the call on that one; I was too new at the time. But I remember it. What has he done to put him in your crosshairs?"

Portia explained the events of the past week.

"Shit," Annie said. "I'd never heard that he'd been suspected of killing so many children. Interesting that he responded so strangely to your inquiry about the unidentified boy. Are you sure he wasn't just holding off in hopes of making another trade?"

"I didn't get that impression."

"What impression did you get?"

"That this boy is someone he'll never give up."

"Which of course implies that the boy is very special to him."

"We'd thought of that. That maybe the boy was his first kill, or his last."

"Maybe. It's obvious that this one was very personal to him." Annie paused before asking, "What are you going to do about it?"

"I'm going to find out who he is. One way or another, I'm going to give him back his name," Portia told her without hesitation. "I was just hoping you'd have some insights into the case. Or into Woods."

"Without reading all the reports, I'm afraid I'd be blowing smoke, and I really try to avoid doing that. The best advice I can give you is to speak directly with the profiler who handled the case back then."

"Dr. Rollins is retired but I can probably get his number from someone at headquarters."

"Don Rollins? I have his number. I just spoke with him a week or so ago. Give me a second to find it . . ."

Portia heard some rustling of papers before Annie got back on the line and gave her the number. Portia repeated it to make sure she had it right. "I'm going to call him right now. I'm sure he'll remember the case."

"No doubt. This was one for the books, literally. At one time, I'd heard Don was planning to write a book about Woods. I don't know if that ever got past the talking stage, though."

"There are quite a few books out there on the case. Maybe one was his." Portia thought for a moment. "But we probably would have heard about it if one of our own published."

"Most likely. I'm sure he'll be happy to discuss the case with you. Give him a call."

"I'm going to do that right now." Portia bit her lip, then asked, her voice almost breaking, "Annie, what happens to make people turn out like that? Like Woods? Why this insatiable need to inflict such pain? To brutalize a child?"

"Honey, that's a question for the ages. If I told you I had the answers, I'd be lying. Each case is different, and yet there are always similarities in their backgrounds. For killers like Woods, the history almost always reveals terrible abuse. I don't know his story, but Don would have details." There was a long silence before Annie spoke again. "I've spent my life studying human behavior, and I've come to believe there is no one explanation, no stock answer. When it comes to the predators, the sociopaths, we take them one by one, and try to make some sense of the chaos. I wish I had a better answer for you, but the truth is, there isn't one."

"It's so depressing."

"Yes, it most certainly is." Annie sighed deeply. "Let me know if I can help out in any way. I'm heading to Maine tomorrow but you can always get me on my cell if you need me."

"My sister left for Maine yesterday."

"Yes, I know. I'll see her there. I heard she was assigned to the case."

Annie proceeded to discuss the case in Maine for another minute or so, but Portia's heart wasn't in the conversation. She wanted to get off the phone. The minute they hung up, she immediately dialed the number Annie had given her for Don Rollins. The number rang five times, and though disappointed, Portia was mentally preparing her speech for voice mail when a gruff male voice answered.

"Dr. Rollins?" Portia asked.

"Yes? Who is this?"

"My name is Portia Cahill. I'm a special agent with John Mancini's unit, and I . . ."

"How is John these days?"

"He's very well. I called because . . ."

"And that pretty wife of his?"

"Genna's fine. They're both fine."

"Good, good. Now, which one of my old cases are you calling me about?"

"Actually, I was calling about Sheldon Woods."

Ther silence on the line lasted so long, Portia was prompted to ask, "Dr. Rollins? Are you still there?"

"Yes, yes. I'm still here." Portia heard a sharp intake of breath, as if he'd been taken by surprise. "What exactly did you wish to talk about?"

"A few days ago, Woods gave up the location of another grave, and we recovered another of his victims." She explained the circumstances, then added, "Actually, we recovered two of his victims, but he refuses to identify one. When I asked him for the boy's name, he said, 'This one is mine.' "

" 'This one is mine'?" Rollins repeated the phrase thoughtfully.

"Yes. I thought it was an odd choice of words."

"Odd, but not at all out of character for Sheldon Woods. He was—apparently still is—a controlling little son of a bitch. And yes, before you ask, that was my diagnosis back then." Rollins sighed. "Sheldon Woods is as typical a pedophile as you'll ever meet. He fits the stereotype so closely one might think he'd posed for the poster. Low self-esteem, though he hides behind a veil of arrogance. He likes to appear to be in charge, likes others to think he's a powerful personality. He's a bully in this respect. Sexually, he's inadequate. Can't form mature relationships with women. Started abusing other boys when he was twelve."

"What was the family history?" Portia asked. "I know it's in one of the files somewhere but I haven't come across it."

"Again, it's exactly what you'd expect. He claims to have been sexually abused as a child, but refused to identify his abuser. He would never go into detail, wouldn't discuss what exactly had happened to him or when."

"Do you believe the abuse actually occurred?" Portia asked thoughtfully. "I mean, if some terrible things had really happened to him as a small child, wouldn't that have been his excuse for what he'd done later? Wouldn't he have hidden behind that?"

"Well, yes, you'd expect him to attempt to use his own abuse as part of his defense, but he never did. He was a very odd study, Agent Cahill. Very odd."

She reached for a pad of paper and wrote a note to herself. *Ask Cannon if Woods had ever mentioned that he'd been abused.*

"Woods had an older brother if I remember correctly," she recalled. "Could he have been the abuser?"

"It's possible. I think the brother left home when he was sixteen and lived with a relative until he graduated from high school and enlisted in the Navy. Woods once made some offhand comment about his brother having been embarrassed by him and leaving town."

"Embarrassed . . . ?"

"By Sheldon's antics. Sheldon began exposing himself to younger boys when he was about ten or eleven—often the first step toward aggressive sexual behavior. His acting out escalated quickly. By the time he was twelve, he was already sexually abusing kids from the neighborhood."

"I read about that. He'd been picked up a few times but got off with a slap on the wrist time after time."

"Parents didn't want to press charges because they were afraid it would stigmatize or traumatize the victims." Rollins snorted. "As if those kids hadn't been traumatized already."

Portia opened her mouth to comment, but before she could speak, Rollins said, "Douglas. That was the brother. Douglas Nicholson."

"Different father?" Portia raised an eyebrow.

"Mama was a rolling stone," Rollins quipped. "Or so I'd heard. Married a number of times."

"So it's very possible that the abuser could have been a stepfather." To her previous note, she added, *Who was Woods's stepfather when he was twelve?*

"It's certainly possible."

"Any other siblings, half siblings, stepsiblings, besides Douglas?"

"I was never really clear on that," Rollins admitted. "There was always a question in my mind that there may have been another brother. Or there might have been a sister. He was always very vague when it came to his family."

"Wouldn't that make you wonder if perhaps his own abuse was at the hands of a relative?" *Ask Cannon about siblings.*

"It so often is, yes."

"Where is the mother now, do you know?"

"She was living in Vegas back then, but who knows where she might be now. You'd have better luck tracking down the brother."

"Good point. He's more likely to have kept the same last name." *Track the mother—maybe Las*

Vegas?—and brother. "Did you ever speak with him? The brother?"

"Oh, yes. At least, I tried to. He wanted nothing to do with Sheldon. Or his mother, for that matter. Told me he'd had no contact with anyone in his family after he left home and had no interest in discussing anyone related to him."

"I wonder if anyone actually interviewed him," Portia thought aloud.

"Someone did, maybe John. I do recall seeing something in the file but there was no substance to it, nothing that would give us a picture into their home life or the relationships within the family. The brother clearly burned his bridges and never looked back."

"I haven't come across that report, but I'll look again." *Ask John if he interviewed Douglas Nicholson—if so, where is the report?* "I'll see if I can track him down. Maybe after all these years, Douglas might be willing to talk a little more."

"Well, good luck with that."

"Thanks for speaking with me, Dr. Rollins. I appreciate your time."

"Not at all. It was one of those cases you never forget. I have to admit I've thought about Sheldon Woods many times since I left the Bureau."

"Really? Why's that?"

"It isn't often you have an opportunity to get up close and personal with the devil, Agent Cahill. I'd seen a lot of really nasty people, but I never came across anyone who came close to equaling Sheldon Woods's level of depravity." Rollins cleared his throat. "The best advice I can give you is, if you have to deal with the man, keep your distance. Don't let him get to you, don't let him ever see that anything he says or does has gotten to you. He'll see any show of emotion as a weakness, and he'll be more than happy to use it against you. Everything is a big game to him."

"I'm not planning on having any more to do with him." *Not, at least, until I've identified my lost boy and I see Woods's ass prosecuted.* "And I have no intention of playing any of his games."

"Man plans, God laughs, as the saying goes," Rollins said softly.

"What's that supposed to mean?" Portia frowned.

"It means that, when it comes to Sheldon Woods, you may not have a choice. If he wants to play with you, he'll find a way to make you take part in the game. Whether you want in or not, if it's in his best interest, he'll find a way."

TEN

"How did it go?" Portia poked her head through John's doorway. She knew he'd been at the Williams home that morning and had just heard him come in. "Is Mrs. Williams all right?"

"She was very grateful, very relieved," John said as he tossed his lightweight suit jacket on the back of a chair. "Lisa, her daughter, is already making arrangements with their local funeral parlor to have Christopher's remains transferred to Palmer. They want to have a memorial service as soon as possible."

"Is Mrs. Williams up for that?"

"I asked her the same question. She said after all these years, she would bury her son if it was the last thing she did on this earth." John grimaced slightly. "I'm afraid it just might be, but the woman is certainly entitled after all she's gone through. She's an exceptional woman, very strong emotionally, even in her frail state. She did request that everyone who took part in the recovery be invited to the cemetery." He started sorting through the phone messages that Eileen had piled on his desk. "I'd like you to plan to attend."

"Yes, of course. I'll be there. Maybe I should call the chief of police in Oldbridge and see if she and her techs would like to be there as well. They're the ones who actually recoverd the remains."

"Excellent idea. Go 'head and make that call."

"I'll do it right now." She waited to see if he was going to add anything else. When he did not, she said, "By the way, did you happen to meet with Sheldon Woods's half brother, Douglas Nicholson, at some point either before or after Woods was arrested?"

"Yes, I did. After the arrest." John looked up from the notes he'd separated from the pile. "Why?"

Portia filled him in on the previous evening's conversation with Dr. Rollins.

"There was no love lost between him and his half brother, I can tell you that." John moved the stack of messages aside and rested his forearms on the desk. "It was all I could do to get the man to admit they were related."

"Dr. Rollins suspects that Woods was abused by someone in his family," Portia said from the doorway. "Any chance it might have been Nicholson?"

John shook his head. "Highly unlikely. When I say Nicholson wanted nothing to do with Sheldon, I mean nothing. Didn't want to hear about him, didn't want to know about him. Said the guy disgusted him and as far as he was concerned, Sheldon didn't exist."

"That could be his way of denying that he'd molested Sheldon. Maybe that's why he wanted to put so much distance between them. If he had been the abuser, maybe he thinks he's responsible for what Sheldon became."

"Possible, of course, but not probable. I really never got that vibe from him at all. He knew about Sheldon's arrest, of course, it made national news because it was so horrific, but he said he wasn't a bit shocked. Said Sheldon was a creepy little kid and it was no surprise that he'd grown up to be a creepy little adult, and that's all he had to say about his half brother."

"What about the mother?" Portia asked. "What did he say about her?"

"Very little. He said when he left home, he left that part of his life behind him. Period. He had nothing more to say about any of them, actually. My notes should be in the file."

"I couldn't find them, so I thought I'd come right to the source. Fortunately, the source was only a few offices away."

"Sorry I can't help you more, but Nicholson really didn't want to talk about his family."

"I'm going to try to track him down anyway. Maybe now that so many years have passed he'll be a little more open."

"Good luck."

"Thanks." At the same moment Portia turned for her office, Eileen called out to her.

"Agent Cahill, the warden from Arrowhead Prison is on the line for you."

"Really?" Portia frowned.

"Line seven," Eileen told her.

"Take it in here." John gestured to his desk phone.

Portia came back into the room and leaned across the desk for the receiver.

"This is Agent Cahill," she said.

"Agent Cahill, this is Warden Sullivan out at Arrowhead. One of our prisoners has requested that I get in touch with you."

"Oh, let me guess who that could be . . ."

"Yes, I'm sure it'll be a stretch."

"I don't have anything else to say to Sheldon Woods, Warden."

"Funny, he said you'd say that. He told me to tell you that he might be willing to make another deal for something else that you might want."

"Son of a bitch," she muttered under her breath.

"What's that?"

"I'm not at all surprised."

"What would you like me to tell the inmate?"

"Tell him I'm busy and I'll get to him when I can."

"He asked me to try to get you in here this afternoon before three."

"Oh, did he now?" Portia grinned at John and shook her head. *Do you believe this guy?* "Well, you tell him I might make it by tomorrow afternoon if I can fit him in."

"I'll do that, Agent Cahill. What time should we look for you?"

"Let's make it around one."

"He'll miss his exercise hour outside." Sullivan sounded as if the prospect didn't bother him a bit.

"Tough. He wants to talk to me, he'll do it at my convenience."

"I like the way you think, Agent Cahill," the warden said. "I sure do. I'll give Inmate Woods the message."

"Thank you, Warden. I'll see you tomorrow." Portia returned the handset to the cradle.

"What do you think he's up to?" John asked.

"I think he's going to want to make another deal. Something he wants for something I want."

"The identity of the second boy in the grave?"

Portia nodded. "That's what I'm thinking."

"What do you think he wants from us?" John frowned.

"I guess we'll have to wait until tomorrow afternoon to find out," she replied with a shrug. "In the meantime, I'm going to see if I can track down Doug Nicholson."

"See if Will can help you," John suggested.

"Will's out of town for a few days," she reminded him.

"Oh. Right. Well, try Jim Cannon." He turned back to the file he'd been reviewing. "He might have some thoughts on that. Oh, and tell him about the memorial for the Williams boy. It was good of him to give up his time to make sure that Woods went through with the deal last week. He should be given the option of attending."

"Doug Nicholson?" Cannon repeated the name after Portia explained the reason for her call. "I don't know that I ever had an address or phone number for him, but I can take a look in my files and call you back."

"I'd appreciate that, thank you. My cell is . . ."

"I have it from the last time you called."

"Right. Well, just let me know if you find something."

"Will do." He paused. "Would I be out of line asking why you want to speak with Woods's half brother?"

"Not at all. I'm just looking for some background information, that's all."

"Something I might have?"

"I don't know." Portia stood and peeked through the blind on her office window. She had a great view of a leafy branch of the adjacent magnolia tree, long out of bloom. "Do you know who might have molested Woods as a child?"

"Whoa." He laughed awkwardly. "That came right out of left field. What's that all about?"

"Last night I spoke with Dr. Rollins—the profiler who handled the case for the Bureau back then. He suggested that very possibly Sheldon Woods had been abused as a child and therefore grew up to be an abuser." She dropped the blind—the sun was blazing hot even through the partial shade of the tree. "I was wondering who the abuser was, and I thought it was interesting that Woods didn't use this as part of his defense."

"Not that it would have made any difference. The bottom line is that he admitted to having raped and killed thirteen boys. Fourteen, if you want to count Christopher Williams. There isn't any reason good enough to make that anything other than what it was."

"I'm not arguing that fact. I happen to agree that there's no excuse for what he did. I'm just curious about the family, that's all."

"Why?"

"Why?" she repeated. "I guess I'm just trying to complete the picture."

"Woods barely spoke about his family. The brother never came to court, and the mother, only a few times."

"What was she like?"

"She reminded me of an aging showgirl. Think dyed, very black hair. False eyelashes. Heavy make-up. A dress fifteen years too young and a couple of sizes too small. She might have been pretty once upon a time, but she looked like she'd led quite the life. Hard to tell her age, but Woods was in his thirties back then. I remember thinking that she was very young when she had Woods. Would have been younger still when she had Douglas—he's about three years older than Sheldon. I'm guessing she must be in her late fifties to midsixties by now. She was sort of full blown, if you know what I mean."

"Sort of. How did she and Sheldon interact?"

"I didn't see any interaction between them at all. Except for a few exchanged looks."

"What kind of looks? Dirty looks? How would you characterize the expressions?"

"Again, tough to say. Maybe a just little on the smug side from him. Disdainful from her."

"Odd choice of words," she remarked. *"Smug. Disdainful."*

"Those are the words that came to mind. He definitely looked unapologetic. She looked like she wanted to toss out a few *tsk-tsks* in his direction. I can promise you that my mama would have had more than a *tsk* or two for me under those circumstances."

"Like I said, odd, but we'll go with that for now." She made a note of his observations and penciled in ODD in large block letters. "By the way, you wouldn't happen to know who Woods's stepfather was when he was around twelve, would you?"

"I don't. He never mentioned anything about his childhood to me. Just wasn't interested in discussing it. You're wondering if the stepfather was the one who abused him? If in fact he had been abused."

"It seems a logical place to start. And you don't have a record of any siblings or half siblings other than Douglas?"

"Nothing off the top of my head, but I can check back over my notes to see if there's something there."

"I'd appreciate that. Thanks."

"You're welcome. Oh—before I forget—have you heard back from the ME in Maryland who was examining the remains?"

"Yes. It was Christopher Williams. John went to meet with Mrs. Williams and her daughter this morning."

"How'd she take the news?"

"He said it went well. They were very grateful for everyone's efforts. We've all been invited to a memorial for Christopher, by the way." She paused. "That would include you."

"Any idea when that will be?"

"Later this week sometime. I can give you a call when I find out."

"I'd appreciate it. I might have to move some things around on my schedule, but I would like to be there."

There was an awkward silence. Portia broke it by saying, "One more thing you might be interested in. I got a call from the warden at Arrowhead a little while ago. Sheldon has requested my presence at the prison ASAP. I told him I'd stop in tomorrow afternoon if I could work it into my schedule."

"That little shit had the warden call you and ask you to come in tomorrow?"

"Actually, he wanted me there today, but I didn't see any reason to jump on his say-so."

"What do you think he wants?"

"The message I got was that he was willing to make a deal for something I might want."

"The name of the second boy?"

"I'm hoping."

"Well, last time we talked, you were determined to find out who that kid was. Now you won't have to waste any more of your time trying to match him up, so you should be happy that he called."

"I'm not happy to have to spend any more time in his presence, but I am looking forward to being able to give the boy a name and return him to his family." She fell silent. "He was such a little thing."

"Hopefully, by this time tomorrow, you'll be able to cross one more name off your list."

"Yes. I'm looking forward to it."

"What do you suppose he wants this time?" Cannon asked.

"Maybe more of the same. He really seemed to enjoy riding that horse."

"You didn't stick around for the full hour. I'm telling you, he was enjoying that ride a whole lot more than I was comfortable with."

"What do you mean?"

"I mean that he was just way too happy the whole time. Grinning from ear to ear . . . it was pretty sickening. And if you want to know the truth, it pissed me off to know that I'd had a hand in making him that happy."

"Is there any consolation in knowing that he gave up more than he got?"

"I am happy for the Williams family," he conceded. "Look, I have to run, gotta be in court in thirty minutes. I'm glad to hear that the Williams family is able to put this to rest. I'm sure it makes Mrs. Williams's burden lighter."

In the background, Portia could hear papers shuffling, and thought maybe he was putting something into his briefcase.

"Thanks for your time, Jim. I'll get back to you as soon as I know when the memorial for Christopher is going to be held."

"Great. Thanks. And I'll let you know if we're able to come up with any info on Nicholson. In the meantime, if you can think of anything else I might be able to help you with . . ."

"Sure. I'll give you a call."

"Well, I guess I'll see you soon."

"Yes," she said, not quite sure how she felt about that. "I suppose you will."

ELEVEN

Her quest for the name of her lost boy apparently no longer necessary, Portia put the file containing the lists in her bottom desk drawer. She made the call to Elena Duffy and left a message with the department secretary giving the Oldbridge police chief a heads-up about Christopher Williams's memorial service and promised to call back with details when she had more information. She sat at her desk, tapping her fingers on the worn wooden surface and wondered what to do next.

Identifying the boy had consumed her for the past several days. Now that she no longer had to piece together the puzzle of his identity, she felt a slight letdown. She'd been thinking of the boy as *hers* since the moment Woods had refused to give up his name.

When Woods had said "This one is mine," her thought had been *No, he isn't. He's mine.* Now the boy was no longer lost, and he was no longer hers. She'd wanted to be the one to find him, wanted to be the one to send him home. She would still do *that,* she reminded herself. She'd still be instrumental in identifying him, but . . .

She knew she should be happy that the boy would be going home after all these years, happy that his family would be able to lay him to rest at last. And she *was* truly happy about those things. But for some reason, she'd seen him as her personal challenge, her quest, and that bound her to him in a way she could not explain or describe. Woods naming the boy would seemingly sever the tie: She was no longer relevant to the boy's identity, and that saddened her.

She probably should have just picked up and gone out to the prison, as Woods had asked her to do. By now she'd be there, and tonight another family would be getting news about their lost boy. But she'd done the one thing she'd told Woods she wouldn't do: play games.

She opened the drawer and pulled out the file. One boy was about to be named, but there were others who were still missing. She'd follow up on the calls she'd made on Saturday and see if she could cross any names off the list.

She was disappointed at having to spend the rest of the afternoon leaving messages for the same people she'd tried to contact two days earlier. At six thirty she was about to shut down her computer for the day when her cell phone rang.

"Hello, Jim Cannon," she said after glancing at the phone's display.

"Ah, I love caller ID, don't you?"

"I do. Lets you send all those unwanted calls right to voice mail where you can delete without even listening to your whiny cousin or obnoxious neighbor or that character you met in a bar the night before. What's not to love?"

"After that, I guess I suppose I should feel flattered that you picked up my call," Jim said, and she wasn't sure if he was kidding or not.

"Well, this is business. I'm assuming this is about your attempts to find some contact information on Doug Nicholson?"

"Right." Was there a trace of disappointment in his voice? If so, he didn't dwell on it. "I had Danielle look back through the files that we have here in the storage room. So far, she hasn't been able to come up with anything, but there are quite a few boxes of material and only so many hours in a day. I did ask her to keep looking, and I'll take a spin through them if I have time this weekend."

"I appreciate your help."

"Sorry I wasn't able to put my hands on something right away. If it helps at all, Danielle seems to remember that he lived somewhere up around Scranton back then."

"Danielle's worked for you that long? She looks so young." As soon as the words were out of her mouth, Portia wanted to bite her tongue. This was a business conversation. The age of his cute little blond receptionist or assistant or whatever was totally irrelevant.

"She's been with me since I opened my first office. Back then, she was my only employee, and she only worked part-time because she was still in school."

"Oh. Well. Nice that she's been so dependable and loyal." *What?* She fairly shrieked at herself. *Could you have said anything more lame?*

"She is that." Jim continued on as if he hadn't noticed. "I can't imagine how I'd get along without her."

She decided she was better off not even trying to respond to that. For some reason, the thought of Danielle being totally indispensable just seemed to set her off. She didn't want to question why, didn't even want to go there.

"Well, thanks for the tip about Scranton. Maybe we'll get lucky. Maybe I'll ask Sheldon about his brother tomorrow and see what he has to say."

"Ask him about his mother while you're at it."

"I planned to. Dr. Rollins mentioned that she was living in Las Vegas."

"You're going to have to find out what her current name is."

"Her current name?"

"She changes husbands a lot. When Sheldon was first arrested, her last name was Lewis. By the time he was sentenced, it was Davey."

"Charming."

"What was her first name again?"

"Rhona."

"Her maiden name?"

"No idea. Don't think I have that."

"I'll see if I can locate her with what I have."

Portia sat in front of her computer and searched first for Douglas Nicholson in every conceivable way, but all she turned up was an eighty-seven-year-old man in Erie, a twenty-two-year-old in Johnstown, and a thirty-year-old woman in Bedford. There was nothing for a Rhona Woods, Rhona Lewis, or Rhona Davey in any of the databases.

Damn, she thought, where was Will with his mad computer skills when you needed him?

She turned off her computer for the day and gathered her notes to take home. There was always tomorrow. In the morning she'd go through a contact at Pennsylvania's Department of Motor Vehicles and see if there was a hit. And, she reminded herself, there was always Sheldon, though she'd rather conduct her search for his family without his knowledge.

For some reason, talking to Portia Cahill always set Jim Cannon on edge. He'd tried analyzing why; she was hardly the first beautiful woman he'd ever seen. And it wasn't that she was an FBI agent. He'd had dealings with others over the years. The federal tag didn't intimidate him. In the end, he decided, it didn't really matter why. It only mattered that she set off a buzz in his head that he'd felt only once or twice before in his life.

Was it his sparkling wit, his sharp intellect, his athletic build, that kept her calling?

"I wish," he muttered as he packed an unfinished brief into his worn brown leather case.

"What's that?" Danielle stuck her head into the office. "Are you talking to me?"

"Just thinking out loud."

"Something going on?" She narrowed her eyes as she came into the room. "Anything you want to talk about?"

"Nope. But thanks." He finished packing up his papers. "By the way, were you able to find the rest of the Sheldon Woods files?"

"I wasn't aware I was supposed to be looking for them." She sat on the arm of one of the wing chairs.

"If you didn't find them all when I asked you the first time, then one would assume you're still looking for them."

"I'll go down to the basement tomorrow and take another look. We're still looking for something on Woods's family? The brother? The mother? The father? Any other siblings?"

"I don't know that there were other siblings, but yes, that's pretty much it."

"This is for that FBI agent, right? Cahill? The woman who was here the other day?"

"Yes."

"She called again."

"I know, I spoke with her a little while ago."

"No, I mean since then. About ten minutes ago."

Jim frowned. "Where was I? Why didn't I get the call?"

"I think you were in with Jordan going over the Lasher file. I started to write you a note but then I saw you were getting ready to leave, so I . . ."

"What did she say?"

"She said the memorial would be on Saturday morning at eleven at the cemetery, and she left directions." Danielle handed him a slip of paper. "I was going to e-mail them to you."

"Thanks." He glanced at the directions. The cemetery was in the Williamses' hometown, about an hour or so away. Certainly doable.

"Are you going to go with her?"

"Who?"

"You know who. Portia Cahill." She paused. "What kind of a name is Portia, anyway?"

He recognized the tone as that of a younger sister looking out for the interests of her older brother.

"You don't like her, do you?" he asked.

"She's just all cool and professional. And she doesn't like me. I can tell."

"Maybe if you'd take that stick out of your butt where she's concerned you'd get along better."

Danielle made a face and he laughed.

"You're not yourself when you talk to her."

"Oh? Who am I?"

"Some starstruck teenager is what you look like to me."

"I admit she intrigues me."

"Intrigues you?" Danielle snorted. "Is that what they call it these days?"

"Say what's on your mind, Dani."

"She's going to be nice to you until she gets what she wants out of your files and then she won't return your calls because she's moved on to the next case and doesn't need you anymore and you're going to feel like a chump."

"There's a word I haven't heard in a long time." He grinned. *"Chump."*

Danielle glared at him.

"It was one of Dad's favorite words," she reminded him. "I like to haul them out every once in a while just so I don't forget."

"I heard Finn call one of his friends a little weasel the other day." Danielle's son—Jim's nephew—was so like their father.

"Another one of Dad's." She got off the chair and patted him on the arm on her way out of the room. "Just keep reminding yourself it's only business between you and Miss FBI, okay?" She paused in the doorway. "It is just business, right?"

"Right."

"Right," she repeated, the word dripping with more than a little skepticism. "I'll see you later at the house. Finn has play practice tonight, so I'll be a little late."

"Aren't you late picking him up?" Jim glanced at his watch.

"He had tee-ball this afternoon. Sean's mother was picking both boys up from school and taking them to the field. I told her I'd pick them up after, so I need to get going."

"Okay." He turned off his office light and walked with his sister through the dimly lit reception area. When they reached the elevator, he said, "Hey, Dani? I appreciate the intentions, but you don't really have to watch my back."

"Someone has to." She punched the down button.

Later, when he should have been working on a brief he had to file in the morning, he found himself in the attic, looking through the storage boxes he'd stashed up there when he first moved back home the year his father died. At Jim's urging, Danielle had left an abusive relationship, taking her six-month-old son with her, and moved into the house they'd grown up in. She was eighteen years old at the time, the last of his family, and Jim was determined to protect her and her son from Dani's ex-husband. He knew a restraining order was useless against a man like Steve Bennett, who wouldn't give a rat's ass about the consequences if he got it into his head to come around and see what kind of damage he could cause. Jim's presence in the house was more of a deterrent than a piece of paper—

he'd long ago recognized Bennett for the bully and the coward that he was, and Bennett had always backed away whenever Jim was around.

So while it had pained him somewhat to give up the independent life he'd made for himself before their father's death, the need to keep an eye on the last remnants of his family was more important to him. Besides, he told himself, it wasn't forever; it was just for now, or until he believed that Bennett had lost interest and moved on with his life.

"Jim, are you up there?" Dani called from the foot of the attic steps.

"Yes. I seem to recall putting some files up here when we moved out of the old office in the city." He leaned over the railing at the top of the stairs. "I thought I'd take a look before I had you tear up the storage room tomorrow."

"Hey, Uncle Jimmy!" The force that was his six-year-old nephew flew up the steps. "I hit the ball every time today! Every time!"

"We're going to have to start calling you Babe."

"It's hot up here." Finn made a face. "I'm not a babe."

"That's Babe as in Babe Ruth. One of baseball's all-time greatest hitters. And he was a lefty, just like you. And it is hot. I opened the window but there isn't much of a breeze tonight."

"Oh." Finn thought it over, then raised a freckled face to Jim's. "I thought Ruth was a girl's name."

"Ruth was his last name."

"And his first name was Babe? That's silly."

"His real name was George. Babe was just a nickname."

"Why?"

Jim sat on the top step. "That's a good question."

"That means you don't know."

"Right. I guess we'll have to look it up."

"But not tonight," Dani said from the second floor. "It's already past Finn's bedtime and he still has homework."

"He's too young for homework," Jim told her.

"Yeah, well, tell that to Mrs. Ramsey." Dani gestured to her son to come down.

"I want to see what Uncle Jimmy's doing," Finn protested.

"I'm just looking through some old boxes of papers," Jim told him. "Nothing very exciting."

"If it's not exciting, why are you . . ."

"Finn Bennett. Now." Dani's hands were on her hips, a sign of her impatience.

"Okay." Finn turned to his uncle. "Will you come in to say good night?"

"I will," Jim promised, resisting the urge to tousle the boy's hair.

"Maybe we could read the book about Max again," Finn said hopefully as he hopped down the steps, pausing on each one.

"You read that one last night," Dani reminded him as he neared the bottom. "And the night before, and the night before that."

"Yeah, but it's our favorite, right, Uncle Jimmy?"

"That's right, buddy. Can't get me enough of those Wild Things."

"See, Mom?" Finn's chatter faded away as he and his mother made their way to the first floor.

Steve Bennett may have been a colossal ass, Jim thought, but the child he'd fathered had been pure joy since the day he was born.

Jim stood and went back to the box he'd pulled out from a stack that he'd tucked into a corner under the eaves a few years ago. He knelt down and resumed leafing through the files, pausing now and then to wipe the sweat from the back of his neck. In one of the folders he found a notebook in which he'd jotted down some observations during the Woods arraignment.

He'd noted that Sheldon Woods appeared younger than his stated age, which at that time was thirty-five. Blond and slender, with small hands and feet, it had occurred to him at the time that Woods's victims could very well have mistaken him for a young teen. *Put a baseball cap on him and a pair of jeans, a baggy sweatshirt, sunglasses . . . he could pass for thirteen or fourteen,* he'd written back then. Parents warned their kids against talking to strangers, but that meant strange adults, didn't it? Did anyone think to warn against kids who were just a few years older?

"Probably not," he murmured.

Woods hadn't liked talking about how he lured

his victims, only what he did with them once he had them. The hunt hadn't seemed to interest him very much; it was the kill that he'd reveled in.

He tucked the notebook under his arm, thinking he'd offer it to Portia. It might give her some insights. Maybe he'd give her a call in the morning, let her know what he had, offer to bring it with him to Christopher Williams's memorial on Saturday. Maybe he'd even talk her into dinner afterward.

Jim frowned. What were the chances she'd be without a date two weekends in a row?

He flipped through several more files before coming across one in which he'd listed the names of all the reporters who'd sought private access to Sheldon Woods. Vultures who couldn't get enough of the story from their seats in the courtroom, they had to get up close and personal with the monster. He noted the names of a handful who'd gone on to write books about Woods. It had disgusted him then and it disgusted him now that anyone would want to ride on the demon's coattails, cash in on the misery and heartbreak Woods had caused to so many. *Why are so many fascinated by the dark side?* Jim wondered as he tossed the file back into the box.

The reporters and the crime writers had been bad enough, but then there were the fans—male and female—who wrote to Woods, and the women who showed up at the prison hoping to meet him, drawn by the sick nature of his celebrity.

What the hell was wrong with those people? He shook his head. He'd hated every minute he'd had to spend in the company of Sheldon Woods. That anyone would eagerly seek out the man's company turned Jim's stomach.

The combination of heat and dust finally got the best of him. He closed the windows he'd previously opened in the front of the house, and made his way to the one that faced the backyard. From this vantage he could see the entire back of the property, the old playhouse where he and his friends had played on endless summer nights so long ago, and the swings where he and Peter, his older brother, used to swing Dani as a toddler.

Thinking about Peter caused his heart to hurt, as it always did. He headed back downstairs, welcoming the cool air of the floor below, turned off the light, and closed the attic door.

TWELVE

"So what have you got for me, Woods?" Portia leaned back in her chair as the little man shuffled into the room.

"Now, that wasn't a very nice way to greet an old friend." He frowned. "How about, 'Hello, Sheldon. Good to see you again. My, you're looking good today.' "

"Don't hold your breath. And we're not friends, Woods, and it's not good to see you. If I never see you again in this lifetime it would be too soon. Don't ever think for one second that my interest in you goes beyond what you can give me." She watched him maneuver gracelessly into his seat, the manacles making him clumsy. "So I repeat, what have you got for me?"

"Not even a pretense at niceties. I don't think I like you very much, Agent Cahill."

"Gosh, Woods, that hurts me. It really does."

"You're a snooty thing, aren't you." It wasn't really a question. For the first time, she was aware of his close study of her face. It took all of her willpower not to recoil. "Made me wait an entire day for you to come here, when I specifically wanted you here *yesterday*. All you too-pretty-for-your-own-good girls are like that. Think you can have your way with anyone, anytime you like. As if anyone would be grateful for your attention."

"Well, now, that's an odd remark, coming from you." She rested her elbows on the table, a half smile on her lips masking her revulsion. "I thought you only noticed pretty little boys."

"You'd be surprised at what I notice, Agent Cahill."

"Like I really care." She gestured impatiently with one hand. "Get on with it."

"I want another hour with Molly Blue."

"I figured as much. And in return, you're going to give me the name of the boy you buried with Christopher Williams."

He stared at her, his small eyes darkly smoldering. "Are you stupid, Agent Cahill, or do you just enjoy provoking me?"

"Provoking you is always a pleasure, Woods, but what's your point?"

"Did you think I was kidding when I said I'd never give him to you?"

"Why not, Woods?" She stretched partway across the table, lowering her voice as she moved closer to him. "What is he to you? Why the secrecy?"

"Do you want another boy, or not? It's all the same to me."

She stared at him for the longest time but she couldn't get him to blink.

"Same terms as last time," he told her. "Cannon in the car with me, over and back. Immunity."

"I have one new condition," she countered. "I want to know who and where. Now."

"It doesn't work that way. Not until I get my ride."

"I'm changing the rules. No name, no ride."

"My, we are in a snit today, aren't we? Got your bitchy pants on, don't we, Agent Cahill?"

"Who. Where." She ignored the barb.

"You know that if you renege, there will be no more names for you. No more lost little boys for the kindly agent to take home to their mamas."

"I don't go back on my word. Talk."

He sighed deeply. "So now we're down to trust issues, it seems, and frankly, I think . . ."

"I don't care what you think. Name. Place."

"Oh, all right, then." He shook his head in a put-upon manner. "Joseph Miller. Outside of Lancaster, Pennsylvania. Nineteen ninety-seven. There's a farm on Three Crow Road off Route Eight ninety-six where they have black-and-white cows—at least, they used to have them. Behind the main barn is a stream, and beyond that, some woods. I planted tulips right where I planted him."

She raised an eyebrow. "That's it? A farm on

some road in Lancaster where they have black-and-white cows? You call those directions?" She laughed derisively. "Gosh, how many farms do you think there are on any given road in Lancaster, Pennsylvania, Woods? And how many of those farms have black-and-white cows, for Christ's sake?"

"It's the third farm on the left, and the cows are very distinctive," he said smugly. "I don't know the name for them—the breed—but they're black with a wide white band like a stripe around the midsection."

"Striped cows," she said skeptically.

"You'll see. Well, if they still have them, you'll see. I wouldn't make that up."

"Oh, God forbid you should lie about something." She rolled her eyes.

"It's Wednesday," he told her. "I want my ride tomorrow or there will be no more deals. Call your boss—this mysterious Fletcher person—and make it happen."

"See you then." She rose, nodded to the guard, and left the room.

"And don't forget Cannon!" Woods shouted to her as the door closed behind her.

It had rained briefly while she'd been inside, a short summer shower that did nothing to cool things down but everything to make the day even more humid and miserable than it had been when she left her sister's house that morning. The thick, humid air smelled of summer rain and hot asphalt. Portia picked up her gun, which she'd surrendered on her way into the prison, and was on the phone with John before she hit the parking lot.

"So can we do it? Can we make it happen again by tomorrow?" she asked anxiously.

"Let me see what I can do," he replied. "It shouldn't be a problem, given what's at stake."

"The boy's name is Miller. Joseph Miller. Lancaster, Pennsylvania. Nineteen ninety-seven."

"Joseph Miller." John repeated the name thoughtfully. "It's not ringing a bell. And I don't recall any kids from Lancaster."

"Maybe it's one you never knew about. One that isn't on any list we have." She loosened the collar of her white shirt and struggled to walk, talk on the phone, and pull her jacket off at the same time. "The name didn't sound familiar to me, either, but I was thinking maybe I'd just forgotten."

"Not likely, Cahill. Some things you just don't forget."

"True enough. But it tells me that Woods doesn't know who we know about and who we don't. Miller could be one who fell through the cracks back then."

"You promised him immunity?"

"Had to. He's not that stupid."

"God, I hate to see him skate on all this." She could almost see John's face twist with frustration.

"He's not going to skate," Portia told him. "We will get him. It will take time, but he's already slipped up once."

"How do you figure?"

"The boy who was buried with Christopher Williams. Woods won't tell me who he is."

"Has he admitted to killing him?"

"Not in so many words, but he didn't deny it, either. For some reason, he is protecting that boy's identity, but once I find out who he was, we can backtrack, build the case against him. Blindside him . . ."

". . . when we charge him for it," John finished the sentence. "Damn. I like the way you think, Cahill. But how are you going to identify the boy?"

"I haven't quite worked that out yet." She unlocked her car from fifteen feet away. "But I will. Sooner or later, I will."

Portia rubbed her temples, hoping to push back the start of an oncoming headache that promised to be memorable. Since returning to the office, she'd searched the database for Joseph Miller and was surprised that there was no information on the boy anywhere. She put a call into the Pennsylvania State Police and spoke with a trooper who knew the area where Woods claimed to have left the body and agreed to meet her in Bartsville.

"Which way do you think you'll be coming?" Trooper Howard Heller asked.

"I have no idea. I have to look at a map."

"Tell me where you're coming from, maybe I can suggest a route."

Ten minutes later, Portia had relatively straight-forward directions and an idea of how long she could expect to be on the road.

"Give me a call when you cross over from Chester County to Lancaster County," he said be-fore he hung up. "I'll wait for you right there at the intersection of Three Crow Road and Eight ninety-six."

Portia poked her head into John's office to let him know she was leaving, but he wasn't there. She left a message with Eileen, and headed for Mi-randa's townhouse. It was already closing in on three in the afternoon, and she had several hours of driving ahead of her. She packed an overnight bag, since there was no way of knowing when—or if—they'd find the body.

She tossed the bag into the back of the car and re-minded herself that she was still renting the vehicle. *I'll take it back next week,* she promised herself. *I'll do a six-month lease on something—maybe a sedan or a small SUV. Or maybe another sports car. Six months should give me plenty of time to figure out where I go from here.*

What if she was unable to find the farm Woods had described? she wondered as she drove. What if the barn was no longer there? Maybe she should have waited before she called the State in, scoped out the area before involving any other law enforcement agency.

As she drove, she spoke to three police chiefs who were returning her calls—their missing boys were still missing, no leads—and called Elena Duffy to give her the information on Saturday's memorial. She called Will on his cell and asked him for some help tracking down Douglas Nicholson and Rhona Nicholson Woods Lewis Davey.

She put in a call to her friend Larisse Jordan, who worked in the FBI lab.

John called and gave her the thumbs-up for Woods's early-morning ride and arranged for the same team of agents to replicate their previous week's guard duties. She called Jim Cannon and left a message with Danielle, who apparently didn't care for Portia any more than Portia cared for her—why was that? she wondered. She was sorely tempted to ask when he returned her call.

"I found a file of notes that date back from when I first became involved in Woods's case," he told her. "I don't know if there's anything that will be of any great use to you, but you're welcome to look through it."

"No client confidentiality issues, counselor?" she asked.

"There's nothing in the notes that refer to anything he told me about any of the victims, nothing to implicate him. Mostly it's just observations on my part, notes I made while talking to other people, that sort of thing. Again, I can't say that it will help you, but you never know."

"Thanks. I'd like to look through them just the same. As you say, you never know where things might lead with this case."

She pushed a lock of hair behind her ear. "Listen, Jim—what are you doing tomorrow morning around, oh, four or five?"

"Ah . . . let me guess. He's promised to give you your boy but first he wants a pony ride."

"Close. He gave me a boy—not *that* boy, he will not talk about that one. It's driving me crazy, but I have to focus on what I have in front of me. A boy named Joseph Miller from Lancaster County is supposedly buried behind a barn out there somewhere. I'm driving out there now. Woods hinted there could be more in the future, as long as he gets his rides on Molly Blue. He wants the same routine, you in the car on the way out of the prison, you in the car for the return trip, or there will be no more deals."

Cannon swore softly under his breath.

"I know it's got to be a pain in your ass, Jim. I'm sorry. I hate to ask you again. I know you're busy . . ."

"I have to be in court at nine."

"Any chance you could . . ."

"Yeah, have someone else from the office cover for me until I get there, sure." He sighed. "Sure."

"I'm really sorry."

"No, you're not."

"You're right," she readily agreed. "I am sorry to have to inconvenience you, but I'm not sorry that the Millers will have their son back soon."

"I'll let you make it up to me this weekend. Dinner on Saturday. I'll give you the notes, you can tell me all about your recovery of the Miller boy."

"Hopefully, tomorrow, if not today. If we can find the right farm, the right spot behind the right barn."

"So, what do you say?"

"About what?"

"About dinner on Saturday night."

"Oh. Sure. Okay."

"Good thing I have a strong ego. A guy could get a real complex around you. And here I thought we were starting to connect on a whole new level."

"I'm sorry. I'm distracted. I just heard a beep on my phone and I was trying to look at the number of the incoming call. I asked one of our computer whizzes to see if he could locate Woods's mother and brother and I was hoping it was him."

"I thought all you feds had mad computer skills."

"Don't I wish," she laughed. "I do all right, but Will can find things faster than anyone I've ever met. He has great instincts, always seems to follow the right thread the first time."

"Well, good luck with everything. Finding the Miller boy, finding Doug Nicholson and Rhona whatever-her-name-is-this-year."

"Thanks. And thanks again for agreeing to go in the van with Woods again."

"I don't really have a choice."

"Of course you do."

"Not if I want to look myself in the mirror."

"That's between you and your conscience." Did that sound smug, she wondered? She hadn't meant it to come out that way.

"Right." She heard someone on his end come into the room and leave again, the door closing. "I'll look for you on Saturday at the memorial," he said. "If you find something tomorrow, though, I'd appreciate hearing about it."

"I'll give you a call," she promised. "It's the least I can do."

She hung up then speed dialed the call she'd missed.

"Larisse?"

"Hey, Portia. Good to hear your voice. I heard you were back with the pack. You planning on staying around for a while?"

"A while. Not sure how long but yeah, awhile."

"So what can a lowly lab rat like me do for a superagent like you?"

"Lowly, my ass. I know who the power behind the throne is."

Larisse laughed. "So what do you need and how soon do you need it?"

Portia told her about the lost boy.

"So what you want is a DNA test maybe?"

"Yes, but I'm not asking for a rush on it. I don't have anything to test against it right now, but I hope to at some point."

"Sure. Send me what you have."

"Actually, right now I don't have anything. I thought I'd ask the ME who has the body to take some samples and send it to you, but I wanted to check with you first."

"Now, if only everyone were as considerate, what a wonderful world this would be."

"I'm saying thank you and hanging up before you break into song, Larisse."

"A wise move on your part, Cahill. Get me the sample, I'll run your tests as soon as I can."

"Thanks. You're a peach."

"Fucking-A."

Portia laughed and hung up. Next call, the one to Don Rollins, would have to wait. Her GPS announced that Three Crow Road was the next left turn, a mere one hundred feet ahead. As she approached, she could see the state trooper's vehicle alongside the road. She made the turn, and pulled behind the parked car.

"You Agent Cahill?" The tall, lanky trooper got out of his car and walked toward hers.

"Yes. Trooper Heller?"

"You got it." He stepped back as she opened her car door and got out.

"Belted Galloways," he told her.

"Excuse me?" She frowned.

"The black cows with the white stripe around the middle are belted Galloways."

"Oh. There is such a thing?" Woods hadn't made up that part. Maybe the rest would hold true as well.

"Sure enough." He pointed down the road. "I asked around, and just like you said, the third farm down the road here used to have a herd of them, but when the farm was sold about ten years ago, the guy who owned the place sold them all to a farmer in Delaware."

"So he told the truth about that much." She nodded. "Shall we go see if he was telling the truth about the boy he buried there?"

"Let's do it. You just follow me." He began to walk back to his car.

"Wait a minute. Shouldn't we find out whose farm it is? Maybe call them, give them a heads-up?"

He shook his head.

"That's the King farm, ma'am. They don't have a phone."

"No phone?" She frowned.

"The Kings are Amish, Agent Cahill."

"So we just knock on their door and say hey, we heard there's a body buried behind your barn?"

"Pretty much. Though we're more likely to find Amos King in the barn this time of the day."

She glanced at her watch. It was twenty minutes before six.

"Milking time, Agent Cahill." He was grinning as he returned to his car. "Amos King has a whole herd of Jerseys, and somebody has to milk them right about now."

THIRTEEN

"You seem to know Mr. King well," Portia commented after the trooper had located the startled farmer in his barn and explained the situation.

"I've worked this part of Lancaster County for over twenty years, and I know most of the people," he told her. "Amos King is typical of the Amish farmers around here. He's cooperative, friendly, won't get in your way, will help you out when you need it."

"I thought the Amish were a pretty closed community."

"That hasn't been my experience. Most of the ones I know are helpful, and like I said, pretty friendly. They tend to handle their own problems most of the time, don't like to ask for help as a general rule, but are always happy to help out someone else."

The sun had dipped a bit in the sky and the barn's shadow offered them shade as they rounded the corner and stood facing the back of the building.

"Where exactly is this body supposedly buried?" Heller asked.

"He said behind the barn is a stream and behind that there are woods." She turned to look behind her. A dry streambed lay twenty feet behind the barn. "That's probably the stream he referred to, though it's dry now. And there are the woods. He said he planted some tulips right where he planted the boy." She glanced up at Heller. "His words, by the way, not mine."

They walked to the edge of the woods.

"Well, hell. Tulips bloom in the spring, right? It's now August. Even the leaves would have died back." Portia looked around. "How are we supposed to know in summer where the tulips bloomed in the spring?"

"We ask Amos." Heller took off for the barn.

Portia stepped back onto the rocks lining the creek bed, acutely aware that the boy could be buried just about anywhere. She was uneasy about standing over an unmarked grave. A hot breeze came through the trees and rippled the rye grass that grew along the dry bank. She walked to the corner of the barn and looked out over the fields where corn grew tall for as far as she could see. A farmhouse—mostly white clapboard but with one small section of stone—stood across from the barn, its neat flower beds erupting with the colors of the summer annuals that someone had taken much care to plant. The house itself rambled, one wing venturing off to one side and a section off the back going in the opposite direction. She stared at the house for several minutes, wondering what was missing, before it occurred to her that there were no electrical wires leading in off the main road. She wondered if the people who lived here still read by candlelight or gas lamps at night. She'd ask Heller. He seemed to know a lot about the locals.

Heller returned with a bearded man of indeterminable age dressed in a black shirt and black pants held up by suspenders. He wore wire-rimmed glasses and a straw hat that looked as if it had been used to beat out a fire.

"Agent Cahill, this is Amos King, the man who owns this farm." Heller introduced her. "Amos, this is the FBI agent I told you about."

"Hello," he said cordially. "You're wanting to know about the tulips."

"Yes," she said, gesturing in the general direction of the woods. "We were told that some had been planted out here about eleven years ago. I guess you wouldn't know where they grew."

"I wouldn't, no. But my daughter, Lydia, picked some and brought them into the house for my wife a few months back. I can ask her, if you'd like."

"If you don't mind, that would be very helpful." Portia nodded. "Thank you."

"You're welcome, I'm sure. She'd be helping with supper right now. I'll just go get her from the house," Amos King told them.

"We'll be right here," Heller told the man who'd set off for the house.

"So let's say the girl remembers where the flowers were," Heller turned to Portia. "What are you proposing we do next?"

"We ask Amos if we can dig." She shrugged.

"Who digs?" he asked pointedly.

"Oh. I see. 'Who digs,' as in, whose crime scene."

"Right."

Portia thought it over. She could very well bring in an FBI team to process the scene and recover the body. On the other hand, if it hadn't been for Heller, she would not have been allowed access to the farm by the property owner without going through a lot of red tape. Would she have gotten a warrant on such dubious grounds as Woods's word that a body had been buried here eleven years earlier? She didn't know. More important, if in fact they did find a body, she'd need Heller's help in identifying it and notifying the family.

"You bring in your people, your crime scene techs, your ME. The boy was from this area, you should be involved," Portia said. "But I'd ask that there be no publicity whatsoever on this case unless we absolutely need the media's help in identifying the body. I don't want it known that Sheldon Woods is giving up the names and locations of some of his victims. It would be devastating to those families whose boys have not—and will not—be returned."

"I understand, yes." Heller nodded. "I can promise that. If the King girl can point to the spot, I'll get a few handpicked techs out here—people I trust completely—to start the process. Starting with the coroner."

"Thanks. I appreciate that."

"And I appreciate you recognizing that, if there's a local boy buried here, it's best handled by the people the Amish know best, feel most comfortable with."

"You're assuming it's an Amish boy?"

He nodded. "A boy whose disappearance wasn't reported to the authorities—one we never even heard about—who's buried on Amish ground?" Heller lowered his voice as Amos King came across the field with his daughter, who appeared to be seven or eight, skipping ahead of him. "What else do you think he could be, Agent Cahill?"

She'd never considered that the victim might be Amish.

Portia opened her mouth to greet the girl, expecting her to point to a place very near where Portia and Heller were standing. But Lydia went right past her, still skipping.

"Lydia," Portia called to her. "Did your father tell you we were looking for the place where you picked tulips in the spring?"

"Yes," she nodded. "Over here . . . by the little stream" and she continued past the end of the barn, past the fenced-in pasture beyond to where a previously unnoticed spit of a stream trickled over the dry ground.

"Woods said behind the barn." A puzzled Portia turned to Heller. "Maybe the tulips she picked were planted later. Maybe in eleven years, the tulips that Woods claimed to have planted just sort of petered out. It happens sometimes. The bulbs get old and they . . ."

"Oh, it's the old barn you're thinking about, maybe. There was another barn when we bought the farm," Amos King told her. "It burned down about seven years ago, and we never rebuilt it since we had this one to use. We were in need of more pasture, so we fenced in a . . ." He stopped, his attention drawn to his daughter.

Lydia stopped several feet from the fence and was calling to her father in German while pointing excitedly toward the ground.

"What did she say, Amos?" Heller asked.

"She said the ground's all dug up," the girl's father replied. "She said it looks like someone buried some clothes there."

Portia's face drained of color. "Oh, my God. Tell her to come back." She cupped her hands and called to the girl. "Lydia, that's fine, thank you. Come back now. Walk as close as you can to the fence. That's terrific, thank you."

Portia met the child as she walked back to the barn.

"Someone buried a pile of clothes there," she

pointed behind her. "The dirt's all moved around and I saw a shirt. Maybe someone dug up the tulips, I don't know. But that's where they were when I picked them for Mother."

"That could be it, yes, thank you." Portia turned to Heller. "I think you'd better call your people, the best that you have. And call your coroner's office. Tell them there might be two . . ."

After asking for and receiving Amos King's permission to dig, Heller suggested that the farmer take his daughter back to the house while they waited for the techs to arrive.

"Why two, Agent Cahill?" Heller asked after King was out of range.

"The last grave that Woods gave me contained the remains of two victims. Two boys. We knew the first was there going in, but we didn't expect to find a second boy, and Woods refuses to identify him."

"So you think he might have done the same thing here?"

"Maybe." She paused, frowning, then took off for the area Lydia had indicated, Heller at her side. "But of course that doesn't make any sense at all. Whether he buried someone here two or eleven years ago, the dirt shouldn't be disturbed now."

"Maybe some animals . . . ," Heller began, then stopped as they approached the dirt mound.

It was obvious that the digging had been very recent.

Heller knelt on one knee and began to carefully scoop some of the dirt away. A bit of gray T-shirt fabric appeared, then a hand.

"Holy shit."

Portia stared at the fingers. Fully fleshed fingers attached to a fully fleshed hand.

"I'll call the coroner's office." Heller stood and took his phone from his belt.

Portia glanced at the horizon, where the sun was just beginning its descent. "Tell them they'd better bring some lights and a generator," she told him. "Something tells me it's going to be a very long night."

It had taken very little time to uncover the recently buried body of a young boy. He appeared to be eight to ten years old, had brown hair, and was dressed in an *Iron Man* tee and cutoff jeans. His feet were bare, which for some reason unbearably saddened Portia. The techs moved in to carefully remove the dirt as Jason Fritz from the coroner's office stood by watching.

"There will be skeletal remains in that same grave," Portia told him. "Under this victim."

"How do you know that?" he asked.

"The killer told me. It's a boy he killed back in nineteen ninety-seven. We think we know his name, but we'll need some DNA samples to make certain."

She gestured to Heller to follow her to a place where they wouldn't be overheard. "Any thoughts as to who Joseph Miller's parents might be?"

"There are several Miller families out here." The trooper sighed. He stood with his hands on his hips, his dark glasses still covering his eyes despite the fact that the sun was already setting.

"Any idea who might have had a boy between seven and ten who might have disappeared in nineteen ninety-seven?"

"Any one of three or four of them could have had a boy that age back then." He scratched the back of his neck where a mosquito had landed and fed. "Maybe Amos knows of someone. I can tell you there were no reports of a missing kid. I checked our records back fifteen years and there was nothing for a Joseph Miller. If he was Amish, like we suspect, they most likely would not have reported it. They tend to like to handle their own."

He set off for the farmhouse seeking Amos King, and Portia sat on a large rock where she could watch the exhumation, her head spinning, her professional armor starting to crack. She needed to see Sheldon Woods. Now.

She wanted nothing more than to beat the crap out of him, and probably would, if given the opportunity.

He'd set her up.

How, she wasn't certain, but there was no doubt

in her mind that the sick bastard had known exactly what she'd find here.

Had he talked one of his "fans" into taking this boy's life, just to mess with her? Had he been coaching someone to copycat what he'd done? Had he found someone as soulless as himself to follow in his footsteps?

What had Dr. Rollins said about Woods? That he'd find a way to make her take part in his game if he decided it was in his best interest for her to play? "Wrong move, asshole. Wrong, wrong, wrong."

She stood, her anger building, and walked toward the farmhouse, her pace increasing with every step. Heller stood on the front porch talking to Amos King. At her approach, he looked up and nodded to her.

"I'm going to have to leave," she told him, "but I wanted to thank you." She smiled wanly at the farmer. "You, too, Mr. King. I'm sorry . . ."

"I wasn't thinking it was your fault," King said gently.

Because she couldn't think of anything else to say to him, she handed Heller her card. "My cell number's on the back. I always have it with me, but just in case, the office number is there also. I'll be in touch."

He tucked it into his shirt pocket. "Israel Eversole over on Bartville Road lost a boy about ten or so years ago," he told her. "I'm going to hold off talking to the family until we confirm that there are, in fact, other remains in there. Then we'll see about getting some samples for DNA testing, just to make sure."

"The remains will be there. I don't know why this is playing out this way, but Woods's victim will be in that grave."

"How would anyone know about that?" Heller asked, obviously as baffled as she was. "Who besides Woods could have known where he left that body?"

"That's exactly what I intend to find out."

FOURTEEN

The first thing she did when she got into the car was to call John and tell him what she'd found. When he didn't pick up, she left a message on his voice mail. She knew his wife had been due back home late that afternoon, so she gave him the basics and promised to fill him in on the details in the morning. She knew that he and Genna hadn't had much time together lately, and there wasn't much he could do tonight about the boy buried in the field.

She cursed as she drove, long convoluted curses that called the demons from hell upon Sheldon Woods. She tried to recall if she'd ever felt as murderous as she did then but couldn't remember a time when she'd been as angry.

What point had Woods been trying to make? To prove to her that while he may be behind bars, he was not without power? Isn't that what Rollins said? That Woods liked to appear to be in charge? That he liked others to think of him as having a powerful personality? How much more powerful could he be than to have others kill for him?

But who? And how?

She eased her foot off the gas a bit. The roads were winding and poorly lit. Some were not lit at all. Several times she had to slam on her brakes after cresting a hill only to find the ubiquitous glowing orange triangle that the Amish affixed to the back of their buggies smack in front of her. It was too dark to safely pass, and the horse could only go so fast. She slowed by necessity and used the time to call Jim Cannon. It was late, so she dialed the cell number she'd previously captured in her phone.

"Who were the fans? The fans of Woods that you told me about?" Portia wasted no time with pleasantries but cut right to the chase.

"What?" Cannon asked, sounding more than a bit confused.

"You said there were fans who came to see Woods. Reporters, other people. Who were they?"

"I can probably get you a list of names that . . ."

"When? When can I have it?"

"Whoa, Portia, back up a little. What's going on? Where are you?"

"I'm on what is supposed to be a major road out here in Lancaster County, Pennsylvania, but there's not a damned streetlight for miles and I'm stuck behind a horse and buggy and going about five miles an hour and I can't even pass because I can't see a fucking thing out here."

"Calm down." She could hear him walking, and a door opened and closed quietly in the background. "Start from the beginning."

The horse and buggy in front of her slowed as the driver prepared to make a left turn. There were headlights coming in the opposite direction and Portia momentarily held her breath, hoping the buggy driver wouldn't try to beat the car. But he waited until the car passed to make his turn, and she blew out a breath heavy with relief. With what she'd already seen that night, a buggy getting wiped out by a speeding car would have been more drama than she'd be able to handle.

"Portia? Are you there?" he asked when she hadn't replied.

"I was just waiting for the buggy to make a turn." She accelerated, happy to have the road to herself again.

"I'm assuming you found the boy that Woods told you about? That's why you're still in Lancaster?"

"They're still looking for him, but you won't believe what we did find." She told him everything.

"Jesus Christ," he swore. "How the hell . . . ?"

"Yeah, that was pretty much my reaction, too. I was so stunned I could barely think at first. I knew there'd be remains, I was expecting that. But a fresh kill? Uh-uh. Unbelievable." She gritted her teeth. "When I get my hands on that creepy little bastard . . ."

"He sent someone . . . ?"

"Oh, ya think?" She cut him off. "You think it was a coincidence that some child killer picked the back of Amos King's pasture to bury his victim?"

Cannon fell silent, and so did she.

"I'm very sorry," she apologized. "I shouldn't have spoken to you like that."

"I imagine you're a little keyed up right now."

"Dr. Rollins—the profiler who examined Woods twelve years ago—said that Woods wanted people to think he had a powerful personality, even though inside he's a wimp. I'm thinking he talked some poor sucker into killing a boy and burying him right where he'd left Joseph Miller so that I'd find him. He's showing off. Showing me how much power he has."

"Where's the advantage to Woods there?" Cannon asked thoughtfully.

"What do you mean, where's the advantage?" She hit the brake to avoid a deer that was stepping onto the roadway about fifty feet ahead of the car. "He gets to play kingpin, gets to show us he's got minions who will do anything for him, kill for him, even."

"But what does that *get* him?" Cannon persisted. "And why now? Right now, he has you setting up horseback riding outings for him, for Christ's sake. He's enjoying that perk enormously, I can testify to that. Surely he's smart enough to know that if you suspect he has a protégé, his little field trips are going to come to a screeching halt. Why would he want that to happen now, when he's enjoying the first bit of freedom—however limited it might be—that he's had in years? It doesn't make sense to me."

"He's a psychopath. He isn't always going to make sense," she countered. "How would anyone know where to dump a body if he hadn't told them?"

"I don't know, Portia. I honestly don't. But that's why you wanted to know who the 'fans' were. You think that possibly one of them could be the killer."

"Right." She thought as she drove along, mindful of the sides of the road where deer or raccoons might be lurking and cursing the fact that the headlights on her car were woefully inadequate. She was going to have to get herself a permanent ride, and soon. "It's obviously someone who admires Woods, someone who wants to be like him."

"I found a file in the attic where I'd listed the reporters who'd sought private interviews with Woods after he was arrested. We can start with those. I can meet you tomorrow and go over them with you."

"All right, thanks. And I'll ask the warden for a list of all the visitors that Woods has had since he's been in Arrowhead."

"I'll take a look at it if you like, see if any of the

names stand out. There were a number of people who from time to time have written to him care of my office, since I'd been his attorney. What's your schedule tomorrow?" he asked. "I guess you'll be at the prison first thing in the morning to confront him."

"I'm on my way there right now. As soon as I hang up with you, I'm calling Warden Sullivan. I want to see that creepy little fucker tonight."

"You think they'll let you in? It's already eleven-thirty. What time do you figure you'll be getting back?"

"It'll be a few more hours," she conceded. "And Sullivan will have to let me in. There's no way they're going to keep me out . . ."

The guard at the gate was waiting for her, and waved her through after checking her ID. She'd called John, who'd agreed that a middle-of-the-night visit to Woods was in order. He'd arranged for her to be let in whenever she arrived. It was almost two A.M. when she signed in and turned over her Glock.

Just as well, she told herself. *Tonight I'd be tempted to use it.*

She was led to the room where she'd met with Woods in the past, and waited for several minutes before the door opened and Woods was led in, barely awake. His eyes widened in surprise when he saw her, and he paused in front of his chair before he sat. The guard—not the usual CO DeLuca, but a beefy man whose name tag read Connelly or Donnelly, Portia wasn't sure which—stood behind Woods and pushed him into the seat with a finger on each of the inmate's shoulders.

"What are you doing here?" a groggy Woods asked. "It's the middle of the night."

"Oh, did I disturb your sleep?"

He stared at her.

She leaned across the table, her hands tightly grasping the sides of the table. "How did you arrange it?"

"What are you talking about?" He blinked and shook his head as if to clear it. "How did I arrange what?"

"Do not insult me by pretending you didn't know! Just tell me how you made it happen."

"Made what happen?" He frowned.

"The boy in the grave, Woods."

"I don't understand." He shook his head uncertainly. "I told you who the boy in the grave was."

"Not him, asshole. The other one."

"What other one?" Woods was either a really good actor, or he was genuinely confused. There was no gleam of triumph in his eyes, as she'd expected. No smugness in his smile.

"Stop it, damn it. You know what other one. The new one." She smacked her hand on the table and he jumped.

For a moment, he appeared dumbfounded. Then a slow smile began to creep across his face.

"A new one?" he asked, his eyes beginning to take on a glow. "There was a new one?"

"You really didn't know?" she whispered, suddenly understanding that he had not been acting.

"No." His smile widened. "How . . . delicious."

"God, you make me sick," she said in disgust.

"Then our work here is done for today. Guard . . . please take me back to my cell, and find someone to escort Agent Cahill out. I believe she said she was going to be ill."

He stood and she glared at him as he left the room.

"I'm going to find out who he is, Woods," she called to him. "I'm going to find out who put that boy there."

"Oh, good luck, Agent Cahill." He glanced over his shoulder, his teeth gleaming white in the harsh light. "Good luck with that . . ."

"Agent Cahill," the guard called to her. "You're forgetting something." She turned around to find him holding her gun out to her. She was still so angry, rushing to get out of there, that she'd forgotten she'd turned over her Glock when she arrived.

"Thank you." She nodded to him and tucked it back into its holster.

He held out an envelope. "The warden called and asked me to give you this."

She took the envelope and looked inside. There were several pages copied from the visitors' log. John must have asked Warden Sullivan to have the records pulled for her. "Thanks so much. And tell the warden that we greatly appreciate it."

"Will do. He told me to copy as much as I could tonight. I only got back as far as three years, but we can have the rest of it by tomorrow, if you can stop back sometime in the afternoon."

She clutched the envelope to her chest.

"You went above and beyond. Thank you very much. I will come back later today."

"Oh, right." He smiled shyly. "It's already to-morrow."

She forced herself to return the smile, and walked out through the door into the parking lot.

Her stomach still churning with revulsion and outrage, she forced her emotions under control until she got into her car where she figured she could scream it all out, all the way back to Miranda's, and no one would hear.

Her car sat alone in the empty lot. She drove to the gatehouse and came to a stop when the guard flagged her down. She handed over her visitor's pass and started to roll up the window.

"Someone's waiting for you," the guard told her.

"What?" She frowned. "Where?"

He pointed to the Jaguar that was parked just beyond the gate.

"Thanks," she said as she drove slowly through the gate, then came to a stop behind the Jag. The door opened and James Cannon got out. He leaned into the open window of her car.

"Hi," he said, as if it was the most normal thing in the world for him to be waiting for her outside a prison gate at three in the morning.

"When did you last eat?" he asked.

"I don't know." She shrugged wearily. "Maybe this morning."

"That would be yesterday morning. There's an all-night diner not too far from here. Why not park this and let me take you there, get you a little fuel for the next round?"

She nodded, too tired, too vexed with Woods and with the situation as it had unfolded that night to argue. She parked the car next to his and got out.

"I should probably tell the guard I'm leaving the car here for a while," she said.

"He'll figure it out."

Cannon opened the door for her and she slid onto the soft leather seat with a sigh. After the rental's stiff faux leather, sitting in the Jag felt like a caress.

"You can tilt the seat back more if you like, make yourself comfortable," he told her.

"I'd fall asleep." She dropped her bag to the floor but the envelope remained in her hands.

"That probably wouldn't be a bad thing."

"I didn't realize how tired I was until I sat back and rested my head. It's been one hell of a day."

"Why not just close your eyes for a few minutes, just till we get to the diner. You can tell me about your conversation with Woods while we eat."

"There are some things that probably shouldn't be discussed over food." She turned her head in his direction. "This is one of them."

"Okay. Talk now and eat with your eyes closed if it works better for you that way."

She smiled in spite of herself. "He swears he didn't know anything about this boy, the dead boy in Joseph Miller's grave."

"Do you believe him?"

"Oddly, I do. I really think he had no idea."

"Maybe he's just a really good actor."

"That's what I thought at first, but then I watched his face. I could tell at the exact moment when he understood what I was telling him. That someone had left a body in a grave he'd dug for someone else eleven years ago. There was no mistaking that look of joyful—gleeful—surprise."

"So you're thinking he must have put someone up to it. I still don't buy that. I think he has something to lose now that he doesn't want to risk."

"His riding."

"Yes." Cannon hit his high beams and took off down the deserted road. "Maybe there's a copycat."

"How would a copycat know he'd buried a body in that exact spot?" she wondered.

"Good question. And then there's always door number three." In the dark, his facial expression became tense.

"Which would be . . . ?"

"That he had an accomplice before. That he hadn't acted alone back in the nineties."

"I didn't see anything in the files that would have suggested an accomplice." Portia shook her head. "Did you ever suspect that he hadn't acted alone?"

"No." He sighed. "I didn't."

Portia leaned back against the headrest. "An accomplice, or a protégé of Sheldon Woods. What an absolutely terrifying possibility."

He slowed at the entrance to the diner and parked up near the front door. They both got out and went inside.

"Two?" the waitress asked.

"Yes." Cannon nodded. "Maybe someplace sort of off by ourselves."

"Oh, you want to be alone?" She winked at Portia. "How about this cozy corner?"

"Perfect." Cannon smiled and took the menus the woman held out to him. "Thanks."

"Can I get you something to drink?" she asked.

"Coffee?" he asked Portia, and she nodded.

"Yes, please. Lots of coffee. Make it high-test."

"I'll bring you a carafe," the waitress told them. "What's your pleasure? Breakfast, lunch, or dinner?" His eyes scanned the menu. "Looks like a little something for everyone."

"I'm going with breakfast. Eggs, toast, bacon—the works."

The waitress returned with the coffee and they both ordered the breakfast special.

"God, I really needed this." She took her first sip of coffee and sighed. "Thank you so much. I don't know why you did this—why you came out in the middle of the night like this—but I am very grateful that you did. I probably would have kept on driving until I got back to the house."

"Or until you hit a pole, or another car."

She made a face. "It's funny, but when I was in . . ." She paused. ". . . the place I was before I came here, I often went more than a day without sleep or food. It never affected me like this."

"When you were . . . wherever it was . . . were your emotions engaged, like they have been for the past few hours?"

"Not to that extent. I was so filled with rage back there in the prison, I could very well have done serious damage to Woods had I had less control. There's something about this case—something about Woods—that brings out the worst in me."

"He has that effect on a lot of people," Cannon told her. "Look, our emotions can do strange things to us. Especially if they've gone into overdrive."

"Mine were definitely in overdrive tonight," she nodded.

The waitress served their food and asked if they needed anything else.

"I think we're fine, thanks." Cannon told her.

"God, this smells good." Portia smiled and dug in. "I can't remember the last time I had a breakfast like this." She thought, then corrected herself. "Yes, actually, I do. At my dad's house a few weeks ago."

"You don't normally eat breakfast?" He looked incredulous. "What do you have in the morning?"

"Coffee. Maybe a piece of toast if I can steal one from my sister on the way out of the house."

"You live with your sister?"

"Temporarily. She's out of town right now, as is her significant other, so I have their place to myself. Only for another day or so, though. I expect they'll both be back soon."

"Are they on vacation?"

"On assignment." She raised the cup to her lips. "They both work for the Bureau."

He raised one eyebrow but didn't comment.

She took a bite of toast and chewed, a thoughtful look on her face.

"You said you had a list of people who'd wanted to meet privately with Woods back in the day," she said. "The prison is preparing a list for me of all of Woods's visitors since day one. Everyone who's visited since he was incarcerated. So far, they've only had time to pull the first three years," she held up the file she'd brought in with her, "but given recent developments, my guess is that this is probably where we're going to find our man."

She pushed her eggs around on the plate, deep in thought.

"Here's an idea. What if he confided in someone, and now that person is acting under Woods's guidance? Or what if he's acting independently for reasons of his own?"

"If Woods was giving someone else instructions, it would have had to have been recent. He just gave you the Miller boy yesterday, right?"

"Yes, but he could have been planning this since last week. Woods could have planned to give up the Miller boy yesterday, but he could have told his buddy about it a week ago." She pulled the lists from the envelope. "Would you take a look, see if any name rings a bell? Maybe someone who started hanging around way back then who's still coming around?"

Cannon put his cup down and took the sheets of paper.

"I left my list in the car. I'll be right back."

She watched him walk down the aisle to the front door, then to the car and back again. He took the steps two at a time and was back at the table in under two minutes.

Portia finished eating while he read, then poured herself another cup of coffee, watching him from the corner of her eye. Miranda had said she thought he'd looked hot in the pictures she'd seen of him. She'd have to remember to tell her sister how much better the real thing was.

"Huh. So he's still around," Cannon muttered under his breath.

"Who's still around?"

"Neal Harper." Cannon tapped his fingers on the tabletop next to his plate. "He's a journalist—so he said, I don't know that he ever sold a story—who used to show up in court all the time. Looks as if he's been a steady visitor these past few weeks." He looked up from the sheet of paper. "Last visit was on Monday."

"Time enough to have planned this." Portia took a small notebook from her bag. "I'll place Mr. Harper at the top of my to-do list. What do you know about him?"

"Nothing, really. But he's been in to see Woods eleven times since the beginning of the year." He looked up and his eyes met Portia's. "What do you suppose they talked about?"

"I can only imagine."

His eyes moved down that page and onto the next one.

"Here's another familiar name." He took a pen from his pocket and drew a circle around one. "Keith Patterson."

"Another journalist?"

Cannon shook his head. "I don't think so. I think

he was just one of those demented souls who was fascinated by Woods. Used to hang around the courtroom whenever we were there. He tried to talk to Woods on several occasions."

"Why would anyone . . ."

"Oh, here's a surprise." He drew a box around a third name. "Eloise Gorman. Used to hand me letters in court to pass on to Woods." He glanced up at Portia. "Guess she got her message through."

"What message was that?"

"She was one of those women who . . ."

"Wait. Don't tell me. Had a crush on Woods." Portia made a face. "Because he was misunderstood. Suffered as a child. Was being framed by aliens and the CIA."

"All of the above, I think." He handed the papers back to her. "Just those three, the rest are names I'm not familiar with."

"You know, you read about these women who form attachments to serial killers, and you want to smack them in the hopes of waking them up." She tucked the pages back into her bag. "What could any woman—any thinking human being, for that matter—find attractive about a man who has killed children? Not just once or twice, but over and over and over . . ."

"It's a sort of celebrity obsession, I suppose. The media gives serial killers a lot of coverage. There are even prison matchmaking websites, where a woman can go pick out her man and start a snail mail correspondence that could lead who knows where."

"You are making that up." She put her cup into the saucer.

"I couldn't make up something that bizarre," he told her.

"I've been out of the country longer than I realized," she murmured. "Any idea where she lives, where she's from?"

"Ohio rings a bell. I'll check my notes." He frowned. "I should have brought those for you. I was afraid I'd miss you so I left the house in a bit of a hurry."

"Why?" She pushed her plate aside and rested her arms on the table. "Why did you do that? Come out in the middle of the night?"

"Well, for one thing, you sounded like a crazy woman on the phone and I was afraid you'd do bodily harm to someone, if not yourself."

"I'm not going to sit here and say it couldn't have happened. You said one thing—what's another thing?"

"I skipped dinner, couldn't sleep with my stomach doing all that growling."

She shook her head. "Not buying that one. Try again."

"I thought you might need a friend."

She smiled. "That's . . . that's really nice of you, Cannon. I did need a friend tonight." She reached across the table and took his hand. "Thank you. I appreciate it."

"Enough to call me 'Jim' instead of 'Cannon'?"

"Very possibly." She squeezed his hand before letting go. "So was that it? Three things?"

"There is something else." He hesitated, but after a moment of collecting his thoughts, he said, "It's bothering me that, when I was representing Woods, I never considered that he might not have worked alone. I just assumed that he was the sole killer. I never questioned it."

"From what I've read, Jim, no one else did, either. Certainly not John Mancini, and he lived-ate-breathed this case for almost three years."

"I was his lawyer. I should have looked into this possibility." He drew a hand down his face. "I've read that so many kids go missing each year—some could have been victims of Woods's partner. All this time, has someone else been out there? Is someone now training a new protégé, as Woods trained him?"

"Those are some heavy thoughts, counselor." She watched the waitress approach.

"Can I get you anything else?" she asked.

"Not for me," Portia told her.

"Just the check," Cannon said.

"Look, you're getting way ahead of yourself," Portia said after the waitress had slapped the check on the table and was out of earshot. "You're assuming that Woods had a partner back then and that you should have known, but somehow you missed picking up on that. I'm thinking that was not the case. Could you, a recent law-school grad on your first big case, have missed something like that? Sure. You could have." She paused. "But John Mancini? Superagent Mancini? I'd find that real hard to believe. John was inside Woods's head, Jim. He'd have known if someone else had been in there with him."

Cannon seemed to take it all in, but didn't reply.

"Here's what I think is more likely," Portia went on. "I think it's more likely that he's shared his information with someone else. I could even think he's been grooming someone to pick up where he left off, except that he was so surprised. That doesn't fit."

"Maybe the surprise was not the killing itself but at the timing," he suggested. "Maybe Woods didn't expect his protégé to act when he did."

"There's a thought." She nodded slowly, turning it around in her head. "Or maybe it's someone who, unbeknownst to him, has been studying his technique."

"Great." He grimaced. "Just what the world needs. Another Sheldon Woods."

"Yeah. Scary thought." She reached for her bag. "You ready?"

"If you are." He placed a few bills on the table to cover the check and a tip and brushed off Portia's offer to split it with him.

"Next time we have breakfast, you can buy," he told her as they walked into the night that was just moving toward dawn.

"I feel so much better now, thank you again," she said when they got into his car. "Almost human, even."

"You sure you can drive back? You can grab some sleep at our place, I can drive you back in the morning for your car."

"Thanks anyway. I think I should just head on home."

"I'm not hitting on you. My sister and my nephew are home. You don't have to worry about . . ."

"I wasn't. I just have a lot to do, a lot to follow up on." She lowered the window and let some of the cool night air into the car. "You live with your sister?"

"Temporarily." He smiled, echoing back her own response to the same question.

"Doesn't that cramp your style just a little?"

"Does living with your sister cramp yours?"

"I'm afraid right now I don't have any style to cramp." She laughed.

"I don't either, actually."

"I find that hard to believe."

"Heavy workload. One of my associates left about six weeks ago and I haven't found a replacement yet. What's your excuse?"

"I'm the new girl in town," she said. "I've been

busy. Been back two weeks and this is the most social life I've had since I set foot in this country."

"And before? When you were out of the country?"

"I was a little busy then, too." She looked out the
window and hoped he wouldn't press her, was relieved when he let it go.

They rode in silence until they got to the prison
gates.

"You sure you don't want to bunk in with us?
Dani won't mind."

"Dani?"

"My sister. You met her at the office."

"Danielle is your sister?"

He nodded. "When Dani was younger, she went
through a period when she was judgmentally challenged. She made some seriously bad choices. One
was marrying the wrong man. He was pretty rough
with her, and she took it for a long time without
telling anyone. But once she had a child . . . well,
she was more afraid for her son than she was of her
husband."

"So she left him, got a divorce, came home?"

"That's the short version. Somewhere in there we
have threats, a restraining order that he violates
every chance he gets, and the death of our dad."

"So you let her move in with you so you could
keep an eye on her?"

"Actually, I moved in with her. She was already
living in Dad's house. I moved back after he died."

"Is he still around? The ex?"

"He's in and out of jail. I try to keep track of him."

"She's lucky to have you to watch out for her."

"We're a dying breed, us Cannons." He stopped the Jaguar behind her car. "Neither one of us wants to be the last one."

"I sort of know how you feel. We lost our mother about a year and a half ago."

"It's just you and your sister?"

She nodded. "Sometimes we're really close. Other times . . ." She shrugged. "Other times, not so much."

"Must be tough then, since you're living together."

"Only until I decide what I'm going to do."

"In regards to what?"

"Staying with the Bureau. Or leaving, doing something else."

"Something else like what? Law school?"

"Been there and done that."

"Really? Where?"

"Villanova. When I realized I didn't actually want to be a lawyer, I dropped out and looked around for something else and decided the FBI looked like fun. Miranda decided she'd sign up, too."

"Fun," he said flatly.

"What did we know? We were twenty-four and out of touch with reality."

"We?"

"Miranda and I. Did I forget to mention we're twins?"

"There are two of you?"

She nodded.

"Identical?"

"Yes."

"Hard to imagine . . ." he grinned. "I'll bet they sat up and noticed when the two of you showed up at Quantico."

"We had our moments."

"I bet."

She hesitated, then leaned across the console and before she chickened out, kissed him, a quick peck on the lips. "Thank you. I'd forgotten how nice it was to have a friend looking out for you."

As she drew away, he caught her by the back of the head and pulled her close, kissing her full on the mouth, a real by-God doozie of a kiss that took her breath away. What could she do but kiss him back in kind?

When he finally released her, he said, "Just so you know. That friend thing? Not exactly what I had in mind, but we'll let it slide for now."

She nodded. "Right."

"So, you want me to walk you to your car?"

"That's not necessary. It's just right here." She opened the car door and swung it aside.

"I know. But it would give me a chance to kiss you good night again." He glanced up at the sky where fingers of orange stretched upward where earlier there had been stars. "Or good morning."

"Ahhh, that's okay." She got out of the car and slammed the door. She leaned through the window and added, "My mama always told me not to start anything I wasn't going to finish."

"The night's still young," he said, his blue eyes dancing.

"Not all that young," she laughed. "And I'm going to have a very early day tomorrow. I suspect you might, too."

"It would be worth hauling my tired ass into court tomorrow morning to have a little more of your company tonight."

"Another time." She straightened up and walked to her car, fully aware that he was watching her every step.

She put a little extra swing in it to make it worth his while.

FIFTEEN

The morning paper hit the front door with a thump. Smiling with anticipation and still in his robe, the man opened the door and picked it up from the top step where it always landed. He closed the door behind him with his foot and took the paper into the kitchen. Because he wanted to draw out the suspense for as long as possible, he poured himself a cup of coffee and stepped out onto the back porch to take a long deep breath of fresh country air. No doubt about it, this was going to be a great day.

Figuring he'd drawn it out long enough, he set the cup down on the table and slipped the paper from its plastic sleeve, then scanned the front page.

It wouldn't be on the front page. Maybe in one of those Lancaster papers, but certainly not here. He smiled to himself again. *At least, not yet.*

He frowned as he turned one page after another. Nothing.

Well, damn. What was the point in doing something newsworthy if no one noticed?

In disgust, he folded up the paper and tossed it on top of the recycling pile.

Maybe it was too soon. Maybe his handiwork hadn't been discovered yet.

That could be it. Yes, that could very well be it.

He acknowledged that patience was a virtue he'd never had quite enough of. *Another day or so,* he assured himself. Sooner or later, someone would notice something and take a closer look at that mound behind that Amish farmer's fence.

And how 'bout that—he'd had no idea that the farm belonged to an Amish guy! He'd watched the family from the woods, watched the girls in their long dresses—even the little ones—their brown feet and legs peeking out from the hems. The mother, her hair pulled tightly back and covered with a bonnet—did anyone else actually wear bonnets these days?—working in the garden with the youngest as they picked vegetables for their supper. The father and the boys working in the fields, then later in the barns, milking the cows . . . it had made him briefly nostalgic for a life he'd never known.

What must it be like to be them, he'd wondered as he spied on them, to live such a hardworking life? He admired their work ethic, but was just as happy to have a much simpler routine himself. An easier job, one that did not require him to break his back on a daily basis, let him buy his food right from the supermarket. None of that plowing and hoeing, no waking at the crack of dawn to feed the chickens and the cows and whatever else that lifestyle required. No, he was just as happy with his own boring day-to-day, thank you.

The dog next door began to bark as it always did when the guy across the street left for work. Now, *there* was one thing he'd change about his life. He'd get rid of that damned loudmouth dog. He daydreamed for a few minutes about how he might go about doing just that, the possible methods leading him back to thoughts of the other night and what he'd left on the Amish man's farm.

He wondered what condition the body would be in by now. If the insects had moved in yet. He'd seen the TV shows. He'd even read a few books on the subject. He knew what went on once a body was put into the ground. He just wasn't sure how long it took. He felt it was critical that the body be recognizable when it was found, and he began to worry that it might not be. It could conceivably be days before it was uncovered. How could he tip off someone without giving himself away? And he'd wanted that pretty FBI lady to find it, wanted her to be the one to look at what he'd done and know that there was someone to be reckoned with besides Sheldon Woods.

The old cuckoo clock in the hall let him know it was later than he'd realized. He dumped the rest of the coffee into the sink and rinsed out the cup before heading for the shower. It would have to be a quick one. He'd spent too much time looking through the paper.

Hot water splashed around him, hotter than he usually liked it, but he didn't have time to fuss much this morning. He grabbed the shampoo bottle from the shelf and poured some into his cupped hand. He paused to look at his hands. He imagined—he relived—seeing those hands wrapped around that small throat. What had he felt when his fingers began to close ever more tightly?

He had to admit that he hadn't felt what he'd been led to expect he'd feel.

Rather than the ultimate sensation, if the truth were to be told, he'd found the experience some-what lacking. There'd been no jolt of revelation, no sense of ecstasy, no joyful release on his part. Okay, maybe there'd been a spark of something when the light in the boy's eyes went out, but it was minimal compared with what he'd expected. And maybe a twinge when the boy's face reflected the realization that something really bad was about to happen to him. That *he* was the bad stranger parents and teachers had been warning him about all his life. But he'd felt nothing like Woods had described.

Of course, *he* hadn't done to his boy any of that other stuff that Woods had done. Uh-uh. None of that for him, thanks. All of that stuff was for per-verts, like Woods. Definitely not for normal guys like him.

Still, he knew he'd missed something. Maybe

he'd done it too fast, without the right amount of buildup, sufficient anticipation. That was probably it.

He turned off the water and stepped out of the shower and reached for a towel, promising himself that next time would be better.

SIXTEEN

"Uh-uh. Not a chance in hell." John shook his head adamantly. "No way did Woods have an accomplice."

"But maybe there was someone in the background. Someone he confided in." Portia sat opposite her boss in his office and leaned both elbows on his desk. She'd come in extra early hoping to catch him before he got caught up in other cases.

"No one was in the background, and the only person he confided in was me. Trust me on this one, Portia. There was only Woods. I knew how he thought—what he thought—back then. I knew who and what he was. No way was he sharing with anyone. That was all Sheldon Woods, all the time. Him and only him."

She opened her mouth to speak but he ignored her.

"Look, we had his lair. We found the place where he took his victims. We went over that place with a fine-tooth comb. The evidence guys got a ton of trace out of that place. Hair, fibers, skin, blood, fingerprints from the kids. But there was no semen, no sweat, from anyone other than Woods."

"You had enough to pull DNA from the samples?"

"Yes."

"Did you run the DNA?"

"Yes." He paused, then said, "And you're wondering where the results of that testing might be. It should all still be in the evidence file."

"So you were able to match the thirteen original boys with the DNA from trace found in the house . . . ," she said thoughtfully.

"Right."

"But you ran DNA on all the samples you found . . ."

"That's how we know there were other victims. Which doesn't mean he might not have killed elsewhere, of course. But yes, we tested every sample we had. It was years before the lab techs would speak to me again."

Portia could tell from his smile that John had an idea where she was going with this. "So you have DNA results that haven't been matched to anyone yet."

"Which you could use to try to find a match to the boy from Christopher Williams's grave."

"Which could prove that the boy was in fact killed by Woods, but still wouldn't tell me who he is." She bit her bottom lip. "What if we had DNA from a relative of the other boys, the ones who are still missing?"

"You mean the thirty-some boys from the area who'd gone missing between nineteen ninety-six and ninety-nine?" He shook his head. "First of all, you don't know that all of those kids are still missing. Second, you get in touch with the parents or the siblings of those kids and ask for hair samples now, they're going to think maybe you found their kid."

"Maybe we did."

"I don't know. That's a lot of people to get stirred up, get their hopes up."

"But if he belongs to one of them, that's one more boy brought home, John. One more boy with a name." She watched his face, knew he wasn't comfortable with the idea. "And wouldn't that narrow things down? Help us sort out who we're looking for? If we get a match from any of the trace from ten, twelve years ago, with a family of a boy who's been missing, at least that family will know what happened, right? And if we knew the names of the boys, we wouldn't need Woods to tell us who. We'd only need to know where to look."

"If you have the names, he'll never tell you where he buried them. It's part of his game," John reminded her.

"But we'd have something to trade. Cannon says he likes his freedom." She stood up, her idea taking shape. "We change the game. We give him the name, he gives us the place, he gets his little outing."

"The lab people will go ballistic if you show up with a bunch of samples and ask them to start looking for matches."

"They go ballistic a couple of times a week. They don't scare me." She smiled. "Anyway, aren't they there to serve?"

"Right. You be the one to remind them of that. Be sure to let me know how that goes," he said. "Look, let's take this one step at a time. Get some of the boy's DNA to the lab, see if they can match it to any of the DNA results they have on file from the first go-round."

"All right." She shifted uncomfortably in her seat, a clear indication that it was not really *all right*. "But I still think we could be using that DNA to determine if any of those missing boys were Woods's victims."

"You've already got calls into the police departments that filed the reports back then, right? So if they took the initial reports, worked the original missing persons cases, maybe they have something that we could test. Something of the child's that the parents might have given them after the kid disappeared. Maybe you can get the DNA and spare the parents at the same time."

"You really don't want me to contact these families, do you?"

"No. Not if there's another way to get a DNA match. I hate to see you raise the hopes of all those people, make them relive that nightmare all over again."

"I'm thinking those nightmares never stopped," she said.

"Pull all the evidence files from the original cases, see if you can eliminate the ones we already know about. Then talk to the lab. If you can sweet-talk someone into working on this, then you have my blessing."

"Thanks. I'll get right on it." She stood. "There's still the matter of who killed this latest victim. I drove to the prison from the grave site. Got Woods out of a sound sleep. He didn't understand what I was saying at first. He didn't know about the boy, John. I'm convinced of it."

"Portia, the guy's a really good actor. How could anyone have known where that grave was if Woods hadn't told him?"

"I've been asking myself that. There's a copycat element to it, certainly. Is Woods putting someone else up to this, or has someone taken a page from his book and has decided, on his own, to follow in Woods's footsteps?"

"I wouldn't put anything past Woods, wouldn't for a minute think he wasn't capable of talking someone into doing something like that, told him where to leave the body so that you'd find it, mess with your head."

"Maybe whoever killed this boy is messing with Woods's head."

"Which brings us back to the question, how did the killer know where to put the body, if Woods hadn't told him?" John rubbed his chin. "I think we can assume that the killer wanted you to be the one to find it."

"Yeah, I'm pretty sure he did. But why?"

"My guess is that he's trying to get your attention—probably because you have Woods's—but you should talk to Annie about that."

"I know she's out of town right now, but I'll give her a call when she gets back." Portia shook her head. "I was so sure when I went to the prison that Woods was behind this, but after talking to him, seeing his reaction when I told him about the body . . . I just don't know that anyone is that good an actor."

"Figure it out, Cahill," he said as he reached in his pocket for his ringing cell. "It's all yours."

Portia returned to her office and turned on her computer. Her mental list of things to do had grown so large that she could no longer rely on her memory, so she wanted to write it all down. She noted a number of new e-mails, one of which was from Will.

Portia—Douglas Nicholson living on Dufree Island, MD. Builds and repairs boats. Shouldn't be hard to find—it's a small island. Still working on Mama Woods but am closing in. And yes, I am good, thank you.

Dufree Island popped up the minute she typed it into the search engine; Will wasn't kidding when he said it was small. One entry under "eateries"— a crab shack down by the dock—and one entry for lodging: Ida Ann's B and B, which looked like a short row of small, whitewashed cabins. No stores of any kind unless you counted Doug's Bait 'N Beer, which appeared to be located in the same place as the boat repair shop. There was only one way on or off the island, a ferry that only ran three times a day.

She mapped out a route and checked the time. It was still early in the day, but the ferry had already made its morning run and wouldn't run again until the afternoon. Which meant she could get to see Douglas Nicholson, but not until later in the day, and if she missed the evening ferry, she'd have to wait until the next day to make her return trip. Or she could wait until tomorrow, when she could go early in the morning, talk to Nicholson, and take the ferry back tomorrow night. She was debating the pros and cons when her cell rang.

"So how much sleep did you get last night?" Jim Cannon asked.

"Not a whole lot," she admitted. "I tossed and

turned most of the night, but at least I did it on a full stomach."

"You should have called me. I could have read to you from my latest brief. Guaranteed to put you to sleep."

Portia laughed. "I'll remember that next time."

"I'm here for you, Agent Cahill."

"Good to know, Counselor."

There was a brief and somewhat awkward pause. Then they both began to speak at the same time.

"The reason I called . . ."

"I just got an e-mail . . ."

"Go ahead," he said.

"No, no. You called me. You first."

"I did a little checking. Neal Harper is living outside Annapolis. I haven't been able to track down Keith Patterson, but Eloise Gorman—Woods's would-be girlfriend—is living in York, Pennsylvania."

"You've been a busy guy." She glanced at her watch. "It's not even nine yet."

"You're not the only one who tossed and turned last night. Anyway, I have addresses, phone numbers. How about we get together later and I'll hand over the information."

"Or you could give it to me now on the phone."

"Where's the fun in that? The least you could do is take me to dinner."

"I'd be happy to take you to dinner. What are you doing this afternoon?"

"Isn't dinner usually in the evening?"

"The place I have in mind is a few hours away, and if we're late, we'll miss the ferry."

"The ferry?"

"Only way to get there, pal."

"Where is *there*?"

"Dufree Island, off the eastern shore. Our computer guru found that Douglas Nicholson owns a boat repair shop there."

"What time is the ferry?"

"There's one at two, and another one back to the mainland at seven tonight. I think five hours should be enough to talk to Nicholson and have dinner."

"Right now I'm on my way to court. I need to be there by ten, and I have no way of knowing how long I'll be. I suspect this case will go into the afternoon. Any way you could put this off a day?"

"I suppose I could," she said thoughtfully. "It isn't as if I don't have anything else to do."

"Or you could go on your own and meet me somewhere for dinner to tell me all about it."

"Or I could do that." She frowned. "I was thinking that Nicholson might be more willing to talk to me if you came along, since he knows you."

"On the other hand, the fact that I represented his brother might make him less willing."

"That is a possibility." Portia bit the inside of her cheek, knowing that there was more to this than wanting Cannon along. She wanted his company. He was the real reason she'd tossed and turned the night before.

"However, tomorrow I have a pretty light schedule. I have a new client coming in but one of my associates can meet with her. So if there's any way you can wait one more day, I'm there."

"Tomorrow will be soon enough. I have a few things I should take care of today anyway. I guess I was just eager to get to him, see what he knows about Woods's alleged abuse as a child. See if he knows what name his mother is going by these days. Maybe he even knows where she is."

"I wouldn't count on that, unless he's had a change of heart over the past decade. There was some serious resentment toward her, some real animosity between them," Jim told her.

"Maybe we can get him to talk about that."

"I'm here at the courthouse," he said, "and I'm running late. So I'm guessing dinner tonight is actually dinner tomorrow night?"

"Yes, if I'm going to be out of the office all day tomorrow, I should stay late today. But I bet the blue claws on the island are worth waiting for."

"Sounds good. Where do you want to meet me?" She heard the sound of his car door slamming.

"My sister's house is on the way to the ferry. Why

don't you meet me there? I'll e-mail you the address
and the directions."

"Then I guess I'll see you tomorrow."

"Great. Oh—and good luck this morning."

"Thanks. I'm going to need it."

She disconnected and put the phone on the desk.
She pulled up his website, found the link to his
e-mail address, and typed in the information he'd
need tomorrow. Then turning her attention to her
to-do list, she started making calls. First to the lab,
where she somehow managed to talk Larisse into
agreeing to run a test on the DNA of her lost boy.
Her next call was to Tom Patton, the ME who still
had the boy's body. She requested that DNA speci-
mens be sent directly to Larisse's attention at the
FBI lab.

On she went through the day, systematically
checking the list she'd made and crossing off items
as she completed each task. She called the prison
and asked the warden to fax the rest of Woods's
visitor logs to her at the office. She took return calls
from several police departments and made notes in
the computer file she'd started on the missing boys.
None of the officers calling had good news to report, but three of the five did say they thought
there may be something in their evidence locker
that could be tested for DNA, and promised to
send her what they had as long as she returned it to

them along with a copy of the results, which she readily agreed to do.

She requested the evidence file from the crime scene—the "lair" where Woods had taken his victims—and was thinking about what she would ask Nicholson the following day, assuming he'd talk to her, when her phone rang.

"Agent Cahill, Trooper Howard Heller here. I just thought you'd like to know that we were able to positively identify the remains we found as those of Joseph Miller."

"How were you able to do that so quickly?" She frowned. "There hasn't been time for DNA. How were you able to identify him?"

"Joseph Miller was missing the second and third toes on his left foot and had an old fracture of his leg. Broke it in four places when he fell under a plow when he was three. The remains we found matched the injuries to a tee. His parents confirmed it."

"I thought you weren't going to involve the parents until you knew for certain it was their son."

"News travels fast in the Amish community. The Millers were at the farm before the coroner had time to bag the remains. They looked at the leg and said they knew it was their son and they wanted to take him immediately to bury him."

"And the coroner let them?"

"He completed his exam right there in the field,

and yes, out of respect for them, he permitted them to take the remains."

"Cause of death?"

"He said he can't tell for sure, though he suspects strangulation. The hyoid bone was in pieces, but since it hadn't fused yet, he couldn't say that it had been broken. Other than that, there was no sign of trauma. No cracks to the skull, no slash marks on the ribs or sternum that would indicate he'd been stabbed. So it's a tough call."

"Thanks. I appreciate you letting me know." She made notes, then doodled around them with squiggly lines. "What about the other boy?"

"That's gonna take some time. There's a lot more to look at there. There were bruises on the neck— we both saw those—but if there was other trauma, we'll have to wait to hear about it." Heller paused. "I was able to find out one thing, though. According to the coroner's office, there was no sexual assault involved."

"No assault?" Portia stopped doodling. "Is he positive?"

"Said he was. Said right now, that was the only thing he knew for certain. Feel free to give him a call if you want any other information, but that's what he told me."

"Thanks for the call. I really do appreciate it."

"No problem. I'll get back to you when we have a cause of death or an identification."

Portia hung up the call, puzzled. Every known victim of Sheldon Woods had been sexually assaulted, a fact he'd freely admitted. The assaults had been his primary motive when he abducted his victims, the killing had been his means of disposing of the boys when he'd tired of them. For Woods, the assault was the motive.

So if this new killer was a copycat—someone following in Woods's footsteps—why no sexual assault? And if assault was not the motive, what was?

SEVENTEEN

Neal Harper lived in a first-floor apartment in a two-story building, not near Annapolis, as Jim Cannon's research had indicated, but in Stokes, a small town thirty miles from Portia's office. Portia obtained this information from a woman who identified herself as Harper's ex-wife when Portia called the number that Danielle Bennett had faxed to her.

Agent Cahill, the fax cover sheet had read, *Mr. Cannon asked that I fax this to you. D. Bennett.*

Well, that's certainly *short and sweet and to the point,* had been Portia's reaction. The formality of the fax both annoyed and amused her. She couldn't help but wonder how Danielle would have reacted if she'd taken Jim up on his offer to stay the night at their home the previous evening. *His sister is his problem,* she told herself as she dialed the number for Harper. *No need to make her mine.*

Candace Harper had had little to say about her ex, but what she had said was intriguing.

"You're welcome to him, if you like them

creepy," she'd told Portia before she'd identified herself as a federal agent.

"I'm with the FBI, Mrs. Harper."

"Oh, what's he done? Never mind, don't tell me, I don't want to know. And it's Miss Wilson. I've gone back to my maiden name. Hold on and I'll get his new number and address for you."

"When did he move, Miss Wilson?" Portia asked after the woman had given her the information.

"Last month. Good riddance."

"May I ask why you referred to your ex-husband as creepy?" Portia asked before realizing the line had gone dead.

Road work added an extra fifteen minutes to what should have been no more than a forty-five-minute drive. Portia parked across the street from Harper's building and took note of the neighborhood. Old shade trees on both sides of the street did what they could to screen out the blazing summer sun from the yards of the row of small houses, all attached twins. Except for a few small children toddling behind their mothers, there was no sign of life. Portia double-checked the house number, then walked over and rang the bell for the first-floor apartment.

Before she could ring it a second time, a man in a sleeveless T-shirt and baggy blue shorts opened the door. He was shorter than she, and his pale gray eyes looked up to meet hers.

"Second floor," he told her.

"Excuse me?" she asked.

"Donte lives upstairs. You hit the wrong bell." He started to shut the door and she stuck her foot out to keep it from closing.

"I'm looking for Neal Harper."

"Why?" He raised one eyebrow.

"Are you Neal Harper?"

"Yeah."

She held up her badge. "Special Agent Portia Cahill, FBI. I'd like a few minutes of your time."

"What about?"

"May I come in?"

He hesitated, his uncertainty evident on his face. But a car pulled into the drive next door, and several men in their early twenties got out. Their eyes went from Portia to Harper and back again, and one of them whistled. Harper's demeanor changed noticeably. He opened the door wide and stepped back to admit her.

"Sure. Why not?" He glanced over her shoulder, making sure the guys in the driveway saw her enter, his expression smug as he closed the door.

"So what can I do for you, Agent Cahill?" He grabbed a pile of papers from a chair and gestured for her to sit while he looked for a spot to place the stack before giving up and dumping it on the floor.

"Talk to me about your fascination with Sheldon Woods," she said as she sat.

"My what?" His face flushed. "Who?"

"Neal . . . may I call you Neal? Please don't play

games with me." She opened her bag and withdrew several sheets of paper, and began reading off dates and times he'd signed in to the prison as Woods's visitor. She stopped after the first half-dozen dates. "Do I need to go on?" She waved the papers at him. "There's a record of every time you visited Woods at Arrowhead Prison."

"Okay, so I visited him a couple of times."

She raised an eyebrow.

"More than a couple," he admitted. "So what?"

"So what did you talk about?"

"Why is it any of your business?"

She pulled an envelope from her bag and handed it to him.

"Open it," she told him, and he did as he was instructed, a curious look on his face.

"Those are pictures of a young boy whose body was found yesterday on a farm in Lancaster, Pennsylvania. He'd been dead about eight hours before we found him. Which means he was probably abducted and murdered earlier in the morning."

His face froze in obvious horror, and he averted his eyes from her and the pictures.

"So where were you yesterday morning, Neal?" Portia asked, her hand held out to take back the packet of photos he so clearly wanted to get rid of.

"I was here. Home."

"Can anyone verify that?"

"I was here by myself. Why are you asking me . . ." His eyes suddenly went wide. "You're

thinking I . . . you think that I . . ." He began to
shake his head. "Uh-uh. No. Why would you think
that I . . . no way could I . . ."

"Sit down, Neal." She pointed to the sofa and he
sat as if hypnotized. "That boy was found buried
in a grave where Sheldon Woods told me I'd find a
victim of his from nineteen ninety-seven. I did find
that boy, but only after we found this one."

She placed the photos on the table between them
and tapped her index finger on the image of the
boy they'd found buried with Joseph Miller.

"So the question comes up: How would anyone
know to bury a fresh kill in an old grave? An old
grave where Sheldon Woods had buried one of his
more than a decade ago. Got any thoughts on that,
Neal?"

"Uh-uh." He shook his head stiffly, as if still in
shock.

"Well, then, here's mine. The only way anyone
could know that one of Woods's victims was
buried in that exact spot would be if Woods told
him. I mean, that's too much of a coincidence for
anyone to buy. You with me so far, Neal?"

He nodded, less stiffly now, as if understanding
where this was leading.

"So we have to look at who Woods talks to, who
his visitors are. Did you know that over the past
year, no one has put in as many visitors hours with
Sheldon Woods than you have?"

"I don't know anything about that boy. I wouldn't—"

"What exactly do you and Woods talk about, Neal?"

"What difference does it make?"

"You're kidding, right? Give me a break, Neal. I know you're not stupid. You're a journalist, right?"

"Yes."

"So I have to assume you're smart enough to put this together."

"Look." He appeared to relax slightly. "Like I said, I don't know anything about that boy, I swear I don't."

"Tell me what you and Woods talked about during all those visits."

"Okay," he sighed deeply, resigned to having a conversation he'd rather avoid. "I'm writing a book about Woods. I read everything I could get my hands on and I realized that none of it answered the big question."

"Which is?"

"Why he did it. Why he killed those kids."

"I can answer that, Neal. He did it because he liked it. He did it because that's what gets him off. All the time you spent talking to him, you didn't figure that out?"

Portia sensed a change in his attitude before he opened his mouth.

"I said I wanted to ask the question. I didn't say I didn't get an answer."

"So you do understand what drove him."

"He didn't make a secret of it." Neal shrugged. "He liked talking about it, actually."

"And how 'bout you, did you like listening to all Sheldon's stories?" She leaned in his direction, catching his gaze and holding it, refusing to allow him to look away. "Did it turn you on, make you wonder what it would be like to—"

"No!" he growled. "No. I didn't like it. It made me sick. *He* made me sick."

"Then why go back so many times?"

"Because I wanted to write the book."

"Ah, Neal? At last count, there were forty-something books about Sheldon Woods." She lowered her voice to a whisper as if sharing a confidence. "It's been done, pal. The story's been told."

"Not the whole story. No one's written that." He shook his head. His demeanor had changed; his attitude was cocky. "Those other books? All pieced together from other sources. No one knows the whole true story, no one's gotten it directly from Woods himself."

"But you have."

"Yes. I have the story—the whole story—in Woods's own words, Agent Whatever-your-name-is."

"So did he tell you about how he was molested as a boy? Did he tell you who his molester was?"

He stared at her blankly. "He never said anything about that."

"How about his family? Did he talk to you about them?"

He shook his head. "He never wanted to talk about them, no."

"Did he tell you how many children he raped and murdered? Did he tell you where he left all the bodies?"

"Am I under arrest?"

"Have you committed a crime?"

"No."

"Then you're not under arrest."

"You want to know what he told me?" All arrogance now, Neal Harper stood. "You can buy the book."

She narrowed her eyes. "I told you not to play with me, Neal."

"Anything else, Agent . . ." He made circles with his right hand as if to fill in the blank of her name, pointedly dismissing her as unimportant. "Next time you can talk to my lawyer, because I think we're done."

He walked to the door and opened it. She picked up her bag and walked outside.

"Have a nice day," he said as he closed the door in her face.

"I'll show you a nice day, you simpleminded fool," she muttered as she walked back to her car, her cell phone in her hand.

She speed-dialed a number as she unlocked the car door and got in. When the call wasn't answered, she waited for voice mail to pick up.

"Will, it's Portia. Sorry to be such a pain in the ass, but as your future sister-in-law, I do feel entitled to take certain liberties. While you're running down Rhona Lewis and Clark or whatever her name is, could you please run Neal Harper as well? I want everything—I mean, everything—you can come up with on this guy. Thanks, Will. You're a peach. If my sister wasn't going to marry you, I'd consider marrying you myself."

She dropped the phone on the front seat and smiled. Neal Harper had no idea of how far from "done" they were.

"John, are you sure you're all right?"

Genna Snow, John's wife, stood in the doorway of their family room where John was sitting in semi-darkness, the television on but the sound muted. His eyes were fixed not on the screen, where a leopard chased an antelope across a grassy plain, but at a spot on the opposite wall.

"You've been looking at that painting for the past twenty minutes. It isn't likely to change." She sat next to him on the sofa and draped her arm around his shoulders. "What is it?"

Her fingers caressed the back of his neck. "I know it's something to do with Woods, because no one else puts you in this kind of a funk, so let's talk it out and be done with it."

"I don't think I'll ever be done with it, Gen. Sometimes I feel that I'll be carrying him with me for the rest of my life."

"So talk and maybe we can exorcise him, if only for a little while. What specifically is bothering you?"

"Portia Cahill is back, did you know?"

"You told me."

"Did I tell you that she's handling the Woods case?"

"Bring me up to date on that."

He did.

"So Sheldon's telling someone where he buried his victims." Genna shook her head in disgust. "He's such a little prick. Nothing he does surprises me."

"Portia wants to obtain DNA from the parents of all the boys who went missing back then and were never found or never turned up alive. She wants to try to find matches for the DNA we have on file from the house where Woods took his victims."

"And . . . ?"

"And I told her no, not now. I'm thinking, all those families have been grieving for all these years, you come in and ask for their DNA, their hopes rise again. They're going to be on pins and needles waiting to hear that their child or brother has been found. I'm thinking it gets a lot of people riled up all over again. Gets everyone's hopes up, most of them unnecessarily."

"Understandable." Genna nodded. "I take it Portia disagreed?"

"Yeah. And her reasons were good ones. Her thinking is that it's a good way to determine which of those missing boys were victims of Sheldon Woods, that if she has the names, maybe she'll be in a better position to bargain with him to find out where they are."

"Okay. So we have good reasons pro, good reasons con. You're still the boss. That makes you the tiebreaker. So what's the problem?"

He placed his hand on her rounded belly, where their first child was growing.

"I don't know if I'm trying to protect those parents because I honestly believe that it would be wrong for them to get their hopes up after all this time, or because I'm putting myself in their place. Would it be worse to know that maybe my son was a victim of a homicidal pedophile, or would it be easier for me to not have this possibility thrown in my face ten or eleven years after I lost him? Is it easier not to know these things? Am I projecting how I would feel as a father onto this situation, assuming everyone else would feel the way I feel, whether that's right for this case or not? Is that fair?"

Genna's hand slid over John's. "You're the most fair man I know. I don't think there's anything wrong in taking the feelings of the parents and siblings of these missing kids into consideration. Right now, would anyone benefit from knowing that Portia *might* be able to determine the names of some of Woods's other victims? I honestly don't know the answer to that." She thought it over for a moment. "I think that losing a child would be the worst thing that could happen. To know for certain that my child had been the victim of a monster like Woods . . ." She shivered. "Unbearable. I don't know that I could ever put that kind of pain out of my heart. But to be told there was a possibility, but to not know for certain, I agree, would dredge up all kinds of agony, so I can't say that I think you're wrong. I understand where Portia is coming from—she's working a case—but sometimes you do have to put that human factor first."

"I told her to contact the police departments that originally reported the disappearances, see who's still missing and who's not, see if maybe there's some potential source of the kids' DNA in an old evidence file somewhere."

"You mean like a toothbrush, a comb, something personal, from which DNA could be extracted?"

"Yes."

"I think that's a perfect solution for the time being. So no, I don't think you were wrong in telling her this might not be the right time."

"Gen, this is the first time in my career I feel my personal feelings may be coloring my judgment.

Maybe it's becoming a father for the first time that has me conflicted."

"There's nothing wrong with your judgment, my love. And it's okay to put yourself in someone else's shoes. Sometimes you see more clearly from someone else's vantage point."

"Then there's the matter of this being about Woods. It all goes back to him." He ran a hand through his hair. "Was I honestly doing the right thing by passing off the case to another agent? Was I really thinking of what was best for Madeline Williams and the other parents and families who still harbored hopes of having their sons returned when I sent Portia Cahill to deal with Woods? Or was it cowardice on my part because I did not want to revisit that place I'd gone to before?"

"John, there's nothing cowardly in facing the truth. And the truth is that if Sheldon Woods had any idea you were involved in the effort to find Christopher Williams's body, he'd have made everyone's life a living hell. Not just yours, but Mrs. Williams as well." She shook her head. "There's no question in my mind—absolutely none—that if he knew, there'd be no chance to recover any of the others. He'd be too busy playing with you, John. So no, it isn't cowardice, and you did the right thing."

When he didn't reply, she added, "It isn't like you to second-guess yourself. This isn't something you normally do."

"I don't normally deal with the likes of Sheldon Woods."

"Time to put it to bed." She stood, taking his hands and pulling him up with her. "Time to put *me* to bed. Lock up the back while I lock the front. I'll meet you upstairs. This is only my second night home in a week. I intend to make the most of it."

EIGHTEEN

"In here, Miranda," Portia called out from the kitchen when she heard the front door slam.

"Well, isn't this cozy." Miranda took two strides into the kitchen before stopping in her tracks. "Am I interrupting something?"

"No, you're not. Might have been nice to know you were coming home this morning, though, just in case."

"I doubt you'd have wanted me to call when I was leaving at four this morning." She flashed a smile at Jim. "I'm Portia's sister, Miranda."

"Jim Cannon." He extended his hand to her. "Wow. If it wasn't for your long hair, I don't know if I could tell the two of you apart."

"You could if you knew us better. For one thing, I'm the smart one." Miranda smiled.

"Oh, you wish." Portia laughed.

"Don't I, though," Miranda muttered and glanced at the coffeepot. "Is there enough for me?"

"There should be. I just made it." She indicated

hers and Jim's cups. "This is my second cup, but Jim just got here five minutes ago."

"Oh." Miranda frowned. "Pity."

"Jim's here to pick me up. We're going to meet with Woods's brother today. At least we're hoping he'll meet with us," Portia added. "Jim met him once before, back during the trial, so I'm hoping that will get my foot in the door."

"It could get the door slammed in your face," Jim reminded her.

"Been there and done that already once this week," Portia said. "Neal Harper practically threw me out on my ass yesterday."

"Who's Neal Harper?" Miranda asked.

"He's a self-described journalist who has logged almost as much time with Sheldon Woods as the prison guards over the past few years. He claims to have been researching a book he's supposedly writing about Woods," Portia explained. "His wife—soon to be ex—referred to him as 'creepy.'"

"She's got that right." Jim nodded. "He's a very strange little man. Used to hang around the courtroom a lot, called my office every day wanting to interview me."

"Did you let him?" Portia asked.

Jim shook his head. "He told my sister that he wanted to talk about what it felt like to have a client like Sheldon Woods." Jim shook his head. "Not something I wanted to discuss publicly."

"Hey, I'll bet you could have gotten a book deal out of it," Miranda told him.

"If I was going to write a book, it wouldn't be about Sheldon Woods," he said.

Miranda filled a cup and sat at the table across from Portia. "So what did I miss while I was gone?"

"Lots." Portia brought her up to date with the short version.

"Yow. Someone else's kill in one of Woods's graves?" Miranda grimaced. "I guess you're thinking copycat?"

"Yes and no. The profile of the victims is the same, but the MO is not." Portia put her cup down. "The boy we found buried on the Amish farm was not assaulted."

Miranda frowned. "That doesn't make sense. If someone is mimicking Woods, you'd expect him to have the same motive. The sexual assault of the boys was what drove Woods, not the murders, right?"

"Right. He killed as a means of disposing of his rape victims."

"So now you have a killer who's killing because . . ." Miranda paused. "Why is he killing?"

"Not sure. I need to discuss this with Annie. John and I think maybe he's trying to get Woods's attention, or possibly mine. But for what purpose?" Portia shrugged. "Haven't figured that out yet. I'm hoping Annie has some thoughts on it."

"I'm sure she will." Miranda glanced at the clock on the wall, then downed the rest of her coffee. "Gotta run. I need to get in to the office before eleven to give John an update on the Maine case and get my reports all in order." She smiled. "Did I mention that Will and I are meeting up in San Antonio tonight? He got held over a little longer than he expected, and I have time coming to me, so I thought I'd take a few days off and join him." She rinsed out her cup at the sink. "Must go unpack, then pack for Texas, then get into the office and out again by this afternoon." She made a face. "I'll never make it."

"You won't as long as you're standing here talking about it," Portia noted. "But we should be going, too."

"Where are you off to?" Miranda asked from the doorway.

"To Dufree Island. Woods's brother lives there. It's one of those little islands in the Chesapeake," Portia told her. "You know, one of those you can only reach by ferry."

"Oh, a ferry ride." Miranda grinned. "I love ferries. They're so romantic, don't you think?"

Portia ignored her. She turned to Jim. "Ready?"

"I am." He stood and passed his empty cup to her when she put her hand out for it. Turning to Miranda, he said, "It was nice meeting you."

"Likewise. I hope I see you again," she replied. She stepped aside as he passed her on his way to the hall. Behind his back, she mouthed the words to her sister: "He really *is* hot."

Portia rolled her eyes, kissed her sister on the cheek, and said, "Send me a postcard from the Alamo."

"Your sister seems to be quite the character," Jim said as he pulled away from the curb.

"Miranda thinks she's a real comedian," Portia replied drily.

"She certainly amused me."

"Yeah, well, some people will laugh at anything."

He did laugh then. "You were starting to tell me about your impressions of Neal Harper when Miranda came in."

"Right. Did I mention that his wife says she's going back to using her maiden name? Strange, since they've only been separated for a couple of weeks."

"Well, you said she described him as 'creepy.' Did she elaborate on that?"

"No. I asked, but she'd already hung up. After talking to him, though, you can bet I will follow up with Candace Wilson. The negative vibes came right through the phone. She really has a lot of hostility toward him."

"Maybe you can get her to talk about that."

"I'm certainly going to try."

"Do you see him as the killer?" Jim asked as he headed toward the highway.

"I don't know. My impression of him wasn't very favorable, but that doesn't make him a murderer." She turned in her seat to face him. "I can't decide if he's fascinated by Woods or at what he thinks is a golden opportunity to make a killing with this book of his."

"Are you ruling him out as a suspect?"

"Oh, hell no." She shook her head from side to side. "On the contrary, I think he bears watching. Plus he pissed me off big time. I'm going to see if I can get a warrant for those notes he took when he was interviewing Woods."

"He's not going to want to give those up."

She grinned evilly. "I know."

"So, you're saying it doesn't pay to piss off the feds."

"You betcha."

"What exactly did he do?"

"Got snarky. I asked him if Woods told him how many kids he'd killed, if he told him where he left the bodies, and you know what that little asshole said? He told me I could buy his book. Then he threw me out." She was irritated all over again just thinking about it. "We're talking about the lives of children, and he's playing tough guy, Mr. Cool, being cocky about the whole thing."

She shook her head. "This case is bringing out the worst in me, I swear it is."

"Why do you suppose that is?"

"Because I hate it when anyone is cavalier about other people's lives." Her arms were crossed over her chest and she was staring straight out the front window. "It's so easy to be glib when you have nothing at stake. When it's someone else's life that's on the line. It's harder when you know that if you don't do the right thing—if you don't do enough to stop it—someone is going to die."

"I feel the same way."

"You mean as a defense attorney?"

"Yes."

"But sometimes your clients are guilty, right?"

"I suppose sometimes some of them are. I never ask."

"How can you not ask?"

"Because I'm bound by what my client tells me. If he tells me he's guilty, it would be damned hard for me to build a defense to prove otherwise without being deceitful in court."

"But sometimes you know, don't you?"

"Sometimes my gut tells me something my client doesn't, yes."

"So if you know that someone has committed a murder, how can you try to prove he didn't do it?"

"I don't have to prove that he's innocent. I have to show that the prosecutor hasn't done his job in proving his case. He—or she—has the burden of building a stronger case than I do."

"Isn't that rolling the dice a bit?"

"Sometimes. But if the DA is bringing the case to court, he should have the evidence he needs to get a conviction. If he does his job, justice will be served. If the DA gets lazy, doesn't do his homework, doesn't check and double-check the evidence and the witnesses, doesn't make certain that it was a clean arrest, then he's likely to lose."

"Have you ever watched a guilty man walk out of the courtroom because you did a better job than the DA?"

"Why not ask me if I've watched an innocent man be led away in chains?" His words were suddenly clipped, his vexation apparent.

"Because I've had way more experience with the guilty than with the innocent."

"Try seeing it from the other side of the table sometime."

His eyes were fixed on the road ahead, and he drove in silence until they reached the turnoff for the ferry.

"I guess you park over there." She pointed out the window toward the lot where several vehicles had already been parked and two small groups of people stood milling around.

Jim turned off the engine and got out of the car and walked to the small guard station at the end of the lot. When he returned, Portia was standing off to one side, looking down over the pilings into the narrow canal that led into the bay.

"Something going on down there?" he asked.

"I'm just watching the crabs," she replied.

He looked over the edge. "Undersized, too small to be caught this year, so they're cocky, unafraid. This time next year, they'll be out there hiding in the seaweed, trying to escape the traps and the nets. How do you suppose they know?"

"I guess every species has its own form of survival instincts." She looked beyond him, to the dock. "Is that the ferry?"

"That would be her."

"It looks as if there's only one car on board," she observed.

"Must be a resident of Dufree," he told her. "The ferry ride for residents and their cars is free. For visitors, they want a hundred dollars for the car. Each way."

"Two hundred dollars to float your car across the bay?" Her jaw dropped. "Are they kidding?"

"Nope. They're just very conscious of the environment. The guy in the booth said they have few roads, and the ones they do have aren't in great shape. They're afraid the newer, heavier cars, like the big SUVs a lot of people drive, will damage them."

"Then why don't they just ban SUVs?"

"I guess they don't want to discriminate."

"So what are you supposed to do with your car?"

"Lock it and leave it here in the lot."

"Are you okay with that?" She glanced back over her shoulder at the pretty Jag sitting off by itself.

"I don't have much choice."

"Maybe we should have brought my rental. I wouldn't feel as bad leaving that alone here."

"Isn't that government issued?"

"They don't have one for me yet, so I'm keeping the rental until something becomes available." Or until I leave, she could have added, wondering not for the first time if John's inability to find a car for her was due more to his uncertainty about her commitment to the unit than it was to a shortage of vehicles.

"You sure you want to come with me?"

"Now would be a strange time for me to decide that I don't, after driving almost an hour and a half to get here."

She looked out past the ferry. "That must be Dufree Island." She shielded her eyes from the sun with her hand. "The lot doesn't look all that se-cure." She glanced at the guard in his little shelter. "I could take that guy with one hand behind my back."

"I guess he thinks that shotgun he has behind the counter provides all the security he needs."

"I guess that and the police car parked over by the dock could serve as a deterrent."

The groups of people they'd noticed earlier began to move toward the dock.

"Is it time?" she asked.

Jim glanced at his watch. "Right on time. The ferry is supposed to leave at one. The guard said they try to keep to the schedule, but that the captain will shove off if he thinks he has everyone on board."

"What if you're late?" Portia frowned and fell in step with Jim.

"I guess you have to wait for the next trip."

"Or plan on being early."

They walked the length of the dock and stepped aboard the double-decker boat. Aluminum lawn chairs were set up on the lower deck, and on the bow was an observation area with a railing of thick metal.

"What's your pleasure?" Jim asked as they made their way through the small crowd that had boarded before them. "A deck chair, or you could do the *Titanic* thing up there on the bow."

"Maybe we can go up to the top deck and sit."

"Looks like the steps are blocked off." He pointed toward a chain across the bottom of the stairway that led up.

"Right. I guess the *Titanic*, it is." Portia walked toward the bow, one hand on the railing as the ferry pulled away from the dock. "Though I have to say, I did see the movie and hated it."

"What, you don't like the sort of love story that rips your heart from your body?"

"That one ripped a little too hard for me," she

told him. "I like happy endings." When he didn't respond, she said, "You don't like happy endings?"

"I don't know of anyone who's ever really had a happy ending." Jim shrugged.

She stepped up to the bow and leaned on the rail. "My sister is going to have a happy ending," she told him. "She and Will are perfect for each other. They're very happy together."

"That's one."

"John—my boss—and his wife, Genna, are happy. Deliriously happy."

"How do you know? Maybe it's all a show."

"I know because I know John. I've known him long enough to know when he's happy and when he's miserable and when he's faking it. Trust me, they're happy." She paused. "Actually, I know a lot of people who are happy together."

"For now."

"Cynic." She poked at his midsection with her index finger, and he caught and held it.

"Realist," he corrected her.

"So you're telling me you don't know any happy people?"

"I know a lot of people who have professed to being happy for a while, or who thought they were," he said, "but I can't say I know anyone who was happy, in the end."

"Wow. That's really sad." She shook her head and pulled her hand free from his.

"Nah," he said, "that's life."

"Like I said, sad."

She glanced over her shoulder. "Looks like we're almost there. Dufree Island, straight ahead. And look, there's a sign for Doug's Outboards right there at the dock."

"Right under the sign for Doug's Bait 'N Beer." Jim leaned his arms on the rail next to hers. "Looks like Doug pretty much has the dock covered."

She nodded. "A real entrepreneur."

"Do you know exactly what you're going to ask him?"

"Pretty much. I'll have to take my cues from him, though. He might shut down on some things, might be willing to talk about others. We'll have to see how it goes."

The engine was cut and the ferry turned around slowly. The boat backed up so that the stern was level with the dock to permit the lone car to be driven off. Several of the passengers jumped off to tie the ferry securely to the pilings. "Must be regulars," Jim noted as they stepped onto the dock.

The bait and beer shop was a structure of weathered, gray wood that stood at the end of the dock where it met the pebbled walk that led away from the bay. The corners of the windows were home to spiderwebs, most of which held a dead fly or bee, and the frames were thick with dust and old caulk. They walked to the end of the building and looked around.

"I guess he wasn't kidding when he said their roads weren't in good shape. This one isn't even paved," Portia observed.

"Looks like they used a crushed stone down here by the docks, but up there," he nodded toward what appeared to be a small cluster of buildings that sat on a rise, "it looks like macadam."

"That must be the center of town. From the ferry I saw a few houses set by themselves down along the bay, and from here you can see a few more dotted about the island, but that appears to be the only place where there's more than a single structure."

"Maybe we'll have time to explore a little. Right now, let's go into Doug's. If he sells beer, maybe he sells sandwiches or something. It's past lunchtime."

They found the door at the opposite end of the building, and went inside. It was hot, baking under the afternoon sun; the only breeze came through the screens. A cooler with sliding doors stood against one wall, and on another, a chipped counter displayed tins of tobacco, a short stack of newspapers, and sunscreen. The wall behind the counter was decorated with horseshoe crab shells and a couple of handwritten signs. One suggested that you ask for bait and another urged you to ring the bell on the counter if you needed service. A metal bucket on the floor held long-handled crab nets.

Through the back windows Portia could see a very narrow beach of dark sand that separated the bay from a grassy slope. At the top of the slope were wooden picnic tables where three women and two men ate piles of crabs off paper plates. A lean-to on the back of the building had an open counter where a tall woman in a stained apron manned an old enamel stove. DOUG'S CRABS was painted in freehand letters on the side of the structure in blue.

"I guess that's the dockside crab shack I read about on the Internet," Portia told Jim. "Looks like Doug has a finger in every pot on the dock."

"Let's sample the crabs and see if we can find the man."

"Maybe we should ring the bell and see what happens."

"Be my guest." He gestured toward the chrome bell and stepped aside when she reached over to ring it. A moment later a door opened and the woman in the apron poked her head in to ask, "Were you wanting bait?"

"We were hoping to get some crabs," Jim told her.

"You want crabs, you come out here and order 'em." She closed the door.

"Okay, then. Outside we go." Portia led the way out back. "Two orders, please," she told the woman, who was now leaning on the counter and smoking a cigarette.

"And a couple of cold beers," Jim added.

The woman looked up from her smoke. "Beer's inside in the cooler. You go on in and grab whatever it is you want, come on back out here, and pay me for it."

Jim did as he was told. He returned a moment later with a couple of cans of beer and a newspaper.

They watched as the woman stuck her hand in a large galvanized tub filled with water and brought out several blue-claw crabs. She dumped them into a boiling pot on the stove. While the crabs steamed, Jim paid for their meal and asked, "Is Doug around today?"

The woman nodded toward the boat shop. "He's down in the shop, working on a motor. Something I can help you with?"

"No, thanks. We'll stop down when we're finished with our crabs."

"Doug don't like to be bothered when he's working."

"We won't take much of his time." Portia's smile was met with a cool stare from the woman.

Without taking her eyes off Portia, the woman handed Jim a roll of brown paper. "Pick a table and cover it, then bring me back the roll."

Jim did as he was told, with Portia's help, then returned the roll to the counter. He traded the paper for a large basket of steamed crabs and a pile of napkins.

"Wrap up the paper when you're finished, toss it all into the barrel right here." She pointed to the large rusted metal drum that stood at one corner of her hut. "Everyone has to clean up after themselves around here. I don't bus anyone's tables."

"Miss Congeniality, circa nineteen ninety-nine," Portia said under her breath.

"Hey, the beer is cold and the crabs are hot. Count your blessings," Jim told her.

"Good point. It could have been the other way around, and this is no day for warm beer."

They polished off the crabs and beer while watching a couple of teenagers race their sunfish across the water.

"I feel like I've been rolled in Old Bay," Portia grimaced when she finished the last of the crabs. "Delicious, but oh, so messy."

"There was a box of wet wipes on the counter," Jim told her. "I'll get a couple so we can clean up before we go in to talk to Doug."

Portia pushed the discarded crab shells to the center of the table and rolled up the paper from each side until she had a tidy package. She walked to the designated barrel and dropped the debris in. It landed with a thump, and she hoped the woman in the apron heard it. She returned to the table and sat on the bench, watching Jim engage the woman in a conversation. *Miranda was right,* she nodded to herself. *He is pretty hot.*

Better than hot.

He ripped open a pack of wet-wipes and began to clean his hands as he leaned closer to the woman in the apron, as if hanging on every word she was saying. The same woman who'd been so rude fifteen minutes earlier smiled and suddenly seemed to have a lot to say.

"What did you do, hypnotize her?" Portia asked when Jim returned to the table.

"Nah." He tossed her a few packets of wet wipes. "She asked me if I had business with Doug and I told her I'd handled some legal matters for his family. I guess she thinks there might be some type of inheritance coming their way."

"You told her that?"

"That would have been lying. Of course, if she misunderstood what I meant when I said that we wanted to talk to Doug about some old family matters, well . . ." He raised his palms up, a gesture that implied that he wasn't responsible for however the woman interpreted his words.

"She's his wife?" Portia opened a pack of wipes and tried to clean away the smell of crabs and Old Bay.

"Yes. Donna Jo. She said she never got to meet anyone in Doug's family since they all died when he was in his teens."

"Really?" Portia asked. "All of them?"

"Every last one," he said solemnly. "Tragic, eh?"

"Very." She watched the woman behind the counter. "Wonder what she'd say if she knew she had a mother-in-law in Vegas and a brother-in-law in prison serving thirteen separate life sentences?"

"Let's go see if Doug has a few minutes to talk while he's fixing that boat engine." He reached out a hand to her and she took it, allowing him to pull her up. He didn't release her hand, and she didn't make an effort to pull away. Hand in hand, they walked to door marked BOAT REPAIRS and went inside.

Douglas Nicholson worked neatly and he worked alone. The shop was clean and nothing appeared to be out of place. The engine he was working on sat on a makeshift table, a thick piece of plywood set over two sawhorses. Tools were lined up according to size on one side of the table, and the man himself worked in a white T-shirt that looked as if it had just come from the laundry. In one hand he held a wrench, in the other, a cloth he used to clean up each phase of his work.

"Hello, Doug," Jim said as he and Portia entered the shop.

Doug Nicholson looked up and squinted. "Hi," he replied uncertainly, setting down the wrench and putting on a pair of glasses that sat on a nearby bench. He looked Jim over as if trying to place him.

"Remember me? Jim Cannon. I was . . ."

"Oh, Christ. What the hell do you want?" Nicholson asked flatly. "What's he done now?"

Before Jim could respond, the man shook his head. "Never mind. I really don't want to know. So you just go right on down there to the dock. If you hurry, maybe you can catch the ferry back to the mainland. It should be leaving any minute now."

"I haven't come to talk to you about anything your brother did, Doug. I—we—wanted to ask you . . ."

"You don't get it, do you?" He took several steps in Jim's direction, then stopped. "I don't know him. I don't want to know him. As far as I'm concerned, he doesn't exist. So don't ask me anything, okay? I don't know anything about him." He shook his head. "I don't *want* to know anything about him."

"Mr. Nicholson, my name is Portia Cahill," she stepped forward. "I'm with the FBI."

"Jesus, don't you people understand? I don't know him. I haven't known him since he was twelve or thirteen years old and all that craziness started."

"What craziness?" she asked.

He shook his head again, as if to clear it. "Look, I don't like people hanging around while I work. I gotta get this engine done, the guy's coming back in an hour to pick it up." He took off his glasses and placed them back on the table where they'd been. "I don't have time to talk."

Doug Nicholson turned his back and returned to his work.

"I appreciate that you're busy, that you have a job to do, Mr. Nicholson," Portia told him. "I can respect that. We'll stop back later."

"Why?" Nicholson asked.

"Because I have a job to do, too."

NINETEEN

"So what now?" Jim lowered himself to sit on a rock at the top of the grassy slope that overlooked the bay. "We've walked most of the island, and we've walked some parts of it twice."

Portia turned her wrist to check her watch.

"It's almost six. Nicholson's customer should be along anytime now to pick up that motor." She sat next to him. "Unless he was making that up to get rid of us."

"Maybe not." He pointed to the dock where a cruiser towing a smaller boat was pulling into a slip. Three men jumped out and were walking toward the shop. "That might be him now. That bow rider he's towing doesn't have a motor."

The men disappeared into the shop and ten minutes later came out carrying the motor.

"Showtime, Agent Cahill." Jim stood and stretched. "When is that ferry due back?"

"In about an hour." She watched as the men positioned the motor on the back of the boat. One man jumped into the water to secure it and maneuver the motor into place. Finally, the one in the water pulled himself onto the deck.

"I hope he's not a smoker," she muttered. "He'll light up like a Roman candle with all that gas and oil from the water around the dock on his clothes."

"Oh, shit, look." Jim stood and pointed beyond the building that housed the crab shack, the repair shop, and the Bait 'N Beer to where a figure hurried along the road.

"Is that Nicholson?" Portia jumped to her feet. "Son of a bitch. I'll bet he's headed home."

"His wife's still here, though." Jim noticed the woman was behind the counter, serving a plate of crabs to a family that had wandered down one of the paths. "Let's follow him, catch him at home, you have your little chat, and we'll be back here in time for the ferry."

They walked quickly in the direction they'd seen Doug Nicholson take. They found him standing on the porch of a house about a quarter of a mile inland past the small hamlet. There was no welcome in his eyes as he watched them approach.

"I told you I don't know nothing about him," Nicholson called to them.

"And I told you that I have a job to do," Portia called back. "This will take us ten minutes," she said as they drew closer, "and then we'll leave, and no one—not even your wife—needs to know what we talked about."

"What, then?" He sat on one of the two rocking chairs but did not offer Jim or Portia a seat.

"The psychologist who examined your brother . . ." she began.

"Half brother," he corrected.

"The FBI's psychologist who examined your *half* brother ten years ago says that Sheldon told him he was sexually abused as a child. I was wondering what you know about that."

He shook his head. "Nothing. He never told me nothing about that."

"You lived with him and your mother until you were seventeen, he was being abused, and you never knew?"

"He's probably lying. Probably made it up, you know, so it would sound like he had an excuse for all those things he did. If it happened, he never told me. But maybe it didn't really happen."

"You're what, four years older than Sheldon?"

He nodded.

"You must have spent a lot of time together when you were little. Only siblings . . ."

"So?"

"So I was wondering what he was like as a child. Who would know better than you?"

Nicholson shrugged. "He was just a kid."

"A whiny, obnoxious kid? A spoiled, nasty kid?"

"No, he was none of those things. At least not then, when he was real young. He was always small for his age."

"So he must have looked up to his big brother."

"I guess. Back then, anyway."

"When did that change?" she said, sensing that at some point that relationship became different.

"I guess when his father left."

"How old was Sheldon then?"

"About five, I guess."

"How did your relationship with your brother change?"

"He changed."

"How so?"

"He had to be Mama's little man, once his father split."

"Where did that leave you?"

He shrugged again, his face closed.

"I understand that your mother has been married several times."

Jim sat on the top step and let her do her thing. Nicholson nodded.

"How many times when you were a child, do you remember?"

"Three, four maybe. I honestly don't remember."

"Do you remember the names of her husbands?"

"I suppose."

"Who were they?" Portia pulled a chair around so that she sat facing him. "What were their names?"

Nicholson sighed deeply, as if resigned to something he wanted no part of.

"After my dad, there was a guy named Claude

Dwyer. She never married him, but he was around for a time. Then there was Aaron Woods, Shelly's father. He left when Shelly was about five."

"Any idea why he left?" Portia asked, noting the use of a nickname for his half brother. Until now, he had avoided calling him by name.

"You'll have to ask *her*."

"So after Aaron Woods, who came next?"

"Guy named Buck something-or-other moved in for a while, then he left, too. She took up with Andy Lewis, married him."

"How about this guy Davey? What was he like?"

Nicholson shrugged. "I never knew him. He was after my time."

"So while you lived with your mother, there was your dad, then Dwyer, then Aaron Woods. After he left, there was a guy named Buck and a guy named Andy Lewis. Anyone else?"

"There was always someone else," he snorted. "That woman never slept alone one night in her entire adult life."

"What was Buck like?"

"Quiet man." Nicholson looked off toward the bay. "He liked to play blues music on the radio. She liked rock-and-roll. He drank scotch, neat. She drank whatever she could get her hands on. Looking back, I think maybe he was too good for her."

"Looking back, do you think he could have been abusing Sheldon?"

He seemed to be lost in thought.

"Mr. Nicholson?" She touched his arm and he shook his head.

"No. It wasn't him."

"How can you be so sure?"

"He never paid any mind to either of us kids. He came into the house, did what he did with her, and left when he'd had enough of her."

"How about Andy Lewis, then?"

"I don't think so." He rubbed his eyes. "I don't know."

"Sheldon never said that someone was bothering him, maybe an older child in the neighborhood? A relative, maybe?"

"Are you asking me if I molested that little shit, Agent Cahill? Because if that's what you want to know, why not ask me outright?" He stood, his anger building. "No, I never laid a hand on him. Ever. You think something happened to him when he was a child that fucked him up? It wasn't me who did it."

"Then who, Mr. Nicholson?"

"Ask *her*." He stood up and shoved his chair back.

"Mr. Nicholson, after your father left, before your mother met Aaron Woods, were you your mother's 'little man'?"

He went into the house and slammed the door.

"Well, I guess that takes care of that," Portia said.

"Interesting how he speaks of his family using

pronouns. *He* or *him* for his half brother, *her* for their mother."

"I did notice that. I guess it's his way of putting distance between himself and them. Though he did refer to Sheldon as *Shelly* there toward the end. A childhood nickname, I guess." She sat next to Jim on the step. Just as she did so, they heard the ferry's horn. "Oh, shit."

She jumped up and grabbed him by the hand. They ran across the lawn, through a grassy field to the road, then down the shell-covered path to the dock. They rounded the corner of the Bait 'N Beer just as the ferry pulled away.

"Hey!" she called, but the motor drowned out her cries. "Well, shit. Now what? That was the last ferry for the day."

"Before we panic, let's just make sure that it was, in fact, the last trip. I'll go inside and check with Donna Jo. Be right back."

She stood on the dock, her hands on her hips, and watched the ferry glide across the bay.

"Okay, now you can panic," Jim told her when he came out of the building. "That *was* the last ferry today."

"Oh, that's just swell," she grumbled.

"I guess we should see if we can find a place to stay, then catch the first boat back in the morning."

"Maybe someone has a boat for hire," she suggested. "Maybe we can find someone to take us across. It won't hurt to ask."

Together they returned to Doug's Crabs.

"Sorry," Donna Jo shook her head slowly after they'd asked. "Tonight's bunco night down at the church. No one's likely to be going anywhere on bunco night."

Jim and Portia exchanged doomed looks.

"Try Ida's up there on the hill." Donna Jo pointed to a spot behind them, and they both turned. "That white house up there with the fancy widow's walk on top? That's Ida's place. She has some cabins she rents out this time of year. I know some of them are taken—there's a wedding here day after tomorrow and the groom's family has been coming in for the past few days—but she might have something for you."

"That's the only place that rents rooms?" Portia asked.

" 'Fraid so."

"Thanks." Jim nodded.

He and Portia started up the hill. "If worse comes to worse," he told her, "we could always sleep on one of those picnic tables."

"The mosquitoes will eat us alive."

"Maybe in one of those fields, then."

"Haven't you ever heard of deer ticks?"

"Then you'd better cross your fingers that Ida has a couple of cabins," he said as they approached the house in question. A sign on the lawn read WEL-COME TO IDA'S, and a long, narrow path led to the front door. The house was sided with cedar shake that had long ago turned a rich dark brown, and the windows and door were clean and white with fresh paint.

"I don't know why, but I'm getting this really strong Hansel and Gretel vibe," Portia said under her breath as they went up the stairs. "So if anyone starts shoving food at you, don't eat it."

Jim rang the bell, then stepped back to admire the property. "You have to admit, it's a pretty place. As a matter of fact, the entire island is charming."

"If I didn't feel like I was being held hostage here, I'd probably agree with you."

A young girl answered the door and told them that Ida was out back. They made their way around the house to the spacious yard and found a woman tossing bread crumbs into a fishpond. She looked up at their approach.

"You here for Todd's wedding?" she asked.

"No," Portia told her. "We came over for the day and missed the ferry. We're stranded. We were hoping you'd have some cabins available for the night."

"You're lucky," Ida smiled and stood up. When she did, Portia noticed the fish were not koi, but instead looked like trout. "Someone called in a little while ago to let me know they'd missed the ferry over, so they have to find a place there on the mainland. So you can have their cabin, but just for tonight. They'll be catching the first boat over in the morning."

"Great." Portia smiled.

"Come on inside, and we'll get your information, give you your keys." Ida not so much walked as waddled on bowed legs. "Will you be wanting breakfast in the morning? I serve coffee and some muffins out here in the courtyard."

"That would be great, sure." Jim nodded. "Do you serve dinner as well?"

"No, but the crab shack down there does a fish fry on Thursday nights, so you're in luck." She climbed the back steps and opened the screen door. "Looks like your lucky day all the way around. If I were you, I'd be buying some lottery tickets."

"Does anyone sell them on the island?" Portia asked.

"No, you'd have to have done that already. Shame." Ida appeared saddened by the thought that they'd missed their chance at a jackpot.

They followed Ida through the big, old-fashioned kitchen into a small sitting room. She told them the fee for the night's stay, then opened a desk drawer and took out a small brown envelope. When Jim and Portia each took out their wallets and counted out the cash, Ida held up a hand. "No, no, that price was for the cabin, not for each of you."

"Two cabins," Portia said, holding up the bills. "Two payments."

"No, honey. One cabin. That's all I have."

"One cabin?" Portia asked.

Ida looked from one to the other, then shrugged and said, "You two work that out between yourselves. I got one cabin, don't care who sleeps in it."

"Well, maybe there's someplace else," Portia turned to Jim. "A motel or a B and B, or something."

"No other thing, honey. It's Ida's or you sleep under the stars. The bugs ain't too bad yet. We seem to have a lot more bats this year."

They each handed over half of their cash.

"Cabin D," Ida smiled as she tucked the bills into a pocket. "It's a nice one. Has a little sitting area with a couple of comfy chairs."

She gestured for them to follow her out a side door, and chatted away as they walked to the cabin. It stood in a line of others that were obviously designed and built by the same person. The cabins all shared the same weathered cedar, white gingerbread trim, and matching porches that Portia had admired on the main house.

Ida took a key from the brown envelope and unlocked the door, pushed it open, and handed the key to Jim. "Here you go," she said. "I hope you have a real enjoyable night, folks."

"How 'bout we sit up there on the grass and watch the fish jump around in the bay?" Jim suggested after they'd finished dinner. It was still fairly light and neither of them had wanted to confront the issue of who was sleeping where just yet.

"What about the bats?" Portia gazed skyward at the dark shapes fluttering and swooping overhead.

"You heard what Ida said. The bats are doing their part to keep the bug population down."

"No pesticides needed on Dufree Island, that's for damned sure."

He took her hand and they walked up the slope behind the picnic area and sat on the grass. It was still warm from the heat of the day. Portia took her phone from her bag and checked her call log.

"I set the phone to vibrate before we went to see Doug in the shop, and I forgot to turn the ringer back on." She scrolled through several missed calls, then checked her voice mail. When she finished, she was scowling, prompting Jim to ask, "Is something wrong?"

"Howard Heller, the state trooper who met me in Lancaster, called to let me know that they'd identified the boy whose body we found on Amos King's farm. His name is Josh Winston. He was nine years old a week ago Sunday." She drew her knees up to her chest.

"It really gets to you, doesn't it?"

She nodded. "I'd be inhuman if it didn't."

"I thought all you law enforcement types developed a kind of shield against taking it to heart."

"There is no shield. You cover up what you have to so that you can do your job, because if you think about it too much, you can't take it. I never met a cop or an agent who could look at the body of a dead child and not have it tear his or her guts out. Regardless of what you say, or what kind of an act you put on, it rips you up inside."

He put his arm around her and pulled her to lean solidly against his body. The smell of honeysuckle from a nearby hedge floated on a breeze and occasionally mixed with traces of the saltiness of the bay. She closed her eyes and tried to lose herself in the scents and the softness of the air, attempting to exorcise the image of Josh Winston lying in the makeshift grave, dirt filling his open eyes.

Jim's phone rang and he drew it from his pocket to answer it. Portia took deep breaths and concentrated on the sound of his voice and his soft laughter as he ended the call.

"That was Dani," Jim told Portia. "I should have called her to let her know I wasn't going to make it to my nephew's ball game, but I completely forgot."

"I'm sorry."

"Not your fault. Finn's okay with it. I promised him I'd make tomorrow's game. I'm assuming we'll be able to get off the island tomorrow, right?"

"Assuming there's no hurricane or the ferry doesn't sink on its way over, I think that's a promise you'll be able to keep."

"Good. I told him I'd pick him up at his summer camp. I'd hate to disappoint him."

"You're very close to him, aren't you? And to your sister?"

"It's just the two of us now. Well, the two of us and Finn."

"Since your parents passed away?"

"And my brother."

"You had a brother?"

He nodded.

"Older? Younger?"

"Older."

"How did he die?"

For a moment, she was uncertain that he'd answer, and was beginning to regret that she'd asked.

"Pete died in prison. He was beaten to death."

"Oh, my God, Jim . . ." Portia all but choked on her own words. It was the last thing she'd have expected.

"My brother was brought to trial on a rape and first-degree murder charge. He was convicted and sentenced to sixty years. He was killed the first month he was inside." He spoke in a flat tone, as if by rote. "Eight months later, there was another rape in the same neighborhood. This woman also died as a result of the assault. When the cops arrested the guy who'd done it and searched his apartment, they found articles of clothing belonging to the woman my brother had allegedly murdered. The guy confessed to raping and killing both women."

"Jim, I don't know what to say . . ."

He shrugged. "What's to say?"

"How was he convicted in the first place? What evidence did they have?"

"The only thing they had was a witness—a friend of the victim's—who was in the bar where Pete was drinking that night. She said that Pete came on to the victim, and that she blew him off. She claimed that Pete left the bar right behind them, that she saw him get into a little blue sedan. Pete drove a blue Honda."

"What did Pete say?"

"He said yeah, it was true. He'd tried to pick the girl up but she wasn't interested so he dropped it. He said he didn't notice when the two women left that night, so it could have been around the same time that he headed home." He stared out toward the bay. "He was very open with the cops. They used what he told them to build a case against him."

"She told him to get lost and it pissed him off. He waited until she left, then followed her home." Portia knew how the scenario would have been spun.

"That's pretty much it. There was no DNA to match up, no physical evidence to implicate him, but this witness was real convincing. She just *knew* that Pete had raped and killed her best friend."

"I'm so sorry."

"Thanks."

"That's what influenced your decision to become

a criminal defense attorney." His commitment suddenly made sense to her.

"If we'd been able to afford a better lawyer than we had, he might have been able to prove reasonable doubt. But the guy we had . . . looking back, I think the witness even had *him* convinced that Pete was guilty. I went to law school with the thought that I couldn't make it right for him, but maybe I could make a difference for someone else."

"How old were you when this happened?"

"Seventeen. Peter had just turned twenty-one the week before he was arrested. It was his first night out alone in a bar. He usually went out with his buddies but no one was around that night, so he took off on his own." His thumb idly traced small circles on the top of her arm. That slight touch raised her awareness of just how close they were. "I was in the courtroom for every minute of that trial. There were times when it was all I could do to keep from yelling at Pete's attorney, the judge, the DA, the jury, the witness. I wanted them all to know Pete the way I did. I wanted his lawyer to put me on the witness stand so I could tell the jury. He said it wouldn't do any good." He shook his head. "I couldn't understand how anyone could fail to see what a gentle guy he was."

"It must have been really hard on your parents."

"My mom was already gone. But I do think that's what killed my father. He never got over what happened—the trial, his son going to prison as a convicted murderer, then Pete's own murder. It was hard for my dad to stay in town after my brother went to prison, but he never considered moving away. He said he knew his boy was innocent no matter what had happened in that courtroom."

"He must have felt vindicated after the real killer confessed."

"All the friends who'd turned away from my dad tried to approach him, but it was too late. He just couldn't take it, couldn't deal with all the what-ifs. What if my brother hadn't gone into that bar that night? What if the witness hadn't been so adamant, so convincing? What if that gangbanger in prison hadn't killed Pete? My dad had a heart attack and died two weeks after the real killer was arrested."

His protectiveness toward Danielle made perfect sense. She'd been in a relationship with a violent man, and Jim had to stand up for her, because there was no one else she could rely on. And maybe there was a bit of guilt on his part as well: he hadn't been able to save his brother, but he would not let his sister down. A seventeen-year-old boy would hold himself accountable, would assume a responsibility that maybe wasn't really his, and that feeling of being responsible would stay with him for a long time.

"Is your sister upset that you aren't coming home?"

"Oh, yeah." He nodded and in the last light of

the setting sun, she saw the first trace of a smile touch his lips. "She's convinced that you're out to seduce me. Actually, Dani thinks every woman I meet is out to seduce me."

"Are they?"

"Sadly, no." He smiled down at her. "Which doesn't mean you shouldn't give it your best effort."

"And if I did?"

"I'd have to fight you off, of course. Give it *my* best effort, to counteract yours."

She turned in his arms, her face turned up to his.

"Well, then. Perhaps we should see whose effort is, in fact, the best."

"I'm always up for a challenge."

He lowered his lips to hers and kissed her, softly at first, then more demanding, his tongue teasing the corners of her mouth. She held his face in her hands for a moment, then wrapped her arms around his neck to draw him even closer. He eased her back onto the ground and lowered himself next to her. With his mouth he traced the softest part of her neck to the top of her cotton shirt and back again.

Portia felt like she was falling, slowly drifting downward, like a leaf on a summer breeze, unable to catch herself and not wanting to try. Warmth spread through her, head to toe, and she welcomed it. It had been a very long time since she had wanted a man in this way, and suddenly, she wanted Jim very much. Wanted his mouth and his hands on her skin, wanted to feel his body on her and in her. When his mouth closed on her breast over her shirt, her head fell back and she ran her fingers through the hair on the back of his head, urging him on. Her breath caught in her throat and she wanted to rip her shirt off with both hands. His fingers slid beneath her clothing, and the need that swept through her was unbearable. She wanted him, and wanted him now, right there. She tugged on his shirt until it came free from his khakis and ran her hand up his chest. He slid her breast free from her shirt and bra, and when his mouth captured it, she arched her back and moaned, offering him more, begging him to take more. She pulled on her skirt, forcing it up, and his hand followed, slipping under the silky fabric there and finding her core. She closed her eyes when his fingers slid inside her and let the rhythm begin.

"Just ride it out," he whispered, his breath jagged, and she did, until the stars behind her eyes exploded.

She reached for his belt to undo it and he caught her hand. "I think now might be a good time to head on back to the cabin," he said. "Anyone could come along right about now and see more of me than they might like to."

"Everyone's down at the church," she reminded him. "Playing bunco."

"What is bunco?" He smoothed her skirt and straightened her shirt, then stood and pulled her up. "Is it a card game?"

"I think it has something to do with throwing dice. Someone in the office plays every week with a bunch of friends."

She started to tuck her shirt back into the waistband of her skirt, then decided against it. Her body felt soft and spent, but she knew it would take very little for the edge to return. She took his hand, and together they walked up the slope in the darkness and found their way back to the cabin. Jim unlocked the door and started to turn on the light.

"Don't," she said as she drew back the curtains. "We have moonlight. I've never made love in the moonlight before."

"Well, then, moonlight it is."

She backed up to the bed, leading him with one hand. With the other, she unbuttoned first her shirt, then her skirt. Soon her clothes were in a heap on the floor along with his. She lay back against the pillow and he followed. She wrapped her legs around his waist and without a word, drew him inside her. He groaned when she lifted her hips to meet his and he sank into her, the fullness of him taking her breath away. The sweet tension filled her and mounted, higher and higher, and she sought his mouth, wanting to feel his tongue on hers when their tension crested.

"You win," Jim gasped after release had shaken them back to earth.

She pulled back to look into his face. "What?"

"Your best. Better than mine."

Portia smiled in the dark. "Hell of a fight you put up, though."

TWENTY

He held his head in his hands and tried to stop the sound of blood pounding in his ears. He'd spent days searching the news for even a hint that his story was out there. But there'd been nothing. He'd gone so far as to drive to Lancaster every other day to buy copies of the *Intelligencer Journal* and he'd checked the Lancaster *New Era* online about three times a day. But nothing. Not a word.

Oh, they could report on the opening of a new restaurant in downtown Lancaster, and the softball playoffs between two rival summer leagues. The morning paper carried the story of a buggy accident on Route 30 that tied up traffic for four hours one day, and on the opening of the newest outlet stores. But the murder of a young boy whose body was found in the grave of a serial killer's victim from ten years ago . . . *you'd think they'd find a little room for that one, wouldn't you?*

He fumed as he paced from one room to the other and back again.

Back in the day, they'd covered every move

Woods had made. Every damned move. Every victim, every suspected kidnapping. Every fucking thing he'd done. You couldn't turn on the TV or pick up a magazine or newspaper back then without reading about Sheldon Woods's latest victim.

So why were they ignoring his?

Intellectually he knew the authorities could be suppressing the story for a reason, like maybe trying to figure out how to release it without causing a panic. Maybe they didn't want rumors of a crazed child-killer loose in Lancaster at the height of the tourist season. *Yeah. Yeah. That had to be it.*

He contemplated the possibilities presented by the thousands of visitors who came into the area every summer to go to the outlet malls. And then there were all those kitschy attractions. The amusement parks. The Strasburg Railroad. The Amish Village. *What the hell?* He snorted. He'd never known the Amish to live in a village.

The more tourists the merrier. The more to witness his cleverness, to fear him, to watch in horror as he had his way with them all. With the press. With the police. With that pretty FBI agent. Oh, yes, above all, he wanted her to notice. She really thought she had it all together, that one did. So dedicated to her work. So sure of herself.

How best to get her to sit up and take notice? He poured himself a glass of water and sipped it, pondering the situation. Perhaps if he knew her better, the answer would be more obvious. He'd have to work on that. Knowledge was, after all, power.

For now, he had to wonder how many dead boys would it take before she—before all of them—started paying attention to him. Two? Three?

There was only one way to find out.

TWENTY-ONE

"Did you folks sleep well?" Ida went from table to table in the small courtyard, serving coffee to her guests and offering fruit and freshly baked muffins. "We made these this morning," she told everyone. "My grandson picked the berries himself late yesterday afternoon."

"And how 'bout you folks?" She smiled at Portia and Jim. "Everything satisfactory?"

"Perfect." Portia smiled.

"Absolutely," Jim assured her. "I can't remember when I had a better night."

"Good, honey. I'm glad to hear that." She patted him on the shoulder and moved on to the next table.

"A perfect night followed by a perfect morning." He rubbed the inside of her wrist with his thumb.

"Please, Counselor," Portia feigned protest. "We have a ferry to catch."

"There's another this afternoon."

She laughed, knowing that he had to get back to his life as surely as she had to return to hers. As if on cue, her phone rang, causing the others in the courtyard to shoot her dirty looks. She glanced at the number of the incoming call.

"Hey, Will. How's it going?"

"Great, good. Listen, I only have a second. I'm late for a meeting." Portia could have guessed that. Will was always the last to arrive. "I found the woman you were looking for. The one in Vegas."

"You found Rhona Davey?" she whispered excitedly.

"It's Rhona Naylor now. She left Mr. Davey in the dust a long time ago. Along with Mr. Fogarty. But yes, I found her. Write this down."

"Hold on, let me find a pen." She opened her bag and began to search. A second later, she said, "Shoot." She wrote down the address and the phone number.

"You are the best, buddy," she said sincerely. "You are the absolute, positive best."

"Truer words were never spoken. Let me know if you need anything else. Gotta go."

"I take it that was your soon-to-be brother-in-law," Jim said after she ended the call. "And that he found Rhona."

"Rhona is two husbands past Mr. Davey," she told him. "No grass growing under her feet."

"She must be some woman."

"I'm going to call John and make arrangements to fly to Vegas today before she runs off to one of those wedding chapels and changes her name yet again."

"I'm sorry I won't be able to tag along. I'm sure it will be . . . interesting."

"Yes. I'm thinking it will be."

"Well, if you're finished, let's head to the dock to wait for the ferry. I can tell by the look in your eyes that you're eager to get on with it."

"I am, yes." She touched her napkin to the corners of her mouth and pushed her chair back. "I'll make my call to John on my way to the dock. And I guess I should try Annie again, find out what she thinks about this latest twist."

"You mean the second killer."

She nodded. "My gut is telling me he isn't finished."

"You think he'll kill again?"

"I think he's just getting started."

The ride back to Miranda's house was quiet, the mood quite different from the drive to the ferry. The previous tension between Portia and Jim had been broken. Their new relationship was fraught with uncertainty and a new tension all its own. Portia had never been into one-night stands, but she was hesitant to read too much into what had happened between them on Dufree Island. Better to let it take its course, she told herself as the Jag buzzed along the interstate, better to go where it leads and not try to force it. She sighed, thinking of how awkward intimacy could be between people who were just starting to really know each other.

"What?" Jim asked.

"What what?" she replied.

"What's making you so pensive?"

"Oh, just thinking about things."

"What things?" He reached for her hand. "Tell me what things so I can think along with you."

Portia smiled. "Actually, I was thinking about . . ."

Her phone rang. She checked the number before answering. "Hey, John."

"Sorry I missed you earlier. I just heard from Lisa Williams. Her mother is in the hospital, so they've had to postpone Christopher's memorial service for a few days. She said she'd get back to me and let me know when they'll be having it."

"Will Mrs. Williams be able to attend?"

"We're all hoping. It would be a damned shame, after all these years, if she wasn't able to see her son laid to rest." He cleared his throat. "So how'd it go with the brother?"

"All right. I can't say that he shed any real light on Woods, but I did find out who all the fathers and stepfathers were. At least, I think I did." She shifted in the car seat and gazed out the window. "I need to go to Las Vegas. I'd like to make the trip as soon as possible."

"I'll see what we can do. You may have to fly

business class, and you may have to wait until to-morrow."

"As long as I get there."

"What's in Vegas?"

"Sheldon Woods's mother. Nicholson says he doesn't know anything about Sheldon having been abused. I couldn't get a good enough read on him to know if he was lying or not. But he seemed . . ." She searched for the word she wanted. "Smirky whenever he spoke about her. Whether that was because he was embarrassed by the number of times she's been married, I don't know. I think we know of six or seven husbands and a couple of live-ins."

"What's the point of this trip, Portia?"

She frowned, put off by his question. "For one thing, I want to find out if she knows who was abusing her son. I think his abuse was what started him down this path. For another, I think we need to know her if we want to know him."

"We do know him," John told her. "I've known him for years."

"You don't know who he confides in. Who knows his secrets. Who knows where he buried the bodies," she reminded him. "But someone does, and that's the person we need to find."

"You think his mother can point you to that person?"

"No. I don't think there's been any contact be-tween them for years. Her name doesn't appear on the visitor's log, so we know she hasn't been to see him since he was incarcerated." She hesitated. "I just have this feeling that somehow she's at the bottom of it all."

"You might want to talk to Annie after you've met with the mother."

"I'd planned on doing that."

"This most recent victim . . . what do we know?" he asked.

"All I know right now is that the boy's been identified as nine-year-old Josh Winston and the state is handling the case. They'll get back to me with their findings."

"And the other remains there in Lancaster—were we able to determine whose they were?"

"Just as Woods said, it's Joseph Miller. That's been confirmed by his parents. They were able to identify him from some old leg fractures."

"Good. That's good." He sighed. "Now, about the other boy—the second boy from the grave where you found Christopher Williams . . ."

"Nothing on him yet. But I haven't given up. I will find out who he is. I want to send him home."

"Well, let's see how many more we can send home."

"That's my goal, John. That, and maybe nailing Woods for a murder he doesn't have immunity for."

"Give Eileen a call in about an hour or so. By

then she should have flight arrangements made for you."

"Thanks. I'll call her when I get back to Miranda's."

She kept the phone in her hand even after the call had ended, thinking about how she'd approach Rhona and what she'd say to her, when she realized the car had stopped. She looked up and found they were parked in front of Miranda's house.

"Oh. We're here already," she said.

"Time flies when you're having fun."

"I was having fun, thank you."

"For the past ten miles, you've been far, far away."

"Vegas. Arrowhead Prison. Swell places like that."

"I wish I could go with you to meet Woods's mother." He turned toward her in his seat and took her hands. "As a matter of fact, I wish I didn't have to leave you at all."

"But you have that tee-ball game today," she reminded him.

"Oh, yeah." He glanced at the clock on the dashboard. "I have just enough time to pick up Finn and get him to the field. Thanks for the reminder."

"You would have remembered. It's important to you."

"So is this." He leaned forward and kissed her on the mouth. "Call me when you get back from Vegas."

"I will. Thanks for going with me yesterday."

"You have to admit, I was of no use at all to you with Doug Nicholson. You could have gotten to him on your own. But I wouldn't have missed it. Not for anything."

"Me either." She opened the car door and got out before she said anything else. *Best to just let it be for now.* "I'll call you."

She walked around the car and crossed the street, turning and waving to Jim before hurrying up the walk and unlocking the door. She waved again when he passed by and entered the house, thinking how she couldn't wait to change her clothes, since she'd been wearing them since the previous morning.

She closed the door behind her, oblivious to the old brown coupe that pulled from its parking space across the street and faded into the line of traffic behind Jim's Jag.

TWENTY-TWO

Portia welcomed the dry heat of the Nevada desert after the high humidity of the Maryland summer. She took a cab from the airport to the condo where Rhona Naylor lived. The street was lined with identical two-story stucco buildings. Portia walked to the first-floor unit and rang the bell. On the step were several chipped clay pots, each holding a thriving cactus, and copper wind chimes hung from the wall. The door was answered by a tall woman wearing white cutoff shorts and a T-shirt that was the same shade of red as her hair. On her feet were sandals adorned with fake jewels. Three fingers on each hand were encrusted with rings with various colored center stones.

"Mrs. Naylor?" Portia asked in the politest possible voice.

"Yes?" the woman replied through her bright-red lips.

Portia held up her identification. "Special Agent Portia Cahill, FBI. I'd like to talk to you about your son Sheldon Woods."

Rhona Naylor slowly blinked her mascara-coated eyes. "What the hell's that boy done now?"

"Nothing. Well, nothing new, anyway. May I come in?"

The woman hesitated for a moment, then ushered Portia in. "You'll have to forgive the way the place looks," Rhona told Portia. "I've been having migraines and haven't been able to keep up with the housework."

"Oh, I'm so sorry," Portia said with as much sincerity as she could muster. "Migraines are the worst, aren't they?"

"You have them, too?"

"Since I was in my teens," Portia lied through her teeth and poured on the sympathy. "I know how you must be suffering. If you'd rather I came back—"

"No, no, hon. It's all right." Rhona plunked herself down on a chair and pointed out a place on the sofa for Portia. She fished a pack of unfiltered cigarettes from her pocket. "Mind if I smoke?" She lit up before Portia could reply.

"Of course not." Portia wondered if it would make any difference if she'd said yes, she did in fact mind.

"So what's that boy up to these days?" Rhona searched the cluttered coffee table for an ashtray.

"He's still in Arrowhead Prison, as I'm sure you know."

"We've been out of touch, Shelly and me. After

what he did . . ." She shrugged. "Well, some things are hard to forgive."

"True enough, but he's still your son," Portia reminded her.

"My little man." Rhona nodded.

"What was he like as a child, Mrs. Naylor?"

"Oh, please, call me Rhona. I'm a divorced lady, you know."

"I didn't know." Portia tried to keep a straight face as she tried to count the number of divorces Rhona had gone through. "I'm so sorry."

"Don't be." Rhona made a face. "Good riddance to bad garbage. He wasn't the man I thought he was. I'm just such an easy mark, you know? I never seem to see the worst in anyone until it's too late. I just get taken advantage of, left and right."

And did pretty damned well by it, too, Portia thought, her eyes scanning the well-decorated room. Rhona appeared to have taken her exes for all they were worth.

"That's what happens when you're too tender-hearted." Portia smiled gently and tried to think of how she was going to get the conversation back on track.

"Oh, isn't that the truth?" Rhona nodded vigorously and blew out a long blue curl of smoke. "You know, my mother always told me that I needed to be tougher when it came to dealing with men. But no. Why, I—"

"Oh, is that a picture of Sheldon as a little boy?" Portia interrupted her and rose to walk to a marble-topped table on which a number of photos were displayed. She picked up the first one she came to and held it up. "What a cute little boy he was."

"Oh, he was such a sweet thing," Rhona said sadly.

"And this would be . . . let's see, I'm guessing this is Douglas?" Portia held up a photo of a boy who was obviously not Sheldon.

"Yes. A sweeter boy you never met."

"And this is . . ." Portia frowned. The boy did not look like either Sheldon or Douglas.

"That's Teddy. He was my youngest."

Teddy? Portia didn't remember having heard about a third brother.

"How old is Teddy?" Portia asked.

"He would have been seven on his next birthday." She pulled a wadded-up tissue from a pocket in her shorts and dabbed at her eyes. "We lost Teddy when he was just a little guy."

"I'm so sorry," Portia patted Rhona on the hand and dodged the lit end of the cigarette. "What happened to—"

"Oh, all my little men." Rhona sighed dramatically. "All of them lost to me, one way or another. Sheldon . . . well, we know about Sheldon, don't we? And Dougie, my first baby boy. Do you have children, Portia?"

"No, I . . ."

"There's nothing like the love between a mother and her sons." She dabbed at her eyes again. "Nothing like it. It's truly sacred."

"I'm sure. Now, Rhona—"

"You asked what Shelly was like as a child. He was an angel. A more beautiful child you'd never hope to see. And he was a good boy, Portia. He was a very good boy. He always did what he was told, he never talked back. He provided such solace to me when his daddy left us." She sighed deeply. "He was the best of all my boys. He was special."

"Rhona, the psychologists who examined Sheldon say that he told them he'd been assaulted as a young boy."

"Assaulted?" Rhona frowned as if she'd never heard the word before.

"Sexually abused."

"That's nonsense." Rhona flipped her hand dismissively.

"Well, he'd made the statement, and since so many men who . . ." Portia chose her words carefully. ". . . men who do the sort of things that Sheldon did, many of them had been abused as children. It's actually very common—"

"Who did he say abused him?" she asked abruptly.

"That's one of the reasons why I came to speak with you. We thought perhaps one of your exhusbands might have been the abuser." Portia watched as Rhona Naylor's entire demeanor changed. "I'm sure you would have been unaware of it at the time, it isn't something you would have necessarily known about, so we're not saying that you—"

"You're implying that one of my husbands did something unnatural with my son?" She stood and rose to her full height. "What kind of a mother do you think I am, that I would let any man touch my children in such a way?"

"Rhona, the allegation has been made, and we need to—"

"You need to get out of my sight." She stubbed out the cigarette violently and stormed to the door and opened it. "Now. How dare you come into my house and say such a terrible thing to me? Don't you think I would have known if something like that had been going on? Don't you think a mother would know if someone was touching her boy?"

Portia walked to the door because she had no choice. "Rhona, your son has said this happened. You're telling me you didn't know. I believe you. I'm not accusing you of anything, I swear I'm not. No one is. But at some point in Sheldon's life, when he was a child, something inappropriate happened to him, and that, whatever it was, contributed to—"

"Out. Of. My. House."

Defeated, Portia walked through the front door, flinching as it slammed behind her with vehemence.

"You have a nice day, too, Rhona," she muttered as she looked in her bag for her cell, and called for a cab.

"He never mentioned having another brother, or half brother," Jim told her when she called him from the airport, where she awaited a flight home. "Are you sure she said this kid was her son?"

"Positive. Yet neither of the older boys ever mentioned this younger brother. And she referred to Douglas, Sheldon, and Teddy as her 'little men.' Kinda creepy, by the way."

"She was always a little strange in the courtroom, I think I might have mentioned that. Never spoke to her son the entire time."

"Which is odd, since, to hear her tell it, she and her Shelly were like *this*." She crossed her fingers.

"You think she knew that something was going on with him?"

"I don't know. There's something there . . . I can't put my finger on it. Maybe it was Woods's father."

"Nicholson said that he left when Sheldon was about four, right?"

"Yeah. I don't know what I think, to be honest. On the one hand, she comes across as a fierce lioness of a mother. On the other hand . . ."

"On the other hand, she comes across as strange."

"Exactly."

"So what's your next move?"

"I'm going to have dinner with Annie McCall, our profiler, when I get back tonight, then I'm going out to the prison first thing in the morning. I want to see what Sheldon has to say about his younger brother who died."

"She say what happened to him?"

"No, I tried to ask but she sort of talked over me. Past me. I thought I'd have time to work back to that, but I pissed her off and she kicked me out of the house."

"Bodily?"

"Damn close. Anyway, I'm curious to see what Sheldon has to say about it all."

"I'd love to be a fly on the wall."

"You could be."

"I'm in court all day tomorrow. As a matter of fact, I'm going to spend some time thinking up the perfect opening argument as soon as we're done here. I took Finn and three of his buddies for pizza so that Dani could go out with a couple of her old friends tonight."

"That was nice of you."

"She really doesn't go out often enough, doesn't see her friends often enough. Besides, I've had fun."

In the background, Portia could hear the voices of small boys all talking at once.

"I need to hang up," Jim told her. "One of the boys just spilled his drink in his lap."

"Better take care of that. I'll talk to you later."

The first call for her flight was announced, so she took the notebook she'd bought in the news store and tucked it under her arm. She'd been making notes on the case and all the things she still needed to do, from following up with Larisse on the DNA results to the things she wanted to discuss with Annie.

By the time the plane landed, her list of things to do had expanded to include things she wanted to ask Sheldon. At the top of the list she'd printed one word: *Teddy*.

It was almost nine P.M. when Annie McCall rang the doorbell at Miranda's townhouse. She carried a briefcase in one hand and a bottle of wine in the other.

"I don't know about you," she said after Portia welcomed her into the house, "but after the week I've had, I could use a nice glass of Pinot and some good conversation with an old friend."

She kissed Portia on the cheek as she passed her on her way into the kitchen. "So good to have you back, Portia. How's it going?"

"It's going okay." Portia followed her and opened several cabinets until she remembered where she'd seen the wineglasses. She took down two, set them on the table, and proceeded to search for a corkscrew.

"Brought my own," Annie told her as she popped the cork out of the bottle.

"You're prepared for everything, aren't you?" Portia laughed.

"I have to be. My life is spent in the midst of chaos. I can't be stopping every five seconds to look for something."

"You are surrounded by the most shit, I'll give you that." Portia took the glass Annie held out to her.

"Well, then, here's to us." Annie raised her glass. "To those of us who chase the shit down, and those of us who have to figure out how it became shit in the first place."

"That would be you."

"True enough, child." Annie sat on one of the kitchen chairs and kicked off her shoes. "What nibbles did Miranda leave for you?"

"Some salsa, some hummus that Will made but it's about a week old so it's questionable."

"All the garlic he puts in, it'll never go bad."

Portia got the hummus from the refrigerator and a new jar of salsa and an unopened bag of pita chips from the pantry.

"Looks like dinner to me," Annie told her.

"We could call for a pizza and have a real dinner," Portia said.

"Do you realize how pathetic your life is when your idea of a real dinner is pizza?"

"If you have spinach on it, it has all the food groups, right?"

"Good point." Annie opened the pita chips and dug into the hummus.

"How's Evan?" Portia asked.

"Evan is wonderful. Tough being married to a cop, though."

"I guess he thinks it's tough being married to an FBI profiler."

"No doubt. He keeps it to himself, though." Annie grinned. "He's pretty much the perfect husband."

"Nice." Portia got out two plates and handed one to Annie. She poured a hill of salsa onto hers, grabbed a few chips and dug in.

"It is nice," Annie agreed. "What about you? Did you leave behind a string of broken hearts over there—wherever *there* was?"

Portia made a face. "Not much time for romance. Though you'd think with those odds—the odds having been eleven men to two women—someone would have at least asked for my phone number."

"Pity." Annie nodded. "What is it with men these days?"

"Might have had something to do with the fact that we were all dirty and smelly from sleeping out in the open most nights."

"That will put a damper on romance, so I hear." Annie put her feet up on the chair next to hers. "So you're not seeing anyone at all?"

"I didn't say that." Portia frowned. "I . . . actually, I don't know what I'm doing. There is someone, but I don't know what we are doing. Dating, I guess." She nodded. "I think we're dating."

"Who is he?"

"His name is Jim Cannon."

"Why is that name familiar to me?"

"He was Sheldon Woods's defense attorney."

"Oh, yeah." Annie nodded. "Very good-looking; right? Tall, nice build?"

"That would be him."

"I've seen his picture in the papers a couple of times. They always refer to him as one of the 'big guns.' "

They munched chips and drank wine for a few minutes, then finally Annie said, "So are you going to elaborate? Give me details?"

"Probably not." Portia shook her head. "Not yet, anyway. Not until I figure things out a bit."

"Okay, then. Fair enough," Annie said. "Let's talk about your case."

"The case is a mess," Portia told her. "On the one hand, we have Sheldon Woods. No introduction needed. On the other hand, we have someone who seems to have mimicked Woods, except in one vital area."

"Which is?"

"As you know, Woods raped his victims, then when he'd finished with them, he killed them."

"Right. We've talked about that before. He's a classic pedophile."

"The victim of the second killer was not sexually assaulted. There was no rape."

Annie frowned. "And this was the victim that was found in the grave that Sheldon Woods gave you directions to?"

Portia nodded.

"You'd think if he was mimicking Woods, he'd have played out the entire script." Annie was still frowning. "So why didn't he?"

"I was hoping you'd have some insight into that."

"He strangled his victim? Like Woods did? That much was the same?"

"Yes."

"But he didn't sexually abuse him."

Portia crunched a chip, which seemed to echo, the house was suddenly so quiet.

"One kill doesn't tell us much. But the fact that he left his victim in a grave Woods dug for one of his tells me he's sending Woods a message."

"We thought so, too, but we didn't know what it was."

"Maybe he's saying 'I can do what you did—abduct and kill—but I'm not like you. I don't rape little boys, and that makes me better than you.' " She helped herself to another mound of hummus and a few more chips. "It's a way of putting Woods down, maybe. And it's probably a bid for attention."

"From . . . ?"

"Woods. The press, the media. Maybe even you." Annie topped off their wineglasses. "He's someone who's had access to Woods, obviously."

"The other day I went to see a guy named Neal Harper. He's visited Woods more than anyone else has over the past few years. He says he's writing a book about Woods, that he wants an answer to the question of why Woods did it."

"And Woods is telling him?"

Portia nodded. "Harper says he did."

"So there's one strong possibility. What was your impression of him?"

"That he's one creepy guy. But a killer?" She shrugged her shoulders. "I don't know. He's shorter than me and soft, no discernible muscle tone. He didn't strike me as very strong physically."

"How strong do you have to be to overpower and kill a small child?"

"Strangulation actually takes some effort, and you have to figure that the kid is struggling. Then again, he really seems to be fascinated by Woods."

"If Woods has told all to him, he'd know where the bodies were hidden," Annie reminded her.

"Tomorrow I'm going to ask John to see if we can get a warrant for his notes. Anything that pertains to his dealings with Woods. Then we'll have an idea of what Woods told him or if he's just blowing smoke. He could just be bragging."

"Also a possibility. Anyone else with an abnormal interest in him?"

"A guy named Keith Patterson—we don't really know anything about this guy except that he's shown up at the prison to see Woods on several occasions. And a woman who apparently has a thing for Woods."

"Oh, spare me," Annie grumbled. "These women who get into these jailhouse romances make me crazy. I'm assuming you're going to talk to these people?"

"They're on the list. The killer is fascinated by Woods, and both of them seem to be fascinated, too. I'm also trying to track down the other visitors that Woods has had over the past year, particularly those who saw him around the time I was going to see him. Woods had to have told someone that he was giving up some of his victims in exchange for favors. He had to have told someone the exact location of the grave in Lancaster in order for the killer to have gotten there just hours before I did."

"He wanted to show you what he could do. Maybe it *is* your attention he's after."

"I don't even want to consider that." Portia shivered.

"I don't think he's doing it solely for you, but I think it's playing into his motive somehow."

"Ugh. The very idea makes me sick."

"Then find him. Stop him." She put down her glass. "What have you learned so far?"

"Sheldon Woods has some really screwed-up relatives." Portia told Annie about meeting with Douglas Nicholson and Rhona Naylor.

"Now this is interesting stuff." Annie's eyes lit up. "Mama's got issues, doesn't she? Multiple husbands, never without a man in her life."

"She refers to her sons as her 'little men.' Icky." Annie's eyes narrowed.

"What?" Portia said.

"She denied that Sheldon was abused?"

"Totally. Tossed my ass right on out. Second time in a week that someone did that to me."

"Who was the first?"

"Neal Harper."

"What did you do to piss him off?"

"I'm not sure. I think maybe he thought I was trying to trick him into admitting something. He actually lawyered up."

"So back to the mother. In denial. Maybe because she knew it was happening and she didn't make any effort to bring it to an end because she didn't want the man to leave?"

"They all left her anyway. Or maybe it was she who left them."

"Track down the ex-husbands. One of them could be the abuser, or could know who was. Could be someone might be able to shed some light on what went on in that house. I'm betting any one of them would have a whole lot to say."

"And then there's the issue of this third son. Teddy. Funny thing. Neither Sheldon nor Douglas mentioned another brother."

"Odd. How does he fit into all this?"

"I don't know. Rhona said they'd lost him when he was a child but she didn't say what happened. I'm assuming he's dead, but maybe she meant literally lost. I asked but she changed the subject to what an angel Sheldon was as a small boy, and then I asked about the abuse, and she showed me the door."

"Curiouser and curiouser," Annie murmured. "When are you going to ask John to give you some help? The stage is starting to get pretty damned crowded. No way you're going to be able to track down and interview everyone—the ones who've been hanging on Woods, all the ex-stepfathers— before this guy strikes again."

"I hate to ask for help. I haven't been back for very long. He'll think I can't handle anything on my own."

"He'll think you're smart enough to know when you're outnumbered. Right now, you are."

It was quiet in the kitchen, so when Portia's cell rang, they both flinched.

"Speak of the devil," she said when she answered.

"Portia," John's voice was both weary and tense, "there's been another one."

"Where?"

"Outside of Frederick, Maryland. Another small body found partially sticking out of the ground in a picnic area."

He read off the directions he'd been given by the police department reporting the find.

"I'm on my way." Portia looked under the table for the shoes she'd kicked off earlier.

Annie already had her car keys in her hand when Portia got off the phone.

"How far from the last one?" she asked. "That was Lancaster, right?"

"About thirty miles," Portia replied.

"And the one before that?" Annie gathered her things and stood and stretched.

"Maybe forty or so in the opposite direction."

"You might want to map it," Annie suggested. "Killers often like to stay in their comfort zone. You might be able to narrow down the field a little."

Portia rinsed the wineglasses and left them in the sink.

"True enough. We'll see if we can find his . . ." She reached for her bag, then stopped. She'd mentally drawn a map and recognized the territory. "It's the prison. All three sites—the one in Lancaster, this one near Frederick, and the one where we found Christopher Williams—they're all within about fifty miles of the prison."

"Which doesn't really help at all. You already know that several of your suspects have made repeated visits to the prison." Annie shook her head. "If the killer is trying to get Woods's attention, what better way than to leave the victims right under Sheldon's nose?"

TWENTY-THREE

Portia knelt to one side of a pile of soft earth that had already been removed from the shallow grave. The child lay on his side, his eyes closed, a thin layer of brown dirt on his blond hair and his blue-and-white cotton shirt.

"Dig around him." She caught the eye of one of the crime techs. "Dig very carefully, a few feet down in each direction."

"What are we looking for?" the tech asked.

"The remains of another child." She stood and brushed her hands on her thighs. "Old remains. But be very careful with him. I'm going to need DNA on the other remains I think you're going to find. Tell the ME to pull a tooth and send it directly to Larisse Jordan at the FBI lab."

"You sure there's another body?" All the techs stopped what they were doing to stare at Portia.

"I'd bet my life on it." She turned to the officer who was in charge of the crime scene and handed him one of her cards. "Make sure they check for sexual assault when they do the autopsy. I want to know as soon as they know. And I'm going to need DNA on this one as well, but tell the ME for God's sake, don't get them mixed up . . ."

She drove in a fury to the prison, so eager to get to Sheldon Woods she almost cried with the frustration of knowing she couldn't lay a hand on him. She handed over her belongings—her bag with her gun—to the guard and stormed down to the small interview room where she paced like a caged animal until she heard the door unlock. She saw Woods start into the room accompanied by CO DeLuca, who smiled at Portia from the doorway.

DeLuca, she thought. *He'd know who Woods talks to.*

"Well, isn't this a pleasant surprise," Woods said. "You're certainly the early bird, aren't you? It's barely . . ."

"Who would it be, do you think?" she interrupted him, not the least bit interested in his banter. "Who would want to be you, but better?"

She watched him shuffle to the chair and sit awkwardly.

"The profiler thinks that by not assaulting the boys, he's telling you that he's a better person than you, a better man. One who does not rape little boys."

"What would be the point of that?" he said idly.

"So who do you think it would be, Woods? Give me your best guess. Harper? Patterson?"

"Who?"

"Keith Patterson."

He shrugs.

"How about your girlfriend?"

"My girlfriend?" He laughed. "What girlfriend?"

"Eloise."

He snorted. "Eloise is a very odd not-so-young woman. She's a virgin, did you know?" He leaned across the table and whispered, "She's saving herself for me."

"Does she know you're never getting out of here?"

"She's hoping for conjugal visits," he said, still whispering.

"Dear God," she muttered.

"My thoughts exactly, if you want to know." He giggled as if they were conspirators, and she grimaced, recalling how he'd once thought the same of John Mancini.

"So Sheldon," she said, her face tightening. "About Teddy."

His face blanched.

"What about him?" he asked.

"Why didn't you ever mention him?"

Woods shrugged.

"I paid a visit to Douglas, by the way. He says he doesn't know who abused you and wasn't aware that you'd ever been abused." She smiled sweetly. "He thinks you made that up."

"Does he, now?" Woods's face set in the mask she'd seen before. No emotion, his eyes and voice flat.

"Yes, he does. He didn't mention Teddy, either. And you know, I find that so odd, that neither of you ever mentioned that you'd had a younger brother."

Woods shrugged nonchalantly. "Dougie was long gone by the time Teddy came along. He never knew him."

"So what happened to him, Sheldon? What happened to your little brother?"

Her questions were met with silence. "Did he die?" She watched his face but it remained immobile. "Your mother gave me the impression that he did."

His eyes flashed fire but he did not respond.

"Okay, then, where was he born? What was his last name?"

Nothing. She stood, angry, and pushed back her chair.

"Was that Teddy in the grave with Christopher Williams? Did you kill your own brother, Sheldon?"

Woods sat still as a stone.

"Did you rape him, too, before you killed him?" She shoved the chair and it slammed into the table, but Woods never moved.

"Of course you did. Otherwise, as you said, what would have been the point?"

Portia stopped to retrieve her belongings at the desk.

"You look overheated, Agent Cahill," noted the morning guard, a middle-aged woman with soft brown curly hair and a pleasant smile. "Can I get you a bottle of water?"

"That really would be appreciated, thank you. As long as it isn't any trouble." Portia was still fighting to get control of her emotions. A cool drink might help.

"No trouble at all. I have a small fridge back here, so I don't have to leave my post." The woman turned in her seat and leaned down. When she sat back up again, she had two bottles of spring water in her hands. "Here you go."

She passed a bottle over the counter to Portia.

"Thanks so much." Portia twisted off the cap and took a long drink. "God, I really needed that."

"It's a hot one out there today. Every time someone opens that door, I feel that hot rush even with the air-conditioning on."

"I heard it's going up to ninety-five or better," Portia said as she took another drink before putting the cap back on. "It's a good day to stay inside and keep cool. Thanks for the water."

"Anytime, Agent Cahill. You have a good day."

Portia went through the sliding doors and felt the heat the second she stepped outside.

"It's a scorcher, isn't it?"

Portia turned to the man who stood smoking a cigarette at the side of the building.

"Oh, Officer DeLuca. I was hoping to have a few minutes to talk with you. And here you are."

"Morning break," he told her. "We can't smoke inside anymore, so I have to come out here to grab a smoke on my fifteen minutes a couple times a day."

"Officer DeLuca, how long have you worked here at Arrowhead?"

"Oh, it's going on twenty-two years. If I can hold out three more, I get to retire." He laughed self-consciously and added, "Actually, that's what I'm holding out for. They got a real nice retirement package."

"You're here almost every day, aren't you?" she asked.

"Five days out of every seven, but they vary as to which days. There are three shifts each day so my days and hours vary from week to week."

"Do you always work Sheldon Woods's block?"

"Yeah, that's my block. That and one other one."

"So you know who comes to see him, what they talk about?"

"Pretty much, sure. On the days when I'm here, he don't see anyone I don't see."

"Has Neal Harper ever come in on your days?"

"That the guy who says he's writing a book about Woods?"

Portia nodded.

"Yeah, he's in a lot. He and Woods sit in that room with their heads together. Mostly Woods just talks and Harper writes it down. Hangs on to every word, too."

"What do they talk about, you ever overhear?"

"Sometimes just a little. I try not to listen. It's pretty sick stuff, you know?"

"What kind of stuff?"

"You know, the stuff Woods did to those little kids. I don't want to hear about it, but it doesn't seem to bother Mr. Harper. He just writes it all down. Thinks he's going to sell that book, sell the story to the movies, make a fortune."

"Who else does Woods talk to?"

"There's this woman who comes in, sometimes twice a month. She has a thing for Woods."

"You mean Eloise Gorman?"

"I think that's her name. Woods calls her 'Weesie' when she's here. The other names he calls her, behind her back, aren't fit to be repeated to you." The officer smirked. "She thinks they're in this big romance, but he laughs at her behind her back. I guess it's really kind of sad, for her."

"Does he talk to her about his victims, about what he did?"

"Oh, yeah." He took a long drag from his cigarette. "She's one of these religious nuts, you know?

Talking all the time about how confession is good for the soul. She's always telling Woods to talk it out, get all the poison out of his soul. She pretends to be real pious, but when he's talking about what he did to those kids, she gets this look on her face . . ."

He shook his head. "I probably shouldn't have said that. Forget that part. I'm probably wrong about that anyway."

"You're just giving an opinion, Officer DeLuca. You're entitled to that."

"I guess. Well, anyway, before she leaves, she gets him to pray with her. She holds his hands and closes her eyes—she thinks his eyes are closed, too, but I see him watching her—and she prays for his soul. She's always talking about how they have this totally pure relationship and how it's so spiritual and stuff like that. Weird, if you ask me."

"Anyone else come to mind?"

"Over the years, there's been some others, can't remember all their names. Some I never knew who they were. For a while there, it seemed like everyone wanted to interview him, do a story on him, write a book." He flicked his cigarette to the ground and stepped on it.

"How about Keith Patterson?"

"He comes around sometimes, yeah. Another strange one, if you ask me."

"How so?"

"He comes in to tell his dreams to Woods."

DeLuca picked up the cigarette butt with two fingers and tossed it into a nearby trash can.

"What kind of dreams?"

"You can imagine, probably. Same sort of stuff Woods likes to do." He shook his head. "I guess creeps attract creeps, you know?"

Portia turned the car's air-conditioning up high as she passed through the gate, pausing to hand over her visitor's badge and exchange some brief pleasantries with the guard. She'd been distracted almost to the point of rudeness when she'd arrived that morning and wanted to make it up to the young man who was always so nice to her and greeted her by name.

As soon as she hit the road, she dialed John's private line to bring him up to date.

"So I'm going to need a warrant for Harper's notes, his computers, anything he has pertaining to Woods and his interviews with him."

"I'll have it taken care of," John assured her. "Anything else?"

"I need someone to track down as many of Rhona Naylor's ex-husbands as possible. And while they're at it, see if they can get anything on Teddy . . ." She blew out a breath in frustration. "I don't even know his last name." She tried to recall the order of Rhona's husbands and lovers. "Maybe Lewis. Maybe Davey. Just guessing here. It could have been anyone after Aaron Woods. Or it could have been someone she never married."

"Got it. What else?"

"I need someone to find this guy Keith Patterson. I had a nice chat with one of the regular guards on Woods's cellblock, and he tells me that Patterson likes to come in to see Sheldon and share his dreams."

"I'll put Will on it. No one's better than he is at finding people who don't want to be found." There was a pause, then John said, "I'm waiting."

"For what?"

"For you to tell me you could use another hand out there in the field." Before she could respond, he said, "Livy Bach just got back from Dallas a few days ago and turned in the rest of her reports. I haven't given her anything new yet. I'll have her give you a call, see what she can help you out with."

"That would be so appreciated."

"It's okay to ask when you need help, Cahill. That's what we're here for."

She started to thank him, and realized he'd already hung up. She was just thinking how lucky she was when her phone rang again.

"I'm getting teeth right and left here," Larisse Jordan said. "What the hell's up with all these damned teeth?"

"They're all from different sets of remains. I'm

sorry, I should have called you to let you know I've been giving out your name all over the place."

"Apparently. So what am I looking for?"

"You're looking to match the DNA to profiles you already have. I'm looking to see if there's a match to any of the victims from Woods's house."

"The old profiles we have? From like, ninety-eight, ninety-nine?"

"Yes."

Larisse sighed. "All right. Anything else while I'm at it?"

"Well, now that you've asked, yes."

"I should learn to keep my big mouth shut," Larisse grumbled—but only halfheartedly. Larisse knew how important Portia's work was.

"The DNA I sent you last week, from the first boy I found . . . see if anything matches up to Woods."

"You think they're related?"

"I think they're brothers."

TWENTY-FOUR

The house Eloise Gorman lived in outside of York, Pennsylvania, was a tiny one-story with a neatly kept yard, in the middle of which was a well-tended rose garden. The shades on the windows were drawn to keep out the midday heat, and a small package sat on the top front step, looking out of place. Portia followed the tidy brick path to the front door. Before she got there, two identical black-and-white cats fell in line behind her.

"How nice," she murmured as she rang the bell. "Feline escorts."

The door opened immediately and Portia found herself looking up into the eyes of a tall, sturdily built woman with short, carefully trimmed brown hair.

"Agent Cahill, I've been waiting for you. You're precisely on time." Eloise Gorman smiled approvingly. "I feel that promptness is so important, don't you?"

"I do," Portia agreed and took the meaty hand that her hostess extended. She noted its strength.

"Well, come on in. Not you two." The woman laughed and shoed away the two cats. "Ruth and Esther, you play outside for a while. Go ahead, go . . ."

She closed the door and brought Portia into a small living room that had a sofa, two club chairs, and a fireplace that Portia would have bet a month's salary had never been used. The fire box was pristine.

"You have a lovely home, Ms. Gorman. Everything's so . . . neat." Portia sat on one end of the sofa.

"Neatness is next to cleanliness, and we all know what cleanliness is next to, don't we." It wasn't a question.

"Oh, yes." Portia nodded.

"Do you read daily?" Eloise Gorman sat on the edge of her seat and leaned forward slightly.

"Well, no. I don't have a lot of time to read anymore. I do try to take a quick pass through the *New York Times* when I can, maybe a magazine or two . . ." Portia sat her bag on the floor next to her feet and looked up in time to catch the look of disapproval on Eloise's face just before she noticed the open Bible on the coffee table in front of her. "Oh. You meant . . ." she gestured toward the Bible.

"A good reading sets the tone for the entire day."

"I'm sure it does." Portia crossed her legs and set her elbow on the armrest. "Ms. Gorman, on the phone I told you I wanted to speak with you about Sheldon Woods."

"Dear Sheldon." She smiled as if the rapture were near.

"You, uh, seem to visit him often."

"I'm helping him find his salvation."

"Do tell."

"He's seeking redemption. He's going to be welcomed into heaven by a choir of angels, because he's repented. He's asked for forgiveness. I'm so proud to have been the one to have brought him to the light."

"You spend a lot of time talking, do you, you and Sheldon?"

"Oh, yes." She was still smiling. Portia was beginning to wonder what sort of happy pills the woman was taking. "There's nothing we can't talk about, Agent Cahill. We're soul mates."

"Soul mates," Portia said flatly.

"Yes. He's confessed the secrets of his heart to me. I understand him, I know him, better than anyone."

"Then he's talked to you about having been abused as a child?"

"Of course. We talk about everything. He's told me all about that. How his soul was destroyed by that evil person." She hastened to add, "Of course, he has forgiveness in his heart now, but I know that was what set him down that terrible path."

"Did he tell you who his abuser was?"

"He said he could not speak the name."

"Did he ever discuss his kills with you?"

"You mean those wayward boys?"

"Ms. Gorman, there was nothing 'wayward' about those boys. They were his victims."

"Oh, he told me about them. How they were the ones who . . ." The smile was gone, and the face began to harden.

Please please please do not even say what I think you're going to say, Portia pleaded silently.

". . . who enticed him. He tried to resist, but there was a demon at work in him then."

They were children. Innocent children. He took their innocence, he took their lives, Portia thought.

"There was a demon in him?" she asked.

"*Then* there was. We've exorcised it, he and I. Working together." She smiled with self-satisfaction. "That's the power of love."

"Did he tell you where he buried the bodies of his victims?"

"No. Oh, he told me *how* he buried them . . . how he found just the right place to lay those poor unfortunate souls to rest. And of course, I knew where his thirteen victims were buried."

"Everyone knew where they were buried, once they were found," Portia reminded her. "I'm asking you if he told you where any of his *other* victims were buried."

"What other victims?" Eloise looked blank. "There weren't other victims."

"Ms. Gorman, Sheldon is suspected of having

murdered many more children than were originally found. He hasn't denied it. We've recently found several of them, but we'd like to find more."

The woman looked confused. "I don't believe you. Sheldon said . . ."

"Sheldon lied."

"He wouldn't lie to me." She rose, five feet ten inches of sheer indignation. "We're spiritual soul mates."

"Your soul mate is a murdering pedophile, Ms. Gorman. He murdered innocent boys because he liked it. He raped them because he liked it."

"I don't have to listen to this. How dare you. You don't know him . . . you don't know what a pure soul he is . . ."

"God help us all," Portia muttered as she opened the front door and walked through it.

"He does, Agent Cahill. He helps us all," Eloise called to Portia from the top step. "Even poor wretched misguided nonbelievers like you!"

It took almost the entire drive to the office for Portia to calm down. She went to a drive-through for a burger, fries, and a soda for her first meal of the day, acknowledging that she was too hungry and stressed to care at that moment about the state of her arteries. She picked up phone messages from Eileen on her way in, then went right to her office where she sat, turned on her computer, and opened the bag of food at the same time.

"Boy, someone's buzzed." A soft voice with a hint of the South drifted through the doorway.

Portia looked up to see Livy Bach—Special Agent Olivia Bach—standing in her doorway. "You'd be buzzed, too, if you'd driven all day to talk to a woman whose head is as far up her butt as the one I was with today."

"Did you learn anything from her?"

"Yes. I learned that man has an infinite capacity for self-delusion. That you can sell anyone just about anything if they think you love them." She thought for a few seconds before adding, "And I learned that God will help even wretched souls like me."

"Well, John said you needed an extra pair of hands on this case of yours." Livy grinned. "Looks like your prayers have been answered."

"Hallelujah. Eloise Gorman was right." Portia gestured to her old friend to take a seat.

"Who's Eloise Gorman?"

"Would-be lady love of Sheldon Woods."

"I thought he was a pedophile."

"That was the *old* Sheldon. Eloise has exorcised that demon. They're soul mates. She's brought him to the Lord."

"Dear God in heaven help us all."

"That was pretty much my reaction. Eloise assured me that God does in fact send help. And she obviously knows what she's talking about, because, hey, here you are."

"You do understand what you're putting into your body, eating that junk." Livy pointed a well-manicured finger in the direction of Portia's lunch. "Trans fats, cholesterol, and dear Lord . . . who knows where that beef came from?"

"Please, I'm aware of the dangers, but right now, I don't care." Portia waved a french fry. "Want one?"

"I thought you'd never ask." Livy reached across the desk and pulled the fries closer. "So tell me about your case. John just gave me the basics."

An hour passed before they'd finished discussing the case and the information Portia was still seeking.

"Will's tied up in Texas right now," Livy reminded her.

"He is if he's still with my sister," Portia quipped.

"Hey, good one. I always heard she was the kinky one." Livy looked back through her notes. "I don't know that we should be depending on Will to locate all these people . . . Woods's mother's ex-husbands, this guy Patterson. Who knows when he'll be able to get to it? Not to mention the brother without a last name. This is going to take some time."

"I know. If I knew someone else as good . . ."

"Well, I suppose you can be excused, since you've been out of the country for a while."

Portia looked at her quizzically.

"I've become quite proficient myself." Livy grinned. "Maybe not 'Will Fletcher proficient,' but on a scale of one to ten, where Fletcher is a fifteen, I'm probably an eight and a half."

"Sold." Portia printed out a copy of her computer file for Livy and pushed it across the desk. "Just in case you need a refresher. I'll be adding the notes from my recent interviews this afternoon and will e-mail them to you."

"Thanks. I can't wait to hear more about Eloise and her rehabilitated pedophile. And thanks for sharing the fries. I can feel the plaque sticking to my arteries even as I speak." Livy stuck her hand in her pocket and took out a card. "This has all my numbers on it. Call me anytime, day or night. I'm with you on this, Portia. Let's get this bastard."

"That's the plan."

It was after seven when Portia looked up from her desk. She'd spent most of the afternoon typing up her notes on her meetings with Neal Harper, Rhona Naylor, CO DeLuca, and Eloise Gorman. What a motley crew, she thought as she forwarded a copy to Livy.

She was thinking how good it was to have a partner. Livy was a good agent, smart and even-tempered, and good-natured about the kidding she got about looking like a fashion model and always being dressed to kill. Years ago, there'd been a story going around about how Livy went to interview a suspect in the field while dressed in a designer suit, and ended up being covered with mud when she'd had to chase the escaping suspect during a rainstorm through several suburban backyards after he'd taken off. Livy had cuffed the fugitive and gleefully brought him back. When someone pointed out that her pretty suit was most likely ruined, Livy had grinned and drawled, "So what? I got this piece of shit off the street." Portia smiled at the memory.

Portia started to pack up for the day, looking forward to getting to bed early, since she still had to catch up on that sleep she'd lost the night on Dufree Island. Then her cell rang.

"I was just thinking about you," she told Jim as she answered.

"Somehow I knew that."

In the background she could hear what sounded like cheers.

"Where are you?" she asked.

"Tee-ball."

"Having fun?"

"You betcha. I'd be having more fun if you were here, though." Jim paused. "How was your day?"

"Oh, swell. I'll tell you about it sometime."

"Sometime soon, I hope."

"I hope so, too."

"Where are you?"

"Just leaving the office."

"You're about what, ten miles or so from Parker?"

"That's the opposite direction from where I was going, but probably about ten, twelve miles from here, yes."

"Why not swing by the field here—we're at the park right off Route Forty—and you can meet my nephew. If you're nice to me, I'll even let you have pizza with us after the game." His voice dropped. "I know you're busy, and we're both going to have busy days tomorrow, but I'd like to see you, even if it's just for a little while."

"Sure. Give me about fifteen minutes."

"We're on the side of the field with the blue uniforms. I'll be the tall guy in the green shirt watching the parking lot for you."

"I'll see you then."

Tired as she was, the thought of seeing Jim—even, as he said, for just a little while—made her smile. She felt the tension slip away from her shoulders just a bit as she turned off her office light and headed for the elevator. Once outside, she tossed the briefcase holding her notes into the backseat and got behind the wheel. She turned on the radio and began to sing along as she drove toward the highway, blissfully unaware of the brown car that pulled out from the curb across the street after she passed by.

* * *

As promised, Jim was standing at the end of the lot with one eye on the field and one eye on the parking lot, when she arrived. He greeted her with a kiss on the mouth.

"That didn't take very long." He smiled and took her hand. "Come say hi to my sister. You can meet Finn after he bats. He's up soon."

"I don't know anything about tee-ball. What's the point of the game?" She fell in step alongside him.

"Just to hit the ball. They're only six- and seven-year-olds," he explained. "They're just learning how to line up the bat with the ball."

He guided her to the sidelines where Danielle stood with several other women, mothers of other players, Portia assumed. When she saw her brother approach with Portia in tow, Danielle's face darkened but she said nothing.

"You know Portia Cahill," Jim was saying, and his sister merely nodded.

"Hello, Danielle." Portia smiled as pleasantly as she could. "Nice to see you again."

Danielle smiled and turned back to her friends. Jim seemed not to have noticed Portia's odd reception, as his nephew was coming up to bat.

"There's Finn, Portia. He's just up now."

Cheers went up from the sideline as a small boy in the blue shirt took a swing. The ball sat on top of what looked to Portia to be a tube that held it roughly at eye level with Finn. He connected with the ball on the first try, and as he ran the bases, the cheers and applause were led by his proud uncle.

"He's got a good swing," Jim told her. "Did you see how far into the outfield that ball went?"

"Does he enjoy playing?" Portia thought back to hours spent playing softball on the local girls' club team in the town where she and Miranda grew up. She'd hated every minute of it.

"He loves it. He'd play all day, every day, if he could. The camp he goes to has ball games in the morning and every other day they play soccer or lacrosse. He's really into it all."

"Were you, as a kid?"

"I played everything. Pete taught me everything that he learned. He was good at it all," Jim told her.

At the mention of their deceased brother's name, Dani glanced over her shoulder at Jim, but did not comment.

The rest of the boys on the field took their turns at bat, running the bases after getting a hit. Some got tagged out at second. At the end of the game, Finn's team had won by a considerable margin.

"You're staying for pizza, right?" Jim asked Portia as they watched the boys line up to congratulate the opposing team on their play.

"You're taking the boys," Danielle said. "Did you forget?"

"No, I didn't forget," he turned to his sister. "Did you forget your manners?"

For a moment Danielle glared at Jim. Then she turned on her heel and walked away, calling to her son to gather his friends.

"I'm so sorry," Jim said apologetically. "I don't know what's gotten into her."

"You're her protector, her brother." Portia shrugged. "Maybe she sees any woman you date as a threat to that relationship. You said yourself that your family is down to the three of you now."

"That doesn't excuse her bad manners," he said, his hands on his hips. "Especially to you."

"You said she hasn't liked any of the women you've dated, Jim."

"You're not any woman."

"I like the sound of that. So I think I'll just choose to not take your sister personally, and we'll go join the team for pizza." She took his hand and tugged him toward the parking lot. "What do you say?"

"She still owes you an apology." He let her lead him to the car.

"She'll offer one—or not—when she's ready. In the meantime, introduce me to this fantabulous nephew of yours."

Finn didn't seem overly impressed to be meeting one of his uncle's girlfriends until they reached the restaurant. They'd pushed together several tables so that the entire team could eat together. Portia found herself seated across from Jim, and between two of Finn's teammates.

"What do you do, Portia?" one of the mothers asked from the opposite side of the table.

"I work for the FBI," Portia replied.

"Like, an FBI agent?" Finn asked.

"Exactly like that, yes."

"Wow." Justin, the seven-year-old to her left, looked up at her, wide-eyed. "You get to carry a gun and all that?"

"Yes."

"Where is it now?" he asked. "Where's your gun?"

"I'm wearing it."

"Can I see it? Please?" he pleaded.

"Yeah, let us see your gun," Finn chimed in.

"I don't think that's really appropriate," Danielle said somewhat sternly. "I don't think you should go to dinner with a bunch of first-graders carrying a gun."

"Sorry, Danielle, but it's part of my job." Portia forced a smile and concentrated on the slice of pepperoni pizza on her plate.

"All the same, I don't think guns belong at the dinner table," Danielle snapped.

Jim started to speak, but the look Portia shot him—*I can handle this myself, thank you*—was loud and clear.

"I'd agree, if I were flashing a weapon around, it would be inappropriate. But I was asked about it, and I answered. If Justin hadn't asked, no one would have known."

"Can I just have a peek?" Justin whispered in her ear.

"I'm afraid not," Portia told him. "I think Finn's mom is right in one respect. I have to have it on, but I shouldn't be showing it around. It isn't a toy."

"Nuts," he muttered.

A few minutes later, he asked, "Is it in a holster?"

"Yes, it is."

They finished eating and the crew of boys was gathered up to leave. Once outside, Justin tiptoed up behind her and pulled on one side of her jacket.

"I saw it!" he called to the others. "I saw the gun."

"You little monkey," Portia laughed, ruffling his blond hair. "And for the record, all you saw was the holster."

"We want to see, too," the other boys sang.

"Oh, for heaven's sake," she said, lifting her jacket. "There. Now you've all seen what Justin saw. Which was mostly brown leather."

"I saw it," one of the boys said as the crowd dispersed into their respective vehicles. "I saw the gun in the holster."

"Me, too. I saw it," another said.

"Dear Lord." Portia laughed in spite of the situation.

"I saw it, too," Jim said, taking her hand. "And if

I play my cards right, I'll get to see it again some-time."

"I'd say your chances are quite good, Counselor."

He walked her to her car and opened the door for her. He stopped her from getting in by putting his arms around her and kissing her deeply. "How does the weekend look for you? Think we could spend a little time together?" he asked.

"I think we could work something out."

"I have a trial starting on Tuesday, and I need to prepare for that, but I could take a break."

"All work, no play, yada yada yada."

"Exactly." He started to kiss her again, when Finn called to him. "Uncle Jimmy, Tad has to go to the bathroom."

"Better take charge there, Uncle Jimmy." She eased from his embrace and got into the car.

"Be careful," he said when she rolled down the window.

"I'm always careful." She backed out of the parking space, and turned to wave good-bye to Jim, Finn, and the boys gathered around his car, waiting for their ride home.

On her way out of the lot, she drove past a brown sedan parked near a grove of trees, all but hidden from view.

He felt a certain sense of purpose driving home. He'd been unsure for a while, but now he was more focused. It had been a good idea to follow her, to follow the man. It helped him find his sense of direction, like following a good map to a destination you'd been unsure of.

Well, he wasn't unsure anymore. She knew he was watching, she must—otherwise, why would she have paraded all those boys in front of him? Wasn't she tempting him . . . challenging him? Daring him to take one?

Of course she was. She was more clever than he'd given her credit for. He'd have to be even smarter, though—if she was using the boys for bait, he'd have to be very smart indeed to not get caught.

He had to think on this awhile.

Soon enough, he was home, turning on the lamps in the living room. He walked past the old upright piano that no one ever played anymore and banged on a few of the keys. He smiled, remembering how that always drove his mother crazy, when he'd bang out chords instead of playing the songs she'd spent hours teaching him.

He wondered why he kept the damned thing. He'd hated playing it, hated all that it stood for.

"A piano is a beautiful instrument," she'd chastise him. "You should treat it with respect."

"Yes, Mom. Sorry, Mom."

"Come back in here and practice your lessons," she'd yell at him when he'd sneak outside to play. "You'll never be a famous pianist if you don't practice."

"I don't want to be a pianist, Mom."

"Of course, you do. You want to be special, don't you?"

"No. I want to . . ."

Smack.

"Don't you?"

"Yes, Mom. Sorry, Mom." His face stinging from the slap, he'd sit at the bench and try to concentrate, try to remember what she'd taught him, his trembling fingers hovering over the keys before he'd start to play.

"That was the wrong chord. Play it again," she'd demand.

"Yeah, sorry, Mom," he smirked and turned her photograph facedown on the piano top. Usually, it worked to shut off her voice in his head.

You'll never be much of anything, you know that, don't you? Not smart like your brother. Not good-looking like your sister. You really don't have a whole lot going for you, you know? I tried to teach you to play, tried to give you something that would make you special, but you just weren't good enough. Just how do you think you're going to make your mark in this world, if there's nothing special about you?

He felt the humiliation rise within him; all he heard in his head was her voice, shrill and demanding, drowning out his own thoughts.

"Shut up, Mom," he said aloud. "Just . . . shut up."

He turned off the light, went into the kitchen,

and filled a glass of water from the tap while his plan took place in his head. When he had it all down pat, he went back into the living room and picked up the photograph.

"You want to see special?" he said. "I'll show you special. Your nothing-going-for-him son is about to turn the FBI on its ass . . ."

TWENTY-FIVE

"I found a couple of the ex-husbands," Livy told Portia the next morning. "Three, actually. Aaron Woods—Sheldon's father—died in 1992. Liver cancer. Andrew Lewis is working for a car dealer in Pittsburgh. He's happily married and has three kids. He may not be interested in rehashing that time in his life. Bob Davey is in Maine, works in a restaurant, but I'm not sure what he does there. I e-mailed the addresses, phone numbers, and pertinent data to you about two minutes ago."

"Terrific. Thanks a million." Portia turned on the computer and waited for her e-mail to appear.

"I haven't found anything on the brother yet, but I'm searching under each of the ex-husbands' surnames. It's taking a while," she said drily. "I have a few more avenues to explore, though, so let me get back to you on him.

"Great. Thanks." Portia printed out Livy's e-mail and reached for the phone. She called the number for the car dealership where Andrew Lewis was employed.

"I'd like to speak with Andrew Lewis, if he's there," she said when the call was answered.

"One moment, please. I'll connect you."

"This is Andy Lewis. How can I help you?"

"Mr. Lewis, my name is Portia Cahill. I'm with the FBI."

The silence on the other end of the phone was long and drawn out.

"Mr. Lewis? Are you there?"

"I'm here. What do you want?"

"I want to talk to you about your ex-wife."

"Which one?"

"Rhona."

"Oh, wait. Let me guess. This is about that wacky kid of hers, right?" He blew out a breath. "Look, I've worked really hard for a long time to put her and that kid of hers out of my life. I have a nice wife, three really terrific kids . . . I don't know Rhona anymore, haven't had any contact with her in years."

"I'm calling about her son, Mr. Lewis."

"Yeah, well, like I said, the younger one, he was a wacko." He lowered his voice. "I heard all about him. Read about him. All those little kids . . . Jesus, to think I lived under the same roof as him."

"Not that son. The younger one, Teddy."

"Teddy?" he repeated. "I don't remember Teddy. Just the older one, Dougie, he was pretty quiet. Kept to himself a lot. And the younger one. There were only the two of them."

"You lived with Rhona for how many years, Mr. Lewis?"

"Three. Craziest three years of my life, I don't mind saying it. Rhona, she's a trip. She's one hot mama, let me put it that way."

"Mr. Lewis, it's come to light that Sheldon had been sexually assaulted as a child. Would you know anything about that?"

"Huh? He was . . ." There was a deep intake of breath. "Uh-uh. No, no. Did she say I was molesting her kid? Is she totally nuts? Christ almighty, she ought to know I never had time for anything but her. When I said she was a hot mama, I meant . . ."

"Sir? No one's accusing you of anything. Rhona never said it was you, Sheldon never said it was you. I'm trying to find out when this occurred. If you say it wasn't you, I believe you." She did. His reaction had been so instantaneous, so genuine, she thought they could cross him off their list. "We're just trying to get a feel for what it was like in that house, what the relationships were like. Between the two boys, between the sons and the mother . . ."

"Oh, I can answer that one. It was weird. Really, really weird."

"What do you mean, weird?"

"Rhona wanted the boys to sleep in the bed with her when I was gone. I drove a long-haul back then, I was gone a lot. She used to call them her 'little men.' "

"Thank you, Mr. Lewis. You've been very helpful."

"I haven't really told you anything, but yeah, you're welcome. Now please, could you just not call again? 'Cause I wouldn't want it to get out that I knew that guy that killed all those kids . . ."

The story was pretty much the same when she spoke with Robert Davey.

"Rhona's a real nutcase. But she was one hell of a woman."

"Why'd you get divorced, could I ask?"

"Rhona had a roaming eye. We'd been together four years before she found someone else, and I don't mind saying they were four happy years for me. I really loved her. We'd have stayed together, as far as I'm concerned, if it hadn't been for the fact that she was one of those women who are just never satisfied, know what I mean? Always looking out for someone better." He cleared his throat. "I read about the trouble that boy of hers had ten years or so back. Well, I sure saw that coming."

"What do you mean?"

"I never saw such a mama's boy."

"And the other two brothers? What was your impression of them?"

"Other two? No, no, there was only one other kid. The older one, I forget his name. Nice kid. I told Rhona she was setting herself up for trouble, the way she treated them."

"What way was that?"

"She pretty much ignored the older one. Thought the sun rose and set on that younger one, though. I used to tell her, it ain't right. You're supposed to love all your children the same. That younger one, she just doted on him."

"Mr. Davey, Sheldon has told psychologists that he was abused as a child. Do you have any idea of who could have been responsible for that?"

"Abused? You mean, like molested?"

"Yes. That's exactly what I mean."

"I don't know of anyone who would have . . . wait a minute, are you thinking it was me?"

"No, sir. I was just asking if you had any idea of who it might have been."

"I honestly don't know. Like I said, I was gone a lot of the time. Was Rhona sneaking someone in the house when I wasn't there? You'd have to ask her that."

"Anything else you can tell me?"

"No, ma'am. Just that Rhona, she sure did love those boys of hers."

"Thank you, Mr. Davey. I appreciate your time."

Portia put the phone down and looked out the window, studying the picture that had formed in her mind. Douglas—Dougie—was Mommy's little man until Sheldon came along. Then Sheldon became the favorite. He'd been a beautiful boy, Rhona had told her, an angel. So Mommy had favored her beautiful child over Douglas, and Douglas had come to resent it. He'd been an only child for several years, he'd had all her attention, all her love. Then along came Sheldon, and Douglas was no longer number one in Mommy's eyes. Douglas reacted by keeping more and more to himself as he got older, leaving home at the earliest possible time. Years later, when Teddy came along, had he taken Sheldon's place in Mommy's heart, becoming the favored one? Had Sheldon resented Teddy so much that he'd killed him?

And what does that say about Mommy, Portia asked herself. Had she been playing a deliberate game with her sons, pitting brother against brother, playing their love for her against the love they had for each other, stirring up their jealousy until it erupted in murder?

What kind of mother would do such things?

She left the office almost on time and arrived at Miranda and Will's townhouse a little after eight. She stopped at the grocery store on the way, picking up the ingredients for a real dinner. She'd been eating crap for the past week and her body was feeling the effects. She was tired, not sleeping well, and she was afraid that her last really good meal had been those crabs back on Dufree Island. She was tempted to call Jim, to invite him over to share the steak she'd just bought, but she knew he was preparing for his case in the morning. She knew, too, there was a damned good chance they'd end up skipping dinner altogether. At least, if she had her way, they would. Still, she'd debated with herself all the way home. Call. Don't call. Call. Don't . . .

"Hey, there you are." Miranda stepped into the hall from the kitchen.

"When did you get back?" Portia hugged her sister to welcome her home. Just as well she hadn't made that call to Jim after all. "Did you have a good time?"

"About an hour ago, and yes, we had a fabulous time, for the short amount of time we had. Did you speak with John? He's been trying to get you for over an hour."

"I have my phone with me." Portia frowned and searched her bag for her phone. "I stopped at McKenzie's Market on the way home . . ." She checked her pockets. No phone. "I must have dropped it in the car. Did he say what he wanted?"

"Just that it was really important."

"I'll run out to the car and take a look."

Portia looked through the front seat, under the stack of paper napkins she picked up at a fast-food place and under the driver's seat. The phone had fallen between the seat and the console. She had to slide the seat back in order to reach it. When she picked it up, she checked the missed messages, then listened to her voice mail as she walked back into the house. Two of the calls were from John, and one was from Eileen on his behalf.

"He needs to talk to you ASAP, hon," Eileen had said in her always-calm tone. "It's important."

"Then why didn't he leave a message?" she muttered.

She'd just come through the front door, and was about to speed-dial John, when Miranda came out of the living room, holding the house phone.

"It's John," she said, and handed Portia the receiver.

"John, sorry, I just got home and heard that you'd . . ."

"There's been another one. I sent Livy out when I couldn't get in touch with you—she's already on her way to the crime scene, but under the circumstances, you need to be out there, too."

"Where?"

"Kendall Road in Parker, right off Route Forty."

Portia stopped in midstride.

"Portia? Did you hear me?"

"Yes." Somehow she managed to get out the words. "I heard you."

"Hang on and I'll give you directions."

"Never mind," she told him. "I know where it is."

"You do?" He paused. "It's a Little League ballfield, Portia."

"I know. I was there. Last night. Jim's nephew was playing tee-ball there."

There was silence on both ends of the line.

"I hope that's just a coincidence, Portia."

"So do I." She swallowed hard. "What's the victim's name?"

"I don't have the name, just the location. The local police called it in, said they'd gotten an anonymous heads-up that a body was there and that they were to call the FBI in."

"I'm on my way." Suddenly, she couldn't wait to get off the phone and out the door.

"Portia, check on Jim's nephew, why don't you?"

"As we speak, John." Her own phone was in her hand and she was dialing.

"Let me know."

"Will do."

When Jim didn't pick up his cell, she tried his office. An unfamiliar male voice answered.

"I'll see if Mr. Cannon is in his office," he told her.

A moment later, Jim was on the line.

"Portia?"

"Jim, Finn . . . his friends from tee-ball . . . are any of them missing?"

"What? What did you say?"

"Are any of Finn's friends missing?"

"I haven't heard of any . . . wait a minute. What's going on?"

"I just got called out to a scene where another

boy has been found." She could barely get the words out. "He was found in Kendall Park, Jim."

"Jesus God. Let me call Dani . . . she might know. I'll get back to you."

"Jim, find out where Finn is."

"That's the first thing I'm going to do."

TWENTY-SIX

Portia stood next to Livy Bach while the crime scene techs continued their careful work, uncovering the latest victim. One small sneaker jutted through the soft dirt and the sight of it broke Portia's heart. She dreaded the moment when the face would be uncovered, sickened by the thought that she would recognize it. She hadn't heard back from Jim, so she felt relatively certain it wasn't Finn. But just as certainly, she knew it would be someone who'd been at the table with them the previous night, eating pizza and celebrating their victory.

"Jesus, he's escalating at too fast a rate," Livy muttered under her breath. "What do you think is spurring him on?"

Portia couldn't respond. Her mouth felt frozen, her tongue powerless to speak. She prayed whatever random prayers came into her head, begged a merciful God that the face hidden by the dirt would be unknown to her. Yet even as she prayed, she knew that this latest victim was meant for her, not for Sheldon Woods.

The techs were almost forty-five minutes into their task when one of them called for a light. A beam was shined into the channel that had been dug, and Portia had to force herself to look.

"Take him out carefully," the assistant from the ME's office said. "See if he has anything on him we can use to identify him with."

"It doesn't matter," Portia heard herself say. "I know who he is."

Her hands were shaking and it took her several tries to dial the number on her cell phone. When Jim picked up, he said, "I was just coming inside to call you back. Justin McAfee is missing."

"I know," she said softly. "We just found him."

It was a full minute before he could respond. When he did, he merely asked, "Are you sure? You're positive?"

"I saw him" was all she could say without breaking down.

"Jesus," he said, his voice trembling. "What do I tell Finn?"

"Right now, you don't tell him, or anyone else, anything. Let the police contact the family. For now, all you can do is hug your nephew and keep him close tonight." She thought for a moment, then added, "Tonight and every night until we find the killer."

"There's a group of volunteers forming in the neighborhood to go look for Justin. Dani is getting ready to go out and join them."

"Let her go, Jim. Let the police handle this. Justin's family needs to be told in the right way."

"The right way?" he asked. "What's the right way to tell someone their child has been murdered?"

When she could not respond, he said, "Keep in touch, Portia."

"I will," she said before she realized he'd already hung up.

She walked back to the site. "Keep digging," she told the techs, even though something told her that no other body had been buried in this spot. It was too much of a coincidence that Sheldon Woods would have buried one of his victims, ten or twelve years ago, in the very park where Portia had watched Jim's nephew and his friends play ball.

This was personal. This one was meant for her.

She walked to the far end of the park and leaned over, retching until her throat hurt. When she thought she had control, she took her phone from her pocket and called Jim back.

"The restaurant where we ate last night with the kids," she said. "What was the name of it?"

"Torro's Pizza."

"He was watching last night. He had to have seen us there, had to have seen the boys." She swallowed hard, unable to put into words that the killer had seen Justin talking to Portia. In her mind's eye, she saw herself ruffling the boy's hair, and wished she could go back to that moment, and not touch him. Not speak to him. She pushed the wish from her mind. "Maybe Torro's has a security camera."

"Good idea."

"Only if he's on it."

When she returned to the site, she asked the local chief of police if he'd send someone to Torro's to ask about a camera and to obtain the tape if one existed. He dispatched an officer immediately.

"We don't have things like this happening," the chief told Portia, anger radiating off him in waves. "Guess I won't be able to say that anymore."

He smacked a fist into his open palm.

"God help this guy if I find him before you people do." He was almost growling. "I want a few minutes alone with him."

"You'll have to get in line, Chief," she told him.

"You really think there's another body in there?" he asked.

"There has been every other time," she told him. "This time, I don't think so, but we need to be sure."

She walked away before he could ask her what made this time different.

The ME arrived and transported the body. It had been all Portia could do not to touch the boy's sweet face as he lay on the ground.

She left without even telling Livy she was going.

She knew Jim's street address and knew the town was a small one. She figured she could find his house easily enough. She had to apologize for bringing this terrible thing to his door, for tainting their relationship. She slowly turned onto his street. There was a crowd gathered in the front yard of a house near the corner. She knew why they were there, and she looked straight ahead, searching the mailboxes for the number of the house Jim shared with his sister and his nephew.

She found his car parked in the driveway of a 1920s-style four-square with a wide front porch. A row of holly trees grew along the drive, and beyond the Jag, a small compact was parked near a two-story garage. Portia parked out front, and when she reached the front door and raised her hand to ring the bell, she saw that her hand was trembling.

"It's because of me, you understand that, right?" she told Jim when he came to the door. "Annie said the killer might be trying to get my attention and I brushed her off because it was too terrible to think about. I should have thought it through."

"Portia, for God's sake, come inside." He took her arm and led her into the front room.

"I didn't think it through. I never should have been around those boys. He saw me with Justin . . . he was watching and he saw me . . ."

"Don't do this to yourself." Jim shook her gently. "You're not responsible for what this man did."

Dani came down the steps from the second floor.

"You brought this here?" she asked. "This happened because of you?"

"Dani, stop," Jim said. "You don't know what you're saying."

"You knew about this killer and her involvement with him, and you brought her around my son?" White with rage, Dani faced her brother. "It could have been Finn. You're supposed to be protecting us, and you bring a child-killer into our lives."

She turned to Portia and started to say something, but instead shook her head and turned back to her brother. "I'm going back to stay with Jeanette tonight. The police just left. Her husband's traveling and they haven't been able to get in touch with him. I told her I'd stay with her until he gets back. Finn's asleep in his room. He doesn't know about Justin and I don't want him to know until I can tell him myself."

She brushed past Portia and went through the front door.

"She's right, you know." Portia's eyes met his. "He's been watching me, so he knows about you. He's watched you, so he knows about Finn."

Jim reached for her but she backed away.

"He was going to go from me to you to Finn. Somehow, he got Justin instead."

She turned toward the door. He tried to stop her, but she pushed him away. "Danielle is right. I brought this here." She shoved past him and went out the open front door.

"Portia, don't leave." He followed her to her car.

"Stay with Finn, Jim. Don't let him out of your sight. This isn't over yet. He's still out there. If he's followed you, he knows how to find Finn." She shook off his hands. "I need to find him first."

TWENTY-SEVEN

Now, this is more like it.

He smiled happily as he opened the morning paper and spread it across the kitchen table. PARKER BOY FOUND MURDERED! FBI SAYS COULD BE CON-NECTED TO OTHER RECENT HOMICIDES!

Oh, yeah, this was good. This was *real* good.

He turned on the local network affiliates, and was pleased to see that the story was breaking everywhere at the same time.

See, all I needed was the right plan. I was right on target this time, wasn't I? Make it personal to her, and all of a sudden it's big news.

He wished he'd thought of it sooner. *But hey, it's the end result that counts, right?*

He turned back to his favorite morning show and reveled in the coverage. Then on to the cable sta-tions, where he watched and listened and felt really good about himself for the first time in a long time.

"And you thought I'd never do anything note-worthy," he said aloud. "Well, I've got 'em taking note now, don't think that I don't."

He read through the newspaper one more time, then folded it over and dropped it on a chair. He'd need it for his scrapbook. The news had concluded its run and the morning shows were coming on. He went from channel to channel, but the coverage had shifted to a fire in California.

"Fame is fleeting," he said with a sigh. "Is that all there is?"

He remembered a song with that name, and for the first time, understood the letdown of getting what you want and finding that it wasn't enough. Even though it all played out just as he'd planned, it just wasn't enough.

The high was already fading, and he realized that, like all junkies, it was just a matter of time before he'd need another hit.

TWENTY-EIGHT

Neal Harper sat alone in the interrogation room, his eyes darting around, looking for a way out. Portia watched through the one-way glass, thinking maybe they should let him sit and worry for a little longer.

Or maybe not. She was just too tired this morning, too heartsick to play games with the likes of him. Livy had called to let her know she had found Keith Patterson and was having him brought in. No one had been home at Eloise Gorman's but they had someone watching her house and would escort her in once she showed up.

"She's not going to be happy," Portia told Livy.

"That upsets me no end," Livy replied drily. "I'll get back to you as soon as we find her."

Portia put Eloise Gorman from her mind and went in to the small room where Neal Harper was busy staring at his folded hands.

"This was your idea, right?" His eyes shifted to stare at her. "Bring me in here, get me all rattled. Take my computer, my fucking notes. What the fuck, lady? I already told you, I don't know a thing about those dead kids. I think it's a shame, sure I do. But I didn't have anything to do with it. And that's all I'm saying until my lawyer gets here. Just remember, when this is over, and I'm suing your ass for invasion of privacy and false arrest and for confiscating my personal property and for . . ."

"Two words, pal: *governmental immunity*." She sat down opposite him. "I'm just trying to figure out why a guy like you—a smart guy—would choose a loser like Sheldon Woods to write about. Why would you waste your valuable time on someone like him?"

Portia's tapping fingers were the only outward sign of her impatience and annoyance at having to spend any more time in the same room as Harper. "All the people a smart guy could choose to write about, why would you decide that Sheldon Woods was your best ticket to fame and fortune? I just don't get it, Harper."

"I told you. No one else got the whole story from him. Just me. I'm the only person he told it all to."

"How'd that come about, by the way?" She kept her gaze trained on him, but he would not meet it. "How'd you get interested in him in the first place?"

"I heard about him from the time I was a kid. They were always talking about him out at Black Horse Farm. About how this kid was a really good rider and was going to go on to jump in shows and stuff but he just left one day and never came back. And then like twenty years later they heard he was arrested for killing little kids."

"Black Horse Farm?" The name hadn't appeared in anything she'd read about Woods in the past.

"It was a riding stable near where my grandparents live," he told her. "I used to stay with them in the summer when I was a kid and one of the things they let me do was take riding lessons at this farm down the road from them."

"Sheldon used to ride there?"

Harper nodded. "All the instructors said he was a natural, started taking lessons when he was real little, like five or six. Like he could ride any horse, any style. They talked about him like they thought he was going to be great. Everyone was real surprised when he stopped coming around." He smirked. "They were even more surprised when he was arrested."

"Where's this farm?"

"Windsor Cross, out near Sykesville."

"Did they say he lived there? How old was he then?"

Harper shrugged. "I don't know any of that stuff. You'd have to talk to the people there. I just remembered hearing about him back then and his name stuck in my head somehow, so when he was arrested and went to prison, I thought, hey, this could be my big break. The one that puts me on the map, you know what I mean?"

"Did you tell him that you used to ride at the same stable?"

"Sure. That was, like, my in with him, see. That's why he picked me to tell his story instead of someone else. Like I was his homeboy or something."

"I do see." She thought for a moment. "Did he ever talk about his brother?"

"Douglas? Sure. It bugs him that Doug turned his back on him. Sheldon hasn't heard from him in years. He didn't even write to him or come to see him after he was arrested and went to prison. Really pissed him off."

"How about his other brother?"

"What other brother?" Harper appeared puzzled. "He just had the one."

"He had a younger brother, Teddy."

Harper shook his head. "Never heard of him."

Interesting to leave that little bit of family history out of his story, Portia thought. Funny that no one knows anything about Teddy. If she hadn't seen his picture, she'd be wondering if Rhona had been telling the truth about having had a third son.

"And his mother? What did he have to say about her?"

"Only that she was one fucked-up old broad. He said when she came into the courtroom, it was all he could do to not look at her. Said he hadn't seen her in a long time before that and he didn't want to see her then." He smiled knowingly. "I think his childhood was real screwed up."

"He give you any details on that?"

"He never was specific about their relationship, no. I just got the impression that she was real manipulative and relied on her sons a lot. Emotionally, I mean. I think she damaged his psyche."

"Everyone's a pop psychologist these days," she muttered. "Woods was pretty graphic about how he dispatched his victims," she said, changing the subject. "How did that affect you?"

"What do you mean?"

"Did it give you bad dreams, did it make you wonder what it felt like to kill someone? How did he describe it to you? Was he matter-of-fact, mechanical, or did he give you all the nasty little details?"

"You are really going to want to read my book, Agent Cahill."

"Look, you self-righteous little prick. Little boys are being murdered by someone who wants to be just like Sheldon Woods." A sudden flashback from the night before caused her to wince, and she squeezed her eyes tightly closed in the hopes of banishing the image from her mind. "Almost like Sheldon Woods. This guy doesn't mind killing kids—doesn't object to putting his hands around their throats and strangling them, but he doesn't go in for the sexual assault part.

"So it's someone who's gotten close enough to him to know what he's done and how, someone for whom killing doesn't seem objectionable but who views raping little kids with a certain amount of disgust."

"You think I'm that guy?"

"You tell me, Harper. Are you?"

An agent opened the door just enough to stick his head through it.

"Harper's lawyer is here."

"If I'm not arrested, I can leave with him, right? I can go with my lawyer?"

Portia made a sweeping gesture toward the door. "Be my guest."

"When do I get my computer back?"

"Someone will let you know."

"I'm going to tell my lawyer to sue you if I don't have it back by noon today."

"Good luck with that."

She went to her office and looked up Black Horse Farm on the computer. It was still in operation, its website proudly proclaiming that it had been owned by the same family for over sixty years.

Perfect. She dialed the number and explained the nature of her call.

"I'd like to speak with someone who taught children's classes about . . ." She did some quick math in her head. "Anywhere from thirty-five to forty years ago."

"You want to talk to Miz Cawley. She's been teaching the kids' classes for longer than that."

"She still gives lessons there?"

"Sure."

"How can I get in touch with her?" Portia asked.

"She's teaching a class right now, but you can leave your number and I can have her call you when it's over."

Portia repeated her cell and office numbers and hung up, hoping that Miz Cawley would call back soon. It was the first link she had found to Sheldon's past that consisted of someone who wasn't related to him. It was also a bit of information that hadn't turned up before, and explained his desire to ride when he could have asked for anything in exchange for his secrets. Anything within reason, of course.

She went into the breakroom for a cup of coffee. She hadn't had quite enough caffeine yet and hadn't slept the night before. Jim had left several voice mails for her, but she hadn't been up to returning his calls. Livy found her there, smacking the side of the coffeemaker in the hopes of speeding its progress.

"No, no, you smack this one with an open palm," Livy told her. "The one in the second-floor breakroom—that one gets the fist."

Portia corrected her technique. Within seconds, the coffee began to flow faster into the waiting pot.

"I just got a call that (a), Keith Patterson is in interrogation room D, and (b), Eloise Gorman is being brought in." Livy leaned back against the counter and watched the coffee drip. "Want me to take one?"

"If you wouldn't mind taking Gorman, it would help." Portia sat on one of the metal chairs next to the square table.

"Consider it done." Livy reached over and took the mug from Portia's hand and filled it from the pot, then handed it back to her.

"You look like shit, sugar. Almost as bad as you looked last night." Livy poured herself some coffee as well. "Want to tell me what that was all about?"

Portia swept up some loose grains of black pepper that had been left behind on the table. "The boy—the one they found last night—was a friend of Jim's nephew. Jim had invited me to one of the kid's tee-ball games. We went out for pizza. Justin—the boy in the park last night—sat next to me at the restaurant." She looked up, her eyes brimming with tears. "He made a big deal out of wanting to see my gun. We talked a bit outside, after we left the restaurant. The killer must have been there, somewhere, in the parking lot, the restaurant, the drugstore . . ." She swallowed hard. "He watched. He followed Jim home, saw where Jim dropped Justin off, maybe, I don't know. But somehow, the killer got to him between the time summer camp let out and the time his mother got home. Someone got to the kid and killed him."

"I'm sorry, Portia. I knew you were more upset than I'd seen you before, but I didn't suspect . . ." Livy shook her head. "I'm very sorry. I know how you must feel."

When Portia looked up at her, Livy nodded her head. "I've been there—don't think you're the only one who feels like their connection with a case led someone to harm. One thing I've learned in this job is that I am not responsible for the actions of other people. Neither are you." She drained the mug and rinsed it out. "I'm going on down to wait for Eloise Gorman. Anything I should know about her that wasn't reflected in your notes?"

Portia shook her head.

"I'll catch up with you later." Livy walked out the door. "Don't forget you got Keith Patterson waiting on you."

The door closed behind Livy, but Portia made no move to get up. She'd handled some nasty situations in the past—some while working counterterrorism—but she'd never had a case affect her the way this one had. She was thinking perhaps she should talk to John and have the case reassigned. Livy could front it; she had all Portia's notes and would do just as good a job without getting any more kids killed.

But what would walking away from a case say about her? What message would it send to John about her commitment? What message would she be sending to herself?

Questions for another time, she told herself. Right now, Keith Patterson was in a room down the hall, waiting for her. She swallowed the rest of her coffee and headed for interrogation room D.

Keith Patterson was tall and rail-thin, with sparse brown hair that was prematurely gray, and deep-set eyes that were so pale she wasn't certain of their color. He wore a faded blue T-shirt with sweat marks under the armpits and dirty jeans that were too big for him.

"Mr. Patterson?" She came into the room briskly. "I'm Special Agent Cahill." She started to extend her hand but dropped it to her side. His hands were dirty and scratched and looked as if he'd been in a fight in a bramble patch.

"I'm not sure what I'm doing here." His voice was surprisingly deep, and he spoke slowly. "Someone wanted to talk to me."

"That was me, Mr. Patterson."

"Name's Keith."

"Right. Keith. I understand you visit Sheldon Woods at Arrowhead Prison from time to time."

He nodded. "When I have the dreams. He helps me to know what my dreams mean."

"What are your dreams about, Keith?" She sat across the table from him. "Want to tell me about them?"

"You have bad dreams, too?"

"Sometimes."

"You should talk to Sheldon about them. He understands."

"Right now, I want you to tell me about your dreams."

"The boys come out to play and then they die."

"Who are the boys?"

"Just . . . boys."

"Boys that you know?"

"No. I don't know any of them."

"Why do they die?"

"Someone has hurt them."

"Do you know who?"

"Uh-uh. No. I don't see the person who hurts them in my dreams."

"When you tell Sheldon about them, what do you say?"

"I tell him what I see. He likes to hear about it."

"When did you first talk to Sheldon about your dreams?"

"I read about him in the paper. About the things he did. I thought maybe he was the one, the one in my dreams."

"Was he?"

"I don't know."

"How did you get all those scratches on your arms and hands?"

"Picking blackberries."

"Keith, have you ever been arrested?"

"A couple of times," he admitted.

"May I ask what for?"

"Stuff." He shifted uncomfortably in his seat.

"What kind of stuff?"

"Looking through people's windows, mostly." His face reddened. "Mostly I just like to see what people do in their houses."

"Most people like a little privacy when they're in their homes, Keith. They don't like other people to watch them."

"I know. That's why I only look through windows if the shades are up. If people want privacy, they should pull the shades down."

"Have the police ever talked to you about anything else?"

"They talked to me about some stuff on my computer."

"By 'stuff,' you mean . . ."

"Pictures of people doing stuff. With other people."

"Got it." She nodded. "Any of these people doing 'stuff' with kids?"

"Sometimes."

"Keith, how do you know how to find these places on the computer, the places we just talked about?"

"Sheldon told me."

"Sheldon told you?"

"Uh-huh. He said he'd help me understand what my dreams were about if I'd go to these places and watch and then come back and tell him what they were doing."

"Let me get this straight." Portia tried to remain calm. "Sheldon Woods told you where to go on the Internet to find child pornography, told you to watch it, and then come back and tell him what you saw?"

Keith nodded.

"Does he ever tell you to do other things, things involving live kids?"

Keith's eyes shifted from her face to the floor.

"Keith?"

"I don't want to talk about that. Sheldon said if anyone asked I didn't have to talk about the things he told me to do."

Portia took a deep breath.

"I'm warm, Keith, are you? Thirsty? Let me get us something to drink." She stood. "I'll be right back."

Her head felt as if it were about to explode. That Keith Patterson possessed a low IQ was apparent, but how low, she couldn't be sure. Had Sheldon Woods played on the man's weak intellect, taken advantage of the fact that he was easily influenced, and set him up to continue the kind of madness that Woods had relished for so many years? Were Patterson's bad dreams not dreams at all, but killings he'd been talked into by Woods?

Maybe. She played with the idea for a few moments, then ran upstairs and turned on her computer. She ran a search for Keith Patterson's criminal records, driver's license, and sent out quick queries to the arresting departments for more information.

She ran back downstairs, grabbed two Styrofoam cups from the breakroom and filled them with cold water. *At least let's get his DNA,* she thought, *see if it matches anything we already have.*

On her way back, she passed the room where Eloise Gorman was waiting for Livy. The door was open, and Portia couldn't resist having a word with her.

"Hello, Ms. Gorman," she said from the doorway.

The woman turned in her chair and gave Portia a once-over. "Your shoes have dirt on them. Dirt and grass. You should take more pride in the way you dress."

She turned her back to Portia, who looked down at her feet. She was wearing the same black driving loafers she'd had on the night before. As Eloise Gorman had pointed out, bits of mud and grass were clinging to the sides. She lifted her right foot to inspect the sole of the shoe and found red-brown dirt and blades of grass imbedded in the treads. The park had been muddy from an afternoon shower, and the grass that had been cut earlier in the day had washed down to the area where Justin had been buried. Remembering struck her heart all over again.

She walked back down the hall, her shoes forgotten, wondering if the killer of that sweet little boy was sitting behind the closed door of interrogation room D.

TWENTY-NINE

"Let me get this straight," Livy said. "Patterson told you that Woods told him to do 'stuff' to kids and come back and share it with him?"

"That's what the man said." Portia was on her way to the prison, loaded for bear, talking to Livy on her cell phone.

"You think he did it?"

"Sure looks that way. This guy Patterson is not the brightest bulb in the chandelier. Right before I left the office, I got a call from one of the officers who recently arrested him for peeping. Says the guy is slow but not stupid, knows right from wrong. Said he's smart enough to *play* stupid, and he might have been doing that to throw me off."

"Which would make him not stupid at all," Livy noted.

"Exactly. I gave him a cup of water and sent it to the lab to test the saliva for DNA, so we'll see if he matches up with anything we have on file."

"Where is he now?"

"Waiting in D for his hometown boys in blue to

pick him up. He has an outstanding warrant for peeping. They're going to hold him for as long as they can while we check into his whereabouts last night." Portia changed lanes and sped up. She couldn't wait to confront Woods. "Did you get anything useful from Miss Eloise?"

"She's one strong lady, that one. I'll bet she drags out that weight bench at night and presses a couple hundred pounds without breaking a sweat."

Portia laughed.

"Seriously, she's got a grip on her. She could be a contender, Portia."

"For what?"

"She could be the killer. She spends a lot of time with Woods. I'm willing to bet that she knows where it all went down and where he hid everything. She's strong enough to do some serious damage with those hands. And Annie said the killer is trying to get Woods's attention, right? So who wants his attention more than Eloise?"

"Good point. Have someone keep an eye on her. You learn anything else?"

"Only that she's really off the wall with all this soul mate stuff. Which I already knew from you." Livy laughed, then added, "Bless her heart."

"I'm hearing the Carolina coast in your voice again," Portia said.

"You can take the girl out of the South, Cahill, but . . ."

"Yeah, yeah, I know." There was a barely audible beep on Portia's phone. She looked at the number.

"That your phone or mine?" Livy asked.

"Mine."

"Do you want to take the call?"

Portia took a few seconds to consider.

"Someone you're avoiding?" Livy asked.

"It's Jim."

"Why're you avoiding him? He's the good guy."

When Portia didn't respond, Livy said, "Oh, okay. I get it. You don't want to talk to him because of what happened to his nephew's friend, right? Because somehow, that's all your fault, isn't it?"

"In a sense, yes."

"So you're going to guilt yourself into letting go of someone you care about because you feel guilty over something that someone else did? That makes a lot of sense, Cahill. Honestly, I thought you were smarter than that."

"Until we catch this guy, yes, I think it's better that Jim and I don't see each other. I don't want to run the risk of putting Finn in any more danger than I already have."

"Did you discuss this with Jim? That you're dumping him?"

"I'm not dumping him. I'm just backing off for now. But no, I haven't had time to have that conversation with him. This all just happened last night."

"Make time. And do it now. Today. Tonight. If you're not going to take his calls, you're not even going to return them, at least have the decency to tell him why and let him have his say."

"I can't imagine that he'd even want to be around me after what happened to Justin."

"Don't you think you should let him decide what he wants?"

"You're right. As soon as I leave the prison, I'll call him."

There was another beep on her line, and she glanced at the screen.

"This one I do have to take. It's the farm where Sheldon used to ride horses when he was a kid. I'll get back to you." She hung up one call and picked up the other.

"This is Eliza Cawley returning a call from Agent Cahill," the voice on the line said.

"Agent Cahill here, ma'am. Thanks for getting back to me."

"You wanted some information on a former student, I understand. Who would that be?"

"Sheldon Woods."

The silence was deafening.

"Miz Cawley? Are you there?" Portia asked.

"Yes, I'm here. I was just . . . surprised. No one's ever asked about him. Not that I've forgotten him, though. The boy crosses my mind every now and then."

"Because of what he did, you mean?"

"That, certainly, but when I think about him, it isn't his crimes I think about. Sheldon was one of the best students I ever had. He had an exceptional seat, wonderful hands. Loved the horses he rode, always treated them gently and with respect. Never came to the stables without something for the horse he would ride that day. Helped the younger students. Volunteered to help muck the stalls, clean the tack, groom the horses. Around maybe his third year with us, he said he'd be quitting because his mother said they could no longer afford the lessons, so I started giving him credit for all the work he'd been doing around the stables for free. I even gave him extra lessons. He had such promise, and he was such a nice kid. I always felt he could have been a great equestrian, Agent Cahill."

Portia was almost speechless. This was a Sheldon Woods she hadn't heard about before. "What happened?"

"Wouldn't I like to know?" the riding instructor said. "He just stopped showing up. I called his house several times and left messages, but he never called me back and he never came back to the farm. Everyone missed him. Me, the other riders, and the instructors. I believe even the horses missed him."

"You never saw him again?"

"Not until I turned on the TV one day years later and there he was, being led from a police car in handcuffs and that unbelievable story about him . . ." Portia could almost hear a shiver in her voice. "I still can't believe that was really him."

"How old was Sheldon when he started taking lessons from you, do you remember?"

"Five or six. He was around twelve when he stopped."

"Had you noticed anything different about him, any change in his behavior around that time?"

"Actually, I did. He was always a friendly boy, if quiet. For a few months before he stopped coming, he began to withdraw more and more. Looking back, I should have probably tried to talk to him about it, or called his mother . . ." Her voice trailed away.

"You've no thoughts on what might have been causing him to withdraw?"

"None. I'm afraid I haven't been of any help to you."

"You've filled in a few blanks, Miz Cawley. I appreciate the callback."

"He's still in prison, isn't he?"

"Yes. He will be for many, many years."

"If you see him, please tell him I was asking about him."

"I'll be sure to do that."

Well, Portia thought, *here's a picture of Sheldon we didn't have before, and a time frame within which things started going south for him.* She tried to recall the reports she'd read weeks ago. By the time he was twelve, he'd already been arrested for something, hadn't he? Peeping? Assaulting a younger boy? She'd have to look it up when she got back from the prison. And she'd need to confirm who the stepfather was around the time he was twelve.

Right now, however, she had other things on her mind: Justin McAfee, Keith Patterson, and how the two might be connected to Sheldon Woods.

It was late afternoon when she reached the prison. She was waved through the gate and handed her pass without having to show ID. Portia drove up to the main building and parked under some trees near the back of the lot where it was shady, to keep the car cool while she was inside.

She found her favorite guard on duty when she checked in at the desk and handed over her bag and gun without being asked. The halls were familiar to her now and she could have found her way through the maze by herself, but was accompanied by a guard to the interview room. She thanked the young man. As she sat down, she reminded herself that she was here for a purpose. There were things to accomplish before she flipped out on Woods.

"What is it going to take to make this stop, Sheldon?" she asked when he came through the door, CO DeLuca closing the door behind them. "How do we stop this 'fan' of yours from killing again?"

"You think that I'm somehow orchestrating this, that I know who it is? I don't know." He shook his head and for a moment, she almost believed he was telling the truth. Then she remembered who she was talking to. "I do think it's ingenious and that must be driving you insane right about now, am I right, Agent Cahill? For that reason alone, I wouldn't tell you, even if I knew."

"Keith Patterson."

"What about him?"

She stared at him darkly, and after a moment, he began to laugh.

"You think Keith . . . ? Oh, that's rich."

"Those dreams of his sound an awful lot like the real thing."

"That's all they are. Dreams. Daydreams, maybe, but they're not original, and they're not the real thing. He goes to the library and takes out books about serial killers and reads all about it and then comes in and tells me he dreamed it." Woods shook his head. "You think he's capable of doing the stuff that's going on out there?"

"Why not?"

"He's not smart enough to pull it off, for one thing."

"He's smart enough to find the porn sites you send him to," she snapped. "Smart enough to watch and report back to you on what he sees."

A flush crept up Woods's neck. "That was all just in fun. I have to do something to entertain myself."

"You took advantage of him," she said.

"Oh, dear, I did, didn't I?" He sighed deeply. "That'll be the sin that puts me over my limit, I guess. One free pass, straight to hell, for taking advantage of Keith Patterson."

He laughed and stood with help from the CO, his chains limiting his movements.

"I can't take any more of you." She got up and started toward the door.

"See you next time, Agent Cahill," he called to her as DeLuca led him away.

"By the way, Miz Cawley sends her best."

He froze in midstride, then turned to look back over his shoulder.

"She was sorry you left when you did. She thought you had tremendous promise. Apparently she had high hopes for you."

"Yes. Well."

"Why'd you stop going to the stables, Woods? Why'd you leave without telling her why?"

"It was . . . complicated."

"Too complicated to even say good-bye to someone who cared about you, who believed in you?"

"Way too complicated, Agent Cahill." A wave of true sadness crossed his face, and he looked as if he was about to say something more. He continued making his way to the door, his head down, his shoulders slumped.

Portia was halfway to the door when she noticed a clump of grass and reddish clay on the floor. She reached down to pick it up, chiding herself for having forgotten to clean off her shoes before she came into the prison. Then Portia realized she hadn't walked beyond the table. She mentally retraced her steps . . . from the door to the table, from the table to the door. She replayed it over and over in her mind, but couldn't recall having taken steps in any other direction. She sat back down at the table and turned her foot over to compare. The color and the texture of the dirt was the same.

There had been three people in the room. Woods was the only one who would not have been outside over the past twenty-four hours since it had rained.

She headed toward the front desk, the clump of dirt still in one hand and the other in her pocket, wrapped around her cell phone. She was eager to get outside to call in and request a background check on CO DeLuca. She was almost to the first turn of the corridor when she heard footsteps behind her.

"Agent Cahill," DeLuca called to her from ten feet back. *He must have hustled some to have caught up,* Portia thought.

"You pick up something from the floor back there in that little room?"

She held out her hand, where the clump of grass and dirt lay flat on her palm.

"Housekeeping's getting sloppy," she told him.

CO DeLuca shoved her around so her back was to him. Something sharp and hard poked between her shoulder blades.

"I saw that mess of dirt there, went back to pick it up but it was gone. Nobody in there but you, me, and Woods, and he didn't bend over the whole time we were in there. So I guess that narrows it down, doesn't it?" He took her arm and twisted it. "You know, the whole time you were in there, I kept looking at that spot of grass on the floor, and looking at that little bit of grass on the sides of your shoes. Didn't seem like you noticed it, but I guess I was wrong." He jerked her arm so that she was walking directly in front of him. "Now, nice and casual, we're going out through the front door."

"With you holding a knife in my back? I don't think so."

Portia jumped slightly as the tip of the knife cut through her shirt and into her back. She felt a wet trickle run down into her waistband.

"I think so, Agent Cahill. As a matter of fact, I know so." He gave her arm another twist as they approached the front desk. "You just keep on walking, right through that door there. One word out of your mouth and you are a dead woman."

They walked past the desk where the guard was on the phone. When she looked up, she covered the phone's mouthpiece and called, "Agent Cahill, your bag . . . your gun . . ."

"We'll be right back," DeLuca told the guard without breaking stride, the knife sharp against the flesh over Portia's right kidney.

They went through the front doors and into the humidity that often follows a summer storm.

"We'll take my car." He led her toward an ancient Oldsmobile the color of dirt, opened the driver's door, and shoved her across the front seat.

He reached under his seat and held up a forty-four. "You touch the door handle, you make any move at all, and I'll shoot your knees out." Then he smiled. "Just so we understand each other."

"Where are we going?" she asked, all thoughts of going for the knife now moot.

"I don't know yet." He started the engine. "I have to think it out. It has to be the right spot. It has to mean something."

He drove past the guard's kiosk without stopping. The guard stepped into the drive but made no attempt to stop them. Why would he? Employees wouldn't be required to stop at the gate.

"This was all your fault, you know?" he told her. "It took too long for it to make the news."

"Is that what this is about?" She turned to him. "Making the news?"

He didn't appear to have heard her.

". . . Sick of everyone making such a big deal out of him. Books and newspaper and magazine articles. People wanting to interview him. Women throwing themselves at him. Me, I can't get laid on a dare, but he has women coming in there and begging for conjugal visits. A couple of 'em want to marry him." He laughed hoarsely. "You think crazy Weezie is the only one? She thinks she is, but uh-uh. And every couple of years, there's another book.

Someone comes around to do a TV special. Jesus, it makes me sick. Guys like me, we're invisible. Me, I worked my ass off all my life, and I am still a nobody. He kills kids—rapes little boys!—people treat him like he's a celebrity. How the fuck do you figure that?"

"I can't figure it, Officer DeLuca. I don't understand it, either."

"How come when he does it, the story's everywhere. When I do it—nothing. Can you explain that to me, Agent Cahill?"

"No, I can't. I don't . . ."

"You paid attention to him. Why wouldn't you pay attention to me?"

"Is that what this is about, Officer DeLuca? Getting *attention*?" she asked, fighting to keep the incredulity from her voice. "All of this is because you wanted some attention?"

"You kept going back to *him*. Talking to *him*, doing favors for *him*. He raped little boys, that's how sick he is." He snorted. "But I guess that's what it takes to get the world to sit up and take notice, right? You gotta do something really sick."

His head bobbed up and down. "I'm going to show you sick. Then we'll see who everyone wants to talk to. Who gets the books written about them. We'll see who gets the movie. We'll see who's invisible now."

"You killed three boys so that a movie would be made about you?" She managed to catch the words

Are you crazy? just before they slipped out of her mouth.

"Shut up. Just shut up and let me think."

She watched him from the corner of her eye. He was sweating profusely, and his hands were shaking. It wouldn't take much to put him over the edge. He began to mutter under his breath, and she could not pick any intelligible words out of the rant. When she turned her head to look out the window, he grabbed her chin and forced her head around.

"Look at me when I talk to you! Look at me!"

"All right, Officer DeLuca. I'm looking at you," she said as calmly as she could get the words out.

"It was on the news today," he told her, holding on to her arm. "From New York. All those big stations in New York are carrying the story. They're all talking about me now."

"You know, you don't have to do anything else. You give yourself up, you're already famous, but you're still anonymous. If you give yourself up, they'll all want to talk to you. But they can't make a movie about you if they don't know your name."

"Oh, but they will, soon enough," he told her confidently. "By the time this night is over, everyone will know my name."

"What exactly do you have in mind?" she asked, but he did not respond.

Through the windshield Portia saw a grove of mimosa trees that she could have sworn they'd driven by before. She studied the landscape as they drove on, noting the turns that he made and trying to get a feel for the direction they were headed. The third time past the mimosas, she was certain. He was driving in a circle.

She'd just figured out the spot where she could risk jumping out and finding a place to hide when he pulled over to the side of the road.

"Get out." He pulled her by the arm and dragged her to the rear of the car, the gun held to the back of her head. He opened the trunk and took out a piece of rope.

"Turn around." He shoved her up against the car and jerked both arms behind her back.

He placed a piece of rope in her hands. "Loop it around your wrists, then tie it. Tight."

She looped it over her forearms and tried to hold it there as she tied the knot as he'd directed. If he secured the rope where it was, she'd have enough slack to slip her hands out.

She felt the rope tighten, and then he gave it a good tug and tightened the knot, forcing her wrists to cross. He turned her around, lifted her off the ground, and laid her in the trunk on her back.

"Now be a good girl," he said as he slammed the lid, "maybe I'll let you out sometime today."

THIRTY

"Livy, this is Larisse Jordan at the lab. I'm told you're working with Portia Cahill on this case of hers. I've been calling her and leaving messages for her for the past couple of hours, but she hasn't called me back. If you talk to her, would you please tell her to call me ASAP? Tell her to use my private line—she has the number. I have some DNA results from that 'lost boy' of hers that are going to drop her on her ass."

Livy listened to the message a second time, then tried to call Portia herself, but she, too, got voice mail. She called Eileen to see if Portia had checked in since she left for the prison, but Eileen had already left. She tried John, but he hadn't heard from her, either. Puzzled, she called the warden's office at the prison.

"Let me put you through to the guard up front," the warden told her. "If she was here, she's come and gone through the front door, and the times would be noted."

The guard picked up on the third ring. Livy

started to identify herself as an agent working with Portia Cahill, but the guard told her, "The warden already told me who you were and cleared me to give you whatever information you needed."

"I need to know what time Agent Cahill signed in and out from the prison today."

"She signed in here at the desk at . . ." Livy held while the guard checked her sheets. "She signed in at four-fifteen."

"What time did she sign out?"

"She didn't sign out. I was here when she left," the guard told her, "but she was supposed to be coming back in a few minutes."

"How long ago was that?"

"About twenty-five minutes ago."

"Do you know where she was going?"

"No, she and CO DeLuca left together. He was the one who said they'd be back."

"Who's this DeLuca?"

"He's just a guard here."

"Agent Cahill must have forgotten to come back in to sign out," Livy said.

"If she did, she didn't get very far. She left her bag here. She checked it and her gun when she came in, and she . . ."

"Her gun is still there? She left without it?"

"Yes, ma'am."

"Did they leave the premises?" All of Livy's senses went on alert. She didn't like what she was hearing.

"I don't know. I can check with the guard out front at the gate . . ."

"Please do that. I'll hold." Livy walked down the hall to John's office. The lights were out and his door was closed. She tried the doorknob, just in case, but it was locked.

"Agent Bach?" The guard came back on the line.

"I'm here."

"The guard out at the gate said that Agent Cahill and CO DeLuca went through the gate about twenty minutes ago."

"Did he say who was driving?" Livy asked though she was pretty sure she knew the answer.

"Officer DeLuca was driving his car," the guard replied.

"I need a description of that vehicle." Livy began to pace through the darkened hall that ran past the row of empty offices.

"The front gate has a list of the vehicles, including the license plates. I'll be back to you in one minute."

She was. After giving the information to Livy, the guard said, "Would you like me to have Agent Cahill call you if she comes back?"

"Yes, please." Livy was now in a hurry to get off the phone. "Thanks for your help."

She disconnected the call and started back to her own office to get her bag and keys. As she passed by Portia's, she heard a phone ring. Stepping inside the half-opened door, she realized it was the desk phone. She lifted the receiver and answered, "Agent Cahill's office. Agent Bach speaking."

"This is Jim Cannon, I'm a friend of Agent Cahill's. I've been trying to get in touch with her all day, but haven't been able to track her down."

"This is Livy Bach. I've been working with her on this case of hers. I'm also her friend." She took a deep breath and said, "So you haven't talked to her, either?"

"What do you mean 'either'?"

"I can't seem to find anyone who's heard from her since she left for the prison earlier this afternoon."

"She's been out at the prison all this time?"

"I'm not really sure where she is now. Apparently she left the prison in the company of one of the guards about a half hour ago." Livy hesitated. "I was just about to head on out there myself to see what's going on."

"What do you think is going on?"

"I'm not sure, but I'm real uneasy about this," Livy told him. "According to the guard I spoke with, Portia left the building, but never picked up her bag and her gun. She had checked them at the front desk when she arrived."

"Maybe she forgot."

"It's her *gun* we're talking about. She doesn't forget." She was wasting time that could come back to haunt her later. "Look, I'll have her call you if I catch up with her. I have to go."

Livy hung up the phone and practically ran back to grab her bag from the back of her chair. On her way to the elevator, she was already dialing John's private line.

"John, I think we have a problem . . ."

It had been Livy Bach's use of the word *if* that bothered him. "*If* I catch up with her," she'd said. Why would Livy think she'd not catch up with Portia?

Jim was on his way back to the office from court, but without thinking twice, he made a U-turn and started back in the direction from which he'd come. Eleven miles down the interstate was the road that led to the prison. If Portia still hadn't returned, he'd wait for her.

It was killing him that she felt responsible for what happened to Justin McAfee. Worse, she wouldn't return his calls so that they could talk it out. She would never knowingly put a child in danger, of that he was positive. How could she have known that she was being watched?

Had the killer targeted Portia because she had targeted him? Jim hadn't been able to voice his suspicions to Dani, but he believed that Finn had been the intended victim, that the killer had wanted to get to Portia by going through Jim to Finn. When he couldn't get Finn, he'd taken Finn's friend, just to prove that he could, to show how close he could come to what mattered to her. The thought had kept Jim up all night, listening to the old pipes creak, jumping every time a tree branch scraped against a window. When morning came and there was no way to shield Finn from the news, Dani and the other mothers got together and took all of the bewildered boys from the tee-ball team to one home, to keep them all together, to let them talk and learn to mourn a friend. It was a terrible lesson for seven-year-olds to have to learn.

He was surprised to find a state trooper at the prison gates. The officer held up a hand to stop Jim outside the gate.

"I'm sorry, sir," the trooper who flagged him down told him, "but you're going to have to turn around and go back. The prison's closed."

"I'm an attorney," Jim told him. "I need to get in to see a client."

"May I see some identification, sir?" the trooper asked, and Jim handed over his driver's license. The trooper studied it as if debating what to do, and was about to hand it back when a car pulled up next to Jim's. The driver called to the officer and held up some ID for him to inspect.

"Special Agent Olivia Bach," she told him. "I need to get through."

Before the trooper could react, Jim rolled down his window.

"Agent Bach, I'm Jim Cannon. We spoke earlier."

"Go on home. I'll have Portia call you," she told him.

"No way am I leaving until I know where she is."

"Oh, for cripe's sake. I'll probably get into a shit-storm for this . . ." She called to the trooper, "He's with me, sir."

Jim followed Livy through the prison gates. She stopped just inside and waved for him to pull up next to her.

"You go on and park right over there. You're going to stay out of my way, and you're not going to bother anyone. I understand why you feel you want to be here, and I can't honestly say I'd feel any different if I were in your shoes."

"Fair enough. Thank you." Jim parked the car and got out. Livy was talking to the guard in the kiosk when Jim walked up and, without saying a word, stood quietly behind Livy as if he belonged there.

". . . an older model Buick, brown. He usually stops or waves when he's leaving, but today—nothing. He just drove right on past without even looking."

"Did you notice the time?"

"It was around five thirty."

"Was anyone else in the car with him?"

"Yeah. Agent Cahill. I've been on duty a couple of times when she came out here so I recognized her. I started walking toward the car when I saw her, because she had a visitor's pass and she had to hand it in. But he didn't stop, just drove on out through the gate." He leaned on the side of the kiosk. "I figured she'd be coming back and I'd get the pass from her then."

"Thanks." Livy turned and saw Jim standing a few feet behind her. "What did I just tell you?"

"You must believe she's in some kind of danger, or there wouldn't be all this . . ." He waved his arm around the drive, noting the other cars that had pulled up. Several men wearing black jackets with FBI on the back had gotten out. "Who's this guy she's with?"

"He's a corrections officer here. Name is Clifford DeLuca. He's one of the regular guards on Woods's cellblock," she said.

Jim paused while her words sank in.

"If he's around Woods a lot, he'd have heard everything that Woods told . . ." he began, but she cut him off with a curt, "Exactly."

"He took her somewhere," Jim said flatly.

"That's what we're trying to find out," she told him. "Now, if you'd get back to your car . . ."

"You said on the phone that she didn't pick up her bag when she left. Is her cell phone in the bag?" he asked.

"Good question. I'll find out. Now, if you would please . . ."

"Because you can track her cell phone . . ."

Livy turned to the guard. "Can you get the guard at the front desk on the line?"

He dialed an extension, then handed the phone to Livy.

"Do you still have Agent Cahill's handbag there?" she asked. "Would you open it and tell me if her cell phone is inside?"

She waited for a response.

"You're positive? Great. Thanks." Livy handed the phone back and turned to Jim. "The phone is not in her bag."

"So that means she must have it with her, right?" Jim asked anxiously.

"Maybe. Maybe . . ." Livy stuck her hand in her pocket and pulled out her cell phone and speed-dialed a number. "John, we think Portia might have her phone with her. Can you have its location tracked through GPS? No, there's been no sign of them. Did the APB go out for DeLuca's car?"

She wandered off, still in conversation, and Jim waited for her to come back. When she did not, he walked to his car and leaned against the back fender, every once in a while taking his own phone from his pocket and checking for any missed calls.

Almost fifteen minutes later, he saw Livy walking quickly to her car. Jim caught up with her before she could open the door.

"Have they found her?" he asked.

"The phone's being tracked and the information is coming over John's computer. He's forwarding it to my phone. She's moving." Livy pushed past him and got into her car. Jim opened the passenger side door and got in.

"What do you think you're doing?"

"Going with you," he told her. "If she's out there . . ."

"You're a civilian. Get out."

"Drive."

"I can't. Look, we don't know if this guy is armed . . . dear God, I'm wasting time talking to you . . ."

He got out of her car and slammed the door, sprinting to the Jag. He turned on the ignition, threw the car into reverse, and headed out through the gates. He could see Livy's taillights up ahead, and caught up with her in less than a minute. He was pretty damned sure she wouldn't be happy about it, but there was no way he could stand around at the prison waiting to hear Portia's fate. If Livy was on her way to find Portia, Jim intended to be right behind her.

THIRTY-ONE

The old car rocked from side to side. Portia could tell when they were making a turn and in which direction they were heading by the way her body rolled. Her eyes had adjusted to the dark inside the trunk, assisted by the small bit of light that came through the floor where rust had eroded the metal. She looked for something she could use to work the rope free from her hands but there was nothing.

The phone in her front pocket rang and she wished to God she could answer it. She heard the beep that told her the call had gone to voice mail and she wondered if it was Jim, leaving her another message, or her sister, maybe, asking her if she was going to make it home in time to have dinner with her and Will.

She looked at the roof of the trunk and wished that DeLuca drove a newer model car, one with a latch inside the trunk that would come in handy in moments like this. Then she remembered she wouldn't be able to reach it anyway, with her hands tied behind her back, so it didn't really matter.

She tried to imagine scenarios in which she could distract him or disarm him. Not much hope of that without hands, but unless he tied her feet together, she could do some damage. The techniques she'd learned while at the academy years ago had come in handy in the past. She would have to rely on whatever skills she had—martial arts, self-defense, her wits—to best her captor.

The inside of the trunk was stifling and smelled of gasoline and dirty clothes. It occurred to her that perhaps he'd put his victims in just this spot. It saddened her to think that any one or all of those three boys might have laid their heads where hers now lay. Had he placed them in here alive, only to drive them to another place where he coldly murdered them?

It occurred to her that he was planning on her meeting the same fate. It wasn't the first time she'd faced death, she reminded herself. She'd managed to fight her way out of many situations where the outcome had seemed more certain than this one.

Had the boys fought him, too? she wondered. Well, she could do no less.

The car came to a slow stop, and under the tires she could hear a soft crunching sound. She heard the engine shut off and the slamming of the car door. A moment later, the key was in the latch and the trunk lid opened.

"Let's go," he said as he pulled her from the trunk and stood her next to the car.

Portia's eyes searched quickly for the gun. Not seeing it, she took a few small steps backward in anticipation of knocking his legs out from under him, when her phone rang. For a moment, DeLuca froze.

"You got a phone with you?" he yelled at her. "They can find you with that thing! I saw it on TV."

He went through her pockets until he found the phone, then tossed it as far away as he could.

"Now we're going to have to get back in the car and go someplace else," he complained. "They're going to look for you here."

He grabbed at her arm and she jumped back. Hands still tied behind her back, she kicked with all of her strength and landed a foot in his groin. He screamed like a wounded animal and fell to the ground. Portia debated which way to go for only seconds. The back country road was poorly traveled. If she took off in either direction, he'd have no trouble spotting her. She'd take her chances for cover in the woods. If her phone was being traced, sooner or later, help would arrive. Until then, all she had to do was stay hidden.

She took off into the woods, her gait awkward. She could hear DeLuca still groaning behind her, so she figured she could count on a few minutes' head start. With any luck, she'd find a path to follow, hopefully one that would lead to a house. She tripped over a branch and went down on one knee, losing precious time getting back up again. How close behind her was he? She stopped next to a tree and tried to catch her breath, listening for his footsteps. All she heard was silence.

Encouraged, she turned her back to the tree, and started working the rope against the rough bark until it frayed enough to break. She'd make better time, have better balance, and be able to defend herself with the use of her hands. She rubbed and rubbed until the bark fell free and she had to move to a different spot. As she rounded the tree, she heard him crashing along the same path she'd taken. Too late to finish off the rope, she ran as fast as she could, but she knew he was gaining on her.

She knew, too, that once he caught up with her, he wouldn't be kind.

When Livy pulled to the side of the road and got out to inspect the brown sedan that was parked there, Jim was right behind her.

"Are you crazy?" she yelled at him as she removed her gun from its holster. "You need to get out of here."

"I'm already here, so let me work with you to find her." Before she could reply, he said, "I'm going to assume you tracked her and it's no coincidence there's a brown car right here."

Livy nodded. "It's his. The license plate matches. But the tracker says the phone's here somewhere."

"Let's find out." He dialed Portia's number, and almost immediately, they heard it ringing.

"It's coming from over there." Livy followed the sound through the thick grass. "It's here."

She bent down and picked it up and dropped it in her pocket.

"So which way?" he asked, looking around. "Looks like the underbrush is tamped down going into the woods there to the right. I say that's the way to go."

"Mr. Cannon . . ."

"Jim."

"Jim." Livy shook her head. "Oh, what's the use? You're going to follow me anyway, aren't you?"

He nodded.

"Were you in the military?" she asked.

"No."

"Ever shoot a gun?"

"On a shooting range, sure."

"You any good? Truth, Jim. This is no place for cowboys."

"Truth is I'm a damned good shot."

She went to her car, opened the glove box, and took out a handgun.

"My little backup Sig." She handed it to him. "I hope to God I don't regret this."

"You won't. Which way?" he asked. "I'm for the right."

"Good enough. Let's do it."

Side by side, they hurried into the woods, both praying that they were headed in the right direction, and that the path they were following would lead them to Portia.

"Where are we going?" Portia asked.

"There's a lake down this way." She felt the knife jab at her back and wondered where his gun was. "We're gonna see how good a swimmer you are. You ever try to swim without using your arms?"

When she didn't respond, he poked her in the back again with the knife, this time drawing blood.

"I asked you a question."

"No, I never tried to swim without using my arms."

"Well, we're gonna see just how that goes," he said, laughing. "I'm betting you're gonna be flopping around in the water like a fish without a tail. After I have my fun with you, that is. You're gonna pay for bashing in my balls the way you did. You can bet your life you will."

She looked straight ahead, trying to think of the best way to gain an advantage. Right now, the only plan she could come up with was staying alert and looking to exploit even the slightest advantage. The trees up ahead thinned out, and through them she could see the lake. There was a short dock where a rowboat with only one oar had been tied up. The oar would make a good weapon, if she could get to it, but without the use of her hands, there wasn't much chance of that. She'd have to rely on her feet again, but she'd have to wait for the right opportunity.

On the grassy slope leading to the water, she made her move, spinning around and kicking at his left knee as hard as she could. He managed to dodge her, slashing out with the knife and connecting with the back of her calf. She screamed and fell to the ground.

"Now, for a lady who's smart enough to be in the FBI, you're pretty stupid," he said as he forced her to her feet. "For one thing, I got a gun right here in my belt—you didn't think I left that back there in the car, did you? And I got a knife, and the use of both my hands. And I will be using both my hands on you, Agent Cahill. As a matter of fact, I don't think I can wait to do just that."

He dragged her to the dock and tossed her down on her back. "I'm betting I have a lot more fun with you than Sheldon ever had with any of those little boys." He was grinning as he pulled her shirt out from her waistband and groped at her breasts, squeezing them hard. "You're just all woman, aren't you. And right now, and until I'm done with you, you're all mine."

He straddled her, pulled at her jeans, and slapped her face when she struggled against him. "Stop it. Make nice to me or I'll make it very bad for you."

She stopped fighting for a moment, trying to drive away the panic. She knew it was critical that she keep her wits about her if she had any hope of surviving.

"That's better. Now, we're going to have us some fun, you and me."

He was still fumbling with his zipper when a shadow fell across Portia's face.

She heard the click before she saw the man who stood on the dock holding a gun to DeLuca's head.

"You're going to want to stand up very slowly, arms and hands high over your head." Jim poked DeLuca with the Sig. "Higher. That's better. I should probably warn you that, unlike these ladies, I'm not a trained professional, so this piece in my hand could go off at any minute."

DeLuca stood unsteadily. Portia was expecting a string of protests, but there were none. If anything, the guard looked confused at his predicament.

"Jim, there's a handgun in his waistband," Portia told him as Livy ran on to the dock.

"Got it." Livy removed the handgun from DeLuca's middle.

"Nice job, Cannon," she said as she went past him to help Portia up.

"It's about time you guys got here. Get this rope off me." Livy helped her to her feet.

"I don't have a knife," Livy told her.

"He does," Portia nodded in DeLuca's direction.

"Where is it?" Jim asked him.

DeLuca pointed to the deck where he'd dropped it while he was pulling at Portia's clothing.

"I wasn't going to hurt her," the man whined. "I was just going to scare her a little."

"Yeah, right. Save it for the jury." Livy picked up the knife and used it to slice off the ropes.

"Thanks," Portia said, rubbing her wrists. She looked up at Jim. "And thank you," she said.

"Don't mention it," he told her.

Livy called for backup to meet them on the road, then turned DeLuca around and cuffed him. She gave him a shove to start him back toward the woods.

"You watch it," he told her. "I have rights. I'm gonna get a lawyer . . ."

"That's the first true thing you've said since I got here," Livy said. "You sure are going to need a lawyer." She recited his rights to him, and when she finished, she reached into her pocket and found Portia's phone.

"Here." She tossed it to Portia. "You have a lot of messages to listen to."

"Most of them are probably from me," Jim admitted as he took Portia's hand. "So they can probably wait."

"I know there's one from Larisse Jordan at the lab," Livy said. "She said it was really important that you call her ASAP. She said she has to talk to you about the DNA for the lost boy. You know what she's talking about?"

"Yeah, I do." Portia started listening to her messages as they walked back to the road.

"You're limping," Jim noted. "What happened to your leg?" he asked, but she was dialing a number into her phone.

He pulled up the left leg of her jeans and exposed the gash on her calf.

"Your leg is bleeding," he said, frowning. "Let's get you right to the ER and have someone take a look at that cut. I'm betting you're good for about seven, eight stitches."

She heard him but did not respond as the call she'd made had been answered.

"It's Portia. I just got your message. What's up?"

She listened intently for a full minute, a look of horror on her face.

"Dear God, are you sure? You're positive? Larisse, you cannot be wrong about this. Yes, I understand exactly what it means. That's why you have to be one hundred percent certain . . ."

She listened for another minute, then said, "Thank you for letting me know."

She hung up as they reached the road where two

agents waited for them. The agents met Livy halfway and took custody of Clifford DeLuca.

Portia walked directly to Jim's car. "Will you drive me back to the prison?" she asked.

"Sure. As soon as we have that wound tended to," he told her.

"No." She shook her head. "The prison first. There's something I have to do before I do anything else."

THIRTY-TWO

Portia sat at the table in the interview room and waited. Her leg was throbbing terribly and she knew she'd lost a bit of blood, but this could not wait. The door opened and Sheldon Woods entered, smiling, as if happy to see her.

"My, my, twice in the same day. I'm so honored. But this is a very different look for you," he said as he seated himself. "You usually look so pretty, and here you are, come to call, no makeup on, your clothes . . ."

His eyes narrowed and he seemed to take it all in, the disheveled hair, the ripped blouse, the mark on her face where DeLuca had slapped her. If he'd been anyone else, she'd have thought he was actually concerned. For a moment, she almost believed he was about to ask what happened to her, if she was all right. But this was Sheldon Woods, and the moment passed.

"I spoke with our DNA lab today," she told him.

"Oh? And that concerns me how?"

"They ran the DNA for the boy in Christopher

Williams's grave. The one you said you wouldn't give me. The one you said was yours. Turns out he certainly was. Yours, that is."

Woods's eyes filled with the first real sign of fear she'd ever seen, and the bravado began to fade away.

"How could you have done it, Sheldon?" she asked, her voice barely above a whisper. "How could you have killed your own *son*?"

He looked away from her, the pain on his face all but taking her breath away.

"She would have made him just like me," he said after several minutes had passed. "I couldn't let her do that. One monster in the family is more than enough, wouldn't you say? He was a good little boy. A fine little boy," he told her. "I saved him from becoming just like his father. Did the world really need a chip off this block? What do you think, Agent Cahill?"

"It didn't have to be that way."

He snorted. "You don't know Rhona."

"You could have gone to someone for help."

"Someone like who?"

"A teacher . . ."

"What teacher? He never went to school. She never let him out of her sight. No one knew about him, don't you get it? He was our dirty little secret. There was no record of his birth, she had him at home, did it all herself. She never reported it. He's the boy who didn't exist, Agent Cahill. The boy who never should have been born."

"The police . . ."

"Oh, of course! The police! Why didn't I think of that?" he scoffed. "Hello, police department? This is Sheldon Woods. Yes, the same Sheldon Woods you arrested last week for indecent exposure. Yes, yes, the pedophile, that Sheldon Woods. Listen, I fathered a child by my mother, and I'm afraid she's going to abuse him the way she abused me. What can you do for him?" He rolled his eyes. "Please."

For once, Portia was speechless.

"Ah, didn't expect that can of worms you opened to be quite so full, quite so messy, did you? All those dirty, disgusting, squirmy little truths."

He watched her for a moment, then asked, "How did you figure it out?"

"I thought you were brothers. Half brothers. So I had the lab compare your DNA to his. I never suspected you were both brother *and* father."

"Surprise, surprise."

"Your mother is the monster, Sheldon. Rhona needs to answer for what she did to you."

"Hell of a family legacy, wouldn't you say?"

She ignored his attempt at humor. "Will you testify against her?"

"To what end? Will it change anything?" For a moment, Portia caught a fleeting glimpse of the man he might have been. "Will it change me? Will it change what I am?"

"You are what she made you."

"But there's no unmaking me, is there. I am what I am. I did what I did. There's no going back."

He stood, his face white, his eyes the eyes of a man who had been haunted all his life.

"One thing, Agent Cahill. When you see my brother, ask him how he was able to put it behind him. God knows I never could."

Portia watched him turn away.

"Why did you stop going to the stables, Sheldon?"

He glanced back at her. "Is your leg bleeding, Agent Cahill?"

She nodded.

"At first, my riding lessons were my reward from Rhona—for performing well in the ways that pleased her."

She raised an eyebrow. "You started riding when you were six years old."

"Like I said, a reward for doing the things Mommy wanted me to do."

"Why did you stop going?"

"It became all too ironic," he said. "The only time I felt clean was when I was working at the farm. Even mucking out the stalls made me feel cleaner than being at home, with her. But after a while . . . it was harder to face people . . ." He fought for words. "People who thought I was a good kid . . . who thought I was something that I wasn't. People who never saw the ugliness inside me."

"Miz Cawley would have helped you."

"Most of all, I never wanted Miz Cawley to know about the things I did. The thing about children is that you know deep inside that something is bad, wrong, even when someone you love tells you it's good, it's okay. Carrying around that secret—the secret of what she made me do—became more than I could bear. I was so sure that one day Miz Cawley would see what I was. She'd never look at me the same way again."

He turned back to the guard. "I'm ready to go back to my cell now, Officer Kelly. Agent Cahill needs to have that leg looked at."

He left without looking back. A few minutes passed before Portia was able to stand and walk herself out, not because of the pain in her leg, but because of the pain in her heart for the child Sheldon Woods had once been, before unspeakable acts had made him the man he had become.

THIRTY-THREE

The morning of Christopher Williams's memorial service was the first relatively cool day in weeks. The temperature was not expected to go over eighty-five, and the humidity was lower than normal for a Maryland August. Portia stood in the receiving line that snaked through the cemetery where the once-lost child would be laid to rest and watched as Madeline Williams, seated in a wheelchair, personally greeted and had a word with everyone who had come to pay their respects to her son. She looked pale and weak, but even from a distance, Portia could see that the woman's eyes were very much alive.

"How do you think she's holding up?" Portia asked John, who with his wife, Genna, represented the Bureau.

"She's waited eleven years for this day," John replied. "It's what kept her going, what kept her alive."

Lisa Williams stood behind her mother's chair, occasionally patting Madeline on the shoulder or passing her a bottle of spring water. When the few clouds that had shielded them from the sun moved on, Lisa wheeled the chair into the shade under the tent that had been set up for the service. The line moved slowly, because so many had come.

Portia looked around at the crowd, amazed at the people who waited in line. There were detectives, street cops, representatives from the Maryland, Pennsylvania, and Delaware State Police, sheriff's deputies, and district attorneys from several counties. John pointed out the parents and family members of those other boys who had been murdered by Sheldon Woods, the "Baker's Dozen," and the families of those boys who were yet to be found. Portia recognized Chief of Police Duffy from Oldbridge Township and her crime scene techs who had uncovered the bones of the boy they would bury that day, and Tom Patton, the medical examiner who had cared for the bones until they were released to the funeral home Madeline had chosen.

Portia had been so busy watching the crowd, she hadn't realized how far the line had progressed until she heard Madeline Williams's voice.

"Agent Mancini." The woman in the wheelchair reached for John's hands. "I am so happy to see you. If not for you . . ."

John leaned in close and spoke softly, so Portia could not hear what he was saying. She assumed he'd introduced Madeline to his wife, whose hand Madeline now held.

Suddenly Portia felt John's hand on her elbow as he steered her forward, and she found herself standing in front of Madeline Williams, whose hand, dry and brittle as November leaves, had taken her own. She barely heard John's words of introduction, so stricken was she by the irony of life, how burying your only son could be regarded as a good day.

Madeline's fingers were surprisingly strong, though her voice was weak. She tugged at Portia to bring her closer.

"There are no words to thank you for what you have done, Agent Cahill. If Agent Mancini is my knight in shining armor, you are my hero."

And for the first time since she'd taken her place beside her son's coffin, Madeline Williams began to weep.

Jim parked the Jag in front of Miranda's townhouse and turned off the engine.

"Want to come in and meet Will?" Portia asked.

"Sure."

They walked hand in hand to the front door and found Miranda and Will waiting for them in the doorway.

"I can't thank you enough for saving the day." Miranda stepped forward to embrace Jim. "Not to mention saving my sister's ass."

Will extended his hand to Jim. "Thanks, man. Like she said . . ."

"Thank Livy Bach," Jim said modestly. "She was the one who tracked the cell phone and marched into the woods to find Portia. I just sort of followed along."

"That's not the way Livy tells it." Miranda ushered them into the house and closed the door behind them.

Jim shrugged. "The important thing is that Portia is here and she's fine, and DeLuca is in the psych ward being evaluated."

"As long as he's under lock and key, I don't care where they put him," Portia said. "All the heartbreak that man caused because he wanted to be noticed. That says psycho to me."

"How's your leg, Portia?" Will asked.

"Much better, thank you," Portia told him. "Some antibiotics, a couple of stitches, and I was good to go."

"Great," Will said on his way out of the room.

"You were lucky," Miranda pointed out.

"Very," Portia agreed.

"How was the memorial service?" Miranda asked.

"Very sad and yet satisfying at the same time," Portia replied. "There was a huge crowd and I think that helped the family, but I also think it took a lot out of Madeline Williams. She's obviously in very poor health."

"She rallied like a trouper today, though," Jim added.

"Like John said, finding her son's remains meant everything to her," Portia said. "I have a feeling that the next news we get about her won't be good news. I overheard her daughter tell someone that Madeline felt that now she could let go and die in peace."

"We've been saving this bottle of champagne for a special occasion." Will returned with a tray holding a bottle and four glasses. "I think this qualifies."

He popped the cork and poured some bubbly into each of the glasses. Miranda handed them around.

"What are we drinking to?" Jim asked.

"To getting the bad guys, and to the bad guys getting theirs." Will raised his glass.

"I will certainly drink to that." Miranda took a sip, then lowered her glass and said, "Speaking of the bad guys getting theirs, what's going to happen to Rhona of the many last names and the many perversions?"

"I'm meeting with the state attorney's office tomorrow morning. We're going to sort out what we can charge her with."

"How about being a disgusting, immoral, despicable excuse for a human being, not to mention a very sick mother." Miranda started ticking off Rhona's dubious qualities on her fingers. "While I know that none of those are offenses under the law, they do offend me."

"We're going to start with child abuse, corruption of minors, and go on from there. It's going to be tough without a witness against her, though."

"Neither of the boys will testify?" Will asked.

"Sheldon has gone silent on the matter, Doug still denies that it happened to him, and Teddy is dead," Portia explained.

"Is Woods denying that he killed his son? Or his brother . . ." Miranda paused. "Which is it? Or is it both?"

"It's both, actually," Portia said. "Sheldon was Teddy's half brother, since they had the same mother but different fathers."

"Teddy's father being Sheldon. Ugh." Miranda grimaced.

"To answer your question, no, he's never denied it."

"Then there's your chance to bring murder charges against him that he can be tried on, right?" Miranda asked. "Isn't that what you were hoping for? To bring him to trial for a murder he doesn't have immunity for? It should be a slam dunk."

"I guess." Portia nodded. "Though frankly, I don't know that I wouldn't like to see Rhona strapped to a gurney with an IV in her arm."

"Rhona didn't tell him to repeatedly rape little boys and then kill them and bury them in hidden graves," Miranda pointed out to her.

"Granted, Sheldon Woods is responsible for everything he ever did," Portia agreed. "But would he have done those things, would he have become what he is, if his own mother had not been a nymphomaniac pedophile who repeatedly abused him and forced him to have sex with her? If he'd had a normal childhood, would those boys still be alive?" She looked at Jim. "My guess is that they would be. I lay this all at her feet. Not pardoning him, but I think the blame has to go to her as well."

"I don't know," Jim said. "If Sheldon is telling the truth, Doug Nicholson suffered the same kind of assault at their mother's hands. He hasn't become a pedophile. He's not a murderer. He's married, owns his own business. By all appearances, he's managed to overcome the abuse without becoming an abuser himself."

"He wasn't subjected to the years of abuse that Sheldon endured," Portia reminded him. "She abused Doug until she could abuse Sheldon. But after Sheldon, there were no more 'little men' until she had Teddy. By then, Doug had long since moved out. He didn't even know there was another half brother."

"And we don't know what goes on in Nicholson's head," Will noted. "We don't know what demons he faces when he closes his eyes."

"And here's the thing about Woods getting the death penalty. Once he's gone, his secrets—the whereabouts of the remains of those other missing boys—that all goes with him," Portia said. "I don't know if I'd want to deny those parents—many of whom were at the cemetery this morning—a chance to recover their sons."

"That's a call I wouldn't want to have to make," Jim agreed.

"So where is Rhona now?" Miranda asked.

"She's in Vegas. She's being questioned about her sons—it remains to be seen whether or not she'll admit to anything. So far she has not. She has a lawyer, though, and his attitude is, 'bring your charges or leave her alone.' He also hinted that he's having her evaluated by a psychiatrist. He thinks she has a sexual addiction."

"Oh, there's a surefire defense." Miranda rolled her eyes.

"Maybe in time Sheldon will change his mind and will agree to testify against his mother," Jim said, "and maybe someday, Doug will face the truth and be willing to talk about it."

"It won't feel *done* to me until she's behind bars," Portia told them. "There won't be any justice until she's convicted of her crimes."

"You know how it is, though. You can't always make it right. You just do your best, then put it behind you and move on to your next case." Miranda paused. "You are staying around for another case, right?"

"Staying around?" Jim turned to Portia. "Is there

some question of whether or not you're staying around?"

"No." Portia shook her head. "I'm here and I plan on staying. John was right. The fight is the same. I'm on board. One hundred percent."

"Great. We need you," Will told her. "Counter-terrorism has thinned our ranks and has taken some of our best agents. We're happy to have one of them come back to us."

"In that case, welcome home, Sister Love." Miranda raised her glass.

"On that note of reconciliation . . ." Will got up and went to the desk and picked up a flat FedEx envelope that he handed to Portia. "This came after you left for the memorial service this morning."

Portia looked at the return address. "It's from Jack," she said.

"We know." Miranda took another sip of her wine.

Portia opened the envelope and took out a smaller one, from which she removed a handwritten note. She sat quietly and read both sides.

"He's going to be in New York next month," she told them. "Madison Square Garden."

"I heard about that," Will said. "The tickets sold out in something like twenty minutes. You should see what they're selling for on the Internet. Astronomical."

"Wonder what I could get for these little beauties." Portia held up the envelope.

"Are they what I think they are?" Will asked.

"An Evening with Jack Marlowe," Portia read. "Four in the front row. Plus backstage passes, hotel reservations, limo service to and from, and dinner with Jack after the show."

Will bit the back of his hand, and Portia laughed.

"He'd like you to be there," Portia said to Miranda. "What do you say?"

Miranda looked at Will. "It's up to you, babe," he told her.

"Oh, crap, maybe it's time," Miranda said. "Tell him I'll be there."

Will cleared his throat meaningfully.

"*We'll* be there," she corrected herself.

"Yes!" A jubilant Will pumped a triumphant fist in the air.

Quiet until now, Jim asked Portia, "Would I be out of line asking how you rate front-row seats and backstage passes to see Jack Marlowe?"

"He's our father," Portia told him.

"Jack Marlowe. Mad Jack Marlowe?" His eyebrows rose in surprise.

"Yes," Portia and Miranda both said at the same time.

"Jack Marlowe is your *father*?" he asked as if he wasn't sure he understood.

Both women nodded.

"Are you going to explain that?"

"Someday." Portia smiled.

Jim turned to Portia. "Any other bombshells? Family secrets? Skeletons in the closet? Anything else I don't know about you?"

"Oh, there's lots." Portia grinned. "Stick around."

He lifted her hand and kissed the inside of her wrist.

"Count on it."

*Read on to catch an
exclusive sneak peek at*

Goodbye Again

*the highly anticipated second novel
in the Mercy Street Foundation series
from* New York Times *bestselling author
Mariah Stewart!*
*Coming in March 2009 from Ballantine Books
Available wherever books are sold.*

In southern California, a woman leaned closer to her television and listened with great interest to the midday press conference she'd found by accident while she was channel surfing, wasting time until she had to pick up her daughter at summer camp. Intrigued, she went to the Mercy Street Foundation website and read about Robert Magellan's latest brainstorm. Using Magellan Express, the Internet search engine he'd developed and later sold for a king's ransom, she typed in *Conroy, PA*, and found it to be a small, working-class city surrounded by farms and gently rolling hills. She studied the photographs, and liked what she saw. Returning to the website for the Foundation, she filled out the online application for employment.

Fifteen minutes later, she was still deliberating whether to submit the app, when the sound of a slamming car door drew her attention to the street outside. In this mostly blue collar neighborhood, there was little traffic during the afternoon hours. She rose and peered through the front window, and her blood froze in her veins. A late-model car was parked directly across from her house, and two men were standing on her front lawn. Instinctively, she knew what they were there for, even if she did not know their names.

Turning back to the laptop, she hit SEND.

Almost without thinking, she ran up the steps and into her daughter's room, where she grabbed a few things she knew they could not leave behind, then slipped back downstairs. The men were still standing on the front lawn, debating, perhaps, the likelihood of finding her home in the middle of the day. She picked up her laptop from the sofa and hurried into the kitchen. Grabbing her handbag from the counter, she checked for her Glock, stuffed her daughter's things in with it, opened a drawer and searched quickly for her checkbook, then quietly passed through the back door into the yard.

She'd been warned that this day was coming. She just hadn't expected it to be so soon.

Her heart pounding, she ran the length of the backyard to the alley behind her house where she'd parked her car. Driving carefully to make certain she was not being followed, she took a roundabout way to her daughter's day camp. She parked on a side street, out of view of the front of the building, took a deep calming breath, and entered through a side door, just in case.

Once inside, she waved to the head counselor, indicating that she'd arrived to pick up her daughter.

"Hey, you're early today," the counselor said.

"Just a little." She searched the group for her child.

"Chloe, your mommy's here," the counselor called into the next room.

A tiny girl with dark curls and yellow paint on her clothes skipped through the doorway.

"Can I go home with Natalie today?" The little girl flung herself onto her mother's legs and held on. "Please?"

"Not today, sweetie," her mother replied softly. "Go get your things and tell Natalie maybe another day."

"Tomorrow?"

"We'll see."

" 'We'll see' means no." Chloe pouted.

"It means, we'll see what tomorrow brings. And we will. So go get your things now and—"

"I have my things. There, by the door." The child pointed to the pile of backpacks.

"Say good-bye to your counselor, then, and let's go."

"Bye, Miss Maria. Bye, Natalie. Bye, Kelly." The

little girl's voice trailed off as she picked up her belongings. Reaching up to hold her mother's hand, she babbled brightly all the way to the car.

"Are we going home?" Chloe asked as she strapped herself into her seat.

"We're going to Aunt Nikki's for a while."

"Are we eating dinner there?"

"We might even stay all night."

"Yay! I get to play with Mr. Mustache." Chloe's small feet kicked the seat gleefully. "He's my favorite cat in the whole entire world."

"He's a pretty special cat, all right," her mother agreed.

"Mommy, are you having a bad day?"

"Why? Do I look like I'm having a bad day?"

"You're not smiling."

She forced the biggest smile she could muster.

"Better?" she asked.

"Better," Chloe agreed.

She took the long way to her friend Nicole's house, and parked two blocks away. Knowing that cell phones can be tracked, she opened the glove box and set it inside. She gathered up the things she'd brought with her, and locked the door. She'd have to remember to ask Nikki to have the car towed to the police impound lot for safekeeping.

"Why do we have to walk so far?" Chloe grumbled as she trudged along, lugging her backpack.

"Because it's a good day for a walk, and we want to see what we can see."

"It's cold," Chloe complained.

"Then we'll cross and walk on the sunny side of the street." She remembered there used to be a song about that, but she couldn't remember the words. Someone used to sing it to her, long ago, but she wasn't sure who. "But we're almost there already. See? Just three more houses and we're there."

They crossed the street and walked up the driveway to the backyard.

"Her car's not here. She isn't home." Chloe looked as if she were about to cry.

"She'll be here soon."

"What if she isn't? We'll have to walk all the way back to the car . . ." Chloe's eyes widened dramatically at the thought.

"She said she'd be home by . . . oh, there she is, see? I told you."

The blue and white Crown Victoria pulled slowly into the driveway, parked, and a tall woman in her early forties got out. If she was surprised to see she had visitors, Chief Nicole Jenkins of the Silver Hills, California, police department didn't show it.

"Hey, cuteness," she called to Chloe. "What's happening?"

"I'm happening," Chloe grinned.

"You bet your buttons you are." She kissed the top of the child's head, looking over it as if trying to read her friend's expression. "Come on inside.

Let's see what old Mr. Mustache is up to. I'll bet he's sleeping like a big old slug."

"Mommy said we might eat dinner here and maybe sleep here, too." Chloe dropped her backpack inside the door and took off in search of the cat.

"*Mi casa es su casa,*" her Aunt Nikki told her.

"What?" Chloe turned to ask.

"It means my house is your house. It means you are welcome to stay as long as you'd like."

"Yay." Chloe grinned. "Does that mean your cat is my cat, too?"

No words had yet been exchanged between the two women. It wasn't until after Chloe was sleeping snugly in the guest bedroom, the old gray tom curled up contentedly beside her, that Nikki handed her old friend a glass of wine and said, "Okay, spill."

"I brought in a hooker this morning for solicitation."

"And that would be news because . . . ?"

"She offered to trade some information with me in exchange for not booking her."

"By the look on your face, I'd say she had something big to trade." Nikki tucked her legs under her on the sofa.

"She told me that Anthony Navarro knows that the child I adopted four years ago is his daughter, and he's coming after her." She nodded slowly. "I'd say that was big."

"You think she knows what she's talking about?"

"You think there's any chance she could have made that up and just coincidentally got the facts right?"

"Okay, so we pick him up . . ."

"First, you have to find him. Nik, you've been after him for years, and you haven't come close."

"So we stake out your house and we wait for him to show. In the meantime, you and Chloe stay here."

"He won't be coming himself. He won't have to. He's offered twenty-five thousand dollars to the person who brings him his daughter."

Nikki whistled. "Jesus. He's serious."

"As a heart attack."

"So we pick up whoever he sends—"

"They'll just keep on coming, Nikki. He wants his daughter."

"Why?"

"The word on the street is, two years ago he had measles. It left him sterile. No more baby Navarros."

"So he wants the one he had with . . . wait a minute. How did he find out who adopted her? Tameka died while she was in prison. The court terminated his rights because he never showed up for any of the hearings. How all of a sudden does he know who has his kid?"

"He bribed someone at children's services. This

gal this morning, she knew the whole story, Nik. She even knew the name of Chloe's birth mother."

"Well, shit." Nikki stood and began to pace. After a moment, she said, "Okay, we do this. We stake out your house—"

"You'll have to get in line. It's already being staked out."

"You know this for certain?"

"I saw them. Two of them, parked right across the street from my house. Bold little bastards, they thought nothing of walking right up onto my lawn."

"When was this?"

"They were there when I left to pick up Chloe. Which is why I left when I did, and why I came here instead of going home."

"You think Navarro sent them?"

"I'd bet my life on it. I won't, however, bet Chloe's."

Nikki reached for the radio she had strapped onto her waistband, but her friend stopped her.

"Uh-uh. It won't do any good, Nik. It won't stop until he gets her. He'll get her at her school or he'll have someone come into the house in the middle of the night, but he will get her." She shook her head. "As long as we're here, and he knows we're here, it won't stop. There aren't enough police in this part of the state to take on his whole family, and he won't care how many of us or how many of them die."

"So we call in the FBI."

"Nikki, the FBI has been after him for longer than you have."

"So what are you going to do?"

"Let me tell you what I saw on TV this afternoon." She related what she'd heard and what she'd learned from the Mercy Street Foundation website.

"You're thinking about applying?"

"I already did, online."

"You're just going to pack up and move east?"

"No time to pack." She shook her head. "I don't dare go back to the house, Nik. I have to protect my daughter. No way can I let that animal or any of his relatives get within a country mile of her."

"Give me a few days to see what we can do."

"There's nothing you can do. No one's gotten close to him, ever. No one knows where he is. He has a huge network, his brothers, his cousins, his uncles. We're talking about one of the biggest drug families in southern California."

"Sooner or later—"

"Later will be too late for my daughter. I can't give her up to the kind of life she'd have, growing up as the daughter of a major drug dealer."

"So you move across the country, you think he won't be able to find you?"

"He won't be looking for Emme Caldwell."

"You'd change your name?"

"My *name*?" she snorted. "What's my name, Nik? I don't even know what my real name is."

Nikki held her head in her hands. "You know that Emme Caldwell died two years ago."

"Robert Magellan won't know that."

"He will when he checks her references."

"That would be you."

Nikki fell silent.

"I know it's a lot to ask. If you're not comfortable with it, God knows, I'll understand. I can re-apply, with a different name."

"You already applied as Emme?"

"Yes."

"Well, that pretty much seals the deal."

"I know. I should have thought this through a little more. It's just that, after hearing all this from that hooker this morning, then going off my shift and seeing this press conference on TV, then those two goons were outside my house . . ." She blew out a long stream of air. "It just seemed like a sign, like someone was telling me something. Anyway, it's going to be okay, Nik. I'll come up with something else."

"It's not okay," Nikki told her. "You're the best friend I ever had. You saved my life twice in the past five years. I can save yours this once. Besides, if anything happened to you or to that precious girl . . ."

A chill ran through Nikki, and she visibly shivered. They both knew she'd seen firsthand what happened to those who crossed the Navarro family in the past.

"Just tell me what you want me to do."